BESTSELLING AUS~~TRALIAN~~ AUTHOR

Carol Marinelli

Outback Hope

MILLS & BOON

Published by
Mills & Boon
An imprint of Harlequin Enterprises (Australia) Pty Limited
(ABN 47 001 180 918), a subsidiary of HarperCollins
Publishers Australia Pty Limited (ABN 36 009 913 517)
Level 13, 201 Elizabeth Street
SYDNEY NSW 2000
AUSTRALIA

Printed and bound in Australia by McPherson's Printing Group

CONTENTS

Carol Marinelli did her nursing training in England and then worked for a number of years in Casualty. A holiday romance while backpacking led to her marriage and emigration to Australia. Eight years and three children later, the romance continues... Today she considers both England and Australia her home. The sudden death of her father prompted a reappraisal of her life's goals and inspired her to tackle romance-writing seriously.

The Baby Emergency

PROLOGUE

THERE WERE TWO very good reasons Shelly didn't want to be there.

For one thing, the barrage of sympathetic stares and awkward greetings that were sure to greet her she could certainly do without.

And as to the other...

Darting into the changing room, she rather unceremoniously dumped the mud cake she had bought on the bench, before checking her reflection in the full-length mirror.

The pregnancy books had been right about one thing at least—the mid-trimester glow they had promised as a reward for the constant nausea and mood swings had finally appeared.

Glowing was the only word that would describe her.

Even Shelly, with her eternally self-critical eye, acknowledged that for once in her thirty years her skin was smooth and clear with not a blemish in sight. Even her long auburn curls seemed to be behaving for the first time in memory, falling in heavy silky tendrils instead of their usual chaotic frizz, and her vivid green eyes were definitely sparkling.

Funny she should look so good when everything around her was falling apart.

Closing her eyes, Shelly took a deep cleansing breath, trying to settle the flurry of butterflies dancing in her stomach. Even the baby seemed to sense her nervousness, wriggling and kicking, little feet or hands making certain they were felt.

'It's OK, baby.' Shelly put a protective hand to her stomach and spoke softly, hoping her falsely calm voice might somehow soothe the child within. 'We're going to face this together.'

Touching up her lipstick, Shelly fiddled with her top for a moment, the flimsy powder-blue top softening the ripe bulge of her stomach. She even indulged for a tiny moment the still surprising sight of a cleavage on her increasingly unfamiliar body.

This should be such a happy time. The words buzzed around in her head. How she wanted it to be happy, how she wanted to enjoy the changes that were overwhelming her, to be afforded again the luxury of revelling in what had been a very much planned and wanted baby.

Still wanted.

A fresh batch of tears was adding to the sparkle in her eyes and, blowing her nose loudly, Shelly practised a forced smile in the mirror and picked up the cake. Looking down at her bump, her free hand went back for a final comforting stroke of the baby within. 'Come on, little one, let's get this over with.'

'Shelly!' Her name seemed to be coming at her from all directions as her colleagues welcomed her warmly, welcoming her straight into the click of things, but despite the smiles and casual chit-chat, not one of them managed to look her in the eye.

Not one of them asked how her pregnancy was progressing.

Except Melissa.

The playroom on the children's ward was for once void of patients and anxious parents, filled instead with staff, some in uniform, some like Shelly in regular clothes, all clutching cups and paper plates, all there to say goodbye to a certain doctor who in his six-month rotation had brought more vitality and energy to the ward than most did in their whole careers.

Like a radar homing in, Shelly made her way over to her

staunchly loyal colleague, grateful in advance for the quiet support Melissa in her own unique way would impart. 'Quite a spread,' Shelly said, handing Melissa her cake. 'Anyone would think it was one of the consultants leaving, not a temporary intern.'

'I know,' Melissa sighed. 'Ross can't believe it himself. I think he expected a cake and a couple of bottles of warm cola, but just look at the turn-out! People like Ross don't come along everyday, though. We're all going to miss him.'

And there was Shelly's second reason.

She didn't want to say goodbye.

Again.

Didn't want Ross Bodey, who'd breezed into her life at various intervals over the years, to breeze out again. Didn't want the smile that had brightened her day, the funny chats and sometimes serious insights to end.

It wasn't as if she was alone. Not one person in this room wanted him to go. Ross in his own easygoing, light-hearted way had turned the ward around. Even Tania, the rigid unit manager, had somehow loosened up under his good-natured teasing. Everyone here today was going to miss him.

Especially Shelly.

Over the years they'd grown close.

Very close.

Oh, nothing to be ashamed about. They'd been friends for ages. Shelly had met him first when she'd been doing her midwifery training and Ross had been but a lowly second-year medical student.

The occasional coffee in the canteen had been a welcome interlude, listening as Ross had planned his travels, determined to fit the most into his summer semester break, happy too to let Shelly chatter on as she'd planned her engagement party.

Friends, nothing else.

The five-year age gap between them seemingly unfillable. Ross ready to party, Shelly ready to settle down.

Even when Ross had breezed back this time, ready to resume their friendship, Shelly hadn't had a qualm of guilt. There was nothing in their friendship that threatened her marriage. There was a bond between them, that was all: something special that gelled them. They didn't keep in touch or anything, their friendship only extended to the workplace, but it was their unique bond that made Ross call for her when he needed a hand, that made Shelly ring him first if there was a sick child she wanted seen. OK, maybe she did check the doctors' roster with more than a faint interest these days, and maybe she had put up her hand for a couple of extra shifts when Ross had been on, but there was no harm in that, there was nothing wrong in a man and woman being friends.

Ross was twenty-five years old, for goodness' sake, into nightclubs and trendy clothes. A world away from Shelly's contented suburban existence: happily married, excitingly anticipating the birth of her first child.

Till now.

'Fancy coming out for a drink at the weekend?' Melissa's invitation was casual enough but it was loaded with caring and Shelly bit back the sting of tears.

'I might just take you up on that.'

Dear Melissa. For all Shelly's friends, for all the colleagues who had squealed with delight when they had found out she was pregnant, who had beguiled her with horror stories of their own pregnancies and labour, Melissa, fifty, single and childless, had been the only one to call her up again and again when she had been permanently greeted by the answering-machine. The only one who had ignored Shelly's frosty response and had pressed on regardless.

When friends were being doled out, Melissa had been a treasured find.

'Shelly!'

Finally a pair of eyes were actually managing to look at her. Very blue eyes, almost navy in fact; the dark lashes that framed them a contrast to the blond hair flopping perfectly and no doubt intentionally onto his good-looking face.

'Hi, Ross.' The forced smile was still in place and Shelly widened it an inch. 'Given that it's your last day, are you going to finally admit that you do dye your hair?'

'Never.' Ross grinned. 'How would I find the time for all that palaver with roots and regrowth? You're just going to have to accept that I'm naturally good-looking, isn't that right, Melissa?'

'No comment.' Melissa shrugged good-naturedly then she let out a deep throaty laugh. 'Who am I trying to kid? You're stunning, Dr Bodey, you know it and so does everyone else. Just don't let it get to your head.'

Waddling off, she left an open-mouthed Shelly gaping in her wake. 'I do believe Melissa was flirting.'

'Terrifying, wasn't it?' Ross winked.

The smile she had been forcing was coming more naturally now and Shelly took the plastic cup he'd brought over for her and took a quick sip of some very questionable cola.

'Thanks for coming, by the way. I know you're on days off.'

'As if I wouldn't have said goodbye. What are you doing tonight, having a big family send-off?'

'Hardly.' He gave a quick shrug and for the tiniest instant Shelly could have sworn she registered the beginning of a frown, but it soon faded, the nonchalant smile she was so used to soon back in place. 'They're used to me wandering off by now. It'll just be a case of too many beers with a few choice friends. Come if you want.'

In Shelly's present mood, Ross's invitation didn't even merit a response and Shelly didn't bother to try.

'Come on,' Ross pushed. 'I'll even shout you a cola, with ice,' he added, grimacing as he took another sip.

'It's better I don't, I'm not exactly in the mood for a party. Anyway, we're going to the tennis tonight.'

'You lucky thing,' Ross exclaimed. 'It's the quarter-finals

too. I've been trying to get tickets all week—how did you manage to swing that?'

'I didn't,' Shelly sighed. 'We're going with Neil's work, another boring night making small-talk. Still, at least I can distract myself looking at the players. Who knows? Maybe one of them will see me sitting there in the stands and fall head over heels then whisk me away from all this.' She caught his quick grin. 'I'm allowed to fantasise, aren't I?'

'Of course,' Ross said, that quick grin splitting his face now. 'But given that it's the women's quarter-finals tonight, Shelly, that particular fantasy of yours is doing terrible things to my blood pressure!'

'Ross!' Shelly exclaimed, the first laugh she had expended in days spilling out of her lips as she blushed a rather unbecoming shade of claret and quickly changed the subject. 'So, are you all packed?'

'No.' He shrugged as Shelly's eyes widened.

'But you're going tomorrow.'

'So? I'll pack in the morning. I don't think I'll need much in the middle of the outback, a few shorts and T-shirts, a pair of boots. No doubt you'd have had checklists as long as your arm, trying to cram everything into ten suitcases.'

'Probably,' Shelly admitted with a begrudging smile. 'I just like to be—'

'Prepared,' Ross finished with a laugh. 'Super Nurse Shelly Weaver, prepared for any eventuality.'

'Not quite.' The smile was fading now and Shelly took a sip of her drink, eternally grateful to Ross for bringing it over, glad for something to do with her hands.

'Did you find out what the sex of the baby is, then? Or are you going to keep us all in suspense?'

'Sorry?' Shelly looked up, startled, sure she must have misheard him.

'You said were going to find out what you were having when you had your scan. Come on, you can tell me. I'm leaving so it won't get out.' He was still smiling, his grin so broad and his face so innocent Shelly truly thought he couldn't have heard the news.

'I found out a bit more than the sex.' Shelly took another long drink, wiping away her cola moustache with the back of her hand as Ross just stood there patiently waiting for her to explain. 'The scan showed up some anomalies,' Shelly continued, her voice faltering every now and then as she spoke. 'And after further tests the upshot is that I'm going to have a Down's syndrome baby, or a special needs child, or whatever the latest buzz word is for it at the moment.' Her green eyes shot up to his and the tears that were always appallingly close these days sparkled as they brimmed, ready to splash onto her cheeks. The bitter note in her voice was so out of place in her normal sunny nature even Shelly looked shocked at the venom in her voice. 'I'm surprised you hadn't heard already. News normally spreads like wildfire around here.'

'Melissa told me,' Ross said simply. 'I'm sorry for what you're going through. How are you managing?'

'Fine,' Shelly said through gritted teeth. 'It's not as if I have any choice *but* to manage.'

'And Neil?' Ross probed, ignoring her obvious desire to end the conversation.

'Not so fine.' Suddenly her paper cup was coming under intense scrutiny as Shelly fiddled with it in her hands. 'Neil likes to be in control, likes to have choices, a say in things. He's having trouble taking in the fact that no amount of second opinions or dollar-waving is going to change the outcome of this pregnancy.'

'But he's supporting you?'

Shelly gave a very short, very brittle laugh. 'Is that what you call it?' As soon as the words were out Shelly wished she could somehow erase them. Moaning about Neil, no matter how merited, no matter what the circumstances, seemed wrong somehow, but Ross didn't seem fazed by her outburst. Instead he pulled the shredded cup from her hand, his eyes never leaving her face.

'I shouldn't have said that,' Shelly mumbled as Ross stood there patiently, waiting for her to elaborate.

'Why not?' Ross asked simply, when no explanation was given.

'I just shouldn't have said anything, that's all.' She was almost biting through her lip in an effort to keep the tears back, and had the exit door not been located on the other side of the room Shelly would have turned and left there and then. She hadn't come here for this. A quick goodbye was all she'd intended, and now here she was on the verge of letting five days of tortured anxiety burst forth and blubbering like an idiot in front of everyone.

'Oh, Shelly, I'm sorry.' His voice was suddenly serious, the tone directly hitting the final straw of Shelly's reserves. As one large tear rolled onto her cheek a strong arm pulled around her thickened waist as he gently led her out of the playroom and into a small annexe where they stood alone and for the first time in days Shelly felt free to let the emotions she had held in check so painfully finally flow as Ross's gentle voice gently gave her permission to continue. 'Talk to me, Shelly. I know I'm going, but it doesn't mean I don't care. I know there's nothing I can say, but I can listen.'

'There's nothing anyone can say. I'm sick of seeing the pity in people's eyes, sick of everyone adding up how many weeks pregnant I am in their heads and wondering if it's too late for me to have a termination. It's my baby.' Tears were streaming unchecked now. 'It's my baby and I don't want to get rid of him. So he's not going to perfect! It doesn't mean I don't want him. I should still be allowed to love him.'

'It's a boy, then?'

His words were so calm it stilled her, and as she looked up Shelly saw that he was smiling.

'Congratulations.'

'You mean that?'

'Of course I do, Shelly. You're going to have a beautiful little boy and you're going to be a fabulous mum. Yes, he's going to have some problems, need some extra care, but if ever there was a woman who could give a child that then it's you. It might all seem a jumble now, but you'll work it out.'

'Do you really think so?'

'I don't think so,' Ross said emphatically. 'I know so. You and Neil will deal with this.'

'What I said before, about Neil, I mean. I was just letting off a bit of steam. He's upset, which is understandable. It's hard for him too. All the dreams he had, *we* had, have just suddenly gone.' She gave a small laugh, trying to lighten the loaded silence around them. 'I think Neil had our baby pegged to be Prime Minister one day.'

'What's the population of Australia?'

Shelly had no idea where he was leading, no idea where he'd plucked that question from, but her mind whirred away from her problems for a millisecond as she struggled with her appalling general knowledge. 'About twenty million, at least I think that's what it is.'

'The odds weren't great, then.'

Shelly's forehead creased as she tried to fathom where Ross was leading. 'What on earth are you going on about?'

'If you factor in the rising population, increased immigration, well, suffice it to say...' His hand moved forward, gently reaching the soft swell of her stomach as Shelly stood smiling at his strange logic. 'This baby was never going to be Prime Minster. But you can still have dreams for him, Shelly, still cherish his life.' His hand was still there, she could feel the warmth spreading through her top. The baby was motionless, perhaps feeling the quiet confidence Ross so effortlessly imparted. If only over the awful past few days she had endured Neil could have said just one of the comforting words Ross had conveyed so easily,

'You'd better get back.' Her voice was strangely thick. All she wanted to do was lay her head on that chest, feel those strong arms around her, for just an ounce of his strength to somehow rub off on her. 'And I've got to go.'

'Not yet,' Ross moaned. 'I'll get stuck with Tania. If you think Melissa was bad, just wait till you see how Tania's behaving. I swear she's wearing lipstick. I think she's got a crush on me.'

'She has.' Shelly laughed. 'So watch yourself.' Pulling her bag over her shoulder, Shelly swallowed hard. 'I really do have to go. I just popped in to say goodbye. I've got an appointment with Dr Forbes at two.'

'I thought Dr Lim was your obstetrician.'

'He is. This visit is for Neil. I know it's not going to change anything, but he just wants another opinion.'

'Come on, I'll walk you out to your car and say hi to Neil. It would be nice for us both to put names to faces and maybe I can answer some of his questions. His mind must be working overtime.'

'Neil's at work.' She saw a hint of a frown mar Ross's near-perfect features and instantly jumped on the defensive. 'He can't take an afternoon off work every time I see a doctor, he'd never get anything done.'

'Of course not.'

There was a tiny awkward moment as Shelly turned to go. What should she do, shake his hand? A casual wave as she got to the door? Ross answered the question before it had even formed in her mind. Pulling her towards him, he held her for a moment, her bump pressing against his toned abdomen, until he moved away just enough to place his hand on her swollen stomach. 'Look after that mum of yours,' Ross whispered to the babe beneath his hand. 'She's one in a million.'

A tiny kiss was aimed at her cheek but Shelly moved nervously, his lips grazing hers for less than a second, but it felt as if they were both moving in slow motion, every tiny movement magnified, the soft warmth of his mouth on hers as unexpected as it was welcome, and Shelley swallowed hard as he pulled away, biting back tears as he squeezed her shoulder in one final supportive gesture and then he was gone. Off to his party, off on his travels again, off to the outback to impart and absorb, a million miles away from Chisholm Hospital, from the beach and the world he'd become so much a part of in the six months he'd been back.

Her lips were burning from his briefest touch and Shelly shook her head as she walked, her speed increasing as she pushed the unwelcome stirrings from her mind.

Of course Ross Bodey was going to say the right thing, he was a doctor, for heaven's sake! He'd just spent the last six months on a children's ward, dealing with anxious parents and sick kids. Of course he knew how to handle her, that was his job. She was being unfair, comparing his reaction to Neil's.

Neil was the one living it. Neil was the one whose life had changed for ever when they'd found out the news.

Still…

Starting her car, Shelly pulled off the handbrake and indi-cated to turn right, gliding into the afternoon traffic as she headed for her doctor's appointment, for an afternoon of scans and blood tests, an afternoon of being prodded and poked in a futile attempt to obtain a different version. A little piece of news that might brighten Neil's day. But no amounts of scans, no amount of technology or statistics were going to change the outcome. Their baby was handicapped, and no amount of wish-ing was going to change that fact.

But she could still have dreams for him.

Ross's words washed over her, a soothing interlude in an awful day. And in the weeks and months that followed they comforted her with increasing regularity, a life raft to cling to in the turbulent times that followed.

She could still have dreams for her son.

CHAPTER ONE

'SORRY, DARLING.' MARLENE put down her basket on the hall floor and haphazardly deposited a kiss on Shelly's cheek. 'The match went on for ever.'

Shelly gave her mother an easy smile to show there was no harm done. 'I've got plenty of time before my shift starts. Is Dad still there?'

'Of course,' Marlene replied crisply, with a slight edge to her voice. 'This twilight tennis competition is supposed to be a combined effort for the two of us to get fit, yet your father undoes all of the hard work in one fell swoop. He's in the clubhouse guzzling beers and eating lamingtons as I speak. Goodness, Shelly,' Marlene said, finally looking at her daughter properly for the first time since she'd arrived. 'You look nice—very nice, in fact! What have you done to your hair?'

'I just put a bit of mousse in it in when I washed it,' Shelly answered vaguely as Marlene gave her a rather sceptical look.

'I'll have to try some. Where's Matthew?'

'Asleep.' Shelly rolled her eyes. 'At long last. But I think this new routine is finally starting to work. I gave him his bath at seven, read his blessed book five times and now he's out like a light.'

'Oh, really?' Marlene's face broke into a wide grin and she gestured behind Shelly. 'So who's this, then?'

'Matthew,' Shelly wailed. 'You're supposed to be asleep.'

Holding up his dog-eared book, Matthew's podgy little face broke into a wide and very engaging smile, instantly dousing Shelly's irritation. '*Wun, wun,*' he begged.

'No more run, run,' Shelly corrected, smiling despite herself. 'The little gingerbread man is fast asleep now and so should you be.'

'*Wun, wun.*' Matthew insisted, his grin widening as he saw Marlene. 'Nanny.'

'Yes, darling.' Marlene scooped her grandson into her arms. 'Nanny's looking after you tonight while Mummy goes to work.' Marlene pulled Matthew closer, whispering loudly in his ear so that Shelly could hear. 'Or at least that's where she says she's going, but I've never seen Mummy looking quite so stunning for a shift on the children's ward!'

'Mum,' Shelly moaned. 'Don't talk like that—you'll confuse him.'

'I'm just teasing,' Marlene soothed, turning her attention back to Matthew. 'Now, give Mummy a big kiss goodnight and we'll wave goodbye to her, then how about we go and see if there's any nice biscuits in the cupboard?'

'Mum.' Shelly's voice had a warning note to it which Marlene dismissed with a wave of her hand.

'The biscuits are for me, darling. Why should your father be the only one ruining his waistline? I'm going to have a nice cuppa then I'll read Matthew his story. You go off to work. Don't worry about us two, we'll be fine.'

'I know,' Shelly admitted, giving Marlene a quick kiss before lingering a while longer with Matthew's. 'Love you, Matthew.' He smelt of baby soap and lotion and as she kissed him gently Shelly wondered, not for the first time, how she could bear to go to work and leave him. Reluctantly Shelly picked up her bag and, turning in the doorway, she forced a cheerful wave. 'If one of those biscuits does happen to find its way to Matthew...'

'I know,' Marlene sighed. 'Make sure I brush his teeth.' Holding up one of Matthew's hands, she guided him into a wave as Shelly opened the car door, the tempting scent of a neighbour's barbeque wafting over the fence. Even though it was nudging eight-thirty, it was still so light Shelly wouldn't even need to put on her headlights, and it would have been so tempting not to go, to curl up on the sofa with Matthew and read him his beloved book.

Not that Matthew would thank her for it, Shelly mused as she turned onto the freeway and headed towards the hospital, Matthew would be having the time of his little life right now, gorging on biscuits and dancing around the lounge with his eccentric grandmother, who would end in one night the routine Shelly had been so painfully attempting to implement.

'Who are you trying to kid?' Shelly mumbled, rallying slightly as she caught sight of herself in the rear-view mirror, her pale eyelashes gone for ever, or at least the next couple of months, thanks to this afternoon's tint. As tempting as a cuddle on the sofa with Matthew might be, tonight, for the first time in ages, she couldn't wait to get to work. Putting her foot down slightly, Shelly felt a tremble of excitement somewhere in the pit of her stomach as the signs for the hospital loomed ever closer, the brightly lit building coming into view, the hub of staff outside Emergency indicating something serious was on its way in. A security guard indicated for Shelly to clear the entrance road. Pulling over, she sat in her car patiently waiting as an ambulance flew past, its flashing blue lights adding to the theatre of it all, watching as the emergency staff leapt forward to greet it. Shelly felt the bubble of excitement in her stomach rapidly expand.

Chisholm Hospital had never looked so exciting!

'Thank goodness you're on tonight, Shelly.' Melissa patted the seat beside her at the nurses' station. 'I've had agency staff with me every night this week—it will be nice to have someone who actually knows the place.'

'You smell nice.' Turning, she smiled at Shelly who sat blushing as red as her hair. 'You look lovely too—been to the hairdressers?'

'No,' Shelly lied. 'You're just used to seeing me coming on an early shift at seven in the morning.'

'Hmm.' Melissa looked at her knowingly but didn't push further. 'So, how many nights are you down for?'

'You're stuck with me for a month.' Shelly rolled her eyes. 'I've been avoiding it for ages so it had to catch up with me sooner or later. Tania rang me at home this morning and told me you were tearing your hair out.'

'I was and I know it's probably the last thing you need right now, but I for one am glad you said yes to a stint on nights.'

'I really didn't have any choice.' Shelly shrugged. 'There's been a big fat zero beside my name where night shifts have been concerned recently. Bring back the old days, I can't stand internal rotation.'

'Sounds painful!'

Shelly let out a gurgle of laughter and stood up delightedly. 'Ross!'

'The one and only.'

'Only you could find a sexual connotation with the nursing roster! So how are you finding it? Back in civilisation after all this time?'

'I've had a very civilised couple of years, thank you very much,' Ross corrected, wagging his finger playfully. 'There's a bit more to the outback than tents and billy tea but, yes, it's good to be back, I think.'

'You think?' Shelly questioned with a grin. 'I would have thought they'd be treating you gently on your first day back.' She was blushing to her toenails now, shamefully aware that the perfume, the hairdresser's, even the shaved legs and smooth bikini line had been done entirely for the benefit of this quick delicious moment at handover, to show Ross somehow that she hadn't completely let herself go just because she'd had a baby. There was nothing like an old friend reappearing after a prolonged absence to force a critical look in the mirror, and now that the vague chance she'd catch Ross on his way off duty had materialised, Shelly was taken back by the rush of emotion that had engulfed her.

Ross Bodey was back in town, and he looked absolutely divine, his blond hair practically white now, courtesy of the hot Australian sun, and his face brown and smooth, accentuating the impossibly blue eyes.

'I've only just set foot in the place.' Ross grimaced. 'Luke Martin is off sick so they rang me at the crack of dawn this morning to tell me I'm going to be stuck on nights for the next week, so there goes my social life. How about you?'

For a second Shelly's eyes flickered to Melissa who sat innocently staring at the whiteboard, jotting down the names of the children and babies under the care of the ward that night. 'I don't have a social life, Ross. I've got a son to think of now. Wine bars and nightclubs are but a distant memory these days.'

'I meant what shift are you on?'

'Nights.' Shelly had to forcibly remove the grin from her face and remember she was supposed to be disgruntled about the fact.

'So we're stuck with each other?' Ross wasn't even pretending to look disgruntled. He was grinning from ear to ear, teasing her with his smile.

'It looks that way.'

'So you don't have a social life.' Smiling, he tutted a few times. 'Haven't you heard of babysitters?'

'Not with the tantrums my son's been throwing lately. I wouldn't inflict that temper on anyone just yet.'

Ross just laughed. 'So Matthew's hitting the terrible twos with a vengeance?'

'That's an understatement.' Shelly's voice stayed light, her grin stayed put, but her mind was whirring as the beginning of a frown puckered her forehead. 'How did you know his name?'

Ross shrugged. 'Melissa told me. So who's looking after him tonight?'

Her frown deepened. Melissa had obviously told Ross a bit more than Matthew's name. 'My parents are, they've been really good. You know about Neil and me, then?'

Ross nodded. Moving away from the desk slightly, they found their own private space in the corridor, slipping so easily back into their ways of old. 'It can't have been easy for you.'

Shelly gave a slightly brittle laugh. 'That's an understatement.'

Ross didn't comment at first, the silence around them building as Shelly stood there wondering how much to tell, scuffing the highly polished floor with her rubber soles and leaving little black marks that would have the cleaners in hysterics in the morning.

'Neil told me he was leaving us the day I was due to be discharged from hospital, the day I was supposed to bring Matthew home.' Her voice was shaky and she couldn't even look up as she recounted her story, sure the inevitable pity she was so tired of seeing in people's eyes would send her into floods of tears. 'He said he couldn't cope with a handicapped child, that it just wasn't what he was cut out for.'

'Then you're better off without him.'

Shelly looked up with a start. There was no pity in his voice or in his gorgeous blue eyes, just the cool sound of reason.

'So everyone keeps telling me,' Shelly sighed. 'And they're all probably right. But is it better for Matthew? Surely he needs a father?'

'Not that sort,' Ross said quickly, his voice strangely flip, a defiant jut to his chin. Suddenly he looked older than twenty-seven. He certainly didn't look like the carefree backpacker she'd built in her mind. He looked every bit the man he was. 'Children need to feel loved, safe and wanted, which are the three things Neil can't give him, so if you ask me, Matthew's better off without him. You, too, so I'm not going to make small-talk, passing on my condolences about the demise of your marriage when your divorce obviously agrees with you. You look the happiest I've seen you in a long time.'

'I am,' Shelly said slowly, the words a revelation even to herself. The divorce had hurt, but her grief had been expended long ago. The tears she cried now when she thought about the end of her marriage weren't for herself and what she'd lost but for her little boy, a two-year-old child whose father simply didn't want to know. Yet for all the angst, for all the struggle, both financially and emotionally, for all the responsibility of being a single parent, for the first time in over two years Shelly actually realised just how much she had moved on.

That she was finally making it.

Not happy exactly, but definitely getting there.

As Melissa stood up Shelly picked up her notepad. 'I'd better go and get the handover. I'll catch up with you later.'

'No doubt about that.'

Her cheeks were burning as she took handover, her mind flitting as she desperately tried to concentrate, tried to ask intelligent questions and make sure she had all the drip rates and drugs due diligently written down in her usual neat handwriting as Annie, the sister in charge of the late shift, told the night staff about the patients on the ward. But there was no chance of that. Her mind was saturated with Ross, going over and over their brief but long-awaited exchange. Still, when Annie gave the details of the latest admission, Shelly's ears pricked up and all thought of Ross flew out of the window, momentarily at least.

'We've got a new patient direct from Theatre—Angus Marshall, twenty months old with a spiral fracture of the femur.'

Shelly's eyes shot up as Annie continued. A spiral fracture in a child was an injury that sounded alarm bells and Shelly's were ringing, but Annie quickly shook her head to dispel any worries.

'The staff in Emergency are happy with the story—they don't

think it's a non-accidental injury. Apparently he's just started walking so the injury could have happened when he fell.'

'Could have?' Shelly questioned, knowing that injuries like that were sometimes caused by an abusive parent.

'They're not sure how it happened, there's a big sister and a new baby at home so it's obviously a busy house. Apparently Angus was very grouchy and reluctant to weight-bear and his mum noticed the swelling so she took him to their GP who sent them over to us. They're nice people, the child's beautifully looked after.'

'That doesn't mean anything.' Melissa's stern voice matched Shelly's thoughts exactly.

'I'm going on what I've been told. They've been interviewed extensively by Dr Khan down in Emergency and he's satisfied that it was a simple accident, so it's not up to us to go jumping to conclusions.'

'Nobody's jumping,' Shelly said in a calm voice, trying to diffuse the undercurrents. 'But with an injury like that, child abuse has to be considered.'

'Which it has been,' Annie answered stiffly. 'And it's been discounted.'

'So, how many beds does that leave us with?' Shelly asked when she realised the discussion was going nowhere.

'One bed and two cots,' Annie said, closing the folder she was reading from. 'But Emergency just rang and they're probably going to be sending up a three-month-old boy with bronchiolitis, which will leave you with just the one cot.'

'Probably?' Shelly checked.

'He's quite sick, they're still deciding whether or not to transfer him to the Children's Hospital in case he needs an ICU cot as our intensive-care beds are all taken. Ross is just heading off down there to see him.'

'Well, I hope Ross takes into account there's only three night staff on and Nicola's only a grad,' Melissa said with a warning note to her voice that had Annie again ducking for cover. Melissa was a straight talker and didn't care who got hurt along the way. Feelings didn't come in to it when she was dealing with her beloved babies. 'It's not like on days where staff are falling over themselves. One critical baby is bad enough but there's a couple more here that could go downhill quickly.'

'Ross knows all that,' Annie said defensively. 'But this baby has been down in Emergency for eighteen hours now, and there's hardly a paediatric intensive care cot left in Melbourne, so someone's going to have to take him. Anyway, Emergency just had a big multi-trauma come in and they need to start moving some of the patients.'

'Well, maybe you should have thought of that earlier,' Melissa carried on, without even blinking. 'You know as well as I do that we're going to get this baby. He should have been admitted and settled by now while there were enough staff to do it comfortably, not left till Emergency's bursting at the seams and there's no choice but to move him.' And without another word she headed out onto the ward, leaving the rest of the staff chewing their lips and rolling their eyes.

'Good luck with her tonight,' Annie said with a grimace. 'She's in a right old mood.'

'I don't blame her,' Shelly said quickly, and to the other staff's obvious surprise. 'That baby should have been admitted ages ago, not just left for the night staff.'

Minor bickers like this were uncomfortable but commonplace on a busy ward. Even though Shelly hadn't done a stint on nights for ages she knew how busy it was, and also knew that as much fun as Annie was to work with she was also very good at putting things off for the next shift to deal with. Melissa had been right to say something and Shelly was only too happy in this instance to defend her. As the day staff departed Shelly gave a comforting smile to a nervous-looking Nicola.

'When Melissa said you were "only a grad" she wasn't aiming it at you personally, just pointing out the staff levels,' Shelly said, moving straight to the point.

'I know that. It's just that she seems so fierce. I know I haven't worked with Melissa but I've seen her in handover and it's enough to put anyone off. I've been dreading coming on nights.'

'You haven't worked with Melissa yet,' Shelly pointed out. 'You've only seen her in here. She's nothing like that out there.' Shelly gestured to the ward and gave Shelly a reassuring smile. 'Any bad feeling stays in the handover room, that's an important rule on the children's ward. The patients pick up on bad vibes otherwise. Anyway Melissa's as soft as butter really. Once the day staff are gone you'll see that for yourself. As fierce as she can be, Melissa's also the best nurse here, you can learn a lot from her. There's nothing about sick children Melissa doesn't know. She's been doing this job for more than thirty years now, so if there's anything you're worried about don't sit on it, just tell her, OK?'

'OK.' Nicola nodded but Shelly could see the poor girl was still terrified.

'It will be fine, you'll see.'

It *was* fine. The obs and drug round went smoothly. Even the raucous older children, some bored from weeks in traction, seemed fairly settled, exhausted from too many visitors and computer games and a day spent good-naturedly teasing the nurses.

Melissa was in charge so she worked both sides, overseeing all the patients and keeping a watchful eye on Nicola as she settled the children and did the late round. Shelly took the cots, which consisted of eight airy rooms all surrounded by glass, which meant at any given time she had an uninterrupted view of her patients but they were all effectively isolated so as not to spread any infections. Six were occupied and Shelly checked each child carefully, smiling to herself as she did so, taking in the little bottoms sticking up in the air, thumbs tucked into mouths, the babies sleeping on blissfully as Shelly watched over them. A couple of the cheekier babies had extensions on their cots to stop them climbing out, but for now they all looked like cute little angels.

Angus was sleeping and Shelly roused him gently, carefully checking his observations and the little toes sticking out of the damp plaster, making sure the circulation to his foot was adequate. Annie was right, Shelly thought as she flicked on the cot light and checked him more closely, Angus *was* beautifully kept—his little nails short and clean, his hair soft and shiny, no rashes or bruises, nothing to indicate he was anything other than loved and cherished.

'Is he all right?' Mrs Marshall's anxious face appeared at the end of the cot. 'I was just getting a coffee.'

'He's fine,' Shelly reassured her. 'He'll probably sleep soundly for the next couple of hours. He was given a strong painkiller so he's quite comfortable. Would you like me to get you a camp bed? We can set it up beside the cot.'

Mrs Marshall shook her head. 'Thanks, but no. The day nurse, Annie I think her name was, already offered, but I'm going to go home. I've got the other two to sort out and it's been an exhausting day.'

'I'm sure it has. We can always ring you if there are any problems, if he gets too distressed,' Shelly said.

'Of course.' Mrs Marshall gave a tired smile. 'But he normally sleeps right through.' The mobile telephone ringing in her bag made them both jump and Shelly waited patiently as Mrs Marshall took the call.

'That was my husband, Doug. He's come to pick me up.' Walking over to her son, she gave him a tender kiss and stroked his little lock of hair. Shelly knew she should mention that mobiles were supposed to be turned off on the ward, given her little lecture about the interference they could cause with the equipment, but she didn't. Trying to put herself in Mrs Marshall's place for a moment, she figured it could wait for the morning.

Shelly had always been a quick worker and was grateful for the chance to make up a few bottles for when the babies inevitably awoke and to prepare some jugs of boiled water and change the sterilising solutions. Happy she was on top of things, Shelly set up an oxygen tent for the inevitable new admission and prepared the sterilising equipment and nurses' gowns along with some literature on bronchiolitis for the undoubtedly anxious parents.

'How's it going?' Melissa popped her head in the darkened room and smiled as she saw Shelly setting up the room. 'Finally, someone who doesn't have to be told! How are they all?'

'Settled. I've put the new admission in here so it's nearer the nurses' station, but cot six needs an eye kept on—she's still a bit wheezy even after her nebuliser. Cots two and four are due for a feed at eleven so I've left their obs till then. Their mums aren't staying, so if they wake up at the same time I might need you or Nicola to feed one of them—their bottles are all ready.'

'Good.'

'How's Angus?'

'Fine.'

'And the mother?'

'She's fine too, she's gone home.'

Melissa shot her a shrewd look. 'So what's the problem?'

'I don't know,' Shelly admitted. 'I know lots of mums go home, that it doesn't mean anything at all...'

'Just that you wouldn't?'

'I've only got one child.' Shelly flicked her eyes down to her handover notes. 'Mrs Marshall's got three and one of them is a young baby. She might be breastfeeding so it's totally understandable that she had to go home.'

'So why aren't you convinced?'

Shelly shrugged. 'Her husband rang her from the ambulance bay. Surely he'd want to pop up and see Angus and say goodnight?'

'Maybe he's got the other two asleep in the back of the car,' Melissa pointed out. 'Imagine if Security found two children unattended in the car park. The social workers would have a field day!'

Melissa was right, of course. There was a perfectly reasonable explanation and Shelly gave her head a small shake, determined to concentrate on the facts. But she'd misjudged Melissa, the conversation wasn't over yet.

'Just keep your eyes and ears open. I'm not entirely happy myself.' For a moment their gazes lingered on the sleeping toddler, both women deep in their own thoughts for a moment. 'Come and have a cuppa before they wake up,' Melissa said finally with forced cheerfulness. 'I'll go and put the kettle on.'

'Sounds marvellous.'

'Wait till you taste the cake I've made. Ross is already champing at the bit.'

'Melissa?' Shelly called as Melissa made her way out of the ward. 'Just what did you say to Ross exactly?'

'That I'd baked a cake!' Melissa gave Shelly a quizzical look as if she'd gone completely mad!

'I'm not talking about the cake, Melissa.' Shelly took a deep breath. She didn't want to ruffle any feathers but the fact Melissa had taken it on herself to tell Ross so much about Shelly's personal life needed addressing—the very last thing she needed was Melissa playing Cupid. Ross Bodey had enough women after him without thinking he had Shelly on his list of swooning fans. 'Ross knows Matthew's name, he seems to know all about the divorce, I just wondered how.'

'I might have said something…' Melissa shrugged.

'You mean you gave him a life update on me the second he entered the ward. Why?'

'I didn't,' Melissa said quickly. 'I hadn't laid eyes on Ross until I saw him when I was with you, honestly,' she insisted as Shelly gave her a disbelieving look. 'Believe it or not, as riveting as your life might seem to you, it's not my favourite topic of conversation. Ross and I have kept in touch while he's been away, I probably said a few things then in passing.'

'Oh.' Thankfully the room was in semi-darkness and Melissa couldn't see the blush flaming on her cheeks, but with the heat it was radiating Shelly was sure she must be able to feel it winging its way across the quiet room.

'He's rung a few times at night when he's needed something looked up or wanted a bit of advice on a patient. He's a good doctor is Ross, not too up himself to ask a nurse for advice, and when he rang we'd have a chat. He'd ask what the gossip was, who was seeing who, who was pregnant, who was leaving, that type of thing. We didn't just talk about you, Shelly.'

Suitably chastised, Shelly wished the ground would swallow her up whole.

'I'm sorry,' she mumbled. 'I was just taken back that he knew so much about everything.'

'That's Ross for you.' Melissa shrugged. 'You know he loves all the gossip.'

'Sure.' Fiddling with the oxygen tubes, Shelly kept her voice even. 'Go on, then, get the kettle on, I'll finish up in here.'

Once alone, Shelly sank onto the camp bed she had made up for the baby's mother. Sitting perched on the end, she buried her burning cheeks in her hand, trying for the life of her to fathom why Ross keeping in touch with Melissa had upset her. Why was she feeling like a jealous schoolgirl all of a sudden?

'Blast,' she muttered, then flicked her eyes open to check the coast was still clear. As if Ross would be that interested in her marriage problems. As if Melissa was going to rush to fill him in on the latest saga.

She really wasn't that important.

It had just been a casual chat, a snippet of gossip Melissa had imparted to a bored doctor stuck in the middle of nowhere, eager for a chat, happy to while away the lonely hours on call with an old friend. She should have been relieved, relieved that Melissa hadn't embarrassed her, that she hadn't bent his ear about the divorce with a nudge and a wink and a load of innuendo.

But...

The green-eyed monster was rearing its ugly head again.

Why hadn't Ross rung her? Why had he kept in touch with Melissa over the last few years?

And why did it matter so much?

'Damn,' Shelly said more strongly, the words whistling through her gritted teeth as she forced herself to take a deep steadying breath as realisation finally hit.

The hairdresser's, the perfume, the long overdue meeting with her razor hadn't been a coincidence. Hadn't even been a vague attempt to show an old friend she hadn't completely let herself go.

Of all the stupid things to go and do...

Of all the ridiculous, ludicrous things she had done in her time, this one certainly took the biscuit.

Developing a king-size crush on a certain Ross Bodey was the last thing Shelly needed to deal with. Her cheeks scorched with embarrassment at the thought of him finding out, that the dependable, organised Shelly, his on-duty friend and confidante, had succumbed like legions of others to his blue-eyed charm.

He was miles out of her league, young free and single, not just a world away but an entire galaxy from Shelly's routine existence, and it would serve her well to remember the fact.

Ross Bodey was way out of bounds.

CHAPTER TWO

PULLING UP A chair at the nurses' station, Shelly smiled at a now much happier Nicola.

'She's great, isn't she?' Nicola said, happily munching into a huge slab of walnut cake.

'Told you. Melissa's bark is far worse than her bite. Once the day staff are gone she relaxes—and feeds us,' Shelly added, helping herself to a generous slice.

'Save some for me!' Ross perched on the edge of the desk, depositing a mountain of files and X-rays as he did so.

'How's the baby in Emergency?'

'Heading this way,' Ross sighed. 'He's pretty sick but he's holding his own at the moment. The children's hospital has got an ICU cot but not a general one, whereas we've got a general but no ICU. I can't believe I'd managed to forget the constant battle with the bed state.' He rolled his eyes. 'Looks like we're in for a long night. Hopefully Melissa will go easy on me, I didn't really have any choice but to admit him. Emergency's steaming down there, it's no place for a sick baby.'

'I agree.' Melissa, coming up behind Ross, caused him to jump. 'I don't mind being busy, Ross, it's just the general thoughtlessness that annoys me. Annie should have had him up here hours ago. Instead, we've got a sick baby to assess and an overwrought mum to deal with in the middle of the night. A little bit of foresight wouldn't have gone amiss.'

Ross nodded his head in agreement. 'Right, what have you got for me? I'd better clear the pile before Kane gets here. Who knows when I'll find time otherwise?'

'Just a couple of IV orders that need updating, and I think Shelly wants some antibiotics written up for cot five—his blood culture results are back.'

Ross nodded. 'Yeah, the lab just paged me.' One hand tapped away on the computer as he brought up the results. 'This is the life,' he sighed. 'Pathologists on call, X-Ray just a stone's throw away.'

'I thought you said it was civilised where you were,' Shelly teased, desperately trying to resume normal services despite her internal bombshell.

'It was. The clinic I worked in at Tennagarrah was comparable to a luxury caravan. All the basics were there but you weren't exactly spoilt for choice and you had to work for everything. This in comparison is a five-star hotel.' With an exaggerated whoop of delight he jumped down and opened the drug fridge. 'And just look at the mini-bar, where do I start? Bactrim, flucloxacillin, gentamicin, vancomycin. What can I get you, Sister?'

Shelly peered at the monitor in front of her, reading the blood results and the antibiotic sensitivities. 'Well, a large dose of flucloxacillin would hit the spot.'

'Coming right up.

'Anything else I can get you?' Ross asked, carrying on the joke as he pulled the vial of antibiotic out of the fridge. 'Have you had a look at the room service menu yet?'

'This will do just fine.' Picking up her cake, Shelly effectively ended the playful conversation. Images of five-star hotels and bubbling spas and four-poster beds weren't exactly doing wonders for her blood pressure, and the sight of the porter wheeling in the gurney carrying the baby provided a very welcome diversion.

'Kane Anderson,' the emergency nurse informed them as Shelly pulled down the cot side and greeted Kane's mum with a warm smile. 'He's been down in Emergency so long he's part of the furniture now. This is his mum, Angela.'

'Hi, Angela, we're just going to get Kane into the cot and then I'll get the handover from Emergency. Once that's done I'll come and settle you both in.' Gently she lifted the infant over, handling him deftly and with minimum fuss so as to avoid any unnecessary exertion.

Although the handover was important and the emergency nurse was obviously in a rush to get back to her department, Shelly took a moment or two to explain how the oxygen tent worked, realising how alarming it must look to Angela.

'This monitor tells us the oxygen concentration in the tent, it's very safe.'

'He can't suffocate?' Angela checked.

'Definitely not,' Shelly said firmly. 'If the level drops in the tent the alarm goes off, and this little probe I've attached to his foot tells us Kane's own oxygen levels. I'll be back in a couple of moments. I'm just outside but if you're worried at all just bang on the window or call.'

'She's being a bit difficult,' the emergency nurse started.

'No doubt because she's worried and exhausted,' Shelly said quickly, refusing to get drawn into a discussion on the mother's emotional state, preferring to make her own observations. 'And eighteen hours in Emergency wouldn't exactly have helped matters. What's the story with the baby?'

The story wasn't very good. Three days of a worsening cough and struggling to feed, two different types of antibiotics from the local GP and a long wait in Emergency. 'His respiration rate is still very high and his heart rate's elevated. He's very grizzly, which isn't helping his breathing, and he just won't settle.'

'Any wet nappies?' Shelly asked, flicking through the obs chart.

'Three. He was moderately dehydrated when he came to us but the IV fluids have kicked in now. He's still very sick, though.'

Shelly nodded in agreement. Her brief assessment of Kane had done nothing to reassure her. He was working hard with each rapid breath, using his stomach muscles, his tiny nostrils flaring, all dangerous signs. 'I'll get Ross to have another look at him,' Shelly concluded, anxious to get back to her small charge. 'Thanks for that.'

Ross was already at the cot side, rubbing his stethoscope between his hands to warm it before placing it gently on the baby's rapidly moving chest as Angela stood anxiously wringing her hands, every bleep of the monitors making her jump slightly, every tiny jerking movement Kane made causing her to step forward anxiously, bombarding Ross with questions as he tried to listen to the baby's breathing.

'He's hungry,' Angela said the second Shelly entered. 'The sister in Emergency said he might be able to have a bottle once he got up to the ward.'

Pulling the stethoscope out of his ears, Ross straightened, carefully zipping up the oxygen tent and pulling up the cot side. 'He can't have a bottle at the moment, Angela, he's too exhausted to feed.'

'But he isn't settling.'

Shelly could hear the slightly hysterical note creeping into Angela's voice and stood back quietly as she carried on with her outburst.

'They said they were going to put a tube down his nose and give him the milk that way, but they haven't even done that. No one seems to be doing anything. He's not even on any antibiotics!'

'Look, why don't you sit down for a minute?' Ross started, but his well-meant words only inflamed Angela further.

'I don't want to sit down,' she shouted. 'I want someone to tell me what's being done for my baby.'

'I know you're upset—' Shelly started.

'Oh, what would you know?' Angela snapped, turning her fury on Shelly, her face livid.

'That you're exhausted, and terrified?' Shelly ventured, her stance relaxed, her voice calm and sympathetic. 'That you've probably had more people offering their opinions and telling you what might be, could be, should be done than you can even count?'

Mistrusting eyes finally made contact and Angela gave a grudging nod.

'Well, you're on the children's ward now, and Ross is the doctor and Melissa and I are the nurses looking after you and your son tonight. If you'll let us, we can tell you what we're going to be doing, but shouting and getting upset is only going to unsettle Kane—can you see that?'

The nod Angela gave wasn't so grudging this time, more sheepish, and Shelly felt her heart go out to the other woman as she burst into noisy tears. 'I'm sorry, it's not you, I'm just so scared, he keeps getting worse.'

'He's been sick for a few days, hasn't he?' Shelly asked gently.

'Since the weekend. I thought it was just a cold at first then he got this cough and then he started wheezing. I haven't slept for the last two nights.'

'Kane has bronchiolitis,' Ross broke in, gently taking Angela's arm and guiding her to a chair before pulling one up for himself. 'It's a respiratory virus that can be particularity nasty in young babies. Now, because it's a virus antibiotics aren't going to do any good, none at all,' he emphasised as Angela opened her mouth to argue. 'What Kane needs at the moment is what we call supportive care. That means he needs to be kept warm and rested, with lots of oxygen to help him breathe and fluids through a drip to keep him hydrated. All of this we're doing for him, and this in turn gives his body a chance to concentrate on fighting the virus. If we give him a bottle now he wouldn't be able to cope with it, he simply hasn't got enough energy to feed. If we give him one at this stage he could become a very sick little boy indeed.'

'What about the tube they were talking about?' Angela asked hopefully, her mind still focussed on her baby getting fed, but Ross firmly shook his head.

'The tube we would pass is very small and fine, but it would still upset him while we passed it and I don't want to cause him any more distress, that's why I'm going to try and not to do any blood tests or anything that might upset him, for now we just want him to rest. Kane's getting what he needs from the drip and we can give him a dummy to settle him.'

'He keeps spitting it out.' Angela's voice was rising again, her shredded nerves ready to snap at any moment, but Ross carried on chatting, his voice amicable and easy.

'We can soon fix that.'

'How?' Angela snapped.

'Glycerine.' Ross gave an easy shrug as Angela immediately shook her head.

'You're not supposed to put anything on their dummies, it says so in all the books. The child health nurse said—'

'Kane's very sick,' Ross interrupted gently. 'He needs to rest, and if a smear of glycerine on his dummy achieves that, then it's merited.'

'Ross.' Shelly gave him a wide-eyed look and Ross frowned slightly at the interruption. 'Can I have a quick word, please?'

'What's up, Shelly?' Following her outside, there was a slight impatience to Ross's stance. 'I'm trying to calm the mother. Pulling me outside isn't really helping.'

'I know that,' Shelly responded. 'But putting anything on the babies' dummies really is frowned on. Tania will have a fit…'

'Tania isn't here,' Ross pointed out. 'And if she was I'd tell her what I'm about to tell you. That baby's sick—any further slide in his condition and he'll be on a ventilator in intensive care. Now, given this hospital hasn't even got an intensive-care cot, that will mean sending him and Angela for a ten-minute jaunt in a helicopter. Now, if a bit of glycerine on a dummy can prevent that, I'm all for it.'

'But, Ross.' Shelly pulled at his sleeve as he turned to go, the contact tiny but enough to throw her, the sleeve of his white coat new and crisp, the solid bulge of his forearm, even the scent of his aftershave wafting over as he turned to go, all enough to distract her. Shelly fumbled to finish her argument.

'I know it seems petty, but the department has strict guidelines on this. The dental damage—'

'Shelly.' Ross's voice was quiet, but his words were very clear as he spoke, his eyes looking right into hers, unblinking, unwavering. 'Let's get this little guy through tonight, huh? Lose this battle and tooth decay will be something Angela can only dream about.'

Shelly's eyes were wide with surprise as Ross turned and went back to Kane. His words made sense, good sense, and in truth Shelly felt ridiculous arguing about such a tiny detail, but rules were rules... But it wasn't Ross's little lecture that had left her reeling.

The few years in the bush had changed him. That easygoing, eager-to-please guy was gone, and in his place, just as gorgeous, just as stunning, was a rather more confident version, a man who knew what he wanted, and would make sure he got it.

Heading to the treatment room, Shelly took a while to find the little-used jar.

'The contraband's arrived,' Ross said dryly as Shelly joined him at the bedside, Angela looking on anxiously, still dubious that it would work.

'It's just while he's sick,' Shelly said confidently, noting the tiny smile of appreciation on the edge of Ross's lips as she put aside her own misgivings and beckoned for Angela to come closer. 'What's more, it's something *you* can do for Kane to help him settle.'

Her words hit the mark. As Angela took the dummy, Shelly went into greater detail, showing Angela how to open the tent, how she could slip her hands in and even put her head in the cot to cuddle and speak to her child. Thankfully the glycerine worked and after a few goes baby Kane finally took his dummy. With the tent delivering a high dose of concentrated oxygen, he lay back exhausted, his little arms and legs flopping outwards like a washed-up frog as he drifted into a spent sleep.

'How's he doing?' Melissa's knowledgeable eyes scanned the monitors and baby in a moment.

'He's asleep, his saturations are ninety-two on thirty-five per cent oxygen.'

'Turn it up to forty per cent,' Melissa said after a moment's thought. 'Let's give him as much help as we can.'

Ross nodded his approval as Shelly fiddled with the flow meter.

'Come and have a cup of coffee,' Melissa offered to Angela.

'I'd rather not leave him. Can I have it in here?'

'Sorry, but the last thing you or the staff will be thinking of if Kane gets worse suddenly is a hot cup of coffee balanced on the locker.'

'Fair enough.' Angela was positively meek now, but even Shelly thought Ross was pushing things with what he said next.

'Go and have a coffee.' Ross's voice was assured. 'And then come back and have a lie-down.'

'I'm not sleeping,' Angela flared. 'How can I sleep when he's this sick? What if he gets worse?'

'He probably is going to get a bit worse.' Ross's eyes held Angela's terrified ones. 'And then he's going to start getting better, and when he does he's going to have you running in circles, feeding him, amusing him, spoiling him rotten...' He gave a tiny smile and to Shelly's amazement Angela gave a reluctant one back. 'You need some rest, you need to try and trust us to look after your baby, and you're going to be right next to him.'

He gestured to the camp bed, his eyes never leaving Angela's face. 'And if anything happens, we'll wake you.

'I promise,' he added.

'You've got the A team on tonight,' Melissa broke in, her brisk, efficient voice such a contrast to Ross's calm one, but somehow the balance worked. 'Your baby's in good hands. Now, come and have a coffee with me while we go through the admission forms. I need to know his little ways, what formula he has, how you generally settle him, that type of thing.' Technically the job was Shelly's, she was looking after cots tonight so the admission was hers, but Shelly was more than happy to defer to Melissa. They were a team and Melissa was what Angela needed right now—someone a touch more authoritative, less close in age, someone to lean on.

'She'll be right now,' Ross said quietly as Melissa led Angela out. 'That's why I wanted to just get them up here. The poor woman was beside herself down in Emergency. A slice of Melissa's cake and a bit of a rest and she'll be a new woman.'

He was right, of course. Ross was always right when it came to dealing with women, Shelly mused, fiddling again with the flow meter to get the concentration right now that the cot was zipped up and Kane was quietly resting. Someone must have given Ross a glimpse of the rule book the day he hit puberty, told him how to turn on that winning smile and work that velvet voice to gain maximum impact. Oh, he wasn't a flirt, he didn't turn on the charm to beguile people, it was all just so damned effortless with him and it would be so, so easy to let it go to her head.

To forget that the smile she was privy to right at this very second was the same gorgeous smile he used on everyone.

Even Kane.

'Cute, isn't he?' Ross murmured. 'I love fat babies.'

Shelly gave a little laugh at his simple description, her eyes taking in the sleeping infant as a woman for a moment, not as a nurse. 'Matthew was like that.' Her voice was soft, her mind dancing backwards, remembering him soft and warm in her arms, that delicious baby smell filling her nostrils, Matthew's dark curls soft and warm against her arm as she'd held him close and nursed him. 'The child health nurse even had to tell me to cut down on his feeds he got so big.'

'A little Buddha?'

'That's what I used to call him.' Shelly looked up with a start then righted herself. It was hardly an original nickname. 'He's nothing like that now, though, he's the fussiest eater in the world.'

'Unless it's ice cream?' Ross caught her eye as she gave a small nod. 'I'd love to see him.'

'I've got some pictures in my bag,' Shelly said lightly. 'I'll get them out when we've got a moment.'

'I meant I'd like to meet him.' Suddenly the tension was palpable, his eyes not moving, taking in every flicker of her startled reaction. 'See for myself if he's as cute as his mum.'

'Flatterer.' Shelly shrugged off his compliment with a smile and picked up the obs charts, which really didn't need filling in just yet. Holding his gaze would just have been too hard. 'Anyway, he's a bit tricky with strangers.'

She wanted this to be over, didn't want Ross working his winning ways on her, didn't want their friendship moving out of the safe confines of the ward, terrified her cool façade might slip and he'd register the shift in her feelings. But Ross simply refused to take the hint, whipping the safety net from under her with one stroke of his silver tongue and sending Shelly into freefall.

'That's easily solved.' His words were slow and measured but the effect was instantaneous. Shelly's heart rate surely matching the monitor bleeping rapidly beside her as Ross plunged her world into confusion. 'Don't let me be a stranger, then, Shelly.' Wrapping his stethoscope around his neck, he gave her a tiny questioning smile as she stood there, trying to think of something to say, eternally grateful when Melissa appeared with a very groggy Angela and the awful loaded silence was broken.

'One exhausted mum,' Melissa fussed, tucking in the sheets around Angela as she climbed gratefully into the camp bed, 'and one sleeping baby.'

'You'll wake me,' Angela checked as Melissa flicked off the main ward light, leaving only the cot-side lamp on, and gestured for them all to leave.

'Of course we'll wake you,' Melissa said assuredly. 'Ross promised, didn't he? And, believe it or not, you're looking at a guy who actually keeps his word.'

CHAPTER THREE

'WHAT'S THE PROBLEM?' His eyes bleary from sleep, his blond hair anything but immaculate, Ross huddled into his white coat and yawned loudly as he took a seat next to Shelly at the nurses' station.

'No problem,' Shelly said, barely looking up, concentrating instead on getting Angus to finish the training cup filled with milk that she was trying to get into him. 'Why?'

'My pager just went off.' Pulling it out of his pocket, he peered at it closely. 'Or at least I thought it did. I woke up with the most terrible fright.'

'You were dreaming.' Shelly laughed. 'I thought you'd have grown out of that by now.'

'I wish,' Ross muttered. 'Every time I've got a really sick one it's the same. I lie there half-asleep waiting for my pager to go off, and when it doesn't I wake up with a jump thinking I've slept through something.'

'Well, you didn't,' Shelly said matter-of-factly. 'Kane's still sleeping.'

'Any better?' Ross asked hopefully, but Shelly shook her head.

'Not really, that's why I'm feeding Angus up here at the desk, so I can keep an eye on him. Nicola's on her break and Melissa's in room five with a child having a nightmare.'

'Must be the night for it,' Ross muttered, glancing at his watch. 'Five a.m. already. It's not even worth going back to bed—I'll never get back to sleep now.'

A loud angry wail made its way down the corridor and Shelly let out a moan. 'Well, if you're not going back to bed, make yourself useful and go and put cot four's dummy back in for me—she's been keeping me running all night.'

'Sounds like she wants a bit more than a dummy,' Ross yawned as he stood up.

'Tell Tayla she'll just have to be patient. Her bottle's warming and as soon as I've finished this little one, she'll get her turn.

'And wash your hands first,' Shelly reminded him as he wandered off. 'Hey, little guy.' Tickling Angus under his chin, Shelly attempted to raise a smile, but his solemn eyes wouldn't meet hers. 'You really wanted that milk, didn't you?'

'What are you doing?' Shelly grinned, looking up from Angus as Ross wandered back, dressed in a white nurse's gown and holding an angry pink bundle in one hand and pushing a portable bassinet with the other.

'What female knows how to be patient?' Ross asked good-naturedly, settling himself in the chair and holding out the bottle. 'Check the temperature for me.' He shook a few drops onto her wrist and when Shelly nodded he balanced the baby on his knee and attempted to offer her the bottle, which Tayla promptly spat out, her wails of protest increasing.

'You need to cuddle her in.'

'In what?' Ross asked, bouncing her up and down on his knee as Tayla's cries gained in momentum.

'Into your chest. Wrap her up more tightly in the blanket and hold her against you.' She watched, fighting the urge to put her own patient down and interfere as Ross clumsily wrapped the baby up, leaving her little pink feet kicking in the air. Ever meticulous, Shelly liked things neat and organised but baby Tayla didn't seem to mind Ross's haphazard methods, her cries instantly stopping as one blond-haired arm wrapped firmly around her and pulled her in close.

Lucky little thing, Shelly thought reluctantly.

'It worked.' Ross grinned. 'She likes it.'

'For now,' Shelly warned briskly. 'But that good mood won't last long if you don't follow it up with her bottle.'

Ross did as he was told and soon Tayla was guzzling, batting her little blue eyes at her enthralled admirer and somehow managing to coo and drink at the same time.

'Another female you've won over,' Shelly said dryly.

'If only they were all so easy.' Looking over, he gave Shelly a slow smile. 'It's like having twins, isn't it?'

'Heaven forbid,' Shelly said lightly, deliberately shooing away the rather cosy little images fluttering into her mind. The beginning of a shadow was dusting his chin, his eyes blinking with tiredness as he stifled regular yawns, and he looked so completely adorable Shelly felt like joining Tayla and cooing in blatant admiration.

Sure, the odd doctor had in his time given a baby a bottle at night, and sitting at the nurses' station nicking biscuits and cake was an annoyingly regular occurrence, but it was the *way* Ross did things. His absolute delight in the simple things in life made moments like these precious, made sitting feeding two little imps at five o'clock in the morning on a hushed children's ward so special it almost brought a lump to Shelly's throat.

Ross looked over as Shelly pulled Angus in for a cuddle.

'How's he doing?'

'Good. He's had all his milk, he hasn't made a murmur all night.'

'Has he had any paracetamol?'

'He hasn't needed anything,' Shelly said lightly, but her voice trailed off as she saw a frown pucker Ross's face.

'Give him some anyway.' Ross's voice was suddenly thick, a serious look Shelly had never yet witnessed marring his normally happy face. 'Maybe he's in pain and has just given up complaining about it.'

'You think he's been abused as well?' Shelly looked down at the dozing child in her arms and her heart ripped another inch. 'But Dr Khan seems to think—'

'Forget what Dr Khan "seems to think",' Ross interrupted bitterly. 'Look at him, Shelly, look at him. Why isn't he cooing like Tayla? Why isn't he smiling or even crying come to that? Why isn't he asking for his mum?'

There was such a raw note to his voice, such an edge of urgency that Shelly looked up from Angus, startled. Never had she seen Ross like this. Sure, he was a caring and compassionate doctor; sure, he got upset at times, they all did, but something in his voice told Shelly that Angus had touched a nerve, a raw painful nerve, and Shelly was momentarily at a loss as to how she should react.

'Ross...' she started, but he shook his head.

'Leave it, Shelly.' He took a deep breath and looked back down at Tayla. 'Please.'

Which pretty much ended the conversation.

Standing, Shelly held Angus closer as she found his prescription chart from her neat pile on the desk and opened the drug cupboard, measuring out the medicine with one hand, a feat she had mastered to perfection after so many years on the children's ward.

Angus took the syrup without a murmur of protest, but instead of putting him back into his cot, Shelly sat back down. In the scheme of things one extra cuddle wouldn't make much difference, but it surely couldn't hurt!

'So how was your first night back?'

'Not the best.' Ross shrugged, his usual smile noticeably absent. 'Nothing changes here, does it?'

'Of course not,' Shelly quipped. 'Why change the habits of a lifetime?' Still Ross didn't smile, and Shelly felt her own smile fading as Ross continued.

'After I left here I had to go over to the postnatal ward and check the lab results on a baby with jaundice. She needs to go under the phototherapy lights and when I told the mum she started crying because she doesn't want her baby in the nursery away from her for the next thirty-six hours.'

'It happens all the time, Ross,' Shelly said lightly. 'Why on earth would that upset you?'

'Because it's so unnecessary. I suggested to the midwife we move the lights into the mother's room, she's in a side ward, the equipment wouldn't bother anyone else...'

'What did the midwife say?'

'She agreed with me,' Ross sighed. 'Trouble is, she's been having the same running argument for the last three years and hasn't got anywhere, because policy dictates that phototherapy takes place in the nursery. Apparently if we make allowances for one, all the mums will be demanding side wards if their babies need the treatment.'

Shelly sat deep in thought for a moment, her first instinct to sigh and agree with Ross, the pettiness of hospital protocol achingly familiar, and yet...

Green eyes darted upwards and suddenly Shelly felt defensive, longing to reassure him, for Ross to feel as enamoured of the place as she did, because if he didn't...

The alternative was too awful to contemplate.

'Doesn't it ever get to you?' Ross asked, breaking into her thoughts.

'Sometimes,' Shelly admitted. 'But it's a big hospital, Ross, there's always going to be a policy that irks if you go looking for it. I just try not to let it get to me. I enjoy my work on the children's ward, I do my job to the best of my ability and then I go home, that's enough for me.'

'Is it?' Ross questioned, and Shelly took another moment as she pondered his question.

'It has to be, Ross. I've got a mortgage, a child to think of. I can't go around demanding changes, questioning the wisdom behind every decision. Sure, sometimes I get frustrated, some-times I'd like to be able to do my own thing, but in a hospital this size it's just not going to happen.'

'It would in Tennagarrah.'

Shelly heard the shift in his voice, the slightly wistful note as he moved in his chair and smiled down at Tayla.

'You really miss it, don't you?' She watched the slight nod of his head then ventured further. 'If you loved it so much, how come you came back?'

'I had my reasons.' His eyes found hers then, but they didn't dart away, didn't turn back to a contented Tayla or relax into a smile. Instead, he held her gaze, not blinking or wavering as Shelly felt her colour deepen, felt the weight of his stare and the dearth of unanswered questions behind it.

Confused, self-conscious under his scrutiny, Shelly broke the moment, tore her eyes away and looked down at Angus who was sleeping peacefully now. 'Let's get you to bed, little guy.'

Angus's room was quiet and Shelly lingered a moment as she tucked him in, brushing the blond curls back from his face and placing one of the hospital's teddy bears under the blan-ket beside him.

But it wasn't just Angus keeping her there. Suddenly she was strangely reluctant to go back outside without the easy diversion of feeding a baby, unnerved by the blatant openness of Ross's stare. But there was a pile of notes waiting to be written, and hiding in a cubicle wasn't going to get them done!

'I didn't know you wore glasses.' Ross grinned as Shelly opened a folder and started her nursing notes, relieved at the shift in tempo. 'When did that happen?'

'Sometime after I hit thirty,' Shelly said grimly, her forehead creasing as she concentrated on the paperwork.

'They suit you.'

His observation went without comment as Shelly worked diligently away, Kane's history too important to be sidetracked by small-talk.

'Talk to me, Shelly,' Ross grumbled as she worked on in silence.

'I'm working.'

'So am I,' Ross responded, placing a sleeping Tayla into the bassinet beside him. 'Come on, Shelly, talk to me. I haven't seen you in well over two years.'

'You're worse than Matthew,' Shelly sighed. 'At least *he* can amuse himself for five minutes. Look, I'm busy right now, Ross. Make yourself useful and put the kettle on.'

Which took him two seconds flat.

He really was worse than Matthew, leaning over her shoulder when she wrote, correcting her spelling and generally buzzing around like an annoying fly. A gorgeous diversion he might be at times, but right now a diversion wasn't what Shelly wanted or needed!

'Can I see the photos?'

'What photos?'

'The ones you said you had in your bag.'

'They're in my purse,' Shelly mumbled, chewing on her pen and gesturing to the bag, but Ross just sat there, annoyingly close, his blue eyes boring into her rapidly darkening cheeks. 'What now?'

'I can't just go through your bag. You'll have to get them for me.'

'You really are annoying, Ross, do you know that?' Kicking the bag in his general direction, Shelly pointedly turned back to her notes. 'I promise there's nothing exciting in there. If there is, we'll halve it.'

But for all her nonchalance, for all her supposed annoyance, as Shelly sat there, writing, her heart was in her mouth as she focussed on the blur of words in front of her, struggling with an overwhelming desire to turn her head to see Ross's reaction when he saw Matthew for the first time, though why it should matter, why his opinion should count for much, Shelly truly couldn't fathom.

'He's beautiful, Shelly.' Ross's voice was quiet and there was a difference she couldn't pin down, a subtle shift from the observations he had so readily imparted about Kane and Tayla. She acknowledged him then. Turning, she caught her breath as he took in the pictures, his eyes scanning each shot, a flickering smile lighting up his tired face.

'He's just gorgeous.'

She waited, but the words she silently dreaded didn't materialise, didn't impinge on the moment. No ifs or buts, no sighs or if onlys.

Ross in his own sweet way had said the three little words Shelly really needed to hear.

CHAPTER FOUR

'HOW WAS YOUR night, sweetheart?' Marlene flicked on the kettle the second a weary Shelly pushed open the front door.

'Busy,' Shelly answered, a huge smile splitting her tired face as a pyjama-clad bundle dived off the couch and ran the length of the hallway. 'Hi, Matthew.' Her instinct was to scoop her son into her arms and kiss the Vegemite-streaked face but, ever mindful of bringing germs home from work, Shelly settled instead for a quick kiss on the cheek. 'Just let Mummy have a quick shower, darling, and I'll be with you in a moment.

'Two minutes,' she added to Marlene, before darting into the bathroom and taking the quickest shower in history and dressing at lightning speed.

Everything seemed to be done at lightning speed these days.

Work, crèche runs, cooking, cleaning, even mothering.

'How was he?' Running a comb through her long auburn curls, Shelly scraped her hair into a scrunchy before taking a grateful sip of her coffee.

'Fine. Once he went down, he slept all night.' There was a long pause, which struck Shelly as unusual. Marlene was normally regaling her with tales, not necessarily about Matthew. They could be anything from the movie she'd seen, the newspaper headlines, to what she was cooking for dinner that night—anything other than silence.

'What's wrong, Mum?'

'Nothing.' Marlene's voice didn't sound particularly convincing as she busied herself stacking dishes before turning around, a worried frown out of place in her usual sunny face. 'You know there's a group of our friends going to Fiji on Saturday?'

Shelly nodded. 'That's right. You didn't want to go.'

'We did want to go.' Her voice was wary and Shelly jerked her face up as Marlene continued. 'We just didn't think it would be fair on you.'

'What on earth made you think that?' Shelly wailed. 'Of course you should have gone. I'd have managed.'

'How?'

'Matthew's in crèche now. I'd have worked my shifts around and if not I'd just have taken annual leave. You and Dad do enough for us, you deserve a holiday. I can't believe you'd pass one up without talking to me first.' Shelly was gesturing wildly in the air, the longed-for cup of coffee quickly forgotten as she struggled with what her mother was telling her.

Ken and Marlene had been wonderful.

Wonderful.

When Neil had dropped the bombshell that their marriage was over, Ken and Marlene had put their hands up straight away. Had picked up a shell-shocked mother and her newborn from the hospital as if it had been the most natural thing in the world, and had practically spoon-fed Shelly through those blurry postnatal days until gradually her reserves had strengthened. They'd helped her find a new house, decorating it for her until it had become a home, babysitting endlessly, there at the drop of a hat or a ring of the telephone, sleeping over in Shelly's house when she'd worked nights so as not to disrupt Matthew's routine and generally going way beyond the call of any dutiful parent.

And it was starting to show.

Marlene and Ken were getting older, and co-raising a boisterous toddler, exhausting at the best of times, was a hard feat as they neared their sixties. The endless guilt Shelly felt as she saw her own parents suspend their lives in the name of love surfaced at that moment and she struggled with tears that welled in her eyes.

'Why didn't you talk to me, Mum?'

'I am talking.' Marlene forced a smile. 'June and Roland can't go. She's got to have a little operation, and if she puts it off, heaven knows when her name will come up again. If they back out now, they'll lose all their money...'

'You and dad could take their places,' Shelly said quickly, as Marlene gave a worried nod.

'That's what we were thinking.'

'Do it, Mum. Please.'

'But how on earth will you manage?' Marlene asked hesitantly.

'Like every other single parent!' Shelly exclaimed. 'How long will you be gone?'

'A week,' Marlene said doubtfully.

'I can manage for a week, for goodness' sake!' Shelly exclaimed. 'If you pass this up I'll never forgive myself and I'll be furious with you. I'm furious already that you didn't even discuss it with me the first time around. Look, Matthew's my son, not yours. You and Dad have been wonderful but I don't want you to give up your lives for us. Dad should be enjoying his retirement, not worrying about crèche runs and babysitting duties...'

'We love doing it,' Marlene protested.

'I know that, Mum,' Shelly said wearily. 'And, to be honest, I don't know how I'd have managed without you, but I have to start standing up on my own two feet a bit more, I have to start holding the reins by myself, and a week without you will be a good practice run. When do you have to let June and Roland know by?'

'This morning.'

Shelly deliberately didn't sigh, purposely kept on smiling as the cosy image of her warm bed was pulled from under her. 'Good. You go and tell them yes and I'll drop Matthew at crèche then I'll go and speak to Tania, the unit manager, about my roster.'

'But you're tired. Why don't you just ring her and then go to bed? I can take Matthew to crèche for you.'

'No.' Shelly's voice was firm but kind. 'He doesn't like going there and I know how upset you get when you leave him.'

'It's for the best, though,' Marlene's voice was wary as Shelly blew out her cheeks. 'It *is*, Shelly. You know Neil's not my favourite person in the world, but he did look long and hard into the best crèche for Matthew. If he follows this programme, he might even be able to go to a normal school.'

'With an aide,' Shelly pointed out.

'Still, it would be nice.'

'For who?' Shelly started, then bit her tongue. Matthew's education wasn't on the agenda this morning. 'His crèche is on the way to the hospital, and it really would be better for me to talk to Tania face to face than do it over the telephone. Anyway…' Shelly managed a reassuring grin '…you've got to get to the travel agent.'

'Just give him a kiss and tell him you'll be back at five, Shelly. He'll soon stop crying when you're gone.'

When I've abandoned him, you mean.

Shelly knew Lorna, the childcare worker, meant well. Knew from her own nursing experience that invariably once the parents had gone children quickly settled. But Matthew wasn't in hospital, this wasn't a two-day admission with the mum popping home for a shower and freshen-up. This was a Monday-to-Friday occurrence and it was tearing Shelly to shreds.

Crying in the car park over her steering-wheel was another Monday-to-Friday occurrence.

Matthew should be at home with her, making fairy cakes,

or mud cakes in the garden, sleeping in his own bed for his afternoon nap. She should be working part time for pleasure, not full time to support them.

Bloody Neil and his big-shot ideas.

Turning on the engine, Shelly wiped the back of her damp cheeks with a shaking hand.

Early intervention, integration. Neil relieved his guilt by paying half of the crèche fees and he had the gall to think he was helping. Shelly didn't want intervention—she wanted to care for her own child in her own home. And as for integration!

'Don't get me started,' Shelly muttered to herself.

Why should going to a *normal* school be the ultimate goal? Why should matching his peers in their milestones be the be-all and end-all?

Matthew *was* different, and it would seem Shelly was the only person in the world prepared to accept the fact.

Tania didn't exactly roll on the floor laughing at Shelly's request to yet again juggle the roster, but the incredulous look she imparted as Shelly falteringly outlined her parents' plans pretty much made the message clear.

'I'd love to help,' Tania sighed, running her eyes down the roster, 'but I just don't see how I can.'

'If I can go back onto days for just a week then I could drop Matthew at crèche early. I couldn't do the late shift, though,' Shelly mumbled. 'The crèche is only open until six...' Her voice trailed off as Tania shook her head.

'The whole point of implementing internal rotation was to share the load, and I'm sorry to say this, Shelly, but in your case this simply isn't happening. You can't expect the other staff to keep covering for you—they've got families of their own to worry about.'

Cheeks flaming, Shelly deliberately didn't rise, her parents' holiday enough incentive to force the issue. 'Can I have some annual leave, then?'

'You've used up all your annual leave, Shelly,' Tania pointed out, running her eye along the holiday schedule. 'In actual fact you owe the ward eight hours.'

'Then can I take it as unpaid leave?' Shelly pushed, hating the fact she was reduced to begging, but there really was no other alternative. 'I hate asking, but it's important.'

'It always is with you, Shelly.' Tania sighed as she put down her pen and fixed her junior with a firm stare. 'I'm sorry, but in this instance my hands are tied, there's just no one to cover you. I've just received yet another memo from Admin about cutting back on agency staff.' Her voice had a slightly pained edge. 'Last month it was Matthew's grommets, the month before chickenpox…'

'I know,' Shelly muttered, scuffing the floor. 'We've had a bad run.'

'I have enough trouble accommodating my staff's holiday requests without having to take into account their parents! I need dependable staff, Shelly, this is a children's ward and it has to be run by competent, reliable staff.' Her words were delivered in a relatively calm voice but Shelly felt the sting of them as surely as if she'd been slapped. To date she'd always prided herself on her competence, her organisation and her meticulous attention to detail, and suddenly here she was being told that even that saving grace was being taken from her.

'When you're here, you're wonderful.' Tania added more gently, the evident shock on Shelly's face softening her stance. 'I know you've had a lot of problems, I know you're home life's rather difficult, and it's a credit to you that you manage to leave your problems at the ward door and deliver excellent nursing care, but I can't keep juggling the roster to fit in with your domestic issues.

'I'm sorry,' she added as Shelly stood up and left the office and in her haste to get out of there didn't even attempt to say goodbye.

'Hey, Shelly, I thought you'd be safely tucked up in bed by

now!' Ross was grinning, as laid-back as ever, walking alongside her effortlessly even though Shelly was marching briskly, hoping to make it to the car park before she broke down in tears.

'I had to sort out my roster,' Shelly replied, without looking. 'How come you're still here?'

'I wanted to have a word with the boss about Angus.'

His words stopped Shelly in her tracks and she turned abruptly to face him.

'I'm still not happy with the story,' Ross said with a tight shrug. 'Not that my opinion counts for much.'

'They're not going to report it, then.'

'Dr Khan doesn't think there's any need. "Accidents happen" were his exact words.' His voice was flip, but Shelly knew the words that were coming out of his mouth weren't Ross's. 'I've also been delivered a short sharp lecture on my over-zealous nature. Dr Khan seems to think that as I've been stuck in the bush for the last couple of years I'm chafing at the bit to get my hands into some "real" medicine. Hell, if only he knew what I'd dealt with out there. I tell you this much, Shelly, I don't get any kick out of exaggerating things, but there's something going on with Angus, and I'm the only one who can see it.'

'You're not, Ross,' Shelly sighed. 'I'm not happy either. I've written it all up in my notes and I've handed it over...'

'That's all we ever do.' The angry edge to his voice shocked Shelly and for a second the man that stood in front of her seemed so far away from the Ross she knew that Shelly barely recognised him. But almost as soon as the words were out his expression changed, the easy smile was back and the Ross she knew so well was smiling down at her. 'So, did you get it sorted?'

'What?'

'The roster.'

Pulling her bag high on her shoulder, Shelly resumed her angry march. 'No. In fact, I got my own short sharp lecture this morning, except in my case it would seem I'm not zealous enough. Apparently the ward's been making allowances for my lack of dependability, given my "domestic issues", but it would seem the goodwill has run out now.'

A warm hand was on her arm, a hand that was pulling her back, turning her around to face him.

'Tania can be a right cow sometimes. Don't take it personally, Shelly.'

'But it is personal,' Shelly hissed. 'My mum and dad have run themselves ragged looking after Matthew and the one chance they get to go on holiday I can't even take the time off to look after my own son.'

'You'll work something out.'

'How?' Shelly snapped, her exasperation brimming to the surface.

'Because you always do. Come on, Shell, let's go and get some breakfast in the canteen, have a chat and see if we can come up with something. Two heads are better than one.'

'Oh, spare me the proverbs.' Snarling at Ross was the last thing Shelly wanted to be doing, he didn't deserve it, but she was past caring. If he'd just let her go she could get to the car park, and if he didn't, well, Ross would just have to wear the steam she was blowing in all directions.

'Come on,' Ross pushed. 'At least for a coffee.'

'I don't want a drink, Ross, I want to go home and sleep. I've got to come back here tonight.'

'So do I,' Ross pointed out, his laid-back calmness only exacerbating Shelly's volatile mood.

'Yes, but no doubt you'll get up at eight, hop in the shower and pour some boiling water over two-minute noodles then rock across from the doctors' mess around nine.'

'I don't like noodles.'

'I, on the other hand,' Shelly carried on, ignoring his grin, 'will get up at four, pick up my son and then prepare a dubiously delicious but extremely nutritious dinner, packing in as many omega oils as I can along the way to supposedly increase his brain function. Then I'll try to squeeze in an hour of quality time before I bathe him and attempt to have him tucked up in bed before my mum gets over, and then…' Shelly took a deep breath, her angry, tired eyes finally meeting Ross's. 'Then I'll come and start work.'

He stood there for a moment, eyeing her thoughtfully, as Shelly's colour darkened, stunned at the venom of her own outburst, waiting for him to crush her with some cutting remark.

'Was that a no to the coffee, then?' A lazy smile was tugging at the corner of his mouth, and to Shelly's absolute amazement a reluctant smile was wobbling on the edge of hers.

'Yes, it was a no,' she mumbled, scarcely able to believe after her anger only seconds before she was now almost smiling.

'Some other time maybe?'

Shelly nodded. All the fight had gone out of her and she ached, literally ached for her bed, the vented steam leaving her curiously calm.

'Come on.' His lazy arm slung itself around her and for the tiniest second Shelly let herself lean on him. 'I'll walk you to your car.'

Surprisingly, the steering-wheel wasn't privy to a second batch of tears. In fact, idle fingers drummed on it as Shelly drove home, listening to the radio and singing tunelessly.

She didn't even toss and turn as she lay in bed, her mind didn't throb as she tried to fathom the hows and whys of arranging childcare in her parents' absence, she didn't lie there fretting about Matthew and the beastly crèche. Instead, she pulled the curtains closed on the midmorning sun, slipped into the welcomingly cool sheets and closed her eyes with only one sleepy thought on her mind.

Ross was back.

And how good it felt.

'What's this?'

Shelly shifted in her seat and quickly folded the papers she had been reading in front of her. The last few days had been spent simultaneously assuring Marlene she had everything in hand and panicking at her inability to organise Matthew's child-care.

So desperate was Shelly, she'd even swallowed every last shred of pride and rung Neil, taken the bull by its very reluctant horns and dialled his office. But even before he had stopped huffing and puffing, even before Neil had admitted there was no way his new wife would even consider having Matthew for a week, Shelly had decided that he wasn't going there anyway.

She'd rather pay someone to look after him than expose Matthew to such blatant apathy!

Which was why Ross had found Shelly sitting at the nurses' station engrossed in the pile of brochures the crèche had provided her with, reeling somewhat at the hourly rates. It wasn't just the money that was the problem—the thought of a stranger looking after Matthew in her house at night while she worked was giving Shelly palpitations! Folding up the papers, Shelly pushed them away on the desk before turning her frown on Ross. 'Don't you know that it's rude to read over people's shoulders?'

'No, it isn't.' Ross laughed. 'Maybe for an uptight puritan like you, but as to the rest of us...'

Shelly swung round on her chair, her jaw dropping incredulously. 'That's a bit strong, even from you!'

Ross just shrugged and spooned three sugars into his coffee. 'Possibly,' he conceded with a grin. 'But it got a reaction. Anyway, you can't afford it.'

'Can't afford what?'

'A live-in babysitter.'

This was getting way too personal and Shelly pulled off her glasses, snapping them firmly in their case before heading off towards Kane's room.

'That's right,' Ross called good-naturedly, 'run off, why don't you? One mustn't discuss money or personal problems or any other social taboos.'

'I'm not running off,' Shelly corrected. 'I'm checking on Brody in cot two.'

'You did that ten minutes ago and, anyway, Melissa's just been in.'

Reluctantly Shelly sat back down, her back rigid, her lips disappearing into her face.

'You can't afford it,' Ross said again. 'Because if you had that type of money to burn, you wouldn't be at work in the first place.'

His irritating logic was unfortunately spot on.

'Ring in sick,' he suggested lightly. 'You get two weeks with chickenpox when you work on a children's ward.'

'Oh, very helpful, Ross.' Shelly gave a slow handclap. '"Hi, Tania, I know I sat in your office and begged for unpaid leave, but it really is just a coincidence that I've come down with chickenpox and can't work for a week. Yes, I know Matthew had it a few weeks ago and I didn't catch it then. Funny, that. And I know you think I'm undependable and are probably about to sack me, but can I take this opportunity to assure you that I'm really very reliable?"'

'All right, bad idea,' Ross shrugged. 'How about I babysit for you?'

'You?' Shelly gave a rather undignified sniff.

'I am a doctor,' Ross pointed out. 'Almost a paediatrician even! I can look after Matthew at night while you work, then you can take over in the day, the same as you're doing with your parents now.'

'But you've never even met him.'

'Neither have any of this lot.' Picking up the brochures, Ross flipped them in the wastepaper basket.

'Why on earth would you want to do this?'

'Because I can.' Perching on the desk beside her, he tapped his thigh with a pencil, his leg so close it occasionally brushed Shelly's as he distractedly swung his feet. 'You need help,' he pointed out. 'And I'm only too happy to give it. Mind you, you'll have to feed me a lot. You already know I don't like noodles, but apart from that I'm pretty easy. I'm not very tidy, though.'

'I'd never have guessed.'

'And I'm a morning person. You can't just march home after a hard night at work and demand silence. I like someone to talk to over my breakfast.'

The image of Ross sitting at her breakfast table was doing terrible things to Shelly's concentration.

'It would never work.'

'Why? I've only got a room at the doctors' mess, it would take two minutes to pack my backpack.'

'It wouldn't work,' Shelly insisted in an irritated voice. 'I'd rather pay someone, at least that way I'd know they were doing things properly.'

'Properly!' Ross repeated her last word through pursed lips.

'Yes, properly, Ross,' Shelly snapped, her words coming out way too harsh, but suddenly Ross was getting too near for comfort, making promises he would surely never, ever keep, and perhaps more to the point Shelly was frightened of letting him into her life. Terrified that one look at the real Shelly, the mum, the housewife, the eternal juggling game that her life was at the moment, would have Ross scuttling away in two seconds flat.

Snapping seemed her only option.

'I like things done in a certain way. You'd probably let Matthew stay up half the night chewing on sweets and no doubt then you'd forget to tell him to brush his teeth.'

Ross roared with laughter. 'You've really got an obsession with dental decay, do you know that, Shelly?'

'People would talk.' She shot him a look, knowing exactly what was coming next and keen to get in first. 'And if that makes me an uptight puritan then so be it.'

'Let them talk.' Ross leant across the table, his dark blue eyes dangerously close, very white teeth that he most certainly had brushed glinting at her as she took in his wide sensual mouth. 'Better still, let's give them something to talk about.'

'This is silly.' Standing up, Shelly shook her head. 'I really am going to check on cot two now.'

Brody was fine, better than fine actually. The little boy who had been keeping Shelly on the run with his exacerbation of asthma was sleeping peacefully, his respiration rate finally nearing normal, his heart rhythm settling and his oxygen saturations spot on.

'I think he's turned the corner.' Ross had come up behind her, and they stood there in the darkness for a moment eyeing the baby, sharing a mutual sigh of relief. 'When did he last have a nebuliser?'

Shelly glanced down at her watch. 'An hour and a half ago and it's still holding him.' Pulling her stethoscope out of her pocket, Shelly carefully listened to the sleeping baby's chest. 'Not even a hint of a wheeze.' She smiled, pulling the earpieces out and offering them to Ross. She moved the bulb of the stethoscope as Ross listened, then looked up with a grin.

'Clear as a bell.'

'Which means you can get some sleep now.'

She felt rather than heard him go. Having written Brody's observations down, she pulled a falling blanket around his little shoulders, her cheeks still burning from the conversation only moments before, a frown puckering her forehead as she recalled Ross's offer.

It was all a joke to Ross. His suggestion, however well meant, had irritated her.

As if someone like Ross Bodey was going to take a week out of his life to devote to her and Matthew. Sure, he'd maybe even meant it while he'd been sitting there, but it wouldn't last five minutes. He'd probably already forgotten he'd even offered.

Wrong.

Walking out into the corridor, she jumped as a face came out of the shadows.

'Did you forget something?'

'Your address.' She couldn't read his expression in the darkness but for all the world Shelly was sure she heard a note of nervousness in his voice. 'What nights do you need me for?'

'You're really serious about this?' Shelly checked.

'Totally.'

'Sunday through to Wednesday,' Shelly ventured, watching his reaction closely, waiting for him to baulk at the final hurdle. 'Then back again for one night next Saturday.'

'Fine,' Ross said easily. 'I finish my nights on Saturday morning so I'll have a sleep then come for dinner around six. Don't worry,' he rattled on as Shelly opened her mouth to protest. 'I'll bring the food. You won't have to lift a finger. It'll give me some time to get to know the little fellow and on Sunday afternoon I'll come back to stay.'

'Ross, this isn't going to work,' Shelly said quickly, confused at the turn of events, desperate for some breathing space to think things through.

'Yes, it is.'

He sounded so sure, so confident Shelly felt the frown puckering her brow slip away, and after a moment's more hesitation she took the pad he was offering and scribbled her address, which he deposited in his pocket.

'And it is going to work, Shelly.' One warm hand gently cupped her cheek, the small gesture losing all its innocence as her heart went into overdrive. 'Because we're going to make sure of it.'

CHAPTER FIVE

'HONEY, I'M HOME!'

Shelly stood holding the front door, grinning as Ross barged in armed with white carrier bags wafting delicious smells.

'What on earth are you going on about?'

'I'm practising for our week of domestic bliss.' Kissing her on the cheek, he shot a quick wink at a rather stunned Matthew who was clinging for dear life to Shelly's leg, one curious eye peeping out from behind her far-too-short skirt. 'Can you show me where the kitchen is?'

She should have been nervous!

She had been nervous!

The entire day had been spent in a flurry of cleaning and scrubbing, and not only the house! Her hair had been deep-conditioned, body lotion had been applied, eyebrows plucked and her wardrobe turned up and over as she'd frantically scrabbled for something to wear.

Something terribly casual, of course.

But also absolutely gorgeous.

A mad dash to the shops at four-thirty had for once been a success given that the very short lilac wraparound skirt Shelly had had her eye on all week actually came in her size.

Even Matthew was amazingly clean for six p.m. The usual

sticky fingers for once were gleaming, his jammy face washed and wiped as he stood in very trendy clothes, a world away from the grubby overalls he normally wore around the house. Yet now that Ross was here, now that he'd burst in with his usual wacky humour, Shelly wasn't nervous any more, just very, very pleased to see him.

'How was your day at the office?' She kept up the joke as Ross deposited his wares on her kitchen bench.

'Awful, actually.' For a second the easy smile slipped away and Shelly found herself frowning. 'I had a bit of a run-in with Dr Khan this morning before I finished up.'

'What happened?'

'I'll tell you later.' Ross's eyes shifted to Matthew shyly peering around the kitchen door and his face broke back into its usual wide smile.

'What's that smell?' He sniffed the air, screwing up his nose as Matthew watched.

'Tuna casserole,' Shelly answered primly, awkward in her new skirt and panicking that she was showing too much of her pale legs. 'And don't worry, it's not for you—it's Matthew's dinner.'

'Smells terrible,' Ross quipped as Matthew started to giggle.

'It's very tasty actually.'

'If you like tuna casserole! I've bought Thai for us all,' he carried on, banging around opening cupboards and finding plates. 'Now, that really is tasty.'

'For us perhaps, but Matthew won't like it.'

Well, what would she know? She was only his mother after all.

Matthew, as it turned out, loved Thai food—nearly as much as he liked the cola Ross had bought and the ice cream that followed.

Nearly as much as he clearly adored Ross.

'You'll get bored before Matthew does,' Shelly warned as they engaged in a complicated game of peek-a-boo while Shelly stacked the dishwasher. But yet again her son surprised her—it was Matthew who ended the game. Ross, it seemed, would have gone on for hours.

'Bar.'

'Bath,' Shelly translated easily as she came into the living room, smiling at the two of them lying sprawled on the sofa, watching cartoons. Scooping up Matthew, she carried him out, not even mildly surprised when Ross followed her. 'He always has one around this time.'

'He's his mother's son.' Ross grinned as Shelly stood with there with a questioning look on her face, waiting for enlightenment. 'Bath at seven, bed at eight…'

'He likes to have a routine, all children like a routine, it makes them feel secure.'

'Whatever you say, *Sister*.'

Shelly was prickling with indignation as he followed her to the bathroom. Ross could always do this to her, make her feel uptight, like some antiquated old school nurse.

'Look…' Shelly gestured as she put in the plug. 'Not a trace of carbolic soap in sight.'

'I'm teasing,' Ross said easily. 'Still, you'd better show me where the spare toothbrushes are kept.'

'Here.' Pulling open the bathroom cupboard as she ran the water, Shelly caught his incredulous look. 'What have I done now?'

'I was joking.' He laughed. 'Or at least I thought I was. How many toothbrushes have you got in there!'

'The crèche was doing a fundraiser,' Shelly mumbled as he perched on the vanity unit. 'Each family had to sell ten—it was easier just to buy them myself. I haven't got obsessive-compulsive disorder.

'Yet,' she added with a reluctant grin.

And as easily as that, her awkwardness was gone. The days of frantic preparations, the nights wrestling with the wisdom of having Ross as a house guest disappearing like a puff of smoke as she joined him on the vanity. They dangled their feet and watched as Matthew enjoyed his bath the way only two-year-olds could. Squealing with delight at the mountains of frothy bubbles, filling bottles and emptying them over and over until he worked out that hitting the water directly with the palms of his hands could have the adults present ducking for cover. Ross didn't mind, not at all, and by the end of the bath the two of them were only slightly less wet than Matthew.

It was nice having him there, not awkward, not difficult, just nice. Somehow he seemed to know exactly what was needed, what was wanted, and when Matthew was dressed in pale blue pyjamas, his little eyes blinking as he struggled to keep them open, Ross gave the little guy a playful ruffle of his hair and said goodnight, leaving Shelly to settle the over-excited little boy into his bed.

'*Wun, wun.*' Sticking his thumb in his mouth, Matthew pointed to the much-loved book Shelly was holding, but instead of opening it and getting on with the story Shelly decided to test the water.

'Did you like Ross?' Shelly ventured, knowing Matthew wouldn't answer but hoping for some sort of reaction that would indicate his take on things. 'He's a friend of Mummy's,' Shelly pushed, but Matthew had eyes only for his book. 'He's nice, isn't he?' Climbing on the bed beside him, Shelly pulled Matthew into the crook of her arm as she awaited his response, but a little man made out of gingerbread was all Matthew wanted to hear about now.

'*Wun?*' he said again, his voice more insistent as he looked up at Shelly.

'In a minute, darling,' Shelly said gently. 'I just want to explain things to you. Ross is a doctor,' Shelly explained patiently. 'Mummy works with him at the hospital. He's also a friend, a good friend of mine.' She hesitated then, unsure how much information to give. Telling Matthew now might only upset him but, taking a deep breath, Shelly decided to plant the seed. Matthew's reaction would be the litmus test that would invariably make up her mind. 'While Nanny and Grandad are on holiday, Ross is going to look after you while Mummy works.' She forced a reassuring smile at the innocent little face, half expecting him to burst into tears or break into hysterics, but Matthew's thumb stayed firmly *in situ* as his eyes drifted back to the book.

'*Wun, wun,*' Matthew insisted, apparently none the worse for the bombshell that had just been dropped.

As she took over the story Shelly couldn't make up her mind whether she was disappointed or excited. Disappointed because there was no legitimate reason for calling this ridiculous charade off, or excited because it really looked like it was going to finally happen.

'"As fast as you can…"' Shelly intoned, her mind a million miles away from the page in front of her, achingly aware that Ross was waiting for her in the living room, achingly aware that the night had only just started…

'I thought you said that he was tricky with strangers.' Filling two glasses from the wine bottle he'd brought, Ross handed one to Shelly.

'I meant he's tricky with adults.' Shelly grinned as she took a grateful sip of her wine. 'It's no wonder you got on so well.' Sitting down on the couch, she let out an exaggerated sigh. 'I love him to bits, but it's bliss when he finally goes to bed.'

Ross didn't say anything for a while, just fiddled with the remote as Shelly sipped at her drink, not sure now that her ally was gone how to deal with the sudden silence.

'You've got a lovely home.'

Shelly gave a small shrug, embarrassed at the sudden need for small-talk. 'It's not much.'

'It's great.' His eyes wandered around the room, taking in the jumble of photos filling every available space, the cushions scattered over the sofa, the toys dotted around the floor. 'It's a real home.'

Eyeing him over the top of her glass, Shelly realised then that he wasn't just filling an uncomfortable quiet patch, that his admiration was genuine, and for a reason Shelly couldn't even begin to fathom she felt the sting of tears in her eyes, something in Ross's voice reaching somewhere deep inside. 'So what happened at work this morning that was so awful?'

He didn't answer for a moment but when he did his voice was curiously hollow. 'They discharged Angus.'

Sitting up abruptly, Shelly tucked her long legs under her, shaking her head as she spoke. 'But I thought you went ahead and reported your suspicions...'

'Ah, but I'm just a lowly resident.'

'But surely...' Her voice trailed off as Ross shook his head.

'Dr Khan still insists that I've overreacted, that I'm a bit wet behind the ears, a touch too eager. He overrode my findings.'

'Ross, you're the most conscientious doctor I've ever met. As if you'd just jump right in if you didn't have valid reasons.'

'Not valid enough, obviously. Hell, Shelly, I've been in the outback for two years, I've seem more drama there than that lot can imagine.' He looked at her questioning face. 'I have,' he said insistently. 'I was the only doctor for two thousand kilometres and, believe me, I've had to make my share of decisions on my own two feet. I come back here and I'm treated like some sort of country bumpkin that's been starved of practising medicine, determined to create a drama when there isn't one. Well, I'm telling you that little kid is being abused—'

'Hey, Ross.' It was Shelly breaking in now, slightly taken back by the passion of his outburst but understanding where he was coming from all the same. 'I'm on your side here.'

'I know.' He ran a slightly shaking hand through his hair then forced that smile again. 'Let's watch the movie, shall we?'

But Shelly refused to buy it. Ross was hurting. There was something going on here that she couldn't put her finger on. 'Ross, why are you so upset about this?'

'A child's being abused, Shelly! Of course I'm upset.'

Mentally kicking herself, Shelly rephrased her question. 'I know it's awful, it eats me up too, but it's our job, Ross. Tragedies happen regularly in paediatrics. Any illness in a child is awful, but Angus seems to be really getting to you.' She watched as he shifted uncomfortably, as the shutters came down in those vivid blue eyes, effectively ending the conversation.

'You did everything you could, Ross,' Shelly pushed, not wanting to leave things there when he was so obviously upset. 'You've reported it, you've gone through all the right channels.'

'Fat lot of good that did.' Ross took a gulp of his wine as Shelly looked on thoughtfully. It was Ross not letting Shelly in now, and his obvious hurt not only upset her—it made her strangely uneasy. His disenchantment with the hospital unnerved her, made Shelly feel suddenly twitchy. How easy it would be for Ross to throw in the towel if things weren't going well at work, to head off back to his beloved outback, or wherever the mood took him.

'You can talk to me, Ross,' Shelly ventured. 'You've listened to my problems enough over the years. It goes both ways.'

'I'm fine.' Ross gave a shrug. 'Really.' As if sensing her sudden apprehension, he gave her a reassuring smile, stretching out on the sofa beside her, his winning smile back firmly in place. 'Let's just drop it, shall we? Talking shop is the last thing I need right now.'

She'd have been a fool to push it.

Even watching a slushy film that Shelly had seen maybe a hundred times felt special, sharing it with Ross.

It was so nice having someone to chat to, someone to grab a bag of chips from the pantry, someone to tell you what you'd missed when Mother Nature called and you couldn't wait for the commercials!

Topping up her glass as the movie ended, Shelly went to fill up Ross's but he shook his head. 'Better not. I'm driving.' He turned back to the television, not even a hint of innuendo hanging in the air, so why was Shelly blushing?

'Stay.' The single word was more of a croak really and as Ross turned his head Shelly shook hers. 'On the couch. I didn't mean...'

'But what would the neighbours say?' Ross laughed at the blush flaming over her cheeks. 'A strange man's car parked outside all night!'

'Well, they're going to have to get used to it over the next week and I'm sure they've got better things to worry about,' Shelly mumbled, filling up his glass. 'Anyway, it will be good for Matthew to see you here in the morning.'

A tourism commercial was playing now, inviting Australians to come and see for themselves the wild rugged beauty of the outback, and Shelly couldn't help but notice the way it held Ross's attention, one idle hand lifting his glass as he gazed at the screen.

'You really love it, don't you?' Shelly murmured.

'Oh, yes.' Putting his glass on the coffee-table, Ross stretched out on the floor. Propping himself up on one elbow, he fixed his blue gaze up at her. 'The time I spent in Tennagarrah was easily the best few years of my life.'

'Really?' Shelly shot him a slightly questioning look. Sure, the outback had its charms, but from the rap Ross was giving it, it sounded like he'd been living in paradise. 'But didn't you get lonely?'

'I didn't have five minutes to myself—there wasn't a chance to get lonely. It's like another world, Shelly. The entire community rallies round each other, respects each other. I can't even begin to describe the people, it's like one big family. You'd love it.'

'Oh, I don't think so.' Shelly shook her head firmly.

'You would,' Ross insisted. 'There's none of this arguing about policies, they're just so thrilled you're actually there. Without a doctor or midwife nearby, pregnant women have to leave their homes weeks before their due dates so they can be at one of the clinics when they go into labour. Can you imagine how hard it would be to up and leave your husband and children at the time you need them most, just to ensure a safe delivery?'

'It would be awful,' Shelly gasped.

'It happens there all the time, that's why they're so thrilled to have anyone medical there. You'd be treated like a queen, you being a midwife and everything.'

'I haven't practised for years.'

'You could do a refresher course,' Ross said easily, and Shelly found herself doing a double take. Ross was actually talking as if the idea had some merit! 'They're the most resilient people you'll ever meet, they have to be, which means nine times out of ten by the time they've called for medical attention, they really need it! You're using your brain, working on your own initiative every step of the way.'

'Well, if it's so good, why did you leave?' Shelly asked airily, while privately delighted that he had.

'There was a lot of talk about extending the centre I was at, making it into a small hospital.'

'So why would that put you off?'

'They wanted a three- to five-year commitment.'

Shelly almost laughed. 'And we know how much you hate the "C" word. Why's it so hard for you, Ross? Why, if you so clearly love the place, couldn't you commit to staying?' Her mind was only half on the question. Ross's T-shirt had worked its way out of his jeans, giving a teasing glimpse of a very flat, very brown stomach, blond hairs blazing a golden trail downwards, and Shelly had to force herself to concentrate, anticipating a vague answer about career progression or appalling wages, crippling social life, anything really.

Anything other than what came next.

'Haven't you worked that one out yet?'

Dark blue eyes were fixed firmly on her and Shelly took a desperate gulp of her drink, sucking in air as she realised her glass was empty, her eyes frantically seeking refuge from his direct stare. But no solace was forthcoming, just the decadent glimpse of his stomach, the muscular strength of his thighs and that very attractive bit in the middle that seemed to be working like a magnet to her green eyes.

'Worked what out?' Her voice was high, and she settled for the television. The late night news had started now, a touch of strange normality as her own world seemed to shift out of focus.

'Why I came back.' He'd knelt up now, tipping the last of the bottle into her glass as Shelly desperately feigned disinterest. 'I heard that a certain nurse I'd always had a soft spot for was suddenly single.'

When Shelly didn't respond he carried on regardless, his voice a velvet caress as it delivered his earth-shattering tale, as calm and detached as the newsreader talking easily about fires and bombs. 'More than a soft spot really. I never could quite get over her so when I heard her marriage was finished I figured I'd check things out for myself. Find out if things between us were as good as I remembered, see once and for all if the woman I'd been crazy about for so long was as gorgeous as I remembered.'

'And was she?'

The glass she was clinging to was being gently prised out of her hands, and she watched in stunned silence as Ross placed it very carefully on the table next to his.

'Better,' he whispered, his breath hot on her cheek, his lips moving in for a skilful kill, his lips when they brushed hers rekindling memories, the tiniest kiss they had long ago shared soldered into her subconscious; the rock, the strength he had provided wrapping around her again as Shelly closed her eyes, the soft warm flesh of his lips, the cool shiver of his tongue, the heady, all-embracing scent that filled her, the trembling reaction as his body pressed against her.

His kiss.

It was everything she'd secretly imagined.

And more.

Every electric brush of his hand, every tiny shared smile that had bonded them magnified now; culminating in this delicious lingering moment. Their lips moving, probing, as Shelly's fingers crept into the thick silken blond hair, the scratch of his jeans against her smooth long legs sending her stomach into freefall, the firm touch of his hands on her back as he pulled her closer.

And for a moment it felt so instinctively right it was easier to go with her feelings, to succumb to the moment, to die a little in his arms as his lips traced the hollows of her throat, as one hand worked its magic on the aching swell of her breast.

'Don't.'

The word was so at odds with how she was feeling, for a split second Shelly thought she was hearing things. But the sound of her voice was definitely familiar and it was her hands pushing him away, fiddling with her top, flicking back her hair, and it was her eyes frantically trying to avoid his.

'Why?'

It was a good question and one Shelly struggled to answer for a moment. Why shouldn't she just go on letting him kiss her, why shouldn't she just keep right on kissing him back? 'Because it isn't right.'

'It felt pretty right to me.' His hand was on her leg, fiddling with the hem of her skirt, with one tiny stray thread of lilac cotton. One tiny pull and the whole hem would unravel, one tiny touch and her resolve would weaken, and it was that thought that forced the words to come more harshly perhaps than intended.

'Is that what you're here for?' She looked at his nonplussed face. 'A week of regular sex?'

'What are you going on about, Shelly? I didn't plan for this.'

'Rubbish,' Shelly scoffed, erecting the barriers again, furious at herself for letting him near. 'But then again, you probably didn't. You're not one for master plans, are you? You're just happy to go with the flow, and why not? Let's see if poor old Shelly's fair game, it might make the next week a bit more pleasurable.'

'Let's get a couple of things straight here, Shelly.'

His hand moved, Ross moved, away from her, away from the sofa, and she felt the shiver of the air around her without him near.

'The doctors' mess mightn't be the most luxurious accommodation in the world...' His voice was very measured and deliberate, and Shelly realised Ross was the one in control here. Her heart was pounding in her ears, her mind reeling from the shock of the words she had delivered. She felt like a gauche teenager—one little kiss and already she was demanding explanations. She wanted the ground to open up and swallow her, but no such miracle was about to happen here. All she could do was fiddle with the thread on her hem that Ross had found as he delivered his stern lecture. 'But it suits me just fine. And to clear up another point before it jumps into your mind, neither am I here for your fabulous home cooking. Tuna casserole doesn't do it for me, unfortunately.'

Shelly opened her mouth to argue, to point out that she'd never intended to serve it to him, but she snapped it closed. Best to let him get his tantrum over and done with.

'And as for sex...'

Shelly deliberately tried to keep her face impassive, to think calm thoughts and stop that awful blush from darkening, not take a deep breath or raise her eyebrows or give him any indication that she was struggling with discussing that three-letter word with him.

'It's Saturday night, Shelly. I hate to sound arrogant, but if it's casual sex I want, I can think of several places where I'm more likely to get it...'

Her eyes jerked up for a brief second, not that she needed to see him. Long-limbed, impossibly tanned, that blond hair flopping over one navy eye, he could walk into any bar in Melbourne and half, if not all the women would subconsciously stand up and cheer.

Ross Bodey was one of those men.

One of those men that reminded women they were female.

One of those immaculate prototypes God threw out every now and then to show the world just how good he could make it.

And Shelly hadn't a hope in hell of holding him.

'I like you, Shelly.'

Still she didn't say anything.

'I've liked you for a very long time, you must have known that?' When she still didn't answer he carried on, but the stern assuredness had gone from his voice now. Instead, his voice was almost wary, questioning. 'There was always an attraction?'

'No.' Shelly shook her head. 'I was married.' The lie was audible and Shelly gave a tiny painful shrug. 'OK, I was attracted to you, Ross, like every other female in the hospital. Happy now?'

'I don't care about every female, Shelly. The only person's opinion I'm interested in is yours.

'Yours,' he emphasised. 'Maybe you're right. Maybe I did plan this, but later Shelly, much later. If we're going to have a relationship, it's hardly going to be able to proceed normally.'

Her vivid green eyes were frowning now. Ross talking about relationships was causing a massive mental overload and she had to forcibly drag her mind back to follow the words he was saying.

'We're not going to go to the movies, and have candlelit dinners and go to the theatre.' His grin was back now, almost. 'OK, maybe the movies, but with Matthew sitting in between us munching on popcorn while he watches a cartoon, well, it's hardly...'

'Romantic,' Shelly finished for him, but Ross just shook his head.

'Oh, it would be romantic, Shelly, but it's hardly get-to-know-you time. *This* is the get-to-know-you time. A fast-forward on the awkward dates, a chance to really get to know each other, to see if this attraction we both know we feel equates to the outside world.

'I shouldn't have kissed you then—you're right, it was too soon. I just never figured on this…' His fingers tapped his chest. 'Seeing you sitting there, so adorable, I just went with the flow, just followed my heart. Can you understand that?'

She did understand. His kiss hadn't been manufactured, some contrived move. As skilfully as it had been delivered, it had been loaded with instinctiveness, guided by her very own longing.

'We'll take things slowly,' Ross said tentatively as Shelly's face jerked up.

'You'll still stay?' Her voice was unsure. 'After all the things I said?'

'Shelly, what type of guy do you take me for? We had a minor disagreement, a few short words. Even if we'd had a full-scale row, do you really think I'd just up and go? Leave you and Matthew in the lurch?'

'No, of course not.'

He heard the uncertainty in her voice and knelt back down on the floor beside her, one hand resting on her chin, forcing those reluctant eyes to meet his. 'You don't sound very convinced.'

'I'm sorry,' She let out a long ragged sigh. 'It's me, not you.' She knew he was waiting for her to elaborate and after a moment, wrestling with her own demons, Shelly did her best to verbalise her confused emotions. 'Why would you stay, Ross? Why would you even want to be here? Matthew's own father—'

'Don't ever compare me to him.'

'I'm not,' she broke in quickly. 'You don't compare.' They didn't, Ross with his laid-back ways, his take-it-or-leave-it slant on the world, was a million miles away from the ordered, manufactured world Neil inhabited. A world where a little boy with special needs was just too damned hard, too not what they'd planned, too less than ideal.

Neil had his life planned.

Ross lived for the moment.

There was a question there in itself. Right there at the front of her mind. But gazing into the depths of his eyes, Shelly pushed it away. Pushed away the ordered, neat life she had made for herself and chose, perhaps for the first time ever, to go with the flow.

Sort of.

She couldn't just dive in here, there was too much at stake to throw caution to the wind and to hell with the consequences, but feeling his hand on her face, feeling the quiet strength of his body so very close, Shelly took a deep breath and dipped one very tentative, newly painted toenail into the water.

'I can't just tumble into bed with you.'

'I know.'

'We have to keep things under wraps, especially when Matthew's around.'

'Of course.'

'And I don't want anyone at work getting even a hint that there's romance in the air.'

Ross gave a slight grimace. 'Might have to do a quick renegotiation on that one. I'd say the whole ward knows that there's romance in the air.' He looked at her aghast face and grinned. 'There's sparks coming off the pair of us, Shelly, everyone knows.'

'Everyone except me,' Shelly mumbled.

'Rubbish.' Ross remonstrated good-naturedly, grinning ever wider until even Shelly managed a reluctant smile.

'I just wasn't expecting all of this.'

'All of what?' Ross asked innocently. 'From this moment on, I'm your official babysitter for the next week, nothing else.

'Nothing else,' he added, as Shelly shot him a very disbelieving look. 'You, young lady, can tell me when you're good and ready. My ego can't take being rebuffed twice in a row.'

He was joking, Shelly knew that deep down, but there was an element of truth to it all the same. Men like Ross Bodey wouldn't be turned down too often. Not that Ross seemed particularly bothered. He was picking his car keys up from the table.

'It's up to you, Shelly.'

'Where are you going?' Her heart sank a mile. All that chat about staying had obviously only been if sex had been on the agenda.

'To get my sleeping bag from the car.' He replied simply, not noticing the relieved look that washed over her as he wandered out to the garage, returning a couple of minutes later with the grubbiest offering of a sleeping bag Shelly had ever seen.

'I've got a spare duvet you can use,' she said quickly, wincing slightly as he unravelled the shabby swathe of material over her pale sofa. 'I can wash that for you in the morning.'

'You're not washing this,' Ross said in alarm. 'It would fall apart.'

'Exactly.' She would have pushed, would have nagged just a touch more, but Ross had pulled his T-shirt over his head and was now working on the buttons of his jeans. 'Is that it, then? Conversation over?'

'Yep,' Ross said easily. He was down to surprisingly white boxer shorts now and Shelly struggled to keep her eyes on his face, this blatant display of male sexuality not having the most soothing effect.

He watched her eyes dart down to his boxers and flick back quickly to his face, a furious blush working its way up her neck to her flaming cheeks.

'They accentuate my tan,' Ross said in a feigned effeminate voice.

'I never tan,' Shelly mumbled. 'I just go red and get a load more freckles.'

He was climbing into that disgusting bag now, looking up at her with innocent eyes, forcing an exaggerated yawn he stretched languorously. 'Turn the light off on your way out, would you?'

So that was it.

Not one goodnight kiss?

Not one further word of reassurance?

Not even one further attempt to discover the colour of her very new, very sexy knickers?

"Night, then.' Shelly flicked off the light and stood in the darkness for a moment.

"Night, Shelly.'

She turned, slowly. The bedroom was just across the hall and she walked the few steps rather slowly, her ears on elastic, hoping and simultaneously dreading that he'd call her.

Unzip that bag and pull her right on in.

Oh, she'd have gone.

In a second.

But Ross didn't call, even though she undressed slowly, even though she only turned the tap on to a dribble as she brushed her teeth, so that she didn't miss her summons, but the only sound that filled Shelly's ears was silence.

Slipping into bed almost frenzied with lust, she lay staring into the darkness, concentrating on keeping her breathing even.

All that talk, all that bravado about waiting, had dissolved in a flash the second he had undressed. The sudden low-key way Ross was acting was having the strangest effect.

Staring at the dark shape of the door, she almost willed it to open by mental telepathy, could almost see the outline of his spectacular body in the shadows. But just as she could take it no more, just as one hand was ready to throw back her duvet and call him to come to her, a rhythmic deep sound filled her ears, and Shelly shot back under the sheets like a scalded cat.

Ross was snoring.

Ross Divine-Body Bodey had had the gall to go and fall asleep.

CHAPTER SIX

SHELLY LAY THERE for a moment when she awoke, trying to orientate herself, stretching in the warm bed then rolling back on her side and closing her eyes again. Since Matthew had been born, Shelly had never, not even once, just woken up.

Unless she counted the time she'd had her wisdom teeth taken out and Marlene had moved in for a couple of days, but that had been pain waking her, not the lazy, hazy feeling that came when one's body had actually had enough sleep. Normally little fingers were prodding her face or an alarm clock was buzzing in her ears. Stretching out, Shelly grappled for her alarm clock, her eyes widening in horror as she saw the hand edging past ten o'clock.

Her feet hardly met the carpet as she dashed out of the bedroom, her arms struggling to find the sleeves of the new dressing-gown she had bought in honour of her house guest, bracing herself for what she wasn't quite sure.

Chaos, as it turned out.

Ross's clothes still lay in a crumpled pile on the living-room floor, that awful sleeping bag half on, half off the couch, the curtains still drawn. Padding fast along the hall, she pushed the kitchen door open and the mess that greeted her made the living room look like a display from the Ideal Home Exhibition. Newspapers were everywhere!

Everywhere.

Cereal boxes and milk cartons littered the bench, bread, margarine, honey, Vegemite…

'Morning.' Turning from the bench like a phoenix rising from the ashes, she was privy to a glimpse of a very fetching smile, attached to a more than attractive body.

Ross had changed his boxer shorts, Shelly mentally registered as she took the steaming mug of coffee Ross was holding out for her. Still white, but littered with little red love hearts, and on anyone else they would have looked ridiculous.

'Why didn't you wake me?' Shelly asked, trying to ignore the chaos that used to be her kitchen.

'Because you're working tonight,' Ross replied with annoying simplicity as he guided her to the kitchen table. 'Do you want some toast?'

'Mummy sleep.' Matthew pointed a rather accusing finger in Shelly's general direction then broke into squeals of delighted laughter as she showered his sticky cheeks with a flurry of butterfly kisses. He was sitting at the kitchen table, his little pudgy hands working their way through the cartoon section of the newspaper and the endless reams of catalogues that came with the Sunday papers.

'Yes, Mummy did sleep,' Shelly muttered. 'Someone should have woken me.'

'Why?' Ross shrugged. 'We managed.'

Hot buttered toast was being placed in front of her, and without even bothering to ask Ross took it upon himself to slaver it in mountains of honey.

'Have you changed Matthew's nappy?' Half standing, Shelly sat back down as Ross rolled his eyes and gave an exaggerated sigh.

'Yes, I've changed it.'

'But how did you know where everything was kept?'

'You couldn't lose your keys in Matthew's bedroom.' He was talking with his mouth full, back to reading the papers and not bothering to look up. 'It's so neat I just looked under "N" for nappies. Couldn't quite work out where the talcum powder was kept, though.'

'He doesn't have powder, it's supposed to be bad for children's lungs or something.'

'Amazing we survived to adulthood, all things considered,' Ross said dryly, taking a slug of his coffee. 'We did all right, didn't we, Matty?'

She was about to correct him but stopped herself, not in time, though, for Ross to miss her intake of breath.

'Sorry, Matthew,' he amended.

They had done all right, Shelly conceded, nibbling on the edge of a piece of toast. She knew that she should have felt relieved that they were getting on so well and that Matthew had obviously taken to his babysitter. So why did she feel so edgy?

Because nothing was that easy.

Ross had swept back into their lives with effortless ease, had won over Matthew, installed himself in her home and even forced Shelly to admit to herself that she was hopelessly in lust with him.

There had to be a downside.

'OK, then.' Ross looked down at his watch. 'You can start cleaning now.'

'What are you talking about?' So deep in her daydream was she Shelly thought she must have missed something as she struggled to keep up with the conversation.

'Every day I'm going to stretch it out by another five minutes and by the time the week is up you'll be able to go half an hour without wiping down the benches.'

'You really think you've got me all worked out, don't you?' Shelly looked over the rim of her coffee-cup, a slightly mysterious smile playing on the edge of her full mouth.

'No,' Ross admitted. 'But I'm working on it.'

Shelly didn't clean the benches, didn't grab a garbage bag and start picking up the newspapers. For the first time in living memory, she ignored the mess and actually read the Sunday papers. The three sat in amicable silence, Matthew drawing erratic pictures over his pages, Shelly lingering over the colour supplements as Ross read all the newspapers from end to end, only rising every now and then to replenish their coffee-cups or open a packet of biscuits for Matthew.

And even though in the scheme of things it didn't add up to much, looking up from her magazine for a short moment, Shelly felt the swell of a lump in her throat, the tiny glimpse of domestic bliss such a cherished moment it would surely be etched in her mind for ever.

Her lazy day continued long into the evening. After some persuasion Ross took Matthew back with him to the doctors' mess to collect a few of his things and Shelly was privy to the decadence of an afternoon alone. Throwing together the quickest roast dinner a Sunday had ever seen, Shelly bypassed the usual run under the shower, opting instead for a lazy soak in the bath before closing her eyes for a supposed ten-minute doze.

A bit more than ten minutes as it turned out.

A rather crispy roast was the order of the day, and by the time Shelly had bathed Matthew and put him to bed, Ross had made surprising inroads into the dishes.

'Why didn't you just load them into the dishwasher?'

'Because then I'd have had to embarrass myself telling you I'd no idea how to use it.'

Smiling, Shelly crossed the kitchen. 'It *is* a bit complicated actually.' Putting a tablet in the dispenser, she picked up his hand, leading his finger to the 'on' button.

'OK, Einstein, what are the rest of the buttons for, then?'

'Decoration.' Her hand was still on his and neither seemed in any particular rush to break the physical contact.

'Do you know what would be nice now?' Their hands had moved from the stainless-steel surface of the dishwasher and were now located rather more comfortably between them, Ross standing over her, his teasing grin matching hers.

'What?'

'Chocolate.' His eyes weren't on Shelly's, instead they were focussed on their mutually entwined fingers. 'A big slab of chocolate and a very sad movie.'

'Sounds wonderful.' That was an understatement. Curling up on the sofa with Ross would be the perfect end to a perfect day, and for once chocolate didn't even get a look-in.

'Ring in sick,' Ross grumbled as Shelly let out a gurgle of laughter.

'Which would entirely defeat the purpose of you being here.'

'I guess.' Puppy dog eyes were looking at her now and Shelly even amazed herself by imagining the wrath of Tania if she dared do it.

It would almost be worth it.

'I'd better get moving.' Reluctantly she retrieved her hand and padded off to her bedroom, pulling on her uniform and putting up her hair with indecent haste before applying only the briefest slick of lipstick. Shelly picked up her bag and hovered by the lounge door, watching as Ross, lying long and relaxed on the sofa, snapped in two the biggest bar of chocolate she had ever seen and for cruel effect pressed the remote control with gusto.

It would have been so easy to stay.

So frighteningly easy.

CHAPTER SEVEN

'HOW'S THE HIRED help?' Smirking slightly, Melissa sat down and dived into the box of chicken savouries Shelly had bought. 'Behaving himself?'

'Impeccably.' Shelly met her colleague's eyes, reddening as she crossed the line she had sworn Ross to and elaborated. 'Unfortunately.'

'I thought that was what you wanted,' Melissa was tucking into the savouries with gusto now, as Shelly concentrated on the feed she was giving.

'It is,' Shelly insisted, leaning back in the chair as the baby attacked the bottle. 'Or it was. I don't know, Melissa, I've set the boundaries, insisted he doesn't cross them, and now I'm annoyed that he's keeping to the deal that I set in the first place.' If she hadn't been holding a baby, so exasperated was Shelly she would have got up and paced the floor right then and there.

It was her fourth night on duty. Her fourth night of leaving Ross in her home and heading off to work. And no doubt in just a few short hours it would be the fourth time she would arrive home in the morning to two grinning faces and a house so untidy it was unrecognisable.

A house that felt completely like home.

'I was the one who insisted we didn't discuss things with anyone at work, and just look at me!'

'I'm not just anyone, though.'

Shelly let out the breath she'd inadvertently been holding. 'I know you're not. You must be just about sick of all my dramas by now.'

'On the contrary.' Melissa grinned. 'I love them, just so long as you keep on feeding me. When do your parents get back?'

'Sunday morning.'

'And you're off now until when?' Melissa asked with thinly disguised interest.

'I'm back at work on Saturday night.'

'So is Ross staying at yours for the next few nights, or going back to the doctors' mess in between babysitting shifts?'

Thankfully the baby started to fret and Shelly avoided answering for a moment as she placed the bottle on the workbench and leant the baby forward, massaging his back to bring up his wind.

'Shelly,' Melissa pushed. 'You can wind a baby and talk better than anyone I've ever known.'

'OK,' Shelly snapped, more annoyed with herself than Melissa. It was a question that had been plaguing her for the last couple of days and now as the clock crept toward four a.m. it was make-your-mind-up time. 'It would seem that the ball's in my court.'

'I've never held a tennis racket in my life.' Melissa grinned as she took another handful of savouries. 'You'll have to be more specific.'

'Ross has made it very clear the next move's up to me. If I ask him to stay the next few days…'

'He'll want sex?' Melissa asked eagerly, and Shelly shook her head and started to laugh.

'Melissa!' Shelly said indignantly. '*If* I ask him to stay it will mean I'm moving things forward, that I like spending time with him, that I want to spend more time with him.'

'Which you do,' Melissa said with annoying simplicity. 'And you can rub that back all you like but that baby's not going to burp for you again.'

'Look, what if I ask him to stay and by nine o'clock tonight I realise I've made a mistake? I can't just dash off to work…'

'You mean there'll be no safety net.'

'I suppose. What if I realise the mistake I'm making, what then?'

Melissa stood up and took the dozing baby out of Shelly's arms. Cuddling him in for a moment, she smiled down at the sleeping infant. 'You gave me a scare, little man, and just look at you now, all ready to go home tomorrow!' Her kind, shrewd eyes turned back to Shelly. 'Seems to me you're more worried what you'll do if you realise you *haven't* made a mistake.' As Shelly opened her mouth to protest, Melissa carried right on. 'That you, young lady, are more worried that waking up next to Ross might just be the best thing that's ever happened to you.' Shelly's mouth opened again but Melissa hadn't quite finished. 'What then, Shelly? That's what's really troubling you, isn't it?'

Waddling off, she left a troubled Shelly sitting at the desk and for something to do Shelly picked up the box of savouries, but a salty early morning snack wasn't going to solve her problems tonight. Even the slab of chocolate in her bag wouldn't bring answers.

Melissa, as usual, was spot on with her diagnosis.

What then?

Ross was five years younger than her and though their age difference would barely raise an eyebrow, those five years might just as well stretch to fifty.

Five years had seen Shelly marry, have a baby, divorce. Five years had led her to single motherhood, the only parent of a very special little boy, with all the joy that entailed on the upside but all the responsibility the permanent angst on the downside.

Whereas Ross…

Ross lived his life out of his backpack.

His five years had been spent studying, working, but most importantly living. Dancing, romancing, travelling, hot southern nights and all the promise a body like his would surely attract.

How could she hold him?

And if she did for a while, how could she possibly bear to lose him?

'You know Dr Khan?' Melissa was back. The baby had obviously settled easily and Shelly struggled to concentrate as the conversation turned back to work and the aging consultant that ruled the ward.

'We had an affair.'

Thank goodness she wasn't feeding a baby now! Shelly's jaw literally dropped open as her head swung around, positive she must have misheard!

'Thirty years ago, mind.' Melissa gave a shrug and took the box of snacks from Shelly's limp hand. 'I was in my twenties, a lot prettier and definitely a lot thinner.'

'Dr Khan!'

'Mushat. Mushi I used to call him.' She wasn't really talking to Shelly any more, her usual gruff voice was softer now. 'I knew from the start it wasn't going anywhere, we both did. Once his internship finished he was expected to go back to Pakistan and marry.' A thin, wry smile replaced the needs for words for a moment. 'Mushi wasn't going to rewrite the rulebook. He loved his family, loved his culture and more to the point he loved his wife-to-be. He had a wonderful marriage.'

'Did it carry on after...?' Shelly's voice trailed off as Melissa shook her head vehemently. 'He's a decent man, he'd never have cheated on his wife, it's simply not in his character. He loved her, Shelly, right up until she died last year. But for a while there he loved me, too.' Her eyes found Shelly's then. 'Like it or not, you've got a complicated life and men like Ross don't come by every day. Take your moments in the sun, Shelly, you don't know when then they're going to come around again.'

'Just because I'm a single mum with responsibilities, it doesn't mean I'm going to take any crumbs of comfort…'

'I'm not talking about Matthew.' Melissa ignored Shelly's snappish response. 'I'm talking about you. When Mushi and I broke up I cried like every other woman getting over a broken heart, and though I swore I'd never get over him, deep down I thought there'd be someone else, that one day what Mushi and I had would be just a warm distant memory.

'But that was it,' she rasped. 'That was it for me, Shelly. But as painful as it's been, I'm glad for the two years we had. For the two years I felt as beautiful and loved as every woman deserves to feel at least once in her lifetime.'

Pulling a couple of tissues from the workbench in front of her, Melissa blew her nose loudly and Shelly found herself doing the same.

'Is there any chance for you two?' Shelly ventured. 'Now his wife's…?'

Melissa shook her head sadly. 'There's too much water under the bridge now,' she said sadly. 'Since his wife died he's so brusque, and it's not just me that's noticed, even Ross was moaning about how much he's changed. Sometimes when I talk to him about the patients, or the budget, or whatever the latest drama on the ward is, he's so far removed from the man I used to know I wonder if he even remembers how close we once were.'

'I'm sure he does,' Shelly said gently as Melissa blew her nose again and stood up. 'Perhaps you should try talking to him.' But her suggestion fell on deaf ears. Melissa looked up at the clock and started to pull out the drug trolley.

'And perhaps we should get on with our work.'

Work felt just like that for the rest of the morning.

Like work.

Melissa, embarrassed at revealing so much, turned into the ogre sister from hell and every baby in the place woke at six demanding to be fed, unmindful of the fact that Shelly needed to do some obs and write her nursing notes. In fact, by the time she turned the key in her front door any chance of preparing a speech for Ross was but a distant dream—not that it mattered.

Ross had obviously only awoken as her car had turned into the drive.

'Shelly,' he gasped as she came in and rather disdainfully eyed the lounge. 'I fell asleep. I was going to have it tidy for your last morning...'

'What, and spoil the surprise?' She started smiling as she watched him picking up blankets and toys. He was wearing navy boxers this morning, and if anything they made his tan look ever darker. 'Did the late night movie go on too long?'

'No.' He stopped his flurry of activity then and faced her. 'Matty got up a few times.'

'Matthew?' She wasn't correcting him. Shelly's forehead creased and for a second she felt the surge of panic familiar to mothers around the globe. 'Why?'

'I don't know if he had a dream or was just miserable.' Ross ran an exasperated hand through his hair. 'I checked him over but there was nothing wrong, I read him his gingerbread book, changed his nappy, gave him a drink, but he just wouldn't settle. I gave him some paracetamol just in case.'

'I'll go and check him, he's usually up now.'

'He's probably exhausted. Could he be teething?'

His question went unanswered as Shelly fled towards Matthew's bedroom.

'He's OK, Shelly, I checked him less than an hour ago,' Ross tried to reassure her, following her rapid footsteps, and though Shelly believed him, knew deep down what Ross was saying was true, until she saw Matthew for herself nothing was going to convince Shelly that her son was OK.

'Mum.'

She didn't even make it as far as the bedroom. A delightfully familiar bundle was running towards her smiling a very wide smile, little arms outstretched, dark hair sticking up at every angle—a tell-tale sign of the restless night he had spent.

'Hey.' For once Shelly ignored the fact she was still in her uniform and she scooped him into her arms, one hand instinctively sweeping his forehead, the nurse in Shelly checking for a fever as the mother in her rained kisses on his little pudgy cheeks. 'What's been the matter, little guy?'

'Mum,' Matthew said again, and it was all the answer Shelly was going to get, but all the answer she needed, and turning to Ross she gave him a relieved slightly embarrassed smile.

'I'm sorry you've had such an awful night. Normally he sleeps right through.'

'Don't worry about me.' Ross was standing right beside them, pushing his fingers into Matthew's fat tummy as the little boy giggled and rubbed his face in Shelly's neck pretending to be shy. 'And it wasn't awful. We had a bit of fun for while.' He gestured through the bedroom door to the biscuit wrappers and piles of toys on the floor. 'We had our own little party, didn't we, buddy?' His face turned to Shelly and he gave an apologetic shrug. 'I tried everything I could think of—read him that story he liked, I even sang to him. He wasn't upset or anything, he just didn't seem to want to sleep.' A large yawn ended Ross's sentence and he barely managed to lift his hand to cover it. 'I'd best head off to the shower.'

One final ruffle of Matthew's head and he turned to go.

'Woth.'

Turning slowly, suddenly Ross didn't look tired any more, an incredulous delighted look lighting his face as Shelly nearly danced on the spot in excitement, holding her breath as she waited for Matthew to say it again.

'Woth.' A little index finger jabbed in Ross's general direction and there was no mistaking the word that had spilled from his lips hadn't been an accident.

'Is that supposed to make up for keeping me awake all night?' Even though his voice was loud, Ross was grinning as he walked back towards them, the feigned anger in his voice not fooling Matthew for a second as he squealed in delight at the anticipation of another tickle, which was soon forthcoming. Shelly joined in the laughter, the strangest feeling bubbling in the pit of her stomach as Ross's face was suddenly serious, his voice low and soft. 'Well, guess what little man...? It does.'

Matthew's arms were pointing in Ross's direction now, and Shelly watched in wonder as the toddler slipped easily into his arms, resting his little head for a moment on the strong bare chest as Ross held him close for a moment, the expression on his face unreadable as Shelly stood silently watching this most precious moment. 'Best have that shower,' Ross said finally, reluctantly handing Matthew back. 'I'm sorry to leave you with all my chaos.'

'Don't worry about the mess. I'm just so grateful to you for helping me out, helping *us* out.'

'I haven't finished yet. We're still on for Saturday.'

Shelly nodded, wanting to speak, wanting to break in and tell him he didn't have to go, that he was more, so much more than just a babysitter, but the words simply wouldn't come.

'I'll come back after my shift and collect all my stuff.'

'You don't have to...' Her voice trailed off. The coming back she could certainly deal with, it was the thought of him leaving that hurt...

Ross was staring at her, his eyes willing her to continue, and for the longest time a loaded silence hung in the air.

'You'd better grab a shower. I'll rustle up some breakfast.'

It was such a paltry offer, such a pale offering compared to the words that were screaming from every taut nerve, but it was the best Shelly could come up with, and as Ross walked off she fought the urge to call him back, to somehow erase her last few words. To tell him she was feeling it too.

CHAPTER EIGHT

WITH ROSS HOGGING the hot water, Shelly had to make do with a quick wash in the basin as Matthew danced around the *en suite*, squeezing her expensive moisturiser onto the tiles the second Shelly's back was turned.

'My one luxury in life,' Shelly admonished, picking up the empty tube and trying to scrape up the mess with toilet tissue. 'It will be all your fault if I dissolve into a mass of wrinkles and crow's feet now, and who's going to love me then?'

The innocent, bubbling smile that looked up swept away her vague annoyance.

'Ask a silly question.' Shelly smiled, placing Matthew on the bed as she slipped on some fresh undies and pulled on a skirt and top. 'And I'll love you too!'

Despite the fact Ross looked like a walking zombie—and a gorgeous one at that—Matthew didn't seem remotely tired after his night's exploits, tucking into his breakfast with gusto, then performing his usual disappearing routine as Shelly attempted to dress him, giggling away as she forced two kicking legs into a pair of shorts and two wriggling arms into a T-shirt. 'Now here comes the hard part,' Shelly muttered as Ross collapsed onto the sofa, only a skimpy fluorescent pink towel draped around his hips, his body glistening with the morning dew of his shower. Trying to tie the laces on Matthew's runners was a feat at the best of times, but trying to perform this task suddenly took on monumental proportions as Shelly saw Ross walk over.

He probably thought his assistance would make the task easier.

Flying solo to the moon without an oxygen tank would have been easier than attempting to tie Matthews's laces into two neat bows with six feet three of freshly showered tanned flesh hovering just millimetres away!

One damp, blond-haired arm brushed against her bare thigh as he expertly trapped one little fat leg and Shelly performed the amazing feat of tying a double bow, as opposed to brushing the shimmering drops of water of his forearm, as opposed to looking up and catching Ross's eye...

'I don't know how you do it.'

'Practice.' Shelly shrugged, planting a playful smack on Matthew's rapidly departing bottom as he scuttled away fully clothed.

They were still kneeling on the lounge floor and Ross rested back in his heels. 'Now I know why all the nurses head for the coffee-room as soon as they come on duty. I know that's where I'll be going.'

'Will you be all right—today at work, I mean?' She was genuinely concerned. Ross, for all his hectic social life, was a most conscientious doctor. Having listened with slightly envious curiosity to his party ways over the years, Shelly knew that despite the late nights and frequent dates and parties they were always held well away from a shift on duty.

'I'm wondering that myself. If I was heading off to a nice air-conditioned office and pushing a pen all day, I might try and bluff my way through.'

He gave a small shrug as Shelly chewed her bottom lip nervously. 'It's a bit different to examining children and writing up prescription charts.'

Ross nodded. 'Not much room for error there.

'Hey,' he added, seeing the guilt-tinged concern flood her face. 'I didn't come here for a holiday, I knew what I was letting myself in for. I'm not just exhausted from last night, I haven't really slept well since I've been here.'

'I thought you only got nightmares when you were on call.' It was meant as a small joke, a throw-away comment to fill the tiny space that was between them, but as she saw Ross shift uncomfortably, watched his cheeks darken, Shelly could have bitten her tongue off, realising with regret that she had embarrassed him. 'Ross, I'm sorry,' she said quickly as he stood up.

'Don't be.' Ross gave a brief smile. One hand holding his towel in place, he offered the other, which Shelly accepted, allowing him to pull her up from the floor. 'Anyway, it wasn't just nightmares keeping me awake.'

'I thought he'd been sleeping. You should have told me—'

'He has slept,' Ross interrupted. 'At least, apart from last night.' He sat back down on the sofa behind him and ran a hand through his damp blond spikes, his hair falling easily back into perfect place. 'I was just worried about him.' His blue eyes finally looked up from the floor he was staring at. 'It's different from being at work, isn't it? I just felt so, so…' His lips moved but no words came out and Shelly finished his sentence for him.

'Responsible?'

'That's the word. I kept thinking, What if his blankets have fallen off? What if he's called out and I haven't heard? What if—?'

'The laundry door isn't locked and he's wandered out?' Shelly grinned as Ross looked at her with a start.

'I checked it three times!'

'I do the same,' she admitted. 'Oh, I'm not so bad now, and Matthew wasn't old enough to wander when I first moved in here, but I can clearly remember those first few nights on my own with him after living with my parents. I never slept a wink.'

'So I'm not going crazy?' Ross gave a relieved laugh. 'When

I gave him that paracetamol syrup I must have checked the dosage on the bottle about five times. How many times do I write up paracetamol syrup in a day's work? I guess it's different when you…' He didn't finish the sentence again and this time Shelly didn't jump in and help him, the unsaid word hanging in the air between them. 'I'd better ring Dr Khan and tell him I won't be in.'

'I'm so sorry, Ross.'

'Don't be. I've never had a sicky in my life, I'm too damn healthy. I reckon I deserve one. Can I?'

He gestured to the telephone, that simple polite gesture so completely unnecessary, but Shelly just nodded. 'Of course. I'd better get Matthew off to crèche.'

'Sure. I'll get my stuff together and be out of here by the time you get back.'

'You don't have to go, Ross.' The words tumbled out and Shelly could feel her breath bursting in her lungs as she carried on, speaking quickly. 'You can sleep here.'

'Are you sure?'

His casual question was loaded and Shelly gave a very quick nod. 'Of course.'

His eyes were on her and Shelly was eternally grateful to Matthew for choosing that moment to burst into the room. 'I'd better go.'

'He didn't sleep much last night.' Shelly hovered, as the bows she'd so carefully tied on Matthew's runners were undone and Lorna placed slippers on his feet. 'He might be getting a tooth or coming down with something. If he's miserable today—'

'We'll call you,' Lorna said firmly but kindly. 'Give Mummy a kiss, Matthew.'

His tears started then. Arching his back against Lorna, he held his arms out to Shelly, crying pitifully, calling to her as Shelly, her heart breaking, turned reluctantly to the exit door.

Even the fact she was exhausted and her bed was calling,

even the fact Ross was waiting at home for her, wasn't enough to act as a barrier to the emotions that coursed through Shelly as she sat in the car park and battled the urge to simply run back in, to grab Matthew and just take him home.

Shelly, as usual, didn't even take her bag off as she came into her hallway and picked up the telephone, punching in the well-used number of the crèche.

'He's fine,' Lorna said patiently, though Shelly was positive she must be rolling her eyes as she spoke, wondering when this morning ritual would ever end. 'He settled as soon as you left.'

'Thanks, Lorna.'

'What happened?' Ross's concerned face came straight into view as Shelly put down the telephone.

'Nothing.' Shelly unravelled a very small piece of tissue she had bunched up in her hand and dabbed at her reddened eyes. 'Well, nothing unusual anyway. This is a regular event in this household.

'He hates crèche,' Shelly explained. 'And I hate sending him.' Her tears started again and Ross put an arm around her and pulled her in as she started to weep. 'He should be at home, Ross, with me. He's just a little boy.'

'You have to sleep, Shelly. You've been at work all night. Don't feel guilty for sending him.'

But she shook her head. 'I don't *have* to work. With the money it costs to send him to crèche, I'd almost be better off staying at home.'

'Then why don't you? I mean, if that's what you want to do.'

'Because it's a good crèche and he needs early intervention and stimulation.' Shelly gave a wry smile. 'I sound like the brochure. Look, I'm just tired and, like I said, this little drama happens every morning. You were just here to witness it, that's all. I'm fine really.'

'But are you?'

Shelly shrugged. 'Yes, I am. It's just hard sometimes, like we were talking about this morning. It's hard always being responsible, beating yourself up as to whether or not you're doing the right thing. It's just hard, dealing with it all on my own.'

'Then don't.'

Shelly looked up at him, startled. Her words hadn't been a cry for help, it hadn't been a leading statement, a secret invitation for Ross to help her, but it seemed that was the way he was taking it.

'Let me be there for you, Shelly.'

She shrugged him off, pushing him away. 'I wasn't telling you this in the hope—'

'I know you weren't,' Ross said quickly, one hand pulling her back and wrapping his arms firmly around her as she spoke.

'You don't know what you're saying.'

'Oh, yes, I do Shelly,' Ross said very clearly, but Shelly just shook her head.

'I'm going for a shower, and then I'm going to bed.' This time when she pulled away he didn't pull her back. ''Night, then,' Shelly said, even though it was nine a.m., even though sleeping alone today was the last thing in the world she wanted to be doing. Even though she knew she'd just broken his heart.

Ross just stood there as she left. Stood there with a helpless look on his face as Shelly dismissed him and headed for the bedroom.

Determined to face things on her own.

Five minutes alone was all that was needed. The first two took care of washing, one more to dwell on Melissa's words and two to realise that just metres away was all the man she had ever dreamed of.

A man who cared.

A man who clearly adored her.

Adored Matthew, too.

What on earth was she playing at?

Melissa was right.

If it couldn't or wouldn't work, then so be it, but denying herself the pleasure of Ross's touch, the bliss of being loved by him, even for a moment, for the fear of one day getting hurt was a poor argument, when saying no now would hurt more than Shelly could bear.

'Ross?'

He was sitting there just a step or two away from where she'd left him, the sleeping bag pulled out onto the couch, his shoulders hunched, his head buried in his hands.

'Ross,' she said again as he dragged his eyes up to meet hers. She stood shivering, wrapped in a towel, scared to move, terrified of where her next step would lead but knowing she had to, needed to, and so badly wanted to go there.

She didn't have to take it.

He crossed the room in a second. The message in her eyes displaying the clarity of her feelings, there was no need for words, no need for promises.

The promise was all there in his kiss.

Hot, sweet promises of the love and passion that was so much Ross, the strength the humour all there in the weight of his lips on hers as he held her close.

And how he held her!

Every last inch of skin pressing against her, the soapy musky scent of him dragging into her, filling her from the inside, her fingers coiling through his still damp hair, every touch a discovery of pleasure.

It wasn't just sexual desire that fuelled her, pushed her boldly on to impatiently tug at his boxers to glimpse the splendour of him, to take him in her hands—it was need. An unquenchable thirst for this most intimate knowledge, an irrepressible desire to know, to feel, to see all of him. To see him naked and splendid before her. She stared with aroused fascination, his body so perfect, so infinitely divine, and all hers for the taking. His arousal, an arousal *she* had instigated causing a fission of delight, a surge of feminine power, an overwhelming need to touch, to feel, to have him.

And Ross felt it, too.

There was nothing fumbling in his touch as he pushed away her towel, nothing blasé about the intake of breath as he stepped back a fraction, staring in undisguised admiration at her naked body, a tremulous hand reaching out. Slowly but with breathtaking stealth he moved his hand over the soft peach of her skin. Capturing her face in the palm of his hand, he slipped a finger between Shelly's softly parted lips, and in silent understanding she moistened the tip with her tongue, her breath catching in a strangled gasp in her throat as he teased one jutting nipple with his moistened finger, the pink swelling engorging with delicious pain, the other hand cupping the sweet welcoming warmth between her legs as Shelly groaned, her body arching toward his with an insatiable need to be filled, a voracious desire to be as close as man and woman could ever be.

He carried her to the bedroom, her bedroom, the one room he had been denied, the one area he hadn't inhabited.

Until now.

Now he filled the room as if it were his, laid her on the bed as if it were theirs, the dominant male in him surfacing gloriously as he climbed over her, nudging her legs apart with one powerful thigh, his lips scorching a blaze across her stomach, working their way across her swollen breasts and up ever upwards to her taut arched neck, finding her swollen mouth the second he entered her, her gasp of sweet, sweet pain filling his own mouth as he moved inside her, Shelly's most intimate vice gripping him ever tighter as they moved together, rose together, bucked together, the morning air filled with their gasps as their desires were met, their needs fulfilled. No question of prolonging the moment, their lust too overwhelming, the meeting of two bodies so longed for, so eagerly awaited, to have held back now would have been to deny the sweetest release of all. As he thrust ever deeper, Shelly's body spasmed beneath him, tightening, pulling, wrapping, pulsing, every inch of his gift such a pleasure to receive she gasped his name as her body shuddered beneath him, as he collapsed with exhausted pleasure on top of her, their glistening, warm bodies wrapped together in a mutual embrace.

'I've wanted this moment for so long, Shelly,' Ross murmured, kicking back the sheets and pulling her onto the pillows, covering her tenderly then wrapping his arms around her. 'I've dreamed of going to sleep with you beside me.' He was kissing her closing eyes now, his words so sweet that if they hadn't been so heartfelt they would have been corny, but she could hear the genuineness behind them, his touch so reverent, so wondrous, not for a second did she doubt that he meant every last one of them.

Waking in Ross's arms was almost as blissful as falling asleep in them. The hot afternoon sun blazed through a chink in the curtains, catching one of her long auburn curls that had strayed under his head, watching where the strawberry of her hair met the blond of his.

Melissa was wrong.

Strange, the thought that flicked into her mind.

Melissa was wrong, because one moment in the sun with Ross by her side simply wasn't enough.

If this was all there was, if the hurdles undoubtedly before them ultimately proved too great, if this was all there could be for them, though Shelly could never regret what had just transpired, though she would always remember it with love, the agony of losing him had suddenly magnified, and she shivered at the uncertainty that surrounded them.

Don't.

The word resounded in her ears as surely as if she'd spoken it, but Ross didn't stir beside her and Shelly wriggled onto her side, propping herself on her elbow and wallowing in the luxury of watching Ross sleep. Entrenching each and every feature on her mind, revelling in the beauty of awakening beside him, the gentle silence of the late afternoon, the inner peace she had finally found.

The solace she couldn't bear to lose.

A lazy eye peeped open, and he simultaneously smiled, not a hint of embarrassment, not a hint of regret between them, their bodies stretching languorously together, curious hands exploring each other.

'So this is what a sicky feels like. I think I might just have to ring Dr Khan and tell him I've had a relapse and can't come in again tomorrow.'

'There's still tonight,' Shelly said seductively. 'And still another hour or so before I have to pick up Matthew.' Her hand was tracing the muscular outline of his stomach now, edging downwards to the soft velvet warmth that reared eagerly to greet her.

'Time for some afternoon delight, then,' Ross mumbled into her hair as Shelly disappeared beneath the duvet. 'What are you laughing at?' Pulling her up level to his face, he smiled as she carried on giggling.

'I've been so wrong about you, Ross, so very, very wrong.' Another gurgle of laughter as she dived back beneath the covers. 'You are a natural blond after all!'

He just adored her.

Ross rose from the crumpled sheets while she showered to ensure a welcome cup of coffee met her as she stepped out of the *en suite*, rubbing her hair with a towel, then climbing back into bed to watch with blatant adoration as she dressed and brushed her hair.

'You're beautiful, Shelly.'

Up to that moment in time, Shelly would have blushed, would have laughed off his compliment, waved a dismissive hand, but this was no ordinary moment and this was no ordinary day. Under his loving gaze Shelly was able to accept the compliment with all the sincerity behind it. Putting down her brush, she turned from the mirror, a lump filling her throat as she took in the sight of him lying on her bed.

Her fantasy fulfilled.

'So are you, Ross.'

CHAPTER NINE

'HE'S BEEN FINE,' Lorna said cheerfully before Shelly even had a chance to ask. 'A little bit grizzly after his afternoon nap, but he perked up for music therapy. I think you might have a budding Spaniard here, you should see him shaking the maracas.'

The usual still damp 'painting' was handed to Shelly, along with Matthew's bag, and Shelly, loaded like a pack horse, staggered out to the car.

'Did you have a nice day?' Shelly asked as she strapped him into his seat. 'Lorna said you had fun making music.'

Little blue eyes stared back at her but Matthew didn't even attempt a nod. Driving home, Shelly kept up her usual light-hearted chatter, but for once Matthew didn't chat back happily from the rear seat.

Not that he ever actually said much, his vocabulary was too limited for any sort of in-depth conversation, but usually he babbled away, pointing to the cars, the clouds, anything that took his interest. Even when Shelly popped in a favourite CD and sang along to the music, checking in the rear-view mirror she found herself frowning when she saw that Matthew had fallen asleep.

He's tired, Shelly reasoned. After all, he *was* awake for most of the night.

'Hey, Matty!' Ross came out onto the driveway as Shelly pulled up. Opening the rear door of the car, he helped Shelly with the bags and painting as Shelly lifted her little sleepy-headed boy out of the car.

'He's worn out.'

'I don't blame him.'

Dinner was a quick affair, for Matthew at least, a bowl of his favourite fish fingers, and for once Shelly didn't push him with his vegetables when he firmly shook his head, rubbing his eyes and grizzling as he pushed away the bowl.

'How about an early bath and bed?' Shelly suggested, scooping him up.

'Do you want me to take a look at him?' Ross offered. 'My bag's in the car.'

'You've got a doctor's bag?' Shelly grinned.

'Yep,' Ross said with a just a hint of a blush.

'Did your proud parents buy it for you when you passed your finals?'

'I don't think they even noticed,' Ross said with an edge to his voice. 'I bought it myself.'

Shelly found herself frowning. That dark wistful note that occasionally appeared in Ross's voice was back, but just as she registered the fact, Matthew chose that moment to bring up his half-eaten dinner, crying as he retched, and any hopes of resuming the conversation flew out of the window as the next half-hour was spent bathing Matthew and mopping the floor, then visiting the shower for seemingly the umpteenth time that day.

'I'd hate to see your water bill.' Ross grinned as she came into the living room. He was holding a freshly bathed Matthew in his arms, reading him his bedtime story, and Shelly was grateful she could busy herself drying her hair, such was the lump in her throat.

OK, children were sick all the time, Shelly knew that better than anyone. But the night's mini-drama had been made so much easier with Ross there, and though he had examined him thoroughly, checked his ears and throat, gently palpated his stomach, it had nothing to do with the fact that Ross was a doctor and everything to do with him being a fabulous caring man. An extra pair of hands to help when Matthew was crying, to fetch the mop and make a couple of light-hearted jokes, someone to hold Matthew while Shelly dived in the shower, someone to reassure her that Matthew really was OK.

What a different scenario it would have been without him. Bathing a teary Matthew by herself, reassuring a fretful child alone, tucking him in, knowing she had to come out and face the mess she hadn't had a chance to clear up.

'Should I give him some paracetamol?' Shelly asked.

'He seems fine now.' Ross put his hand on his forehead. 'He's not hot.'

'Maybe he *is* teething,' Shelly said, coming over and sitting beside the snuggled-up duo and casting a worried eye over her son. 'Or maybe he's just overtired.'

'He might be brewing something, it might be better to keep him home tomorrow.'

'As if I need an excuse.' Shelly stood up and picked up her son. 'I'll just tuck him in.'

'Take your time.' Ross gently stroked the little head, a brief motion, a quick goodnight, but it was the *way* he did it, with such genuine tenderness in his voice, such genuine fondness in his touch that Shelly felt the familiar lump Ross seemed to generate fill her throat again. 'You'd better take this.' He handed her the rather dog-eared favourite book and Shelly padded off to settle Matthew, but for once even a little man made of gingerbread didn't raise a smile.

'What's up?' Ross noticed her frown as soon as she came into the lounge.

'Nothing,' Shelly said quickly, and then gave a sheepish

smile. 'He just didn't want me to read to him. I shouldn't take it personally.'

Ross saw through her attempt at humour in a flash. 'Do you want me to take another look at him?'

Shelly shook her head. 'I'm just being neurotic, the poor kid's exhausted.' Forcing a smile, she turned for the kitchen and Ross followed her through.

'What are you doing?' he asked as he watched Shelly pull out various packets from the freezer.

'I was going to make something nice,' she said, trying to keep the weary note from her voice. 'Open a bottle of wine, you know, make tonight special. It's not every day someone like you comes along.'

'It's not every day your kid's sick,' Ross said perceptively. Pulling out a loaf of bread, he held it up. 'And as for making it special...' Her kitchen wasn't the biggest in Australia but it shrank even more as he crossed it in two short strides. Taking her in his arms, he held her for a moment. 'You've no idea how special this is to me. *I'll* make dinner,' he said, pushing her reluctantly away. 'You go and put your feet up.'

Toast and wine probably wasn't a connoisseur's delight, but sitting with Ross half watching the television as they chatted easily, for all the romance in the air they might just as well have been in a five-star restaurant with waiters lifting silver lids on flaming dishes and pouring wine the second their glasses met the tablecloth. And when Shelly started yawning, her four nights on duty finally catching up with her, Ross capped the romantic night off perfectly when she came back from checking Matthew and found him lying in her bed.

'How is he?'

'Sound asleep, he didn't even stir when I kissed him.'

He watched as she undressed, watched as she pulled back the duvet to slip into bed beside him.

'Go and put your nightie on.'

She shot him a quizzical look.

'Or your T-shirt or pyjamas, whatever it is you wear when Matthew's sick.'

His insight again floored her. 'You don't mind?'

Ross shook his head. 'He's the number-one guy in your life, Shelly, it isn't a competition. Go to him.'

'Thank you.' It seemed a strange thing to say, words that maybe didn't belong in the bedroom, but how many men, Shelly wondered as she tenderly kissed Ross goodnight and headed to her son's room, how many men at the very infancy of a relationship would give up a night of passion, would understand a mother's need, would be the one to instigate sleeping apart?

Only Ross Bodey.

At least he was the only one that sprang into Shelly's mind.

Slipping into the cramped single bed, Shelly pulled the warm body of her son near, kissing his soft cheek, pulling him into her. 'Goodnight, darling,' she whispered tenderly, laying her head back on the pillow. 'Mummy's here.'

'Ross!' Shelly could hear her scream echoing through the dark house.

It was her third attempt at calling him, the other two strangling in her throat and coming out as dry rasps as they did in a nightmare.

But, then again, this was a nightmare.

A living nightmare.

The bedroom door flung open and the room flooded with light as Ross flicked on the switch, and she watched the look of horror on his face as she turned her stricken one to him.

'He's having a fit!'

Instantly the horrified look faded, replaced in a flash by the calm, efficient doctor she had worked alongside as they'd cared for so many sick children.

Only this wasn't a patient, this was her son.

Shelly had already turned the rigid, jerking body of Matthew onto his side, but Ross crossed the room and took him from her, sitting beside her on the bed and placing the child across his knees, tipping his body downwards slightly.

'My bag's still in the living room.' His voice was calm but loud. 'Go and get it, Shelly.'

Through the darkened house she ran, obeying his order without question, but her mind was at odds. She should be on the telephone, calling an ambulance, summoning help.

She had help, Shelly registered briefly.

Ross was a doctor, he knew best.

Grabbing the bag, she stubbed her toe on the coffee-table as she dashed back but the pain that seared through her barely merited a thought. 'He'll be all right, he'll be all right.' The words were like a mantra, a steadying prayer, as she raced back to the bedroom.

'He's still fitting!' Her wail as she dropped the bag was verging on hysteria. 'He should have stopped by now, Ross, he should have stopped!'

Ross didn't respond to her cries. Matthew was on the floor now as Ross rummaged through the bag. He should be telling her it was over, that her little boy had stopped fitting. Instead, Matthew was still jerking, grunting noises coming from his distorted mouth, his eyes white as they rolled back into his head, and Shelly literally felt her knees buckle beneath her as she grabbed the chest of drawers for support.

'Go and call an ambulance, Shelly,' Ross ordered, his eyes never leaving Matthew as he undressed the rigid body. 'Tell them he's having a prolonged convulsion, that I'm giving him some rectal diazepam.

'Go!' he added, for the first time an anxious note making his voice waver.

Strange, the things you thought of when fear had got you by the heart. Shelly had picked up the telephone, thousands, probably hundreds of thousands of times, but as she picked it up this time she realised just why those three little emergency numbers were printed there.

The supposedly ingrained numbers seemed to have flown from her mind and Shelly had to physically read them to enable her to punch them in.

'Emergency. Which service do you require?'

How calm the voice sounded, how removed from the drama that was taking place in this very house. 'A-ambulance,' Shelly stammered. 'Urgently.' She wanted to hang up immediately to dash back to Matthew's side to see if he had finally stopped fitting, but instead she had to somehow recall her address, somehow tell them there was a doctor in attendance, the drug he was giving right now as she spoke, to somehow give them a clear picture of what was unfolding to enable an appropriate response.

'If you have an outside light, go and put it on now and open the front door. I'll stay on the line till the paramedics arrive.'

She didn't say thank you, didn't respond to the authoritative calm voice at all. Dropping the telephone, Shelly raced to the front door, fumbled with the lock and flicked on the light before racing back the length of the house, back to her son's side.

'He's stopped,' Ross said immediately, but there was no jubilation in his voice, and Shelly knew with a sinking heart why. The awful jerking had stopped but Matthew lay flat and lifeless. Just the rapid movement of his chest, the awful rattling noises coming from his mouth as he breathed showed he was alive. Lines she had never seen before were around Ross's eyes as he examined the floppy arms closely, tying a tourniquet snugly around one to bring up a vein. 'I need to get some IV access in case he starts again. Hold his arm for me in case he moves.' He made a tiny space for her alongside her son as he set to work. Rows of tiny blood specimen bottles were already lined up in a dish. 'Tell me exactly what happened, Shelly.'

'He woke up a couple of times, he was just grizzling but he settled straight back to sleep.' She could hardly get the words out through her chattering teeth, and though she knew Matthew was past feeling pain, and she had seen the same procedure done so many times before, Shelly winced as Ross stuck the needle in Matthew's arm. Only this morning they had been holding him, but he had been kicking then, giggling and playing, not lifeless, not pale and flat with a horrible grey tinge to his lips...

'What happened then?' Ross dragged her back and Shelly took a deep breath, swallowing back the gulping tears that threatened to overwhelm her.

'Then *I* woke up. He felt hot. I was just getting out of bed to go and get the thermometer and check him when he vomited and then...then he started...' She began to cry in earnest, squeezing the little limp hand she was holding.

'Has he ever done this before?' Ross's voice was sharp. There was no time for sentiment, no time to comfort her. He was pulling back blood into the syringe now, then, replacing the cap on the IV bung, he started to squeeze blood into the various tubes.

'Never.'

'Apart from his Down's syndrome, has he any other medical problems?'

Shelly shook her head without elaborating.

'Any cardiac problems?'

'Nothing,' Shelly wailed. Down's syndrome children, apart from mental impairment and their recognisable features, often had other medical problems but till now Matthew had been blessed with good health.

'Is he up to date with all his immunisations?'

Shelly nodded, too choked up to speak, but as Ross pushed further she started shaking her head rapidly, hating the path Ross was taking.

'Has he had his meningitis vaccine?'

'He hasn't got meningitis.' The words stuck in her throat and she struggled to focus, watching with widening eyes as Ross attempted to push Matthew's head against his chest, checking for neck stiffness. 'He's had the immunisation, he hasn't got meningitis.' But Ross didn't seem to be listening to her. Instead, he was filling up a syringe with antibiotics as Shelly fought against the logic that seemed to be screaming at her, pleading internally for it not to be true.

Somewhere in the distance she could hear the wail of a siren, and she waited with bated breath for Matthew to rally, for the stomping of feet running through the house, for the flurry of activity that filled the small bedroom to somehow rouse her little boy. For him to open his little eyes and smile that endearing smile.

For Matthew to come back to her.

Instead, his beautiful tiny face was lost to her as a suction catheter and oxygen mask took their place, as red dots were placed on his chest and leads attached to a cardiac monitor, as bags of fluid were attached to the drip Ross had inserted. Shelly sank back on her heels, utter, overwhelming despair filling her as Matthew just lay there.

'Come on.' Ross's hand was pulling her up. Guiding her from the awful scene, leading her quickly into her bedroom.

'I don't want to leave him.'

'You're not leaving him,' Ross said firmly, pulling open her wardrobe. As if she were a child, he dressed her, guiding her shaking legs into shorts, pulling a T-shirt over her head, even putting her feet into her sandals, tutting gently when he saw the blood on her foot where she had stubbed her toe. 'Where are your keys?'

His question was so, so irrelevant the usually meticulous Shelly had to think, forcibly rake her mind to think where the hell they might be. 'In my bag.'

'This one?' Ross held it up and as Shelly nodded vaguely, the gut-wrenching nausea that had been ever present since Matthew had started fitting overwhelming her now.

'Ross, I'm going to be sick.'

He didn't even bat an eyelid, just guided her to the *en suite*, running a towel under the tap to wash her face down afterwards, which he passed to her as easily as if he were passing her a tissue. 'Come on.'

The night air was warm as she stepped outside. They were loading Matthew into the ambulance now and Shelly vaguely registered the concerned neighbours standing and watching on the nature strips, dressed in shorts and nighties, brought out by the flashing blue lights of the ambulance and police car that was parked beside it. But she had eyes only for the stretcher and the tiny, precious bundle it carried.

'Just wait here, love.' A policewoman held her arm and gestured for Ross to go inside the ambulance.

'I'm his mother,' Shelly argued, but it was pointless. 'Why are the police here?' she asked, bemused.

'We're going to provide an escort.'

The policewoman's hand was on her shoulder, a quiet gesture of comfort and support, but Shelly was way beyond comforting. Every crackle on the radio, every garbled message making her jump with alarm as she waited, waited to be allowed in to her son.

'What's taking so long?' Shrugging off the hand, Shelly lurched forward as Ross stepped down from the ambulance, his face grim, the blue light flashing, his skin unusually pale, and he took her hand as he spoke.

'He had another fit,' Ross started gently, 'just as they got him inside. We stopped the fitting but...' He was swallowing, trying so hard to look at her, trying so hard to be the strong one. 'He stopped breathing for a moment.' His hands tightened around hers as she gave a strangled sob. 'We've intubated him, he's heavily sedated.'

If he hadn't been holding her she was sure she would have sunk to the ground, but there was no time for dramatics. She needed so badly to see Matthew, however bad he was, and Ross seemed to understand that, gently helping her up into the ambulance, the paramedics nodding briefly as they moved some equipment to give Shelly some room to sit down.

'We've got a police escort,' the paramedic said kindly. 'We're going to have him at the hospital in no time. You just sit there and we'll work on.'

His instruction, however gently said, was clear.

There was nothing now Shelly could do.

The ambulance screeched off, hurtling through the darkened streets, its lights flashing, siren occasionally wailing as they braked near traffic lights then accelerated when the road was clear, playing a strange game of chase and catch with the sleek lines of the police car. And Shelly sat there, her teeth chattering, her body sliding along the seat with the motion of the ambulance, her white-knuckled hands holding the seat beneath, her red eyes staring, pleading at the inert body of her son as Ross and the paramedic worked on, squeezing the oxygen into his little lungs, the steady drip of the infusion, the loud rapid blips emanating from the cardiac monitor, so, so fast for a little boy so very still.

The familiar sight of her hospital only terrified Shelly more. Here the awful dream became a reality as she watched well-known colleagues huddling into their theatre greens suddenly move as the ambulance approached, wrenching open the rear doors before the vehicle had even come to a halt, racing to get Matthew inside, to the life-saving equipment and trained expertise he so desperately needed.

Someone, Shelly didn't even notice who, led her inside, showed her into a small neat room where she was left, trembling, hugging her arms around her, waiting for some news, waiting for someone—anyone—to come and tell her just what the hell was going on.

'Hello, Shelly.' A vaguely familiar face appeared at the door and Shelly frowned as she tried to place it. 'I'm Dianne, the receptionist. I just need to get a few details from you.'

'Have you heard anything?'

Dianne shook her head. 'One of the nurses or doctors will be in to see you just as soon as they can.'

Shelly stumbled through the form, giving Matthew's name, his age, his date of birth, his address.

'Does his father live at the same address?' Dianne asked in the same tactful voice Shelly herself had used so many times before.

'No.' Shelly hesitated. 'We're divorced.' She waited for a ream of other questions but they didn't come for now. Dianne clicked off her pen and slipped it back into her pocket.

'I'm a nurse,' Shelly said in last futile attempt to gain access. 'I'm a paediatric trained nurse, I work here! I should be with my son.'

'You're a mum tonight,' Dianne said gently, the compassion in her voice steadying Shelly for a moment. 'Let them do their work.' Gently she guided her to a chair and handed her a box of tissues. 'Is there anyone you want to call, anyone I can ring for you?'

Shelly shook her head. 'I'd rather wait till I hear some news.'

'Hopefully it won't be too long.' Dianne gave her arm a small pat. 'I'll put my head in as I go past, remind them you're in here.'

'Thank you.'

Till then Dianne had always just been a receptionist, a woman Shelly nodded to sometimes in the car park or someone she grumbled to occasionally when the labels from Emergency were missing from the files, but tonight Shelly realised there was so much more to her job, that the administrative personnel who worked in a hospital were just as valuable as the nurses and doctors, and the patients that came through the door affected them just as much as the frontline staff.

'How is he?' Shelly jumped up the second Ross finally entered, but he gently pushed her back down into the chair.

'The same, Shelly, they're still working on him.'

'Is he fitting?'

Mercifully Ross shook his head, but the elation was soon doused. 'He's very sick, Shelly. Dr Khan's in with him, and he thinks that it *is* meningitis.'

'But I had him vaccinated.'

'Shelly, you know as well as I do that the vaccination only protects against one strain of the disease. Dr Khan seems to think it's bacterial, but we won't know anything for sure until the test results start coming in.'

'Can I go in yet?'

Ross shook his head. 'It's better you stay here, Shelly.'

'What about you? Why aren't you in there with him, doing something?' Her voice was starting to rise again, angry, scared eyes turning on him.

'They told me to wait outside. I was getting upset...' His voice trailed off but Shelly didn't say anything to fill the silence, just sat starting vacantly ahead, waiting, willing, praying for some news.

How many cups of tea went cold Shelly lost count, but the first rays of morning light were filtering through the curtains when the distinguished but weary face of Dr Khan finally sat in front of them. He nodded briefly to Ross before turning his full attention to Shelly.

'Matthew is a very sick little boy.' His words were measured, delivered slowly but surely, and he sat quietly for a moment to let them sink in. 'We're going to move him up to Intensive Care shortly. At the moment we've got him sedated and on a ventilator.'

'Is it meningitis?'

Dr Khan nodded. 'All the signs at this stage point to bacterial meningitis. Now, I understand from Dr Bodey that Matthew, apart from his Down's syndrome, is a well child, that he's got no other relevant medical history.'

'He's fine.' Ross's arm was around her and Shelly allowed herself to sink into him for a moment. 'Or at least he was. He's been a bit grizzly. I should have known, I should have bought him up sooner, should have—'

Dr Khan held up his hand. 'This is no one's fault. No one's,' he reiterated. 'Meningitis can strike very quickly. The early symptoms are vague and mild. No one could have predicted this.'

Shelly felt Ross's arms stiffen around her, and as she sat up slightly she looked at the utter despair on his face, the pain embedded in his eyes, and she knew she should somehow comfort him, say she understood what Dr Khan was telling her, that this horrible situation wasn't his fault. But she was too emotionally raw, too scared, too drained to worry about Ross's feelings at that moment. All she wanted was to see Matthew.

'Can I go to him?'

'I'll ask one of the nurses to come and fetch you.' He stood up and briefly looked down at his notes. 'Shelly…' She heard him clear his throat, felt his discomfort. 'As I said before, Matthew is very sick indeed. We're doing everything we can for him…'

'How long will it be?' Shelly's eyes looked up, pleading for a shred of comfort. 'How long until he stabilises?'

There was the longest pause, for an age the horrible sound of silence filled the room and Shelly willed Dr Khan to speak, to inject some measure of hope, some time-frame to cling to.

'We're taking things minute by minute at the moment. I know that you aren't with Matthew's father, but I think you should inform him that Matthew is here.'

'He doesn't see him,' Shelly said quickly. 'He just pays half the crèche fees and gives the odd present here and there…'

Dr Khan's eyes were back on his notes and Shelly felt her heart sink, the realisation of the direness of the situation magnifying as he spoke.

'He needs to know how sick his son is, Shelly. He needs to be given an opportunity to see him…'

Dr Khan didn't say anything else, his unfinished sentence hanging in the air as he slipped out of the small room, leaving a shell-shocked Shelly sitting there trying to absorb the hell behind his words. As Ross's hand found hers she instinctively tightened her fingers around it, clinging on for dear life to the one comfort in this whole bleak wilderness, her eyes turning to

him filled with despair. 'Is he telling me Neil should be here…?'
Her words caught in her throat and struggled to speak, to articulate the hardest words of her life, mentally willing Ross to
soothe her with a smile, to tell her she was overreacting. But
instead he pulled her close, buried his face in her hair and wept
alongside her as Shelly carried on talking. 'That I should give
him the opportunity to say goodbye?'

CHAPTER TEN

'I WISH IT was you looking after him.' Shelly gave a weary smile
to Melissa as she sat on the empty seat beside her. 'They've told
me to wait in here while they do some chest physio and take
some X-rays, that's as much as I've been told. I don't know if
it's because I'm a nurse they assume I know all the answers, or
that they're worried they'll upset me.'

'Maybe they're just busy looking after him,' Melissa suggested gently, picking up the half-drunk cup of chocolate from
the table and handing it to Shelly. 'And I *will* be looking after
him soon. Once he gets out of Intensive Care he'll come to the
children's ward.'

'If he comes out.' Shelly's voice was flat. The tears had
stopped hours ago and she was operating on autopilot, her mind
almost detached from the true horror of it all in some strange
attempt at self-preservation.

'He *is* going to come out.' Melissa's voice was confident,
determined. 'He's going to pull through, Shelly, you have to
have faith.

'Where's Ross?' Melissa asked when Shelly didn't respond,
just stood up and moved to the glass window, her eyes staring

helplessly to where her son lay, surrounded by doctors, nurses, tubes, machinery.

'He's gone to find the contact numbers for my parents. I was going to let them finish their holiday, they've only got another day...'

Her dry eyes suddenly welled, the gripping fear she was so desperately trying to control suddenly gushing in from all sides with such force Shelly thought she might be knocked to the floor. Melissa rushed over, wrapping her arms around her friend, trying to somehow comfort her, despite knowing there was no comfort to be found.

'Shelly.'

The familiarity of the voice calling her gave Shelly no comfort. Looking up, her whole body seemed to tense as she saw Neil standing in the doorway of the intensive care waiting room, clean-shaven, dark-suited, his shirt crisp and white, a plain navy tie luxurious in its simplicity.

Strange, the things one thought.

Strange, how the tiniest, most insignificant detail could take on humungous proportions.

'You look like you're on your way to work.'

He didn't respond to her statement. Instead, he walked over to the window, nodding briefly to Melissa.

'How are you, Neil?' It wasn't the friendliest of greetings but, then, Melissa had been the one pulling the tissues out of the box for the last couple of years, comforting her friend and colleague through the minefield of divorce, the roller-coaster ride of bringing up a special needs child. She gave Shelly's shoulders a squeeze. 'I'd better get back to the ward. I'll come back up in my coffee-break.'

'So how is he?' Neil was looking through the glass now and Shelly watched with something bordering on compassion as she watched him start as he saw Matthew lying there.

'The same as when I called. Apparently no news is good

news for a while. Until the antibiotics take effect we just have to wait and see.'

'But they'll work?'

Shelly gave a brief but painful shrug. 'There are no guarantees.'

They stood in mutual silence, staring through the window, watching as the radiographer pushed the machine forward to take a chest X-ray. A nurse, looking up, gave an apologetic smile then pulled the curtain on them, blocking their view, assuming perhaps it was less painful that way.

'You'll be able to see him soon.' Vaguely, Shelly registered Neil's discomfort, a slight shift as he moved his feet, taking breath in as if he was about to speak, but she was too wrapped up in Matthew to tread gently. 'What, don't you want to see him?' she asked incredulously.

'It's not that I don't want to,' Neil responded quickly, running an uncomfortable hand across his face. 'Cecile just wanted me to check that it would be OK.' He at least had the grace to blush as he continued, to attempt an apologetic shrug. 'She's pregnant, Shelly. Only just, you know how dangerous things can be during the first trimester.'

'The first trimester!' Shelly gave him a wide-eyed look, the biting sarcasm clear in her voice. 'My, we are taking an interest!'

'Shelly don't,' Neil shook his head. 'You can't blame Cecile for being concerned. Hell, I'm concerned. I don't think I could go through it all again if something went wrong this time.'

His lack of sensitivity shocked even Shelly, who had truly thought Neil was beyond hurting her any more. 'If I remember rightly,' Shelly said, her voice wavering with emotion, 'you didn't go through it the first time.'

'I didn't come here to fight.' He was looking through the glass. The curtain was being pulled back, the nurse gesturing they needed a couple more minutes. Shelly watched as he stared at his son, an expression she couldn't read on his face.

'I'm sorry, Shelly, I didn't mean for it to be like this for the three of us.'

'Do you think this is how I'd planned it?'

'I just couldn't cope when I found out he was handicapped. I thought that maybe once he was born I'd come round, but I didn't, the whole thing terrified me. I couldn't just accept it the way that you did.' He was nearly crying now, but Shelly felt no sympathy. 'You're a better person than me.'

'I'm his mother,' Shelly said in a cool voice that defied the emotions coursing through her. 'My love for him isn't negotiable.'

'You're stronger than me...'

'Don't make excuses, Neil.' There was a bitter note creeping into Shelly's voice, coupled with an emerging resilience. 'You wanted the perfect job, the perfect home, the perfect family.' Her green eyes turned to meet his. 'And I hope you get it with Cecile, I hope for her sake that she and the baby can live up to your expectations.' She looked through the window at Matthew, so small and so innocent, struggling so hard just to stay alive. 'All that little boy wants to do is love, that's it. It's as simple and as beautiful as that.'

'Don't make me the bad guy here,' Neil was crying now, taking out a perfectly ironed handkerchief and blowing his nose loudly. 'I know I'm not perfect. I just couldn't cope. Not everyone's like you, Shelly, not everyone's perfect!'

But Shelly refused to accept his excuses, her tired eyes turning to him. 'He's going to get through this, Neil, and when he does, you can forget about the crèche and the occasional present, you can forget about reluctant access visits. Matthew deserves better. You're in or out of his life, not somewhere in between. His attention span's too short for someone to just drift in and out. He needs constancy, he needs a secure world, and I won't let you hurt him.'

She was letting him off the hook, offering him an out, a

chance to get on with his life, and the disappointment, the pain she felt when he nodded was all for Matthew.

'Can I sit with him?'

Shelly nodded as a nurse gestured for them to come around. 'Do you want some time alone with him?'

'Thanks.'

Shelly watched through the window, watched with a heart that felt it wasn't beating any more as Matthew's own father hovered tentatively by the bedside, an awkward hand patting his son's, a helpless look on his face as he eyed the equipment, blowing his nose and wiping away tears.

She certainly wasn't perfect, Shelly thought ruefully. Perfect people were able to find forgiveness, and as she watched Neil pick up his briefcase and turn away there was certainly no forgiveness in her heart. She couldn't even muster up the emotion to hate him. Instead, she made her way out of the waiting room, sat by Matthew's bedside and laid her cheek on her little son's hand.

No one would ever hurt him again.

'Why don't you try and rest for a couple of hours?' Julie, the ICU sister, offered gently. 'Melissa said you've just finished a stint on nights, and you obviously didn't get any sleep last night. You must be exhausted.'

'I'm fine,' Shelly lied, her ashen face not even looking up at the kind voice. 'I really don't want to leave him.'

'I know.' Julie was perched on a high stool at the end of the bed, massive sheets of observation charts on the workbench in front of her, monitoring every tiny variance in Matthew, his observations, the drugs he was receiving, his fluid input and output, rows of red and blue lines all charting his progress. 'But you need to sleep.'

Shelly liked her. Liked the calm way she responded to the alarms that seemed to go off with alarming regularity, liked the way she spoke to Matthew as she nursed him, the way she let Shelly help wash him and comb his hair and do his mouth care. Julie was very young and very pretty, but the depth of her knowledge belied her youthful face and slowly Shelly was starting to trust her.

Shelly had even accepted that the lack of information coming from Julie wasn't an attempt to keep her in the dark. No one knew the outcome.

'There's a relatives' room just along the corridor. I'll send someone for you the second there's a change, and if he stays the same I'll come and get you myself when I go to lunch. Shelly, you know you're going to be useless for Matthew if you make yourself ill. Hopefully in a few days he'll be running you ragged, demanding drinks and sweets.'

The line Julie was using was so familiar, one Shelly had used herself so many times before, and the exhaustion, emotional and physical, was starting to catch up. Every bell, every alarm seemed to be grating in her brain, everything making her jump, Neil's departure playing over and over in her mind like some ghastly video she couldn't turn off.

'Julie's right.' Ross was back, looking refreshed in comparison to the pale shadow of Shelly. He was wearing shorts and a T-shirt, his tan so ridiculously healthy-looking it made Shelly feel like a corpse in comparison. 'You have to sleep.'

'Hi, Ross.' Julie pulled her charts into line, moved over just an inch to let him see them. Try as she may, Shelly couldn't fail to notice a certain warmth in Julie's voice, a certain perkiness appearing, her pleasure in seeing Ross blatantly evident. 'Did you want to take a look at Matthew?'

Ross shook his head. 'Sorry, Julie, I didn't explain myself, did I? I'm actually here with Shelly and Matthew. I'm off duty today.'

'Oh.' Shelly saw the flicker of confusion on Julie's pretty face, her eyes dart questioningly to Shelly, the tiniest, almost insignificant gesture but with the hugest ramifications.

The impossibility of this couple so evident in her eyes.

Julie hadn't been flirting, at least, no more anyway than every other female in the building when Ross was about. After all, even the most happily married woman sucked in their stomachs in honour of Ross, he was that type of guy. The world brightened a touch when Ross was around, Shelly knew that better than anyone.

'Come on.' Ross pulled Shelly up from the chair where she sat and she hovered for a moment. 'What about you?' she argued, reluctant to leave. 'You've been up, too.'

'I'll have a rest later. Go on. I'll sit with him.'

'How did you go with the travel agent?'

'All taken care of. They're going to tell the rep and check the flight availability before they tell your parents.'

'Thanks for that.'

'Here.' He handed Shelly her own overnight bag. 'I'm not too sure if I've packed all the right things but I gave it a go. Go on,' Ross said gently, 'go and lie down.'

She watched him tenderly stroke Matthew's hair, and it was so, so different from Neil's formal, uncomfortable gestures, so far removed from the wooden emotions of Matthew's own father. But Ross wasn't Matthew's father, Ross didn't need to be here…

'When's Neil coming?'

'He's been…' She watched a frown mar his face, his mouth open to speak, and she carried on regardless. 'And gone already.'

For a second she didn't say anything, just stared at the two people she loved most in the world, the two people who mattered.

Two worlds so far removed.

'Ross, can I speak to you a moment?'

'Sure.'

Back to the waiting room Shelly went, back to the coffee-machine, the magazines, the brown corduroy cushions with the button in the middle missing. She knew every inch of the room, every peeling piece of paint, and Ross stood there in the middle of it, his face full of concern as he waited for her to speak.

'This isn't going to work.'

'What isn't?' He sounded genuinely bemused, as if he had no idea in the world what Shelly was about to say.

And maybe he didn't, Shelly reasoned. Perhaps he hadn't given any real thought to what it was all about. He had just drifted into her life without question, just assumed it would work.

'Us.' She let the single word sink in before she continued. 'Like I said, Neil's just been and I've told him I don't want him in our lives. I don't want people drifting in and out. I want Matthew to have security...'

'I can give him that,' Ross argued, coming over, but Shelly put her hand up.

'You can't, Ross.' Tears were coursing down her cheeks and she didn't even bother to wipe them. 'You're twenty-seven years old, you could have any woman you want, and one day you're going to look at me and Matthew and all the problems—'

'Don't even go there,' Ross interrupted furiously. 'Do you think I'm that weak, that some pretty little thing would just have to bat her eyes and I'd be off? Shelly, I adore you, I'd never betray you.'

He sounded so utterly convinced, so sure of his feelings, Shelly almost believed him, but it wasn't just Ross's drop-dead gorgeous looks on the agenda and Shelly reminded herself of that as she stood her ground. 'How long is your contract here, Ross—three months, six?

'How long, Ross?' Shelly pushed when Ross didn't answer straight away.

'Three months.'

'And what then, Ross? The outback again, Asia or Africa perhaps? One day you'll move on. You might not think it now, but one day you'll look around you and realise just what you've taken on and I can't blame you for that, can't blame you for feeling the way any person would, but I can't put myself through it, can't set Matthew and me up for another fall. I don't think we'd survive.'

'Shelly, look at me,' Ross urged. 'Look at me and for once in your life listen! I don't know where I'm going when this contract ends, that all depends on you. I came back *because* of you, I didn't just drift in. You're tired, you're upset…'

It would have been so easy to give in, to accept his words, but Shelly knew she had to be strong. However unwitting, she'd seen the incredulous look in Julie's eyes, seen the improbable couple they made, and however much Ross couldn't see the bitter end they surely faced, Shelly could.

'You're not what Matthew needs.' She watched his face slip. His eyes seemed to literally sink, his shoulders lowering as he exhaled slowly. All the fight of before seemed to leave him then, the struggle to make her listen, to see his point disappearing as if a light had been switched off. 'Matthew deserves stability, and I'm going to make sure he gets it. You can't provide that, Ross, no matter how much you might want to. What I feel doesn't come into this, Ross, it can't. What I'm trying to say is—'

It was Ross who held his hand up to silence her now, Ross who shook his head. 'Don't, Shelly, I think you've made yourself perfectly clear.' His face had a weary dignity about it. 'You have to do what's right by Matthew and, like it or not, I have to respect it. Hey, who am I to argue with a statement like the one you've just made?' He made to go but at the door he paused, turning for a second, and Shelly had to force herself not to rush over to him, his pain so evident she felt it, too. 'Maybe you're right, Shelly, maybe I'm not cut out to be a parent.' His eyes met hers then. 'But I'd have given it my best shot.'

CHAPTER ELEVEN

IT WAS THE loneliest twenty-four hours of Shelly's life.

Surrounded by friends and colleagues, her parents ringing on the hour every hour as they awaited their flight home, endless trips to the waiting room to update anxious visitors on Matthew's progress, friends who had made the trip despite knowing they wouldn't be allowed to see him. Even Lorna from the crèche came, openly crying when she looked through the glass, wondering as everyone did if she'd somehow missed something, if there was something she could have should have done differently. But despite all the activity, all the concern all the love and concern that surrounded her, Shelly felt isolated. As if she were inhabiting an alien planet, even normal conversations, basic exchanges seemed to be taking place in another language.

The only light moment to an otherwise awful day was when she finally, at Julie's insistence, left the ward for the briefest of showers. Ross, love him, had indeed packed and as she looked at the handful of underwear tossed inside she paled at the thought of him rummaging through her knickers drawer, making a mental note to toss out every sensible pair of undies she possessed the second she got home.

She longed for Ross's easygoing nature, for his insight, for his different perspective. Longed for him to rub her weary shoulders the way only Ross could, to inject his easy optimism into this most awful situation and, Shelly admitted almost guiltily, she longed to lie down on the bed Julie kept suggesting she try, and leave Matthew in Ross's tender loving care.

But it was way too late for that.

There had been such hurt in his eyes, a hurt beyond what Shelly had ever imagined there might be, a depth to his pain she hadn't anticipated.

Neil had been relieved.

Ross had been devastated.

'Darling.' Marlene looked so tanned and glamorous for a second Shelly barely recognised her as she crossed the intensive care unit, but on closer inspection the last twenty-four hours had left their mark, dark hollows surrounding her eyes, lines grooved in her cheeks, and her hands were shaking as she reached out and touched Matthew.

'I'm so sorry,' Marlene sobbed as Ken hovered, wringing his hands in despair. 'So sorry we weren't here for you. How is he? Ross said he was picking up a bit.'

'Ross?'

Marlene was dabbing at her eyes as she looked down at Matthew. 'He picked us up from the airport and drove us straight here. We had no idea who he was, of course. He was holding up a sign with our names on!'

'He's one of the doctors here.'

Marlene nodded, her glassy eyes straying to Matthew. 'He said he'd been helping you out with the babysitting. Oh, Shelly we should never have gone, never left you—'

'Mum,' Shelly broke in. 'It would have happened anyway.' But though she said all the right things, though she comforted her mother, Shelly's mind was whirring. So wrapped up in herself and Matthew it had never entered her head how Marlene and Ken would get from the airport, never even thought about

the angst-filled taxi ride battling peak-hour traffic as they struggled to get to the hospital.

But Ross had.

'He's stabilised, they've stopped all anticonvulsants.' She
watched Marlene frown, the medical terminology that came so
easily to Shelly lost on Marlene. 'He hasn't had any more fits
so they're weaning him off the medication, and the antibiotics
seem to have kicked in. They're going to try and get him off the
ventilator tomorrow.' Shelly swallowed hard, hating to douse
the water on Marlene's hope. 'We won't know for a while yet
if there's been any lasting damage.'

'You mean brain damage,' Marlene gasped as she started to
cry again, but, catching Shelly's strained face, Marlene checked
herself. 'I'm sorry, Shelly, I'm supposed to be being strong for
you.'

'I know, Mum, but it's not that easy, is it?'

Julie came off the stool then. It was long into her third shift
with Matthew, watching Shelly dozing fitfully on a chair by the
bed, and she finally put her foot down.

'How about letting your mum and dad have some time with
him, and you go and get some sleep, some proper sleep?' she
said as Shelly shook her head. 'And I'm not taking no for an
answer this time. You're going to end up being admitted with
exhaustion if you don't get some rest.'

'She's right.' Marlene's insistence, combined with Julie's,
was more than Shelly could argue with, and now her parents
were finally here Shelly felt herself able to hand over the reins
a touch, to finally let down her guard a fraction.

'You'll call me,' Shelly checked.

'In a flash.'

A small, plastic-mattressed bed had never looked more inviting. For once Shelly didn't bother tucking in corners, turning
back blankets. Instead, she threw on the pillow case and a bottom sheet and stretched out, pulling the white hospital blanket
over her. The last time she had lain down she had been hold-

ing Matthew, so blissfully oblivious of the impending disaster, so completely unaware how fate was about to roll the dice and throw up another challenge for her to deal with.

Her mind clicked backwards, reliving the precious hours beforehand when for a short while at least the world had been gentler, kindlier, easier.

When she had lain in Ross's arms...

'Shelly.' For a second or two fantasy met reality. A lazy second where the face filling her dreams was really here, where a strong hand was gently touching her arm. 'Shelly.' Her shoulder was being shaken now, dragging her out of her long slumber away from the bliss of a long-awaited sleep.

'What happened?' Sitting bolt upright, Shelly's eyes flashed open, taking in Ross sitting on the edge of her bed, his face now cleanly shaven, his eyes void of their usual easy welcoming smile. 'What's wrong?'

'Nothing,' Ross said quickly, pushing her gently back onto the pillow. 'He's actually picking up, but I just needed to talk to you for a moment.'

She lay back down, allowing the world to come more slowly into focus, listening as Ross spoke, acutely aware of her unmade-up face and unkempt hair, so drab in comparison to a well-groomed Ross.

'They're going to give him a trial without the ventilator tonight. Your mum's with him.' His hand gently held her down as Shelly's first instinct was to rush back to Matthew. 'And what I've got to say won't take a moment.'

She owed him a moment, Shelly knew that much. Whatever had gone on between them, Ross had been wonderful where Matthew had been concerned. 'Dr Khan thinks if he improves enough overnight they might even send him over to the children's ward tomorrow or the next day.'

'So soon?'

Ross nodded. 'Which means I'll be looking after him.' He watched her face as he spoke. 'If you've got a problem with that, tell me now, Shelly. If I tell Dr Khan now, at least we'll be able to arrange something.'

'Why wouldn't I want you looking after him?' Shelly asked bemused as Ross gave a hollow laugh.

'It's my fault he's here in the first place.'

Shelly shook her head, floored by what he was saying. 'Ross, I'm a nurse, I work on a children's ward, I was there when you examined him, this is no one's fault.'

He gave a brief nod, but she could almost feel the self-doubt churning in his usually confident mind.

'What about what's happened between us?'

'Ross.' Shelly's voice so soft he had to strain to catch it. 'That's no one's fault either, it's just something that can never be...' Uncoiling her long legs, Shelly put her bare feet on the floor. 'I need to go to him.'

'Sure.'

Slipping on her sandals, she made for the door, expecting Ross to get up and follow her. Instead, he stayed sitting on the bed, not watching her, not watching anything, just staring at the bland cream wall. 'Are you coming?'

Ross gave a brief nod but made no attempt to move. 'I'll be out in a minute. I'll catch you on the ward, then?' He held up both hands. 'Fingers crossed.'

Holding up her own crossed fingers, Shelly managed a watery smile. 'Fingers crossed,' she murmured, before quietly closing the door behind her.

With Julie's intervention, they let Shelly stay as Matthew was extubated, but even though it went well, even though he breathed on his own, holding his oxygen saturations with just an oxygen mask, Shelly felt a pang of guilt as a sense of anti-climax washed over her.

For three days and two long, long nights she had prayed for this moment, but in her dreams Matthew had opened his eyes, looked right at her. Instead, he just lay there, and Shelly, if there had ever been any doubt, realised then that this was only the beginning of a long exhausting journey. That the Matthew she had kissed goodnight on Thursday would, at best, return to her only in stages, that the deluge of questions about brain damage and long-term effects wasn't going to be answered in the next few days. It was a matter of wait and see, two steps forward one step backwards, and no amount of questions or tests were going to give Shelly a conclusive answer.

The night seemed to go on for ever. Matthew's consciousness level lightened but there was no joyous reunion, just a teary little boy, uncomfortable, pulling at the tubes, staring blankly at a concerned Shelly who did her best to comfort him, to pull him back to her. And despite the presence of her parents, the level of care delivered, Shelly ached, physically ached, for the presence of Ross, for a partner who would willingly share the load, for that mind-reader who instinctively seemed to know how she was feeling. When Dr Khan did the ward round and agreed Matthew could be moved over to the children's ward, Shelly wrestled with the surge of relief that filled her, the knowledge Ross would now be near, reminding herself she had chosen to go it alone.

She was greeted like a long-lost friend on the children's ward, even Tania, reserved to say the least, managed a welcoming smile and a quick pat on her arm.

'Anything we can do to make things easier for you, Shelly, you just have to say. You know where the kitchen is!'

Shelly suppressed an out-of-place smile. The kitchen on the children's ward was hallowed territory indeed, way out of bounds for the parents of patients, and Tania allowing her to use it was a concession indeed!

'Thanks, Tania, and I'm sorry for all the trouble with the roster.'

'Don't even give it a thought. When Matthew improves we'll have a chat, try and work something out. Now, we've put Matthew in a side room, not because he's infectious but the noise on the ward will make him irritable. It might be better to keep the curtains closed if he's still a bit sensitive to light. Still, don't be a prisoner, you can have the door open whenever you want—he's not in isolation.'

The small side room that Shelly knew so well was amazingly unfamiliar with Matthew lying on the bed. Shelly unpacked her bag, then sat awkwardly on the bed, trying to read the nursing charts from her upside-down stance, trying to see what had been written about Matthew, listening to the happy chatter of the ward outside, the hustle and bustle she was so used to being a part of.

'Only me.' Ross gave a brief knock on the open door as Shelly stood up abruptly. 'I've got to admit him.'

'Sure.'

'I know you've answered all these questions a hundred times, but now he's under the care of the ward we have to go through it all over again.'

'Of course,' Shelly said brightly, her voice coming out way too loud as she struggled not to show how awkward she was feeling.

Ross pulled up a couple of chairs and gestured for her to sit down. Even her legs didn't seem to know how to behave as Shelly crossed them too high then shifted uncomfortably as Ross opened the notes.

'I know most of it already, so it shouldn't take too long.'

Five minutes would have been too long in Shelly's highly anxious state. Trying to remember immunisation dates and Matthew's milestones was worse than sitting her high school exams as Ross sat patiently awaiting her answers. She hated the awkwardness between them, the attempt at being professional, the distance she had insisted upon.

'Ross!' Nicola, the student, back on days now, was smiling at the door. 'Hi, Shelly, sorry to hear about Matthew.' She turned back to Ross her colour deepening as she spoke. 'Tania wants to know when you'll be able to review cot four.'

'Tell her I won't be long.' Ross barely looked up. He probably didn't even notice the breathlessness in Nicola's voice, the reddened cheeks. Ross probably thought the entire female population were created two shades pinker with fluttering eyelashes, such was his effect on women. Standing up, he made his way over to the bed and examined a sleeping Matthew gently. 'Has he spoken at all yet?'

'Nothing,' Shelly said, hovering anxiously. 'He's just grizzling sometimes and pulling at everything.'

Ross nodded thoughtfully. 'He's still got meningitis, Shelly. Just because he's out of Intensive Care, it doesn't mean he's over it. He's still fighting a massive infection, and very sick, so don't be alarmed that he's not responding to you.'

'I know,' Shelly said, then gave a tired smile. 'Actually, I don't. It's hard to be objective when it's your own child.'

'Of course it is.' There was a horrible awkward pause and Shelly so wanted to speak, so wanted to fill it, but she truly didn't know what to say. 'I'd better get on.'

Despite Tania's invitation to keep the door open, Shelly closed it gently behind him and in the days that followed more often than not that was the way it stayed. Far, far easier to shut herself away, to block out the noise of the world around her, than to hear him, to see him and know she couldn't have him.

Visitors were exhausting, and as much as Shelly was grateful for them coming, for caring, she was always relieved when they left. Even Marlene seemed draining. The only person Shelly actually looked forward to seeing was Melissa. Under her quiet charge Shelly slept easily, crawling on the bed beside Matthew, knowing they were in good hands, welcoming the contraband coffee Melissa bought into her room each morning.

'Remember to take the cup out,' Melissa warned, 'or Tania will have a fit.

'So are you ready for the off?'

Rubbing her eyes, Shelly crept quietly out of bed, anxious not to wake Matthew and enjoy her five minutes' peace. 'Can you believe I'm nervous?'

'Of course you are,' Melissa said wisely. 'But you're going to be fine. Once he's back home you'll soon see a huge improvement.'

'There already is.' Shelly looked over at the bed. 'It's hard to believe just a week ago he was in Intensive Care. Now just look at him, demanding the television on. He walked a couple of steps yesterday, you know.'

'I know.' Melissa smiled. 'And he'll no doubt walk a few more today. Just take it slowly, and don't expect too much too soon, and he'll get there.' She paused for a second, her voice lowering a touch as she looked Shelly square in the eye. 'I'm not so sure about you, though.'

'Me?' Shelly checked, giving Melissa a wide-eyed look.

'Yes, you. Holed up in here, barely putting your head out of the door. You can't avoid Ross for ever.'

'I'm not trying to avoid him,' Shelly said quickly. 'I just needed some time out and, believe it or not, it's actually been quite nice being cooped up in here. For once in my life I've had some time to think things through, make a few decisions of my own.'

'Such as?'

'I'm handing in my notice.' She watched as Melissa frowned but Shelly shook her head. 'It has nothing to do with Ross. I don't want Matthew going back to crèche. I've nothing against it, I'm sure it's done him wonders, but I'm going to be a stay-at-home mum.'

'How will you afford it?'

Shelly held up the calculator she had on the bedside table. 'Another thing I've been doing while I've been cooped up in here. I won't be that much worse off. The crèche fees are huge, and if I can do the odd casual shift at weekends we'll just about break even.' Shelly grimaced. 'So long as the car stays healthy and the air-conditioner doesn't finally give in and die on me. But, either way, it's something I have to do, Melissa, we'll have to make do with what we've got. I just want Matthew to enjoy his childhood his way, not Neil's, not Mum's, just his. I'm not giving up on him, I'll do my best but I'm just tired of him being pushed every which way.'

'Fair enough,' Melissa said slowly. 'So long as you're not handing your notice in because of Ross.'

'I'm not that stupid.'

'Good.' Melissa stood up and took Shelly's drained cup. 'But just in case Ross does factor into this little life plan you've just suddenly come up with, you'd best know that Ross has handed his own notice in this week.' She watched as Shelly struggled to look impassive. 'He's going back to the outback, to work at that darned clinic he's always going on about.

'You don't look very surprised. Had he already told you?'

Shelly forced a half-smile. 'We're a bit beyond the confiding-in-each-other stage, we barely manage a good morning. No, the reason I'm not surprised is because deep down I knew all along he wasn't going to be here for ever, and I guess this kind of proves me right.'

'What went wrong, Shelly?' There was nothing nosy in Melissa's question, just genuine concern. 'You two just seemed so right for each other.'

'We are.' Shelly smiled at Melissa's confusion. 'And no doubt in another place, another time we'd have had the best relationship, but it just can't be. We're just too different.'

'But if you love each other, surely you can work things out.'

Shelly shook her head sadly. 'Look at you and Dr Khan. You knew it was over before you even started.'

'That was different,' Melissa argued. 'Mushi had his culture, his family.'

'I've got a son,' Shelly said firmly. 'A son with special needs. Ross is young, carefree, and with the whole world ahead of him it just couldn't work.

'It couldn't,' Shelly insisted as Melissa opened her mouth to argue. 'How can I land all this on Ross? It was hard enough before the meningitis but no one can tell if there's going to be any long-term damage. It's hard enough for me to deal with, let alone anyone else. Even Matthew's own father doesn't...' Shelly stopped talking as Matthew stirred. She knew he didn't understand what was being said, but the words were too cruel to be spoken in his presence. 'It's better we realise that now than in a few months' or years' time when Matthew's devoted to him. I'm not going to let Matthew be hurt again.'

'What about you?' Melissa questioned. 'What about your needs?'

'I'm fine,' Shelly said firmly. 'I've got everything I need right here.' Walking over to the bedside, she smiled as Matthew opened his eyes and gazed up at her, his little face breaking into a smile as he lifted his arms to be picked up. 'Haven't I, darling?'

'It's good to be home.' Turning the key in the lock, Shelly smiled at her mother as she stepped inside. The house was back to its usual spotless self, the carpets freshly vacuumed, the kitchen spotless. Carrying a sleeping Matthew through to his room, Shelly noticed the fresh sheets on the bed, not a single shred of evidence to indicate the awful event that had unfolded the last time she had been here.

'You've been busy,' Shelly said, laying Matthew down on the bed.

'I haven't even set foot in the place,' Marlene corrected, bustling around, pulling curtains and tucking a duvet around the sleeping child. 'That Ross said he was going to pop around and pick up his stuff. He must have had a tidy up. You should make a bit of effort with him, you know, Shelly. It's not every day you find a man who comes house-trained.'

Shelly smothered a smile as she popped a kiss on Matthew's cheek and left him to sleep.

Ross was hardly house-trained. He'd probably hired someone to do the work.

Still...

Looking around at the spotless house, in that second Shelly would have given anything to have it back to the chaos Ross so easily generated. For a pile of newspapers to litter the benches, for his grubby old sleeping bag to be thrown over the sofa, for the inevitable take-away boxes to be spilling over the sides of the bin.

'Why don't you go and lie down?' Marlene suggested. 'While Matthew's asleep. You look completely done in.'

Shelly didn't need to be asked twice. The euphoria of Matthew coming home was tempered with a weary exhaustion. The ten days he had spent in the hospital had seemed more like a month.

Not quite house-trained. Shelly smiled as she stretched out on the bed. Ross's domestic duties hadn't stretched to making *her* bed and as she snuggled into the pillow the scent of his aftershave washed over her, a delicious, painful taste of all she had had, all she had let go.

CHAPTER TWELVE

'HOW'S MATTHEW?'

Everyone was asking—Dr Khan as Shelly turned into the corridor, the domestic mopping the floor as Shelly walked onto the ward. Even Tania managed a rather twisted attempt at a smile as Shelly walked onto the ward for the first time in a fortnight.

'Getting there,' Shelly repeated for what felt like the hundredth time, the two little words enough for now, enough for a busy morning when work was on the agenda, but Tania was obviously in the mood for a chat. 'Who's looking after him while you're working?'

'Mum and Dad. He's not well enough to go to crèche.'

'Time for a quick chat?' Tania never chatted and with a sinking heart Shelly followed her into the office. Her first day back and Shelly felt as nervous as she had when she had just qualified, Matthew's illness having taken its toll on her own confidence. Still, Shelly consoled herself as she made her way to Tania's office, bracing herself for another plea to reconsider her notice. Only two weeks to go and she would be taking care of her own child at long last, and no amount of cajoling from Tania was going to make her change her mind!

'We had an admission last night.' Tania gestured for Shelly

to sit down. 'I wanted to talk to you before you heard it at handover.'

Frowning, Shelly sat down, her frown deepening as Tania continued.

'Angus Marshall, a twenty-month-old…'

'I know the one,' Shelly interrupted. 'So what happened?'

'He "fell" again.'

Shelly heard the quotation marks around the word and held her breath as Tania continued. 'He's got a head injury. Thankfully it's not too serious, but he's been admitted so that Community Services can get involved.'

'They should have been involved last admission,' Shelly retorted, not caring that this was her senior she was addressing, angry and bitter that her observations and concerns had been dismissed, angry that even with Ross's intervention Angus had been allowed to go home for it all to happen again.

'I know you had your suspicions about Angus. Melissa and Ross did, too, but at the time there wasn't enough to go on. Children have accidents. We can't point the finger of accusation based on hunches. The Marshalls' stories corroborated the injury, there was no previous history and nothing on the child to suggest he was anything other than loved and cared for. We still don't know that that isn't the case. Accidents don't always happen once. He may have fallen again but, given his history we'll be investigating.'

'It should have been done last time,' Shelly argued, refusing to back down. 'I know I'm not particularly senior but Melissa is a charge nurse, Ross is a doctor.'

'Shelly,' Tania snapped, 'out there on this ward there's probably another child slipping through the net as we speak and, as abhorrent as that thought is, it doesn't mean that we're not doing our job properly. Child abuse is an insidious disease that doesn't always manifest itself clearly. We can only go on the evidence we have, and in Angus's case frankly we didn't have enough.

'Now, I've called you in here the same way I've called Melissa in, because this type of conversation is better to have away from handover. We've got students and grads and I don't want them treating the Marshalls differently. Of course they have to know that Angus is a child at risk but any steam that needs to blown off is to be done in here, do you understand that?'

Shelly took a deep breath and gave a reluctant nod.

'Now, you'll be pleased to know that Melissa's on days for a while. I've already spoken to her about it, so when you go out there make sure that it's business as usual, please, Shelly.'

Melissa's rolling eyes as Shelly entered handover left Shelly in no doubt she'd just been privy to the same little lecture. The mood in handover was as volatile as ever, particularly when Melissa pulled rank over Annie and delegated the staff to their patients.

'Shelly cots one to four. Ross needs to admit Angus and no doubt Dr Khan will want to be there, but I'll sit in on that interview, it might be better if you just concentrate on nursing Angus.'

'Fine.' Shelly scribbled a few details on her notebook. Normally she would have been present while her patient was admitted, but in sensitive situations like this Melissa was right to pull her away. Undoubtedly the parents would be upset and defensive and the last thing needed was an atmosphere around Angus. If Shelly could distance herself from the investigative side of things, it would make it easier for the Marshalls to relate to her, make it easier for normality to prevail around Angus.

Heading out onto the ward, Melissa caught up. 'Business as usual,' she muttered. 'Tania's little lecture reminded me why I prefer nights.'

'Tell me about it,' Shelly mumbled.

But no matter how she felt internally, Tania's words were the order of the day. Smiling brightly, business as usual resumed as Shelly walked into the room. 'Good morning, Mrs Marshall,' she said, then made her way over to Angus, who was resting quietly in his cot. 'How's Angus?'

'Tired,' Mrs Marshall said, her eyes red-rimmed, her voice shaky. 'We were in Emergency all night, we've only been on the ward for an hour.'

'You must be exhausted,' Shelly said sympathetically. 'I won't open up the curtains, then, I'll just do Angus's obs and then we'll let him rest. He can have a bath a bit later on.'

'The night sister said the doctor will be along to admit him soon.'

'That's right, Dr Bodey's on this morning, it mightn't be for a while yet, though as I think he's still stuck in Emergency. Why don't you lie down and have a rest? We'll wake you when he comes.'

Mrs Marshall nodded and sat wearily down on the camp bed. 'I wonder how Doug's going?'

'You've got two others, haven't you?'

Mrs Marshall nodded. 'The older one will be going to school soon. Doug's going to come by then.'

'Good.'

Shelly didn't say much more, just busied herself doing the obs, and her wooden movements had nothing to do with the rather awkward situation. Instead, she felt like a complete novice. Everything felt new and unfamiliar and every shred of her wanted to be at home with Matthew.

Her other three patients were relatively well. A couple of the babies had bronchiolitis but had long since turned the corner and Shelly spent the early part of her shift helping the mums bath them, mindful of their drips and oxygen and doing their obs. Her other charge, Timmy Dale, was on his way to Theatre for a circumcision and the only thing on his little mind was when he was going to get his breakfast!

'Shouldn't be too long now,' Shelly said hopefully to Timmy's anxious mother.

'He wants a bottle.'

'The babies are put at the beginning of the theatre list for that very reason.' Shelly grinned, offering to hold him while his mum nipped out for a coffee. 'I'll call you if the porters come.'

Shelly felt herself stiffen as through the glass she saw an anxious-looking man walk into Angus's room and Mrs Marshall jump up to greet him. The glass wasn't thin enough to allow her to hear what was being said but from the looks on their faces they weren't greeting each other particularly fondly. 'I'll go.' Melissa popped her head in as Shelly attempted to put a wailing Timmy back in his cot. 'Ross and Dr Khan are here now anyway, we may as well get this over with now. How was she with you?'

'Fine,' Shelly replied. 'I don't know whether or not she realises we're suspicious.'

'Well, she's about to find out.'

A brief glimpse of the back of Ross's head was all Shelly gleaned, but it was enough to throw her into turmoil. But there wasn't any time for introspection, not when the porters were bearing down and Timmy was ready to be wheeled off to Theatre.

Taking him across, Shelly kept up with the porters' lighthearted chatter, handed over her little charge to the theatre staff, even managed to find a box of tissues for Mrs Dale when it all became too much, and for all the world not one person would have guessed she was operating on autopilot, functioning with a broken heart.

'So, is it good to be back?'

Shelly started slightly when Ross came into the coffee-room but recovered quickly.

'No,' she admitted. 'But it's only for a couple of weeks.'

'I heard.' His polite answer was almost dismissive and Shelly gave a small shrug and turned back to her magazine, frowning. She had expected a bit of discomfort between them on her return but Ross seemed a million miles away and not remotely bothered that she was here as he spooned coffee and sugar into his cup and paced around, waiting for the ancient old kettle to boil.

'How's Matthew?' This Shelly had braced herself for, and even though she had decided Ross deserved a bit more than her customary answer, from the forced concentration on his face, his obvious distraction, Shelly took her usual option.

'Getting there.'

'Good.'

Picking up a paper, he started to read it but the insistent tapping of his foot told Shelly he wasn't taking anything in.

'Are you all right, Ross?' Shelly ventured, ducking behind her magazine when Ross gave an irritated sigh.

'Never been better,' he snapped, and Shelly stood up and drained her cup, grateful for the excuse to end this difficult meeting.

'Well, if you've finished interviewing the Marshalls, I'd better get back out there,' she said.

'*They* haven't finished yet, so you can take your time with your coffee.' He was almost snapping and, bemused, Shelly sat back down. 'Melissa and Dr Khan did their usual double act,' he explained. 'She suddenly remembered a drug chart I needed to write and he followed me out, then told me to wait for him in here.'

'Why?'

'Apparently my stance was "too judgmental".' Ross shot her a withering look. 'I'm supposed to sit there like a grinning idiot while I listen to the two of them lie through their teeth.'

'I know it's hard,' Shelly ventured. 'But it's important not to go in there with a formed opinion—'

'Save it, Shelly.' Ross turned back to his paper. 'I don't need a lecture from you of all people.'

She was saved from responding as a furious Melissa appeared at the door. 'Thanks a lot, Ross.'

'Any time,' he snapped, his eyes just as angry as Melissa's.

'You can't be so accusatory. It's not your place. We have to let them give their version of events first, not sit there with arms folded, staring the man down.'

'He's lying,' Ross insisted.

'Probably.' Melissa pushed the door closed. 'But your heavy-handed methods aren't helping matters.'

'What about his heavy hands?' Ross stood up, and Shelly was shocked to see a flash of tears in his eyes. 'And as for my methods, if Dr Khan had listened to me in the first place Angus wouldn't be lying there with a lump on his head the size of an egg.'

'Ross.' Melissa's voice was calmer now, her anger fading as she responded to the genuine anguish in Ross's voice. 'We don't know all the circumstances, and we're not going to know unless we tread gently. We're not just here for Angus, we're here for the whole family. I've been nursing a long time and I've learnt that things are never clear-cut, particularly in cases like this. Who knows what the dynamics are in place there, what the reasons behind his actions are? Mr Marshall may have been abused himself...'

'That's not a reason,' he growled. 'That's an excuse, and you'll never convince me otherwise.' Ross's usually relaxed face was livid now. 'You really think you know everything, don't you, Melissa? Well, let me tell you here and now that you don't. This place makes me sick.' Wrenching open the door, he stormed outside, leaving a stunned Melissa and Shelly in his wake.

'What,' said Melissa, folding her arms and puffing up her chest, 'is that man's problem?'

'I'm not sure,' Shelly said quietly, standing up and rinsing out her cup, defying her instinct to rush out behind him, to comfort him the way he had so many times comforted her.

'Well, I'd better tell Dr Khan to tread gently. With the mood Ross is in, he might just take his backpack and head off to the bush tonight, and where will that leave us?'

It was hard to carry on as normal. The atmosphere on the

ward was awful, Ross furiously writing up his notes as Melissa rubbed everyone up the wrong way.

'She needs a man,' Annie moaned when Shelly met her in the kitchen and they made up a pile of bottles between them.

'She needs a holiday,' Shelly said tactfully. 'We all do.'

'What lunch-break do you want?'

Shelly shrugged. 'The Marshalls are in with the social worker so I'm just going to feed Angus his then I'll probably head off. Can you keep an eye on him for me?'

'Sure, and how's the post-op?'

'About to have his long-awaited bottle.' Shelly held it up. 'And then hopefully a big wee and then home sweet home.'

Angus was lying quietly, staring up at the ceiling, his little face barely turning when Shelly came in and pulled on a gown.

'Hey, Angus, how about some lunch?' Sitting him in his high chair was out of the question with his leg still in plaster, so instead Shelly propped him up in his cot, pulling down the side so she could chat to him while he ate, watching as he tucked into his lunch with gusto.

'Not a big talker, huh?' Shelly smiled as Angus ate on, occasionally shyly looking up at her as she rattled on about teddies and toys and trains and all the things toddlers hold dear. 'That's all right, I can do enough talking for the two of us.'

'Tell me about it.' Ross walked in, an almost shy look on his face, smiling gently at Angus before turning his eyes to her. 'Sorry about earlier.'

'Don't be,' Shelly said easily. 'It gets to all of us, even Melissa, believe it or not.'

'I know.'

'How did it go with Dr Khan?' Shelly asked.

'Good and bad. He gave me a bit of a dressing-down, but I hadn't actually done anything wrong. He was more concerned that I was *going* to say something inappropriate, that's why he got Melissa to get me out.'

'So no harm done, then.' Shelly smiled, wiping a streak of egg off Angus's face, her smile fading as Ross carried on talking.

'I'm finishing up today, Shelly.'

Aghast, she swung around to face him, but Ross was already walking off and because it was a children's ward, because there was a toddler finishing his lunch and cot sides to be put up, Shelly wasn't in any position to follow him.

'Why?' she asked when finally she caught up with him in the doctors' room, ploughing through his notes, his pen working furiously across the paper. 'Why would you leave just like that? We all have our bad days. Dr Khan—'

'Dr Khan has nothing to do with it. Sure, I was out of line so he put me in my place—enough said. I'm not leaving because of that.'

'Because of me,' Shelly ventured as Ross just looked at her. 'But I've only got another two weeks.'

'Because of me,' Ross said simply. 'This place just isn't me, Shelly, and today proved it.'

'So you're running off?'

'Nobody's running,' Ross said, turning back to his notes.

'You know the mess this will leave the staff in.'

'They'll manage,' Ross shrugged. 'They'll get a locum.'

'I was right all along, wasn't I?' Shelly gave a rueful hollow laugh. 'Though I never thought you'd just turn your back like that. I thought that even *you* were a bit more responsible.'

'Well, obviously I'm not.' Ross leant back in his chair. 'So you can pat yourself on your back about your lucky escape, Shelly. You've been waiting for me to show my true colours so you can justify dumping me, well, here they are.' He held up his hands. 'Ross the drifter does it again.'

'I don't get you, Ross.' Shelly shook her head, tears terribly close but she bit them back, determined not to cry. 'I'm leaving so there won't be any awkwardness. You've got so many friends here, a job, a life, and yet you can walk away from it all with just a quick goodbye.'

'Not even that.' Ross stood up and slammed the file he was writing in shut. 'I'm tired of goodbyes.'

'Where will you go?' Shelly sneered, biting back tears, appalled not just at the end of their romance but the terrible, terrible conclusion to their friendship. 'What continent haven't you discovered yet?'

'I'm going home, Shelly.' He clicked his pen off and slipped it into his pocket.

'And where's home this week? What country are you going to bestow yourself on this time, endear yourself to, until the going gets too tough or there's a *policy* that doesn't quite sit right with you?' A heavy dose of sarcasm laced her voice but it disappeared as Ross caught her eye and she saw the pain etched in his features.

'Tennagarrah,' Ross said quietly, his voice a contrast to Shelly's accusatory tones. 'It's the one place on God's earth I've ever really felt I belonged.' He paused at the door, his voice so quiet she could hardly hear it. 'Except for a few nights at your place.'

CHAPTER THIRTEEN

'How was work, darling?'

'Don't ask,' Shelly groaned, peeling off her shoes and collapsing onto the sofa as Matthew clambered over her.

'Leave Mummy, darling, until she's had her shower,' Marlene said, casting an anxious look in her daughter's direction and picking Matthew up. But Shelly just laughed.

'He's fine, Mum. He just spent a week on the children's ward, including a few rounds in the playroom, and didn't even catch a cold. I think I've been being a bit precious.'

'My goodness.' Marlene grinned, kissing Matthew. 'Don't be fooled, darling. It might look like Mummy, might even talk like Mummy, but this laid-back woman lying on the sofa is an impostor!'

'Stop.' Shelly grinned. 'You'll give him nightmares.'

'Nothing could upset this gorgeous boy,' Marlene enthused, tickling him as she spoke, obviously delighted to be with him. 'We've had a lovely day. We've made jam tarts and we've read his book, oh, must be a hundred times now. It's amazing, isn't it, how sick he's been and just look at him now.'

'Kids are like that.' Shelly smiled, holding out her arms for a cuddle. 'One minute they're so sick all you can do is pray then suddenly they turn the corner and they're off. Not like adults. We take for ever to get over things.'

'Still,' Marlene mused, 'he's done very well. All the trauma he's been through and he just keeps right on smiling.'

Shelly looked down at Matthew fondly. Marlene was right. She had braced herself for tantrums and long unsettled nights, but Matthew seemed totally content to slip back into his usual routine.

'He must feel secure,' Marlene said fondly. 'That must be it.'

A lump filled in Shelly's throat. For all the crèche, divorce, for all the tumultuous two years they had spent, Matthew did feel secure. She was definitely doing something right.

'He's happy to be home...' Marlene carried on nattering, but Shelly just sat there, staring at Matthew, a million jumbled thoughts tossing in her brain and landing as one, a clear picture forming, so awful so horrible, Shelly could barely even look.

'Mum.'

Marlene stopped mid-flow, the anguish in Shelly's single word speaking volumes.

'What is it, darling? Whatever's wrong?'

On legs that were shaking, Shelly stood up and handed Matthew to Marlene. 'Can you look after him for me?'

'Of course,' Marlene answered, confused, following Shelly out of the lounge as she grabbed her car keys. 'But where on earth are you going?'

'Hopefully to put things right,' Shelly said, giving Matthew and her a quick kiss before she rushed out into the driveway. Starting the car, she wound down the window as Marlene came over, a worried look on her face.

'How long will you be?'

'A while, I hope.' Shelly looked up at her mother's anxious face. 'I really can't explain things now, Mum, there isn't time.'

'Then you'd better get on,' Marlene said, watching as her organised, meticulous daughter shot out of the driveway, then turning to her grandson.

'That's the first grey hair your mother's ever given me,' Marlene said in a fond voice, wandering back into the house with Matthew hoisted firmly on her hip. 'Hopefully it will be the last.'

Finding the doctors' mess wasn't a problem. Shelly had been there a couple of times for the occasional party, or leaving do, but she certainly hadn't graced the doctors' accommodation and the fact she was still dressed in her uniform had Shelly blushing to her roots as she ran an eye over the rows and rows of mail boxes, hoping Ross's name might jump out of her.

'Can I help you?' One of the female doctors Shelly vaguely knew from Emergency came over, and Shelly found herself stammering as she spoke.

'Oh, hi. Rose, isn't it? I'm trying to find which one's Ross Bodey's room.'

'You and every other woman in the place.' Rose grinned then changed track when she saw Shelly's angst-ridden face.

'I really need to talk to him. Look, I know you probably can't tell me which one it is but can you buzz him?' Shelly gestured to the internal telephone. 'Tell him that I'm down here in the foyer.'

'Don't be daft,' Rose grinned. 'He's in room 202, on the second floor. Good luck,' she called as Shelly darted towards the stairs, mumbling a quick thanks as she climbed them two at a time.

Only at his door did Shelly's nerves truly catch up with her. She had no speech rehearsed, no idea what on earth she was going to say to him, just an urgent, irrepressible need to see him, to put things right, to tell him she finally understood. Screwing her eyes closed, biting hard on her lips, Shelly lifted her hand to knock, almost falling inwards as the door suddenly opened and Ross stood there dressed only in the white boxers with love hearts. Given they were Shelly's personal favourite, she decided to take it as a good omen.

'Do you always close your eyes when you knock on doors?' Ross gestured for her to come in.

'Nervous habit.' Shelly's rather paltry attempt at humour wasn't even rewarded with a smile.

'What can I do for you?'

Not such a good omen, Shelly thought as Ross greeted her like a shopkeeper. The room was amazingly tidy but, then, it couldn't really be untidy, she realised, as apart from his backpack bulging in the corner, the only personal item left was a pair of jeans and a T-shirt tossed on the stripped bed and the stubby of beer Ross was holding.

'It doesn't take long for you to pack.'

Ross shrugged. 'I'm used to it, remember?' Walking over to the small bar fridge, he pulled out a beer and offered it to Shelly who after a moment's hesitation accepted it, struggling to pull off the bottle top and finally taking a nervous sip.

'Not much of a beer drinker, are you?'

Shelly shook her head. 'Not much of a drinker, full stop.' Still with a mouth as dry as sand, Shelly ventured another taste as Ross knelt down and started fiddling with the straps on his backpack.

'When's your flight?'

'Six a.m.' He carried on fiddling with the beastly backpack and Shelly knew he wasn't going to make this easy for her.

'I'm sorry for the things I said, Ross,' she started nervously. 'For insinuating you were irresponsible...'

'I probably deserved it,' Ross conceded. 'I am kind of bailing out.'

'With good reason, though.' For a second she thought he stiffened but he soon shrugged it off and Shelly carried on staring at his bare back as he wandered around the room, which wasn't exactly a hardship. The sight of Ross's bare back actually made even the icy cold beer palatable.

'I just can't go on working in that place.' Ross finally volunteered a conversation. 'I'd barely been back five minutes before I remembered why I'd left in the first place.' His eyes caught hers then. 'Or at least one of the reasons.'

'Which was?'

'I can't stand passing the buck,' he explained slowly. 'I can't stand handing things over, being a small spoke in a big wheel. What happened with Angus today will barely merit a mention, just another cock-up that will be brushed under the carpet, and I'm sick and tired of it. I want to be accountable, Shelly. I want to make my own mistakes, not apologise for someone else's.'

'And you'll get that in the outback.'

'Tenfold,' Ross said simply. 'Look, I know you probably think I'm overreacting, but what happened with Angus…'

Shelly took a deep breath, her hesitant voice forcing Ross's attention.

'Angus's father hasn't been abusing him.' She read the confusion in his face, saw his mouth open to argue with her, but she beat him to it. 'It was his mum.'

'His mum?'

Shelly nodded slowly. 'Mr Marshall was covering up for her so, yes, I guess he was lying. He just didn't know what else to do.'

'His mum?' Ross asked again, his face paling as the news sank in.

'After you'd gone, Mr Marshall asked if he could have a word. Apparently since the new baby came along, she's changed…'

'Postnatal depression?'

Shelly nodded. 'It seems that way.' She saw the pain etched in his face and ached to comfort him, but knew more had to be said. 'At least there's hope, Ross. With counselling, medication, they're probably going to be all right.'

'Oh, God.' A shaking hand raked his hair. 'I read it all wrong.'

'We all did,' Shelly said gently. 'But you know as well as I do, problems like that are never straightforward. Sometimes it's hard to be objective.'

'It's my job.'

Shelly nodded. 'And you'll learn from this, we all will. Angus is going to be OK, the whole family are. There's still a lot of love there.'

He nodded briefly, but it was loaded with agony and Shelly held her breath, knowing what was coming next was going to hurt her like hell.

'I overreacted, and there's a reason, Shelly. What happened with Angus, well, it was...' He shook his head, his eyes tearing away from hers, and he walked over to the window, staring out of it and taking a deep breath.

'Personal,' Shelly suggested gently, and she watched again as he stiffened. Only this time he didn't shrug it off. This time every muscle in his body stayed taut and strained and Shelly did the only thing she could, the only thing her mind and body told her to do—went over and placed a trembling hand on the rock of his shoulder, nearly weeping but holding it back as Ross gave a slow lonely nod, one hand coming up to claim hers, his eyes gazing unseeingly out of the window.

'How bad was it for you, Ross?' Her voice was trembling as she spoke but she struggled to hold it together, knowing that the only tears in place here were Ross's.

'Bad enough.' Still he didn't look at her but the warmth of his hand tightened around hers. 'Pretty much like Angus, except there wasn't any love there beneath the surface. But just like Angus, no one believed it was possible. My father's a doctor, my mother's a teacher. Two more upstanding citizens you couldn't hope to meet.' He gave a low laugh, utterly void of any humour, and turned to face her. 'I'm not a wanderer, Shelly, I'm not some idle drifter. I've been working and studying since I was sixteen years old. The only difference is my home has been wherever I've lived at the time. When I went to the outback I knew I'd found my real home, though. For the first time in my life I knew where I belonged.'

'So why didn't you stay? I mean, they wanted a commitment from you, why couldn't you give it?'

'I've already told you that.' His eyes were staring into her very soul and Shelly felt a shiver of excitement as he crossed the room. 'I had unfinished business with a certain nurse.'

'I thought you were joking...'

Ross shook his head. 'I'd never been more serious in my life. I've loved you Shelly, loved you,' he repeated, as Shelly gave an incredulous nervous gasp. 'I dragged myself off to Scotland when I found out you were engaged to Neil, drowned my sorrows in China the night you got married, and threw in the best job I've ever had when I heard that you were divorced.'

'You really came back for me?' Shelly gasped, the magnitude of his words starting to hit home.

'In a heartbeat. Shelly, Melissa's great and everything, but do you really think I called her to find out about Tania's varicose vein operation or the latest gossip on the ward? I ploughed my way through it so I could casually ask about you. You,' he said, taking her face in her hands and staring into the glassy pools of her eyes. 'And I'm sorry, so sorry that it isn't going to work. And as much as I hate the fact, I have to respect your decision.'

'What decision?' Shelly croaked, dragging him back as he dropped his hands and reached for his beer. 'I didn't know how you felt, I didn't know what you'd been through.'

'Shelly.' Ross's voice was sharp. 'I'm not what Matthew needs. Those were your words and maybe you're right, I misdiagnosed him, for heaven's sake.' He ignored her frantically shaking head, speaking over her until she had no choice but to listen. 'Maybe Melissa's right. Maybe it is all in the genes. Maybe I don't deserve to be a parent.'

'No, Ross.' Shelly realised then the depths of his suffering, the self-doubts that plagued him, and she ached with the desire to right a thousand wrongs, to unscramble his troubled mind and tell him, show him what a wonderful caring man he was. 'You're going to be a wonderful father, a wonderful loving father, and as for what I said...' Her mind was racing, knowing that what she said now had to be right, had to somehow knock down the barriers of self-doubt Ross had erected, had to somehow reach him before he left her life for ever. 'I love you, too. I think I always have,' she gulped, her eyes blinking as she looked back briefly over the years with the benefit of hindsight. 'I always have,' she said more firmly this time, 'and I'm not proud of that fact. I was married and yet I loved you, and when you breezed back into my life, swept me off my feet and into my bed, it was all too easy and I was scared that one day you were going to grow up, one day you'd look around and realise what a mistake you'd made. That's what I meant when I said that you're not what Matthew needs, nothing else.' Her eyes sparkled with tears as she stood and looked at this beautiful man who had been through so, so much yet somehow had managed to hold it together, somehow had managed to defy all the odds, had made something of himself, had kept right on smiling.

'The silly thing is, you've already grown up, haven't you? You grew up a long, long time ago.'

Ross nodded. 'About twenty years ago.' He gave a half-smile. 'What you see is what you'll get, Shelly—if you still want it.'

'Oh, Ross.' Shelly was trembling as he pulled her towards him. Leaning on his chest, she heard his thumping heart, felt his arms tighten around her, and she clung to him tightly, their bodies in blissful contact, no barriers between them now, the fears that had held them apart gone now, leaving them in warm blissful union.

'Come with me, Shelly,' he whispered. 'We can make a home together.'

Her eyes sprang open, her long lashes brushing his chest as the enormity of what he was saying took shape in her mind, which he read in an instant.

What about Matthew?

'Matthew will be fine.' She hadn't needed to even say it. 'Shelly, they'll accept him there for who he is, wrap their arms around him as they did me. It's the most amazing place in the world and we can be a part of it. He won't be the special needs child, he'll be who he is, Matthew Weaver, or Matthew Bodey, if you'll give me that honour.' The world stopped for a moment. The only sound Shelly could hear was the pounding of her temples as Ross lifted her chin and slowly dragged her eyes to his.

Honour, that one tiny word proving the depth of Ross's love. For so long Shelly had worried that if ever love did come her way then freedom would be the price the man would pay for her love. Yet here was Ross turning everything on its head, saying in that one word that Matthew would never, ever be baggage. That he, Ross Bodey, would be proud to be Matthew's father.

She'd have followed him to the ends of the earth on the strength of that alone.

Her answer was in her kiss, sweet and deep and full of passion. Trembling with desire, they melted onto the floor, mindless of the open curtains and of Marlene waiting anxiously at home. It could all wait for the moment.

'Is that a yes?' Ross mumbled as he fiddled with her name-tag and the endless row of buttons on her blouse.

'How could I say no?' Shelly caught his eye and gave a hint of a wicked smile. 'After all, how many men would stay celibate all those years, pining for little old me?'

Ross gave her a slightly startled look. 'Er, Shelly.' His hands froze mid-button. 'When I said I'd always loved you I meant it, but it doesn't mean...' Looking up, he saw she was laughing and Ross joined in. 'You're a wicked woman, do you know that?'

'Very wicked,' Shelly whispered. The smile was back on his face, the easygoing joking was everything she could have hoped for and more. 'And very, very happy.'

EPILOGUE

'PICKED UP ANY good tips?' Ross spoke over the sound of the engine, bouncing an over-excited Matthew on his knee as the small Cessna barely registered a blip as it tore through the massive blue sky.

Looking up from her survival guide, Shelly grinned. 'If I'm lost in the outback, I can flash my ring at the sun to draw attention to myself.'

'Any excuse to look at that thing,' Ross groaned, as Shelly lifted her hand and admired the huge diamond cluster on her finger.

Six none-too-small diamonds glittered back at her—one, Ross had explained, for every year he had loved her. It was larger than life, ostentatious and the antithesis of what Shelly would have chosen, yet she loved it with a passion.

'It really is in the middle of nowhere, isn't it?' Shelly said, her gaze turning to the window, taking in the endless red of the hot earth, the rock formations so immense, so awe-inspiring Shelly knew the endless books she had read hadn't done them justice. Nothing except the naked eye could appreciate the glorious vastness of the outback and Shelly drank it in, scarcely able to believe that this was going to be home.

Home.

The word bathed her in a glow as warm as the hot Australian sun high in the midday sky, and she stole a look at the two men in her life, two people who had shared a rocky start, yet carried right on smiling. A lump surely as big as Ayers rock seemed to fill her throat as Shelly's gazed lingered, watching one blond and one dark head bent over a book, the ties that bound them now unbreakable, her love strong enough, confident enough for them all.

'The welcoming committee's here.' The thick Aussie accent of Bruce, the pilot, forced her attention and Shelly tore her eyes away, blinking as the ground neared, kicking herself for missing the approach, the first glimpse of her new home. Vast properties, white and brown, were beneath them, a petrol station, a pub, horses. She counted them off as Matthew, sensing Shelly's excitement, strained to get over to her, to see what all the fuss is about.

'Who are all these people?' Shelly asked as the plane bumped down, children, adults running alongside, waving, their mouths grinning, mouthing words they had no chance of hearing as the engine died down.

'Like Bruce said, it's Tennagarrah's welcoming committee.' Ross stood up first, helping Shelly up before handing her Matthew, then impatiently pushing the door and stepping down into a throng of people as Shelly stared in wide-eyed bemusement at Bruce.

'He's a popular guy, that husband of yours.'

'Tell me about it.' Suddenly overcome with shyness, Shelly hovered at the door of the small plane, watching as they greeted Ross with like a long-lost brother, waiting for the curious stares to inevitably come her way.

'Shelly! Matty!' Arms were reaching out to her, a mass of limbs pulling them both into the warm embrace of their new community. Matthew was prised from her and Shelly felt a tiny bubble of alarm rise, sure Matthew would wail in horror at the tactile, overpowering nature of the greeting, but instead he was laughing, giggling, revelling in the moment, one eye fixed on Ross enough to make him feel safe.

The welcome didn't end there. Somehow between the high chatter and laughter Ross managed to carry her over the threshold and, despite the audience and revelry, the look in his eyes as they went through the door made the moment as intimate as it should be, and Shelly was only too happy to be entertained in her own home as she was welcomed the way only Aussies could.

'I think I'm finally getting a taste for beer,' Shelly said with a laugh much later when only a few lingering guests remained hovering around the barbeque outside. Shelly finally made her way in and stood watching Matthew through the flyscreen as he rushed around the veranda with his newfound friends.

'So, what do you think?'

There was a slightly nervous note to Ross's voice as Shelly looked around the vast jarrah-floored lounge, the airy high ceilings, the simple beauty of the furnishings. 'I love it,' she said softly.

'Still worried about being lonely?' Ross tested gently, but Shelly just laughed.

'Hardly. I think I'm going to have to make a booking just to cuddle Matthew at this rate. Anyway, Mum and Dad are coming next month, then after that we've got the honeymooners...'

'Don't,' Ross said, yelping in mock horror and putting his hands over his ears. 'Melissa and Dr Khan's bedroom will be right on the far side of the house. I don't think I could stand it if I heard the two of them...' He screwed his eyes closed and pulled a face. 'And if she keeps calling him Mushi, I think I'll die of embarrassment.'

'It's lovely.' Shelly laughed, pulling down his hands and making sure they were firmly wrapped around her. 'I think it's just so romantic...'

'Well, you would,' Ross grumbled. 'What gets me is how they

managed! All those years of being in love, working alongside each other, and they didn't do a thing about it.'

'He loved his wife,' Shelly explained. 'But somewhere at the back of his heart he loved Melissa, too.'

'But how, how can you let all those years slip by...?' His voice trailed off as he looked at Shelly holding her ring up to him. Another excuse to admire it, if ever she needed one. 'That was a silly question, wasn't it?'

'A very silly question,' Shelly answered, her lips moving towards his, melting at the thought of permanent access to his most divine body. 'And one that I'm not even going to try to answer.'

* * * * *

The Bush Doctor's Challenge

For Helen, Andy, Joshua and Louise
With love.

CHAPTER ONE

'WHERE'S THE AIRPORT?' Shouting her question over noise from the plane's engine, Abby was slightly taken back by the pilot's reaction when he started to chuckle. It hadn't been her intention to crack a joke!

'Show me a flat piece of land and I'll land this little lady!' Turning, Bruce grinned widely, showing rather too many gaps in his smile, and Abby forced a rather brittle one back, wishing he would turn his attention to the windscreen or whatever it was called on a plane and get on with flying the thing.

Her apparent aloofness for once had nothing to do with Abby's rather formal nature, for now it was borne of pure fear! The tiny plane that had met her on the tarmac of Adelaide airport seemed woefully inadequate for this long journey, and as they zipped through the late afternoon sky, as Abby struggled to concentrate on the mountain of paperwork in front of her, for the first time in ages there were only two questions buzzing through Abby's overactive mind. How the hell did this thing stay in the sky? And, perhaps more pointedly, how would anyone ever find them if it didn't?

'There's a flight strip near the clinic, we should be there in another fifteen minutes or so, give or take a few.'

'Thanks.'

Bruce's time frame was hardly rigid but, as Abby was fast learning, she might just as well have tossed her watch into the quarantine buckets when she'd left Sydney. The same laid-back nature had been present in the ground staff who had greeted her when she'd landed tense and rushed at Adelaide, sure she was late for her connection. And when she'd finally located Bruce, standing by his plane, sipping on a cup of tea, he had assured Abby she had 'no worries'. Bruce, it would seem, would have been happy to wait all day for her if he had had to.

What have I taken on?

A third question was making itself heard as Abby gave up on the paperwork she was attempting to read and leant back in her seat, gazing at the red landscape beneath her. Mile upon endless mile stared back at her, like the coloured sands in the bottle in her small city kitchen back home. The rings of time indelibly etched on the landscape gaped beneath her, leaving Abby feeling as insignificant and as meaningless as the speck in the sky she surely was.

Mind you, it wasn't as if she'd had a choice but to take it on, Abby mused. Reece Davies, Director of Emergency, long-time colleague and supposed friend, had made his feelings on the subject pretty clear.

'There was nothing you could have done, Abby.'

How many times had he told her that? How many times had he pulled her into his office when Abby had ordered a multi-tude of tests on a patient for the most simple of complaints?

'Try telling that to the rest of the staff.'

'There's no need to tell them,' Reece had insisted. 'No one in this department thinks what happened that night was your fault.'

If only she could believe him, if only she could believe that the silence that descended every time Abby approached a clique of nurses had more to do with her seniority and less to do with David's death.

David.

A vague attempt at a smile inched across her lips as she tried to imagine David's take on all this. What David would say if he could see his Abby, the eternal city girl, on her way to three months in the middle of nowhere. But the start of a smile vanished as, once again, cruel realisation hit.

David was dead.

'So we're ordering abdominal ultrasounds on each and every abdominal pain now?' Reece's biting sarcasm as he'd audited her patient cards had hurt, but Abby had stood her ground, arguing it was surely far safer to err on the side of caution. To be sure, beyond any doubt, that her diagnosis was spot on.

But Reece had begged to differ.

'You need to get your confidence back, Abby,' he'd insisted. 'You need to regain some perspective. No one would have guessed Dave had a drug problem, no one.'

'Perhaps not, but if he hadn't been a friend, hadn't been a colleague, if David had just been a stranger wheeled through the doors, I'd have treated him differently.'

Reece had shaken his head, even offered his sympathies again for the terrible circumstances of that fateful night, but his stance had remained unchanged—if Abby wanted the upcoming consultant position in Emergency, then some grass roots medicine was the order of the day and Reece knew just the guy to teach her. And while she was at it, hell, why not go the whole hog and try making a couple of friends along the way?

'Back to grass roots—but, what grass?' Abby muttered to herself.

'Sorry, love? I didn't catch what you said.' Bruce turned again, his open face ready to join in the first conversation Abby had initiated, and Abby's blue eyes widened in angst, wishing Bruce would at least look as if he was controlling the plane!

'Nothing,' Abby shouted over the noise of the engine, embarrassed at being caught talking to herself. 'I was just saying that the land looks very dry.'

'Does it?' Bruce peered out of the side window for what

seemed an inordinate length of time as Abby forcibly resisted the urge to take over the controls of the plane herself. 'No more than normal, love.'

Picking up her papers, Abby gave herself a mental shake. OK, so she was effectively out of action for three months, but you didn't have to be on the front line to fight a war. If her plans for the department were going to take shape then there was a pile of research to get through, people to be contacted, plans to be made. Her time in Tennengarrah wasn't going to be a total write-off.

She could still keep her promise to David...

As the very occasional buildings started to multiply, Bruce finally started to look at least a little like he was concentrating and Abby braced herself for a rather bumpy descent.

It never came. The only shudder she felt was when the plane touched down and a relieved escape of air came out of Abby's tense lips as they hurtled along the small landing strip.

'How was that, Doc?'

'Excellent!' Abby stood up, her first genuine smile of the day parting her full lips. Stretching her long legs, she plucked at some imaginary fluff on her very crisp, very white cotton shorts then ran a slightly anxious hand through her shock of long dark hair, wishing Bruce would stop grinning at her so she could touch up her lipstick.

'Here's Kell to meet you.'

'Kell?' Abby frowned as she hovered by the door. 'I thought Ross Bodey was supposed to be here.'

'Oh, sorry, I should have told you. Ross is on a call-out. I'll head off and pick him up soon, once I've had a cuppa.' Bruce didn't look sorry, not even remotely, and, picking up a large stainless-steel Thermos flask, he opened the exit door and jumped out easily before gallantly offering his hand as Abby made a rather more tentative descent to the dry soil beneath her. The low glare of the sun hitting her face on forced Abby's hand straight up to shield her eyes.

'Hi, Abby, I'm Kell.' A very deep, very masculine voice greeted her and with her sun-dazed eyes making focussing impossible for a moment or two, Abby's imagination involuntarily sprang into action, images of a cool, suited sophisticate springing to mind. Perhaps there was another young doctor Ross Bodey had forgotten to tell her about! 'It's good to have you joining us.' As the voice's hand gripped hers Abby couldn't fail to be impressed by the strength of its grip and a smile played on the edge of her lips as his image came into focus. Maybe the outback might have some advantages after all!

Wrong.

Never had a fantasy been so quickly dashed. Standing before her, smiling easily, was Mother Nature's original version of the Neanderthal man. A hulking brute of a male, well over six feet, was grinning down at her, dark shaggy black hair that needed a good cut hanging too far down his long thick neck, and dark eyes thickly rimmed with even darker lashes were smiling quizzically at her.

He wasn't wearing a loincloth exactly but the faded denim shorts he wore were a pretty good attempt, considering that was all he was wearing!

Even though Abby was wearing only white linen shorts and a crisp white blouse, coupled with some beige loafers, suddenly she felt terribly overdressed. 'Pleased to meet you,' Abby murmured, her eyes involuntarily travelling the long length of his impossibly tanned body, taking in the dark-haired legs and the chest hair, then blushing as she realised she'd been caught staring.

'Shelly wanted to come and meet you, but I told her to stay put, she's not feeling the best.'

'Is that right?' Pouring out a cup of tea from his well-loved Thermos then lighting up a cigarette, Bruce leant against the plane, obviously settling in for a chat. 'What's the problem?'

Abby fidgeted uncomfortably, anxious to get to the homestead, desperate to have a long cool shower as opposed to standing in forty degrees of heat for a cosy little chat.

'She's acting a bit strange.' Kell shrugged. 'So maybe you should hurry up your smoko and go and get Ross.'

Abby glanced over to Bruce, doubting anything short of a nuclear missile would hurry him up, but as Kell carried on chatting in his laid-back voice she did a double-take.

'If the baby is coming, Ross will want to be there.'

'She's in labour?' Abby gasped, but Kell just gave a vague shrug as Bruce noisily supped at his tea.

'Well, Shelly insists she isn't, but if you ask me she isn't far off. She's been cleaning like a woman possessed this morning, and now she's pacing up and down like a tractor turning the soil.'

'And from that you assume she's in labour?' There was a slightly sarcastic edge to Abby's voice, which she quickly fought to correct. After all, it wasn't Kell's fault he didn't know what he was talking about!

'I'm just saying I'd be happier if Ross was here, and that as much as Shelly refuses to admit it, I think she'd be happier, too,' Kell added, with all the authority of a man who'd no doubt single-handedly delivered a zillion calves! 'She's supposed to be flown to Adelaide in the morning.'

'When's she due?' Bruce asked, slurping his drink in such a disgusting fashion Abby felt like putting her hands up to her ears.

'Three weeks tomorrow, but they'll take her to Adelaide in case the baby comes early.'

'Do all pregnant women go to Adelaide?' Abby asked, curiosity getting the better of her. Though she only half listened to the answer, sure these two bush buddies wouldn't have a clue about maternity arrangements.

'Just the complicated ones.' Kell gave a knowing nod and Bruce scratched his head.

'It's upside down, isn't it?'

'Breech,' Abby said, trying to keep the note of superiority out of her voice. 'She probably won't need a Caesarean section, but it's better to be on the safe side. Breech deliveries can be complicated.'

'Is that right? Rightio, then.' Taking his cue, Bruce threw the dregs of his drink onto the ground and took another moment or two to replace his lid and cup. 'I'd better step on it. Will you be all right? I mean, if Shelly really is about to have the little tacker, do you want me to give anyone a call?'

'Good idea,' Abby said approvingly, then snapped her mouth closed as Kell overrode her.

'Oh, we'll be right.' Kell shrugged again. 'But more to the point, Shelly will kill me if I go summoning the troops. I'll catch you later, then, Bruce.' As Kell turned to go Abby stood there bemused for a moment before calling him. 'What about my luggage?'

'Bruce will bring it in later when he drops Ross back. I've only got the bike.' Gesturing to a massive brute of a motorcycle parked in the middle of nowhere, he didn't seem to notice or, more pointedly, chose to ignore Abby's gasp of horror.

'But my computer…' Her voice trailed off as Kell gave her a curious look.

'It will be fine. Bruce will only be gone an hour or so. No one's going to take it.'

Maybe not, but if Bruce went and fell asleep at the controls, which Abby reasoned wouldn't exactly be far off from where he was now, not only would all her drug rehab research go up the shoot, she'd be stuck in this God-forsaken place without the internet, and heaven forbid, the chance to email every last one of her family to tell them about the worst career move in history.

'I'd like my computer, please.' Standing her ground, Abby watched as Kell gave her another quizzical look, combined with another brief shrug.

'Whatever you say. Hey, Bruce!'

Ambling his way over, Abby watched as the two men exchanged a few words, no doubt moaning about the little princess who needed all her gadgets. Well, let them moan, Abby thought fiercely, she needed her computer, it wasn't exactly a big thing to ask!

'Here you go.' Handing her the black bag, Abby mumbled her thanks, her eyes travelling behind him to the large white building.

'The clinic's bigger than I thought.'

That was the understatement of the millennium. For weeks now Abby had been having visions of a tiny tin shack, with a rickety sign bearing a red cross on the outside. Maybe it was the word 'clinic' that had caused her misconception, conjuring up images of a halfway house, a holding bay until *real* help arrived, but the very white, very large building she was looking at now looked suspiciously like a hospital.

Kell nodded as Abby carried on staring. 'It's getting there. Half of it is still under construction, but it's coming along. I'd take you round for a quick tour, but Ross asked me to keep an eye on Shelly. I can take you in, though. Clara's on duty, she'll be only too happy to show you around.'

'That's fine,' Abby said quickly, suddenly overcome with nerves at the prospect of meeting everyone. 'I'll wait for the doctor.' Her words came out horribly wrong, superior and condescending, but thankfully Kell didn't respond, just climbed on the bike. It wasn't as if he'd be up on the intricacies of hospital hierarchy to be offended by her words, Abby consoled herself, making a mental note to be a bit more diplomatic.

'Do you want me to hold your computer for you?' Kell volunteered as Abby eyed the bike suspiciously and lifted one very wary leg. 'Would that make things easier?'

'Thanks.' He slipped the carry strap over his shoulder and waited patiently, a slight grin on his lips as Abby struggled to mount, her cheeks still burning from the mess she had made of his polite offer to introduce her. But it wasn't only embarrassment and the thought of climbing on the brute of a thing that was giving Abby palpitations, it was the realisation that she had no hope of getting on, straddling the thing and riding the couple of kilometres or so to the homestead without touching Kell. Or more pointedly, without touching the vast expanse of naked skin that she simply couldn't seem to tear her eyes away from.

She wanted to ask him for a helmet, to point out the dangers of riding a bike without one. How dammed irresponsible they were being and how awful it would look in her obituary if an emergency doctor was killed riding a bike without one.

But what would be the point?

All that would achieve would be to make her look even more neurotic. Still, if this was how they got about here, she was going to make damned sure she bought one for herself, order one from the internet if she had to.

At least she had her computer.

'Whoops.' Midway through starting the engine, he stopped. Climbing off, Kell opened the back box Abby was leaning on and took out two of the offending objects. 'Better to be safe. Ross would never forgive me if I killed the new doctor on her first day here.'

The annoying thing was, now that she'd got what she'd only seconds ago wanted, Abby had no idea what to do with the blessed thing. Oh, she could get it on, and hopefully it was the right way around, but the straps on Kell's helmet had clipped together easily, whereas hers…

'Here.' He was standing next to her, clipping together the connection and tightening the straps under her chin. As unwashed and unkempt as he looked, this close up Abby realised it just wasn't the case as she caught the faint scent of his soap mingling with a strong masculine deodorant that most definitely did the job. As he lifted his arms and fitted her helmet, pulling the straps so taut under her chin Abby was sure she might choke, the worst part of it all was that while she suffered this brief indignation there was no place else to look than at his very flat, very brown stomach.

OK, he was sexy, Abby admitted reluctantly, in a sort of overgrown, salt-of-the-earth way.

Very sexy, she conceded, eyes level with his epicentre. Even his belly button was sexy, which up to this point Abby had been sure was an impossible feat. Belly buttons were just that—belly buttons. But Kell's, well, the hair around it circled gently, and Abby found herself momentarily mesmerised by the strange beauty of such a normally nondescript object.

'Third time lucky.' Kell grinned, climbing nimbly in front of her and shouting over his shoulder as the bike sprang into life between her thighs. 'Let's go.'

Abby had never been on a motorbike in her life. In fact, she'd barely graduated to getting the training wheels taken off her push bike before books had beckoned, or a drop of pond water placed under her father's antiquated microscope had held more excitement than riding around the back garden in circles. And now here she was in the middle of nowhere, roaring along a dusty red road clinging on for dear life to a man she'd only just met.

It was terrifying, exhilarating and strangely... Abby's mind clicked over, struggling against the whipping hair around her face to find the word she was looking for.

Sexy.

There it was again.

Thousands of dollars' worth of chrome catapulting them along the rough, unsealed road, and it would be a lie by omission not to recognise the added thrill of Kell's snaky hips beneath her hands, her fingers coiling through the loops on his shorts, and unless she wanted to fall off the palms of her hand had nowhere else to go other than resting on his warm, bronzed skin. Abby kept her body well back, though, leaning against the back box, terrified she might be catapulted forward and forced to touch more of him.

It was over too soon, and vague memories of the waltzers at the fairground surfaced as Abby took Kell's hand and attempted to dismount with at least a shred of dignity. Her legs felt as if they didn't quite know what to do and the ground still seemed to be moving.

'Sorry.' Kell grinned. 'I didn't realise it was your first time, you should have told me.'

'Why?' Abby shrugged. 'Would you have treated me more gently?'

Ouch! The sexual connotation had never been intended, and as Kell grinned ever wider Abby followed him up the steps of a massive house, wondering where her attempt at flirting had blown in from.

Yes, he was sexy, yes, he was a fine specimen of a man and all that, but a farm labourer with a thing about bikes certainly wasn't on Abby's agenda.

She was here to work.

Three months of grass roots medicine and she was out of here, and if Bruce's plane collapsed, no matter, she'd walk if she had to.

'Abby!' A very pregnant, very pretty, red-headed woman came out of a fly door and stood at the top of the steps, the massive laundry basket she was carrying in no way covering up the enormous swell of the baby within her. 'I'm Shelly, we spoke briefly on the telephone. I'm so sorry Ross isn't here to meet you.'

'That's no problem.' Abby smiled in what she hoped was a friendly fashion. 'Kell made me very welcome.'

'Did I?' Kell asked with a vaguely surprised grin. 'I wasn't even trying.'

'I was being polite,' Abby muttered, as Kell's grin widened.

'Tell you what, come to the watering hole with me tonight and meet the locals, we'll show you a real Tennengarrah welcome. I'll even leave the bike at home this time.'

'I might just give it a miss, thanks.'

Even though his offer had been imparted in his usual laid-back style, Abby couldn't help but feel a flurry of butterflies as she said no. OK, he wasn't exactly asking her out on a date, but it was certainly the closest Abby had come in a long time.

A very long time.

'You should go,' Shelly pushed happily. 'If I wasn't the size of a baby elephant, I'd take you there myself.' Putting the basket down, Shelly rubbed her back and gave a weary smile. 'Come inside. We'll have a drink and then I'll take you over to where you'll be staying—it's that one.' She pointed over to any one of about three white houses scattered on the perimeter of the property. 'It's all ready for you.'

Privately all Abby wanted to do was grab the keys and head off but, not wanting to be appear rude, she smiled appreciatively and followed a rather cumbersome Shelly back up the steps, hesitating slightly as she realised Kell was joining them.

'Kell,' Shelly said as he followed them in. 'You don't have to babysit me. I've got Abby here now, she *is* a doctor.'

'I'm not babysitting,' Kell insisted, but Shelly shook her head. 'So why have you spent the whole afternoon painting the baby's nursery when Ross was going to do it at the weekend?'

'When did Ross ever get a weekend off?' Kell said, collapsing onto the couch and placing two massive feet onto the coffee-table before him, which had Abby cringing, though Shelly didn't seem remotely bothered. 'Anyway, I need the cash.'

For some reason Shelly seemed to find this hilarious and picking up a T-shirt she tossed it in Kell's vague direction. 'Well, if you're staying you can at least put some clothes on.'

'Kell thought I needed a rest,' Shelly explained to a politely smiling Abby. 'So he decided to make lunch.'

'You don't have to tell everyone,' Kell grumbled, pulling a very white T-shirt over his head, much to Abby's relief. Now at least she'd be able to look at him without blushing. 'Trouble is he ended up wearing a bottle of mayonnaise.'

'It's not my fault Ross screws the lids on so tight.' He cast a brief look to Abby. 'I don't usually walk around half-naked. Sorry if I scared you.' Fortunately, Abby was saved from answering as he turned back to Shelly. 'Look, if you really don't want me around I'll head off, but I think I've at least earned a cup of coffee.'

Which, Abby reasoned, at the rate Shelly was moving, would probably give Bruce plenty of time to have Ross safely back home. This man took his duties seriously.

'Abby, would you like a coffee?'

'Thanks.' Abby smiled. 'If you show me where things are I'll make it. You look as if you're a bit busy.'

'Just a bit,' Shelly admitted, gesturing to the mountains of laundry adorning every available surface. 'I'll feel so much better when all this is done.'

Abby chose to ignore Kell's upwardly mobile right eyebrow as she fumbled around the kitchen, watching with undisguised bemusement as Shelly proceeded to tear the wrappers off a pile of new baby clothes and bundle them into yet another laundry basket.

'So how was the journey, Abby?'

'Long.'

Shelly laughed. 'Tell me about it. I remember the first time I came here I thought the journey would never end. It's like another planet, isn't it?'

Abby nodded, her smile finally genuine as she warmed to the likable Shelly.

'Hard to believe it's the same country. Just wait till Ross takes you out and you see some of the homesteads, miles and miles from anywhere. They make Tennengarrah look like a thriving city—at least we've got a pub and a few shops, and a hairdresser's...'

'Since when?' Kell asked, perking up a bit and leaning forward.

'Well, not a hairdresser's exactly,' Shelly conceded. 'But June Hegley's niece, Anna, is staying for a few months and apparently she trained in Sydney, so she's going to set up shop at June's house.'

'I must remember to make an appointment,' Kell said, shooting a wink at Abby, who realised with a start she was again staring at him.

That shaggy dark mane that framed his face could certainly do with a cut, but on the other hand it actually suited him, Abby couldn't quite imagine Kell with the short back and sides which was so much part of the uniform of most of her colleagues.

'The clinic's nice,' Shelly chattered on, happily oblivious to the sudden crackling tension in the room. 'It's really come a long way since we've been here. I think you'll be quite pleasantly surprised.'

'How busy does it get?'

Her question was aimed at Shelly. From their brief chats on the telephone and a couple of longer ones with Ross, Abby had gleaned that Shelly was a nurse who until recently had been working, but Kell, who obviously thought he knew everything about anything, decided to answer for her.

'All depends. Sometimes you can go a full day without even getting a new patient, but those days are getting few and far between now. With tourism and everything the town's thriving.'

Sucking in her breath, Abby bit back a smart answer, her eyes pointedly trained on Shelly. 'So, how long have you been here?'

'Just over a year. It took me a while to settle in but I think I'm finally getting the hang of it. Matthew, on the other hand, fell in love the first day he was here.'

'Matthew's Shelly's son,' Kell interrupted needlessly, and Abby didn't even bother to answer him, again directly addressing Shelly.

'How old's Matthew?'

'Three. He'll be up soon, he's just having an afternoon nap, which is great for me as I finally got a parcel today. Mum sent me some baby clothes and a few odds and ends.' Holding up a box of laundry powder, Shelly grinned. 'You'd be surprised the things you miss.'

'They don't sell laundry powder here?' Abby asked, aghast, visions of washing her shorts with a rock in the creek gushing into her mind. What on earth had she let herself in for?

'What's laundry powder?'

It took a second for Abby to register Kell was joking. Blushing, she took another drink as Shelly started to laugh. 'It's not that bad, Abby. I wanted some soap flakes, but the local shop didn't quite stretch, so it was quicker to get Mum to send some than wait till we do our big shop in town next month. Now, if you two don't mind, I'll just go and throw this lot in the washing machine.'

'Go ahead.' Kell nodded, flicking on the television with the remote. 'I'll go and get the other basket pegged out for you.'

Abby tried, she really did. She tried not to roll her eyes but sitting in the middle of nowhere discussing the merits of soap flakes versus detergent was just so far removed from her normal life she couldn't help herself.

'Something wrong?' Kell asked.

'Nothing,' Abby retorted.

'Shelly's great,' Kell enthused. 'And if the conversation's not up to your usual standards, bear in mind the poor woman's about to give birth.'

'I didn't say anything,' Abby protested, annoyed with herself for being caught out, and also irritated with Kell for his uneducated assumptions. Shelly Bodey did not look like a woman about to give birth!

'You didn't have to.'

They sat in uncomfortable silence for a moment or two before Abby succumbed, curiosity finally the getting the better of her. 'Kell, why is she washing new clothes?'

'You're supposed to wash them,' Kell explained patiently, his smile back in place to show her she was forgiven, 'before the baby wears them. It gets rid of any perfume or harsh detergents.'

To Abby's utter surprise she found she was actually laughing. 'What did I say?'

'Nothing.' Taking a sip of her coffee, Abby started to laugh again then forced herself to stop. 'It's just the last thing I expected to hear from a guy like you.'

'A guy like me?' Kell asked as he stood up and picked up the laundry basket. 'What, do you think I'm too macho to know about washing powders and the like?'

Finally she managed to look at him. It should have been so much easier now he was wearing clothes, but even without visual access to that toned body he was still stunning, and something about the way he was looking at Abby had her stomach doing somersaults. He looked so ridiculously gorgeous, six feet five of oozing masculinity with a laundry basket tucked under his arm and a handful of pegs!

'You'd better get on.' Abby smiled. 'If you want to get your washing dry.'

It was Kell laughing this time. 'Now, what would a woman like you know about laundry?'

As the fly door slammed Abby let out a long-held breath and sank back into the deep sofa, staring out of the window, her gaze filtering out the so-called town to the view beyond which seemed to stretch on to infinity. Mile after mile of red soil, no bay view, no skyscrapers, no hum of traffic in the distance, just the aching gap of emptiness. Staring moodily out as the sun bobbed lower in the sky, Abby truly wondered how she could possibly survive.

Three months, she consoled herself.

In three short months she'd be handing her washing over at the dry-cleaners without even meriting it a thought.

In three months she'd be a consultant.

CHAPTER TWO

'KELL!'

Shelly's voice wasn't particularly loud, but the note of urgency in it had Abby on her feet in less than a second.

'Kell!' Shelly's voice was louder this time, more desperate. Putting down her mug, Abby cast an anxious look through the window, catching sight of an oblivious Kell, happily pegging out the washing, his mouth full with pink plastic pegs.

Unsure whether to call Kell or investigate herself, Abby tentatively followed the sound of Shelly's increasingly urgent demands. As she pushed open the laundry door, she swallowed a gasp of shock as Shelly let out a deep guttural groan, two frightened eyes darting up to meet Abby's as she hunched over the washing machine.

'I want to push!'

Please, don't. Abby didn't say it, but she definitely thought it!

Stay calm. Abby mentally steadied herself making her way over and gently helping a groaning Shelly onto the floor. *There's a clinic two minutes away filled with nurses, equipment...* Her mind flashed to her doctor's bag winging its way across the outback, a doctor's bag with artery forceps and umbilical clamps and, luxury of luxury, latex gloves. For that split second she could have cheerfully strangled Kell with her bare hands.

'I'll get Kell to ring the clinic,' Abby said assuredly, pushing herself up from the floor, but Shelly's hand grabbed her arm as she shook her head, her face purple as she started to bear down.

'It's coming now!'

'Then we'd better get on and deliver this baby' Abby soothed, her voice amazingly calm given her rapid heart rate. 'We'll manage just fine.'

Grabbing a handful of folded towels, Abby took a deep steadying breath. She hadn't delivered a baby for years.

Years!

Even then it had only been a token attempt, with registrars and midwives beside her in a delivery room packed with equipment! Still, she reassured herself, fast labours were normally easy, just a steadying hand to help Mother Nature along. But as she examined Shelly Abby's heart sank and Shelly's question reiterated Abby's findings from her brief assessment.

'Is the baby still breech?'

'Yes,' Abby's said, in what she prayed was a confident voice, as Shelly let out a moan of terror.

'I thought it had turned. I said to Ross this morning—'

'Shelly,' Abby broke in firmly, 'the baby's going to be fine. I just need you to listen carefully to what I'm telling you to do.' Her eyes shot up to her new patient and she forced a smile. 'I'm going to shout for Kell. He can get someone over with a delivery pack, so try not to push just yet.'

'What if I can't stop myself?'

Abby took a deep steadying breath then looked up at Shelly, her smile every inch the confident emergency doctor she was. 'Then we'll deal with it.'

'Kell!'

It wasn't exactly a dulcet summons but, given that the television was still blaring and no doubt he was still playing housemaid, Abby wasn't exactly left with much choice.

'What's up?'

He strolled into the laundry and to Abby's bemusement he didn't even look remotely fazed by the sight that greeted him.

'Ring the clinic,' Abby said through gritted teeth, as the baby's buttocks descended lower in the birth canal, Shelly's agonised screams splitting the hot afternoon air like a knife.

He returned moments later, pulling open a large leather bag, and Abby nodded her thanks as he handed her a pair of gloves and started to open a large paper-wrapped pack. 'Did you ring?'

'Yep, Clara's on standby' Kell said as Abby's eyes widened in horror.

'I don't want Clara to be on standby,' she hissed as loudly as she could without alarming Shelly. 'I want her to send a team.' Hell, why didn't this Neanderthal just do as she asked? Yes, she was a doctor but this was a complicated delivery. Beads of sweat were on her brow as she struggled to stay calm. Why was Kell still here? Shouldn't he do the polite thing and go and boil some water or something?

'I've got to push,' Shelly begged, and as the baby moved further down the birth canal Abby wasn't sure what terrified her the most—the thought of a breech birth with no back-up or the fact Kell was pulling on a pair of gloves.

'We are the team, Abby,' Kell said in low tones, bending down so that only she could hear. 'This as good as it gets here.' His voice changed then, coming out lighter and friendly, as he looked up and smiled at Shelly. 'The little one's still bottoms up, Shelly, so I'm just going to move you.'

To Abby's stunned amazement, in one quick motion he scooped Shelly up as easily as if she were a child and deposited her gently on the laundry bench. Then, pulling a basket over, he kicked it upside down and pushed Abby's shoulders firmly down till she was sitting. As the fog cleared from her shell-shocked brain Abby realised Shelly was actually in the perfect position for a breech delivery.

'You're a nurse?' Abby muttered, as the baby edged ever closer.

'And a midwife,' Kell whispered, guiding her hand to take the weight of the buttocks now being delivered.

'You never said.'

'You never asked.'

There wasn't time for a smart reply. Shelly started to groan in earnest now, her frightened screams filling the small laundry. 'I want Ross!'

'He'll be here soon, Shelly.' Kell's smile was far more effortless and, Abby realised, far more reassuring than hers.

'I wanted him to be here!' Shelly's voice was rising as another contraction gripped her, and with a grunt that defied her tiny frame she bore down, but seemed to change her mind halfway, her arms flailing in agony, panic overwhelming her. Breech deliveries required a supreme maternal effort combined with concentration and Abby looked up anxiously, worried by Shelly's lack of focus, knowing she needed her onside here.

'Shelly, listen to me…' Abby started, but a warm hand on her shoulder halted her in mid-sentence and she briefly turned her anxious eyes to Kell, who nodded assuredly.

'She'll be fine,' he mouthed, then turned his attention to the restless woman. 'Shelly, Ross is on his way, and we all know how much you need him right now, but holding back until he gets here isn't the right thing to do. This little one isn't waiting for anyone, so you need to do what Abby says and stay with us, OK?'

There was an air of authority in his laid-back voice, an assurity that to this point had been missing from the room, and Shelly responded to it.

'I'm just scared.'

'Why?' Kell asked easily. 'Abby's got it all covered. You and the baby are both going to be fine.'

There was a strange pecking order in medicine. The fact Abby was a doctor supposedly overrode Kell, and, given that she had started the delivery, if Kell were to rush in and take over it could, by some, be seen as professional discourtesy. But at that moment Abby would have very happily given up her seat on the upturned basket and willingly handed the reins to a far more experienced midwife. This was not the welcome she had expected, and Abby took a deep, calming breath trying to quell the mounting panic inside her before the next contraction came and they set to work again.

'All right?' Kell checked, and Abby felt both embarrassed and strangely pleased that he seemed to sense her trepidation.

'I hope so,' Abby mouthed, and then suddenly it was her turn to benefit from his rather dazzling smile.

'You'll be fine, too,' he said quietly as Shelly pushed for all she was worth as Abby and Kell shouted encouragement. With the lower trunk of the baby delivered, Shelly had a welcome break for a moment or two, but there was no time for Abby to relax. She checked a loop of the cord and nodded to Kell, the steady pulsing of the cord reassuring her that the baby wasn't in distress, but she had the shoulders to deal with next and then the hardest part, the head.

'OK, let's go.' Kell sounded as enthusiastic as he had when he'd started his bike as the next contraction started.

Abby felt a surge of confidence. Surely if Kell wasn't worried she must be doing OK. One strong hand assisted her, gently pushing Abby's hand, guiding her to deliver the baby's shoulder downwards towards the floor. Suddenly Abby felt in control, the textbooks, the deliveries she had observed springing into her mind like a much-watched video. The shoulders were out now and she cast a quick glance up to Kell.

'Hold steady a moment, Shelly.' Coming round to Abby, he guided her arm to the infant, so that the baby was effectively straddling Abby's forearm with its arms and legs. 'Just let it hang for a moment,' Kell said gently, and Abby gave a grateful nod, the weight of the baby allowing gravity to help with the delivery of its head. His hand was back on hers now, guiding her middle finger into the infant's mouth as Abby used her other hand to increase the flexion of the head.

She drew the body of the babe first downward and then forward, the baby over Shelly's abdomen as the last inches of the birth canal were negotiated, until finally, with a relief that literally overwhelmed Abby, the head was out, the baby was out and safe, taking a huge breath, its little eyes blinking in indignation as it was delivered. Abby placed the slippery bundle on Shelly's stomach, whose hands moved down to scoop the babe up to her, tears streaming down her face as Kell rubbed the stunned little baby vigorously with a towel.

'A little girl,' she gasped. 'I've got a little girl.'

'A beautiful little girl, too.' Kell's words were coming out almost as choked as Shelly's and to Abby's amazement she watched as a sparkle of tears flashed in his dark eyes. 'Look how blonde she is—she's her father's daughter all right.'

'And she's OK?'

Better than OK. One little girl was pinking up before their very eyes as Kell continued to rub, her dark red lips parted to allow a furious scream to escape.

As Kell dashed off to find a duvet Abby clamped and cut the cord, the placenta delivering with satisfying ease. Wrapping a bundle of towels around the baby and a large bath sheet around a shivering Shelly, she stood for a moment, just revelling in the sheer and utter miracle of birth.

'Abby.' Kell was at the door, only his face peering around as he pushed the duvet through the gap. 'Cover Shelly up, I've got a little guy here who's woken up with a bit of a fright.'

'Matthew?' Shelly gasped, tearing her eyes away from her newborn as Abby quickly tucked the duvet around the pair. 'He must be terrified.'

'He'll be fine,' Abby said assuredly, but Shelly begged to differ.

'He won't understand.' Her eyes met Abby's. '*You* don't understand. Matthew's got Down's syndrome. Ross and I had planned how we were going to introduce him. I was supposed to be in bed, the baby in a crib, Ross was going to—'

'Do you want me to help you into the bedroom, get you settled a bit before he sees you?'

Shelly shook her head. 'He's awake now, you'd better just tell Kell to bring him in.'

Abby nodded and, doing a quick check to make sure there was nothing that might scare Matthew, she went to open the laundry door.

'Abby.' Turning, Abby smiled at Shelly, her hand on the doorhandle. 'Would you hold her for me? It might make things a bit...' Her voice trailed off and Abby stood there, looking at the mother cradling the daughter she had just delivered, and suddenly the lump that had been missing in her throat till now was so big it threatened to choke her.

'I'd be glad to.'

A mother's love...

Taking the swaddled bundle, Abby stared into the most innocent of all faces. Every fibre in Shelly's being would be telling her she should be holding her baby, and yet a deep maternal instinct also told her that a little guy needed her now. Needed his mum to hold her arms out to him, to tell him what had taken place while he'd quietly slept.

Carefully holding the baby close, Abby pulled open the laundry door.

Two blue eyes met hers, two blue bewildered little eyes in a sleep-crumpled face.

'This is Abby, Matty,' Kell crooned gently. 'She's Tennengarrah's new doctor.' Wisely Kell didn't acknowledge the baby Abby was holding, leaving that introduction to Shelly.

'Matthew.' Shelly's arms were outstretched, her tired face managing a bright smile, her voice, her attention, all focussed on her son. 'Did you get a fright, sweetheart?'

He didn't say anything, just nodded seriously as Kell carefully passed him to his mother. 'There's nothing to be scared of Matthew. Abby and Kell have been looking after Mummy, and look who's finally here.'

Taking her cue, Abby stepped forward, holding the infant where her big brother could get a proper look, and the lump in her throat swelled like bread in water as Matthew peered into the swaddle of towel.

'Baby.' His little face broke into a smile that met each ear and the whole room seemed to relax a notch, the tension seeping out as two inquisitive eyes searched his new sister's face. 'My baby!' Matthew squealed excitedly.

'That's right big guy, it's your baby sister.' Kell laughed, one eye on Matthew, the other on a wilting Shelly. Scooping Matthew out of a tired Shelly's arms, he held the little boy closer, allowing him to touch the tiny face. 'That's right, don't touch her eyes, and just give her little cheek a stroke. I'll bet she can't wait for you to give her a big cuddle, but do you know what, little guy? First we have to get Mummy into bed, and I'm gonna need a hand. Do you think you can help me?'

Put like that, how could Matthew refuse?

Somehow, in a matter of minutes Kell had them organised. A now over-excited Matthew turned back the sheets on the bed and plumped pillows as Kell guided a very wobbly Shelly to the main bedroom. Abby followed, carrying the newborn as carefully as if she were the crown jewels, staring down into that tiny wide-eyed face, unable to believe the feelings this ten-minute-old baby was unleashing.

Oh, Abby had held babies before, well, sort of. She'd examined more tiny chests than most people had had cooked dinners, probed more little abdomens than she cared to remember, even bounced the odd baby or two on her knee during her time on the children's ward.

But to hold one so new, so close and for so long was doing the strangest things to her.

To know that unaided by a huge team, she had brought this wanted, precious life into the world suddenly made that medical degree seem a touch more personal.

'You were great.' Kell was sitting on the bed and Abby did

a double take when she stepped in the bedroom. 'Shelly's just in the loo,' he explained, patting the bed beside him.

'I only did great thanks to you,' Abby admitted, not even bothering to look up. The face of the baby held far too much appeal.

But then again…her eyes flicked up and they were met by Kell's black, coal chips.

'I was just giving myself a big pat on the back about how well I'd done, but I'm the first to admit that I nearly had a full-scale panic attack when I saw the baby was breech. Heaven only knows what would have happened if you hadn't been there.'

'It would have been exactly the same,' Kell said with the same assurance he had used with Shelly. 'A couple of minutes of internal panic and it would have all clicked. You know that as well as I do.'

'I hope so. Were you even a little bit worried?'

'No, I never worry.' Abby gave him a disbelieving look but Kell just stood up and rapped on the *en suite* door. 'Are you all right, Shelly?'

'A couple more minutes,' came the distant reply, and Kell frowned.

'Don't you go fainting on me now, Shelly. Two more minutes or I'll come in and fetch you myself.' Smiling, he came back from the door. 'Hey, Matty, why don't you go and get a toy for the baby to put in her cot?' As Matthew scampered off, Kell sat back down. 'I hope she's all right in there.'

'This is the man who less than a minute ago told me he never worried.'

Kell laughed, but just as he opened his mouth to speak the bedroom door was flung open and they both turned as a tall blond man burst in.

'Where's Shelly?'

It was a strange way to meet your new colleague, strange but definitely not awkward or difficult. As Abby stood up Ross

Bodey's jaw literally dropped, an incredulous look on his face as his eyes locked on the baby Abby held.

'Who's this?' he choked, as Abby stood there, speechless.

'Are you talking about the gorgeous raven, or the ravishing redhead?' Kell quipped, but his voice was thick with emotion as the bathroom door opened and a pale-looking Shelly tentatively stepped out.

'I'm talking about the blonde,' Ross said slowly, one arm pulling his wife towards him as he shakingly took the baby from Abby.

'I'm sorry,' Shelly sobbed, the emotion of the evening finally catching up. 'I tried to hold on.'

'There's absolutely nothing to be sorry for.' His eyes never left his daughter as he gently led his wife to the bed. 'This is the best homecoming I've ever had.'

'Wun.' Matthew was at the door now. Charging in, he placed a battered book in the crib, his face splitting in two as he saw Ross sitting on the bed.

'Hey, buddy, don't I get a kiss?'

'Daddy!'

'I think we might have outstayed our welcome,' Kell whispered to Abby. 'How about you let me buy you that drink now?'

'How about you show me where I can have a shower?'

They said their goodbyes, an engrossed Ross attempting to apologise for landing Abby in it, but his mind was clearly on the latest addition to his family.

'Abby will be fine.' Kell grinned. 'I'll bring her luggage over and show her around. Don't worry about a thing, just enjoy tonight.'

'No problem there,' Ross said, then turned to Abby. 'Look, thank you, I really mean that.'

'It was a pleasure,' Abby said warmly. Stepping out into the now dark sky, a billion stars twinkling down, the warm hand of Kell guiding her along the dusty red soil, it hit her, a heady mixture of relief at what had transpired and utter fear at how different the scenario could have been.

'You're crying?' His voice was questioning, concerned, but not for a second mocking.

'I know.' Abby sniffed loudly as she fished in her pockets for a handkerchief. 'It's never got to me like that—a birth, I mean. It's always been nice, special.' The words were buzzing in her head as Abby attempted to articulate the strange emotions that were assailing her. 'But at the end of the day it's been a job well done. Tonight it just got to me. Seeing Matthew, he was so cute, bringing the baby his book, and then Ross...' Another tear splashed down her cheek and Abby wiped it away then gave in as a few more followed. 'He was so thrilled, so delighted with his new daughter, yet he still managed to make Matthew feel number one.'

As Abby started to walk again, Kell pulled her back. 'You think that's a tear-jerker?' His eyes were searching hers as Abby's returned his stare. 'Wait till you hear this—Matthew isn't Ross's son.'

He watched as Abby's lips parted, as the tears started spilling again.

'They've only been married a year, and you know what? He loves that little guy as if he was his own. That's love for you.'

'She's a lucky woman,' Abby said slowly, but Kell shook his head.

'They're all lucky.' Taking her hand, he led her along the pathway. 'They found each other.'

'This is you.'

Pushing open the unlocked door, Kell stood back and let Abby into her new home.

Her luggage lay higgledy-piggledy on the dark wooden floor, no doubt courtesy of Bruce, and Abby stood a moment as Kell flicked on the light.

'It's pretty basic. Kitchen.' He gestured ahead. 'Lounge.'

Stomping along the hallway, he flicked on another light and Abby was somewhat surprised to find herself standing in a beautifully furnished room. A large wooden fan whirred away overhead bouncing a shadow off the white walls, broken by vast Aboriginal paintings, the native art so much more appropriate in its own setting than the museums Abby was used to seeing it in. The soft-cushioned cane furnishing looked inviting and the huge low table in the middle of the large room would be the perfect spot for her computer.

'Oh.'

'What's wrong?'

'I left my computer back at Ross and Shelly's.'

'Well, I'm not going back to get it,' Kell said quickly. 'That's one little party I'm not breaking up.'

'Of course not,' Abby snapped, kicking herself for even mentioning it. 'I was just saying.'

'So we're back where we started?' Kell turned to her. 'Arguing about a computer.'

'Nobody's arguing,' Abby said defensively, but the closeness that had overtaken them since the delivery seemed to have gone, and to her surprise she missed it. 'I was just...' Her voice trailed off and after a reluctant pause she finally spoke. 'I was just moaning...' A smile wobbled on the edge of her lips as Kell waited for her to finish.

'Again.'

'Ready to see the rest of your place?' His smile returned as Abby nodded. 'Bathroom.' Flinging open the door, Kell carried on walking as Abby poked her head in briefly. 'Laundry.' Opening a cupboard, he gave a wicked smile. 'Washing powder. And if I'm not mistaken, there's even an iron. All mod cons here.'

'Very funny,' Abby retorted, following a very broad back along a very narrow corridor.

'Bedroom.'

Suddenly, Kell's voice sounded thick as if he had a cold or had suddenly developed hay fever, but with a notable absence of flowers and not a sneeze in sight Abby could only assume that the sight of the vast queen-size bed was having a similar effect on Kell as it was on her.

A flimsy mosquito net dusted over the bed, the whirring fan billowing the voile gently against the crisp white sheets, emitting a low throbbing hum in the semi-darkened room, and for an inexplicable moment, never had a bed looked more tempting.

'I think we've earned a drink,' Kell said gruffly. 'And if I know Shelly, there'll be a few in the fridge.'

Eternally grateful he wasn't suggesting the pub, Abby's answer was for once positive. 'Help yourself. I'm going to make my acquaintance with the shower.'

'Better?'

Rubbing her hair with a large towel, Abby stepped into what was supposed to be her lounge and amazingly didn't feel like a total stranger. She hadn't known what to wear, but a pair of too new jeans seemed about right and a black sleeveless T-shirt was surely casual enough.

'Much.'

'I made some supper.' The table had been haphazardly laid, and a slab of cheese surrounded by crackers beckoned her. 'But we could head down to the pub now if you're starving, or there are a couple of steaks in the fridge.'

'This will be fine.'

Better than fine actually. Loading her knife with soft Camembert, Abby scraped it along a cracker before biting in. Never had cheese and crackers tasted so good, and as Kell poured iced water into two glasses Abby rallied at the prospect of more time with him.

'We'll have to go over soon,' Kell added. 'The locals will never forgive me if we don't go and fill them in.'

'What's with the *we*?' Abby questioned, nervous at the prospect of facing everyone, far happier to keep a professional distance. 'It won't take both of us to deliver the news.'

'It took both of us to deliver the baby,' Kell pointed out. 'Don't miss your pats on the back, Abby, it's one of the perks of the job.'

'So, are you always so laid back?' Abby asked, resuming the conversation that had taken place in the warm euphoric glow of the baby's birth.

'Yep,' Kell said simply, before elaborating. 'The only trouble is that it doesn't last. Me, I worry after the event. Give me a drama and I cope. Honestly, Abby, I don't know why, but you can throw anything at me and I'm like a textbook, I just see what needs to be done and do my best to get on with it, I don't even break a sweat. But afterwards...' Kell let out a breath. 'I'll lie awake tonight imagining every possible thing that could have gone wrong. What if I'd still been waiting for your plane to come in? What if the head hadn't delivered easily? What if—'

'I get the picture,' Abby moaned. 'Unfortunately it hits me there and then. I'm constantly picturing the worst-case scenario.'

'It's just the way you work.' Kell shrugged. 'And it probably makes you a great emergency doctor. Hell, if I'm in trouble I want a doctor worried on my behalf.'

'And I want a nurse who's calm and efficient.'

'Hey, maybe we'll make the perfect team.' Those dark eyes were smiling and that brittle exterior Abby normally so effortlessly portrayed seemed to be crashing down around her as she smiled back at the man beside her.

'Maybe we will,' she said softly. 'Maybe we will.'

Everything about him screamed contradiction.

Everything about him had Abby entranced.

'You don't look like a nurse,' Abby ventured, plunging her knife back into the cheese, flustered by her own rather personal observation.

'You mean I don't look gay?' Kell laughed at her rather shocked features, but Abby quickly recovered.

'Actually, add a handlebar moustache to those boots and skimpy shorts and you'd be a wow at the Sydney Mardi Gras!'

'I was decorating!' Kell laughed. 'Anyway, in case you were wondering, no, I'm not gay.'

It had never even entered Abby's head that he might be. Not for the briefest second. Some men might throw up that question every now and then, and a male midwife, oozing compassion and in tune with a laboring woman, might bring about one of those occasions, but somehow Kell wore it all well. 'I wasn't,' Abby said quickly. 'You just look more like a—'

'Labourer,' Kell suggested, totally unabashed. 'Hell, you're a snob, Abby.'

'No, I'm not,' Abby replied hotly, and then gave him a worried look. 'At least I hope I'm not.'

'Well, I'll choose to reserve judgement on that. And for your information I am a labourer and a drover, too, and a few other things in between.'

'A real Jack of all trades?' Abby said lightly, but her forehead creased slightly. 'What's a drover, by the way?'

'A cowboy to you.'

'Oh.'

'Well, almost a cowboy. And while we're making personal observations about each other, you don't exactly look like an outback doctor.'

'I know,' Abby groaned, then checked herself. It wouldn't do to voice her misgivings to a local, so instead she assumed what she hoped was a more positive tone. 'But I'm really excited to be here.'

It didn't fool him for a second! 'That's not what I heard.' Kell grinned, topping up her glass of iced water then his own. 'I was under the impression you were only here under sufferance.'

'You know?' Abby gulped. 'But if you know, that means...'

'It's OK,' Kell moved quickly to reassure her. 'Ross only mentioned the fact you didn't really want to come to me, no one else knows. Reece Davies is a friend of Ross's and apparently he was singing your praises when he volunteered you for the job. Ross just told me to treat you a bit gently and make sure that people didn't give you too much of a hard time until you'd found your feet a bit.'

'Honestly,' Abby checked, 'you're not put out that I only came because I had to?'

'That's the reason most doctors come.' Kell shrugged. 'Let's face it—it's a pretty weird place to be. Ross had a passion for it, but he's the exception rather than the rule. The outback's screaming for doctors…'

'So you have to take what you can get?'

'Not at all,' Kell refuted. 'Reece wouldn't have recommended you if he didn't think you were up to it, and Ross wouldn't have taken you on just to have another name on the staff roster. The outback's precarious enough without carrying people. You're here because you're wanted, Abby. The only person who's not happy with the decision is you.'

'Oh, I don't know,' Abby mumbled. 'I've been practising medicine for nearly eight years now and this afternoon is going down on my list of top ten moments. If there's a few more of them around then it's been the right choice. I can see what Reece was saying more clearly now. It's easy to get caught in all the high-tech stuff, but if this is the buzz grass roots medicine gives, then maybe these next three months won't be so bad after all.'

'Maybe not.'

They shared a smile, a tiny smile but it was loaded with hidden meaning. Confused, Abby stood up, and for something to do she grabbed the water jug and headed off to explore her new kitchen, her mind buzzing, every nerve in her body suddenly screaming. A couple of hours in Kell's company and she was acting like a hormone-ravaged teenager, not a sensible thirty-something doctor.

'What's this?' Abby asked, pulling open the fridge.

'I would have thought a lady like you would know champagne when she sees it.'

'I meant, what's it doing in the fridge?' Abby asked, refusing to jump.

'Shelly would have left it there to welcome you. We could always wet the baby's head?'

It could almost have passed as an innocent question, but there was a look in Kell's eyes and such a heavy throb in the air that Abby knew her reserve would pop with as much oomph as the champagne cork, and that was one path she definitely wasn't going to take.

'We'd better get over to the pub. At this rate we won't even make last orders.'

'You're joking, aren't you? The news of the baby will have the pub pumping to the wee hours. It could be a long night.'

'Not for me.' Abby shook her head. 'I'll have a quick orange juice and say hi, and then I'm out of there. I need to be on the ball, and something tells me Ross isn't going to be around very much over the next few days to ease me in.'

'Then it's just as well you've got me.'

Another simple statement, but again Abby felt the throb of sexual tension, the path of a conversation littered with possible innuendo, and she almost took a tentative step, almost responded with a loaded answer herself. But she pulled back in an instant, Kell's easy smile making her wonder if her mind was playing tricks.

'I'll just go and get changed. You do whatever women do before they go out.'

'But where are you going?' Abby asked as he headed for the front door.

'I rent the house next door.' He either ignored or didn't notice the shocked look on her face, carrying on chatting in his usual easy style. 'I only use it for when I'm on call and if I'm on a late then early shift, but I guess it kind of makes us neighbours.'

She didn't answer, Abby truly couldn't, just stood there dumbfounded as he turned and left; the five minutes it took Kell to wash and change nowhere near enough time to get her head together.

Not only was she going to be working alongside him, he would be living next door to her as well.

Three months.

The words didn't console Abby this time.

After only three hours in Kell's company already Abby's nerves were on fire...

CHAPTER THREE

'PUMPING', WAS A slight exaggeration on Kell's part, Abby decided, but the pub was certainly lively.

Walking in, Abby braced herself for a few curious stares, but the cheer that went up as they both entered almost floored her.

'What's all this for?' Abby gasped as her back was slapped so vigorously that, had she been choking, her airway would undoubtedly have been cleared in two seconds flat. Jugs of beer were being held up in all directions as Kell guided her through to the bar.

'You just delivered Tennengarrah's newest resident, remember?'

Oh, Abby remembered. After all, how could she forget? But never in her wildest dreams had she expected this kind of reception. The births she had witnessed at the hospital had been accompanied with a certain amount of euphoria, a jubilant husband, a few relatives, but the long lonely walk back to the doctors' mess had meant any emotions had been left in the delivery room.

But here! The whole town seemed to be out, cheering and applauding.

'Abby, this is Jack Brown,' Kell introduced. 'Tennengarrah's one and only policeman.'

Another smiling face appeared before her. 'Glad to have you on board, Abby,' Jack grinned, 'playing midwife's not my favourite pastime, you did a great job.'

Another pat on the back, another vote of confidence to make her feel as if she had done something really special. In fact, by the time the obligatory toasts had been made, and her hand shaken by every last person at the bar, Abby found herself starting to agree with them.

It really had been special.

'They'll settle now.' Kell grinned, guiding her to a table. 'A birth's big news here, but when the cricket's starting…'

Abby's eyes followed his to the massive screen in the corner, every head in the place seemed to be turned to it.

'It's all a bit much to take in, I guess.'

Abby took a sip of her juice and gave a small shrug.

'Or perhaps there's not enough to take in?' Kell asked perceptively. 'It must seem a bit of a small world here to you.'

'It's just not what I'm used to,' Abby admitted. 'I'm not saying my way's better than yours or anything, it's just different, that's all.' Taking a breath, Abby decided to deal with a niggle that had been bothering her. 'I'm sorry if I came over as snobby or superior when we first met. It was just nerves, I guess.'

'I was just teasing when I said you were a snob.' Kell was smiling at her. Even though Abby still couldn't look, she could almost feel the warmth of it, almost see the wide dark lips breaking apart in an easy smile.

'I know, and no doubt I'm going to have to get used to it. I'm quite sure there'll be more than a few embarrassing moments. To date I've always lived in the city, always worked in big teaching hospitals, where I just blended in.'

'I doubt that.' The beer glass in his large hand seemed tiny, and Abby found herself staring at it as Kell carried on talking. 'I can't imagine a woman like you ever blending in.'

She chose to ignore that little gem, casting her mind around frantically for something to say. 'Do you ever get fed up?'

Kell shook his head. 'I don't get the time to get fed up.'

'And you've never thought of working in a city?'

Again Kell shook his head. 'I did some of my course units there, but it wasn't where I wanted to be, I was always more than happy to come home.'

'So you've never thought about...' Taking a nervous sip of her drink, even Abby herself could barely believe the personal nature of her question. 'About moving away?'

'Why would I?' Kell shrugged. 'I've got everything I need here. A great job, my family nearby. They run a large cattle station out of town,' he explained, 'so there's never a chance of being bored, and though there are relatively few people here, at least I know most of them. I could never leave this place, Abby. Tennengarrah isn't just a town in the middle of nowhere to me, it's home.'

'So what made you choose to do nursing?' Abby couldn't stop herself. Undoubtedly he was a great nurse, she'd witnessed it for herself today after all, but it just seemed such a strange career choice for a man so in tune with the land, for an *almost* cowboy!

He didn't answer straight away. From the cheers and 'Howzats' flying around the pub, Australia had obviously taken a wicket and Kell stood up to watch the replay as Abby sat there, feigning interest.

'Golden duck,' Kell said, sitting back down with a grin.

'Sorry?'

'You've no idea what I'm talking about, have you?' He grinned as Abby shook her head, then leant forward a touch. 'Mum had cancer.' His voice was still light, but Abby saw the pain behind the frown that flittered across his face. 'Every few weeks we headed off to Adelaide for her chemo. I used to go with her and I guess that's how it started. I'd never even given nursing a thought before, still didn't then really, but later...' Abby watched as his Adam's apple bobbed in his throat, and

Kell took a drink before he carried on talking. 'When it be-came terminal Mum wanted to be at home, and why shouldn't she be? The whole town loved her, wanted to help look after her, be with her...'

'But there wasn't anyone?' Abby ventured.

'Oh, no, we had the clinic. It was tiny then, one doctor and one nurse, Clara. You'll meet her tomorrow, she's great. She made all the difference in the world. Sure, Mum had more friends and neighbours than you could count, all willing to help, but it was Clara who came at two in the morning to up her mor-phine infusion, Clara who turned her, worked out the meds with the doctor, Clara who made all the difference. I went out on a couple of her clinics, saw the work she was doing and I knew then I'd found what I wanted to do with my life.'

'Did you think of studying medicine?' Even as she asked her question Abby winced, wishing she could take it back.

'No,' Kell said, grinning widely at her embarrassment. 'Be-cause, believe it or not, I'm not a frustrated doctor. I harbour no secret desires to step into your shoes.'

'I'm sorry,' Abby said again. 'That came out wrong. It's just that, as you pointed out, the outback's desperate for doctors...'

'It's desperate for nurses, too, and as much as I love this place, ultimately it's *my* life. I'm not going to be a martyr and do something I don't want to.' Leaning forward further, he beckoned Abby closer. 'Just to clear things up once and for all, I got the grades to do medicine and I chose not to. You're look-ing at one happy nurse.'

'Glad to hear it.' Her eyes, which had for so long been avoid-ing his, eventually gave in and met his, and finally she held his gaze, the depth of his stare mirroring the depth of his per-sonality. The multi-layered package she was gleefully peeling back, like a child's game of pass the parcel, frantically ripping off the paper, each layer producing its own small gift, a tiny reward for her efforts.

'Another drink, guys?' Mal, the bartender, broke the moment, flicking a cloth across the table, picking up their glasses.

'Not for me, thanks.' Abby stood up quickly, glad of the intrusion, the chance to catch her breath, to break the heaviness of the aura that surrounded them.

'Nor me.' Kell drained his glass in one gulp. 'I'm on an early shift in the morning.'

Strange the lift that snippet of information gave her.

In contrast to their entrance, their departure went almost unnoticed. A few goodnights, a few cheery waves and they were back to the cricket, leaving Kell and Abby suddenly shy in the warm night air, the ten-minute walk back uncomfortable, and it was a notable relief to finally be at her door.

'Thanks for everything today.' Abby hated the formality of her words, the stilted sound of her voice, but it was the best she could do.

'Hopefully you'll have a gentler start tomorrow.'

'I hope so.'

There was no dead lock to fumble with, no security doors or bolts to pull back, just one push and the door slid open, just one step away from ending the evening. She fumbled for a second in the darkness, trying to locate the light switch.

'Here.' The light that flooded the hallway was a pale comparison to his touch, their fingers meeting on the switch, the embarrassed pull back as a touch that shouldn't matter suddenly did, and the tension that had surrounded them, the distant throb of desire shot into gear, lurching forward a notch as the silence grew louder, the mental music stopping, and Abby knew that the parcel was in her hands now.

The game had ended and peeling back the final layer would reveal the biggest prize of all.

'I've got champagne in the fridge.' Her eyes never left his, testing his reaction, unable to believe her own abandonment.

'I thought you'd never ask.'

The pop of the cork was so loud Abby was sure the whole

town must surely have heard it. Giggling in a way she hadn't for so long, she located two mugs, catching the cascade of frothy white bubbles spilling out of the bottle, running rivers along Kell's strong hands.

Passing him a mug, they raised their hands, the pretty china clinking as the mugs met in a toast. 'To...' Abby gave a small laugh '...whatever her name may be, welcome to the world, little lady.'

'And to Dr Abby...'

'Hampton,' Abby filled in.

'To Dr Abby Hampton. That's a nice name actually,' Kell said, as if it really somehow mattered. 'Welcome to Tennengarrah.'

Catching his eyes, a sudden sense of panic engulfed her, an urge to throw back the parcel, to stop this game before it got way, way out of hand, but it was too late for that now. Everything about him was so damned sexy, so mentally, emotionally stimulating, reason barely got a look-in. All Abby knew at this moment was that she wanted him, wanted Kell more than she had ever wanted a man in her life.

She wanted to be the winner, wanted to unwrap her parcel, wanted to taste a moment in his arms, didn't want to go through the rest of her life not knowing how it felt to be held by a man like Kell. Never had she felt such a connection, experienced such an overwhelming mutual attraction, and though the questions, the warning bells alarming in her head were irrefutably warranted, for once Abby chose to ignore them; for the first time in her ordered life, logic lost to passion, desire overrode reason. Surely Kell was a risk worth taking?

He even made denim look sexy.

Until now, jeans had just been that—jeans. Something you pulled on when you couldn't be bothered or didn't have time to think what to wear, a lazy answer almost. But there was nothing lazy about the way Kell wore them, pale and soft against his strong legs, legs that were walking towards her now, taking a step closer, one firm hand taking the mug from her tense hand and placing it carefully on the kitchen bench behind her before bringing his fingers to cup her face, fingers still cold from the champagne, a contrast to the lips so warm, so full, Abby couldn't help but respond, couldn't help but kiss him right back, melt a little closer into his body as she felt his warm smooth tongue slide between her parted lips. And as she slipped from doctor to woman, she knew, as he pulled back slightly, as those black eyes met hers, that she was lost, that the only possible conclusion to this teasing taste was to sign up for the whole package.

No man had ever carried her before, no man had ever swooped her up in strong arms and taken her to the bedroom, and no man had ever even come close to kindling the passion that overwhelmed Abby.

She had to have him.

It was as basic as that.

Had to have him near her, on her, inside her.

The chore of undressing, the usual clumsiness that broke so many moments didn't even get a look-in. Their T-shirts were discarded in seconds, but every button on his jeans was a pleasure, a slow, unhurried delight, her fingers shaking slightly as she glimpsed the stomach that had teased her only this afternoon, the belly button she had wanted so much to touch. She could now. Her white French manicured nails dragged teasingly around the dark, dark hair as he undid her bra, slipping the lace straps over her shoulders until the cream of her breasts flattened against his chest, the white soft flesh such a contrast to the mahogany of his taut, toned body. Catching her breath, he snaked her own jeans past her hips, brushing her thighs then dusting the scratchy denim over her calves until finally nothing separated them, and as he buried his fingers into her damp, needy warmth Abby groaned in primitive wantonness.

A wantonness that embalmed her, overrode her usual reservations, defied all logic.

Shuddering in his hand, her breath coming in small gasps, she snaked a leg around his thigh, urged him closer. Stretching on tiptoe, she raised herself against his solid manhood, her gasps increasing as he slipped inside. His hands were holding her buttocks now, lowering her down on him, taking her weight with such ease Abby realised then the strength of Kell, that his muscles weren't manufactured in some gym, empty hours pumping iron to earn the perfect body. Instead the grit of hard work had given him this divine body, and how she revelled in the strength. How divine to feel so light, so feminine, every fibre of her being on high alert as effortlessly he lowered her back on the bed, their most intimate parts still entwined as she rested her shoulders on her bed, and pulled him deeper inside, Kell standing, pushing, beckoning her on to a place she'd never been, the peak of her orgasm so intense, such a release, only then did Abby realise the tension that had held her together, the strain of the past few weeks dissolving as she shuddered under his touch, as a sob escaped her lips, as tears she hadn't known were there sprung forth and she wept with sweet release.

Her tears didn't faze him. Instead he scooped her into his arms, held her, comforted her and told her over and over that it was all OK, comforting her like a child, slipping a cool sheet over them, tucking his body into her back and stroking her hair, letting her cry those inexplicable tears until finally Abby fell into the deepest, sweetest sleep.

Oh, no.

Abby didn't say it, but the words resounded over and over in her mind as gradually the unfamiliar room came into focus. The overhead fan was still whirring, the sheet billowing gently in ripples over her body, a lazy hand holding her closely as Abby lay rigid, her eyes clamped firmly closed, determined to feign sleep for a few moments until her mind hopefully made sense of the chaos that she'd awoken to.

How?

The single word was the prelude to a multitude of questions that stamped through her mind demanding answers.

How had she let this happen?

How could she have let her guard down like that? She was here to work, to focus on her medical skills, to get her life back on track, not tumble into bed with the first man she met.

But it hadn't been like that, Abby acknowledged. Something much bigger than sex had happened last night. Kell had strolled into her life and into her heart with such breathtaking ease and it would be so easy, so very easy to let him stay.

And that was what scared her the most.

'Morning!' That hand wasn't being so lazy now. Instead, it was working its way along the curve of her hip, moving leisurely along to her stomach, moving relentlessly upwards toward the soft swell of her breasts, and for a second or two, or maybe a moment even, it felt so good, so right, Abby was tempted again to just flow with it, to let the balming effect of his touch soothe her again, to give in to the mastery of Kell's touch.

'Don't.' Her hand gripped his tightly, but there was no need. As soon as the word left her lips, Kell stopped his relentless, sexy exploration and she felt him exhale, and even though Abby's back was to him she sensed the frown on his forehead.

'What's wrong, Abby?'

Scarcely able to believe her ears, Abby wriggled free of Kell's embrace and turned to face him, scooping the sheet around her and trying to cover a determinedly escaping bosom.

It didn't go unnoticed by Kell. She watched his eyes flick downwards, the sheen of early morning lust in his eyes, and again she was assailed with an urge to stop the fight now, to just make love to him and then deal with the consequences.

'What do you think is wrong?' His frown annoyed her now, and Abby sat up smartly, dark tousled hair tumbling down her back, her eyes aghast. 'You, here in my bed, that's what wrong!'

'It didn't feel wrong last night,' Kell said easily. 'In fact, till about two minutes ago it felt pretty damned good to me.'

'I'm not talking about last night,' Abby said, trying to keep her voice even, desperately trying to cast aside the memories of their delicious love-making. She had to put an end to this here and now, to ring the bell and get off at the very next stop, before this journey took her to a place she definitely wasn't prepared to go to. 'I'm talking about now. How I'm supposed to deal with this.' She looked at his incredulous face, visibly shocked at the hysteria in her voice. 'I'm sure you won't believe this but falling into bed with someone I've just met isn't a regular occurrence. In fact...' She took a deep stinging breath, her cheeks flaming as she spoke. 'This has never happened to me before.'

'Nor me.'

Abby gave him a wide-eyed look. 'Oh, sure.'

But Kell didn't seem bothered by the obvious disbelief in her voice, instead he just propped himself up on his elbow and gave his usual easy smile. 'It hasn't,' he insisted. 'Something happened yesterday, Abby, something neither of us was expecting. The second you stepped off that plane there was...' She watched his full mouth struggle to find the words, to articulate something so impossible to define, but, full credit to him, Abby registered, Kell tried. 'There was an attraction, a reaction, whatever you want to call it, but it was nothing you or I had a say in. What happened last night, well, it was special, Abby. Don't ruin it now.'

'Ruin it?' Her voice rose slightly and Abby swallowed hard, raking a hand through her hair, desperately struggling to stay calm. 'Oh, I can tell you about ruining things! I'm an expert! How am I supposed to face everyone? How am I supposed to exert any semblance of authority when I go and have a one-night stand—'

'Hey.' Kell was standing now, his raw nudity causing Abby to flinch. Sensing her embarrassment, he hastily pulled on his discarded boxers as Abby pulled the sheet tighter around her. He didn't look quite so amenable now. If anything, he looked annoyed, those dark eyes narrowing at the edges, deep lines furrowing his brow.

'Firstly, you don't have to worry about how you're going to face everyone because, apart from you and yours truly, no one else is going to know.' He watched her disbelieving shrug and his shoulders tensed. 'They're not. I'm hardly going to go rushing around the town telling everyone. I happen to think that what happens in a bedroom should stay in the bedroom.'

She believed him, albeit reluctantly. As Abby looked up, she knew, as little as she knew him, that Kell wasn't the sort to shame a woman. The blissful time in his arms had taught her that at least. 'What if Ross and Shelly saw...?' Abby said quickly, refusing to be comforted.

'They've got a brand-new baby to deal with. I'm sure they've got better things to be doing than peering out of the window to check whose house I'm going to.'

Abby gave a grudging nod, but Kell hadn't finished yet. 'Secondly, having not had the pleasure of working with you yet, I can't comment on your methods, but I'll tell you this much, Abby, you can exert as much authority as you like out here, but it isn't going to get you very far. We work on mutual respect here. And thirdly...'

Abby took a deep breath and looked up.

'Is this lecture over yet? I'd like to have a shower!'

'And thirdly,' Kell carried on, ignoring her obvious desire to end the conversation, 'you're the one relegating what happened between us to a one-night stand. For what it counts, it meant one helluva lot more to me than that.'

Abby didn't answer—she didn't really get a chance to. In two seconds flat Kell had pulled on his jeans, T-shirt and boots, and without further acknowledgment stomped down the hall. Only when the front door was none too gently closed, and all that was left was the scent of him, did Abby remember to breathe again.

CHAPTER FOUR

'YOU MUST BE Abby Hampton,' a smiling, friendly, freckled face greeted her as Abby tentatively pushed open the door of the clinic. 'I'm Clara, one of the nurses here.'

That went without saying. Clara was dressed in smart blue culottes, topped with a crisp white and blue blouse emblazoned with various badges, and Abby was somewhat taken aback, immediately regretting her own unusually informal attire. She had expected, what, she wasn't sure, but even in the city rarely were nurses so smartly dressed these days, but Clara looked as if she'd stepped out of a nursing brochure as she let out a gurgle of laughter.

'One of the nurses! That makes it sound like we're spoiled for choice, doesn't it? Apart from me there's Noelene, she's part time, very part time,' Clara added with a slight edge to her voice. 'Then there's Shelly, who I'm sure you've guessed is on maternity leave, and Kell, you've met him already, haven't you?'

That seemingly innocent question had Abby's cheeks flaming and she gave a brief nod.

'He met my plane.'

'And a bit more besides.' Clara was still smiling and Abby thought she might faint on the spot. Surely Kell hadn't told her already! 'I was on yesterday,' Clara said, as if that explained everything. 'And let me tell you, you don't have to worry about proving yourself to the locals, you've already done it. Dealing with a breech delivery ten minutes into your arrival has pretty much sealed your approval rating!' She carried on smiling as Abby let out an audible sigh of relief, scarcely able to believe that the drama of the birth yesterday had been so quickly relegated in her mind.

Kell, or rather her behaviour with Kell, was the only thing on it at the moment.

'Good morning.'

On cue Kell appeared and Abby stiffened at the sound of his voice, turning in what she hoped was a casual manner, but her rather forced greeting died on her lips as she took in the delicious view that greeted her.

Gone was the labourer, the cowboy, the jack of all trades, in his place a smart, very smart, and extremely efficient-looking male nurse. His hair was still damp from his shower but, instead of falling in the chaotic manner of yesterday, it was neatly combed, a touch too much on the collar for the old-school type but smart all the same. A crisp white shirt with dark epaulettes on the shoulders was tucked into a pair of very neat navy shorts, and the Blundstones boots had been replaced with dark brown boat shoes.

Anticipating the laid-back style of the bush, Abby had settled for lilac shorts and a white T-shirt but, looking at Clara and Kell, Abby realised she was woefully underdressed. A bush clinic it may be but the nurses here were serious professionals.

Rather than looking at him, Abby peered at his name badge. Kell Bevan. A rueful smile tickled the edge of her lips as Abby finally dragged her eyes up to meet his.

At least she knew his surname now.

'What's Kell short for?' Abby asked, curious despite herself.

'It isn't short for anything.'

'Well, you two don't need any introductions,' Clara said

crisply. 'I'm sure you got to know each other yesterday. Is she very cute, Kell?'

'Oh, very,' Kell said with a devilish grin as the colour swooped at breakneck speed up Abby's neck. 'I'm sure she'll break her fair share of hearts.' And though it was an entirely appropriate response, though Clara carried on smiling as Kell kept talking, Abby would have sworn on anything she could have put her hands on that Kell wasn't talking about the baby.

'Do you think Ross will be in?' Clara asked, oblivious to the undercurrents. 'Bill Nash's daughter just rang and she's bringing him over. He's got chest pain and insists it's just angina even though the sprays aren't working. I offered to go over but Martha wouldn't hear of it. I think she's hoping for a sticky beak at the new baby.'

'She's driving him?' Abby said, alarmed. 'With chest pain? What if he arrests?'

'We've told them over and over to stay put, but they simply won't listen.' Kell gestured to a room. 'But just in case your prediction's right, I'd better show you where things are, or would you rather wait for Ross?'

Her cheeks were burning again as Abby remembered how she'd tossed aside his previous offer to show her around. 'You'll do fine.'

The room Kell led her into had Abby blinking in surprise as she entered it. She had expected a few stainless-steel trolleys, a couple of antiquated monitors perhaps, but the room that greeted her, though smaller, was better equipped than her own emergency department in the city. Advanced monitors lined the walls, along with electronic blood-pressure machines and saturation monitors. In fact, from Abby's brief assessment, it had pretty much everything an emergency room could need.

'Pretty impressive, huh?' Kell said, noting her surprise.

'I'll say.' Fiddling with one of the monitors, Abby shook her head. 'I think I'm going to need a few lessons to fly this thing!'

'You'll be all right,' Kell said assuredly. 'We have to be well equipped,' Kell explained, turning on the monitor and running through the various commands as he spoke. 'It's not like an emergency room in the city where you resuscitate people then send them off to Intensive Care or Coronary Care…' He pushed a red button. 'The ECG tracing will print off at the desk now,' he continued, then carried on talking where he had left off, as Abby took her turn to work the machine. 'We'll have the patient in here until the flying doctors get here. Or patients,' he added. 'If there's a fire or a crash or any number of things, we can end up with several patients at a time. You can start a shift one day and not surface for the next forty-eight hours.'

'But we're just an hour or two away from the nearest base.'

'Assuming they're free to come straight out. And as I said, we can have multiple patients in here, the plane will only take one sicky.'

A dilemma that had first emerged in Abby's mind yesterday was making itself heard, and though the atmosphere between them wasn't exactly relaxed, there was definitely an emerging professional respect, which made Abby the one to ask. 'What if Shelly had needed a Caesarean?'

Kell turned and looked at her and the shrug he gave wasn't dismissive, but loaded with meaning. 'That would have been your call.'

His words reached her, and Abby stilled, reliving yesterday's drama with renewed gratitude for the positive outcome.

'I've never done a Caesarean. How would we have anaesthetised—?'

'We'd have dealt with it.' Kell let out a long ragged breath. 'We've got back-up, amazing back-up, and they can advise us every step of the way. But sometimes tough calls have to be made, and advice is great and all that, but when it's on the other end of a phone or radio, that's all it can be.

'Now, on to Bill.' The smile and slight roll of the eyes told Abby there was a lot of water under the bridge there. 'He had a triple bypass five years ago, and the bottom line is he needs another one. He's been to the city, had all the tests, and unless he has the operation, well, you know the outcome.'

'So why doesn't he have it?'

'He wants to end his days here in Tennengarrah. He's convinced if he has another bypass he won't make it, and frankly with that attitude he's probably right.'

'How old is he?'

'Forty-eight.'

'Forty eight!' Abby gasped. 'But that's no age at all. Surely he should be...'

'Forced?' Kell suggested, and Abby shook her head fiercely.

'Told,' Abby offered. 'He should be told the consequences of his decision.'

'Which he has been. Look, Abby, the angina attacks are getting more and more frequent, invariably he spends a couple of days here and Clara and I get a heap of overtime, but nothing Ross or anyone can say will get him on that plane and into surgery. He knows the risks, knows that he might die bumping along in a four-wheel-drive on the way to the clinic, but that's the way he wants it. Tennengarrah's his home, he doesn't want to leave it. I know you don't understand, Abby, and I can see why, but this place...' A wistful look came over his face and his voice lowered a touch. 'It's in your blood, Abby. For someone like Bill to leave, it would be a tough call.' A hooting car made them both look up. 'Your first patient.'

'Second,' Abby corrected, following him out. 'Don't forget yesterday.'

She could have bitten her tongue off as Kell paused and turned slowly to face her. 'And here I was thinking that was exactly what you wanted me to do.'

One look at Bill Nash was enough to tell Abby that he was in trouble. She could hear the rattle of his chest as she crossed the room! His skin was tinged grey and though sweat was pouring off him, to the touch he was cold and clammy.

'Bill, I'm Abby, Abby Hampton—'

'The new doc,' Kell broke in, slipping an oxygen mask over Bill's face as he attached him to a monitor then tied a tourniquet around his thin wrist to bring up the veins in his hand. 'So you just try and relax, Bill, and let Abby take care of you.'

Bill gave a weak nod, leaning forward on the trolley in a desperate attempt to draw breath into his lungs while Kell established IV access and his daughter filled Abby in on the drugs her father had taken.

'Normally the spray works straight away,' the anxious young woman said, wringing her hands as she eyed her father. 'Or at least after ten minutes or so. He wasn't this bad when I rang—he got worse in the Jeep.'

'Well, he's here now,' Abby said kindly, deliberately not voicing her misgivings as to the wisdom of driving Bill here. Hopefully there'd be time for that later! As she listened carefully to Bill's chest Abby caught Kell's eye. 'Ten milligrams of morphine, please, and I'd like twenty of Lasix as well.' Even before she had pulled the stethoscope out of her ears an ECG tracing was being pressed into her hands by Clara, and Abby didn't have to look too carefully to see that the recording confirmed her findings. Bill wasn't suffering from angina, he was having a heart attack.

'Bill.' Abby came close to his ear and spoke in calm tones. 'Don't try and answer, I know you're very short of breath, just nod if you understand.'

Bill gave a small nod before Abby continued pushing the drugs through the IV bung Kell had inserted the second Bill had hit the clinic. 'There's a lot of fluid on your chest, which is making it difficult for you to breathe. I'm giving you some Lasix now, it's a strong diuretic and will soon get rid of that fluid and have you more comfortable. I've also given you some morphine, the pain will settle in just a moment or two.'

'I'm having—' Bill started, his words faint, but their meaning clear.

'Don't try and talk, Dad,' his daughter interrupted. 'Just try and do what the doctor says.'

But her words just upset Bill who tore at the mask, trying to make himself heard.

'Am I having—?'

'Yes, Bill.' Abby held his frightened eyes. 'You *are* having a heart attack, but we're dealing with it. You just need to lie back and let us do the worrying.'

Amazingly Bill accepted her words and with some relief Abby watched as he nodded then finally relaxed back onto the pillow as the drugs started to take effect.

'Do you want me to put a catheter in?' Kell asked. Given the amount of diuretics Abby had given Bill, a catheter was necessary and Abby gave a grateful nod just as Ross Bodey arrived somewhat breathlessly at the clinic.

'Sorry, Abby,' he murmured, leaning over her shoulder Ross looked at the ECG. 'I'm already wondering how on earth we managed without you. How about you, Kell?' he asked as Kell came over.

'It's starting to look that way.' Kell smiled, but the smile on his face didn't quite meet his eyes. 'But first things first. How're Shelly and the baby?'

'Great.' Ross's face literally lit up just at the mention of them. 'Although I thought babies normally slept a lot for the first twenty-four hours. Kate's been singing like a lark all night.'

'Kate.' Abby smiled as the word popped out of her mouth. 'Kate Bodey, that's just gorgeous.'

'Thanks,' Ross said with the grinning enthusiasm of a new father. 'She was supposed to be Catherine, but one hour into it we'd reduced it to Kate, so I think that's what's going to go on the birth certificate! Kell,' Ross added, his voice a touch more serious, 'would you mind popping over before you head off for the clinic? Shelly's having a bit of trouble feeding, and she's never...' he gave a small embarrassed cough as Kell listened, totally unfazed '...breastfed. I've tried to make a few suggestions, but I think it might come better from a midwife. Apparently, Matty wasn't well enough to feed when he was born so he got everything through a tube, but Shelly's determined...'

'No worries,' Kell broke him off in mid-sentence. Did nothing ruffle this guy? Abby mused. 'I'll go and see her soon, but for now could one of you have a word with Martha? Bill's daughter,' Kell explained to Abby. 'She's really worked up and it's not helping Bill.'

Ross nodded but Abby moved first. 'I'll do it.'

'Are you sure?' Ross frowned. 'It's a bit delicate. Bill doesn't want surgery—'

'Kell already explained,' Abby responded. 'I'm more than happy to talk to her.'

More than happy, Abby thought as Kell led them both to a small coffee-room. If Bill didn't want surgery that was his prerogative, but Abby wanted to be sure of her facts next time Bill arrived on death's doorstep at the clinic.

'Is this it?' Abby hadn't even closed the door behind him before Martha dissolved into a flood of tears. 'Is this the end for Dad?'

Pulling up a chair, Abby waited for the initial surge of tears to subside, and even though Abby had never even been in this room before, never set foot in the clinic or met Martha until now, she didn't feel uncomfortable.

Grief, fear, the uncertainty of dealing with the human body, was a scene Abby was all too familiar with.

'Your father's had a heart attack, Martha,' Abby said gently. 'And from his history this isn't the first. Am I right?

With a teary sniff Martha nodded. 'He had two before he had his bypass. Dr Bodey warned us that without another operation this was going to happen.'

'Why won't your father have the surgery?'

'He's convinced he won't survive,' Martha said resignedly. 'We've all tried to persuade him, but he's a stubborn old bull, says if he's going to die he wants it to be here, the same as Mum.'

'When did your mother die?' Abby probed gently.

'Two years ago.'

'And Bill, your father, he's been depressed since then?'

Martha gave a small nod then shook her head. 'We've already been there, with Ross. Dad refuses to accept he's depressed, he won't hear of taking any medication, or talking to anyone. He seems resigned to it, as if he hasn't really got anything to live for.' Martha started crying in earnest now. 'I don't want to lose my father, Doctor, he's only forty-eight. Is it too late if he changes his mind? I mean, would he still have a chance?'

Abby gave a tentative nod of her head, but her voice was guarded. 'He's obviously not well, but I certainly haven't written him off. We could stabilise him and the flying doctors could transfer him to a major hospital, but it has to be his decision, Martha, we can't strap him to the plane.'

Martha gave a weak smile. 'Believe me, I've thought about it. So what now?'

'Well, we'll treat the acute heart attack, and the next forty-eight hours will be critical, but if he survives this event, we'll review his meds again, see if we can help make him a bit more comfortable. The medication we'll give him now will hopefully minimise the damage to his heart from the attack, but what's happened this morning certainly isn't going to help his long-term prognosis.'

'Old fool,' Martha said, but not unkindly. 'Why can't he see how much we all need him, how much we all love him?' Standing, she gave Abby a tired smile. 'Thank you, for being direct I mean. Maybe you can try doing a bit more straight talking with Dad.'

'I intend to,' Abby agreed. 'But when he's a bit better.' Her sympathetic smile faded as Martha closed her eyes, paling as she fumbled for the chair behind her. Reaching out her hands,

Abby guided her to the chair behind. 'Hey, are you OK?' Abby asked as Martha took a few deep breaths.

'I'm fine. Too much drama on top of an empty stomach.'

But Abby wasn't convinced. 'Let me take a look at you.'

'No.' Martha's voice was firm. 'I'm honestly fine. Can you tell Dad I'll be along in a minute?'

'Sure,' Abby agreed reluctantly, but an internal voice told her that Bill's stubborn streak was clearly hereditary. 'But if you change your mind, you know where you can find me.'

'How is she?' Kell looked up from the notes he was writing as Abby made her way over.

'Upset, understandably. He really ought to be transferred.'

'I know,' Kell sighed. 'Ross is having another word with him, but it would seem Bill's mind is made up.'

Abby looked over at the thin man, attached to monitors, his face covered by an oxygen mask, shaking his head against the pillow as Ross presumably implored him to think again. Even though Abby knew he was getting the right treatment, she also knew that it was only a short-term solution. Bill needed surgery. As Ross made his way over the news only got worse. 'He wants active treatment for the heart attack, but he's made it very clear that if his heart stops or he stops breathing he doesn't want to be resuscitated,' Ross said grimly.

'Well, I'm not sure Bill's in the right state of mind to be making such decisions,' Abby responded quickly. 'He's scared and in pain and he's also had a hefty dose of morphine. In good faith I can't just stand by and watch if he does arrest.'

Abby watched a quick look pass between the two men and though she'd probably overstepped some imaginary mark for such a new staff member, Abby truly didn't care!

She wasn't here to make friends and influence people, she was here to practise medicine; and medicine, as always in Abby's usually ordered life, came first last and always.

'From the conversation I had with Martha it appears that Bill's depressed.'

'He is,' Ross agreed, but before he could add to his argument Abby stepped in.

'When Bill's medically stable we'll go over his options again. Until then I think it would be unwise to withhold treatment.' To the uninitiated, Abby's statement didn't sound particularly profound, but from the sudden dive in the atmosphere Abby knew her words had hit the mark.

The new girl she may be, but she was also a well-qualified doctor and for Ross to ignore her opinion could have huge legal ramifications!

'I'm sorry, Ross,' she added. 'I understand you know Bill well, but in all good faith I can't suspend my beliefs just because I'm not in my usual surroundings. Maybe a rather more objective opinion is called for. I'll let you know my findings when I've spoken at length to Bill, but until then if anything happens he's to be fully resuscitated!' And turning on her heel, Abby walked off, not really knowing where she was going but hoping it was in the vague direction of the staffroom.

'I don't want to discuss it,' Abby started as Kell followed her in.

'Neither do I,' Kell said grimly. 'It's mobile clinic day today. Ross thought it might be a good idea if you came along, met a few of the locals.'

'What about Bill?'

'There's an emergency bell that goes directly over to Ross's house and Clara will stay with him.'

Abby gave a hesitant nod. A day with Kell wasn't exactly at the top of her agenda, but maybe it was best to get it over with if they were ever going to establish a normal working relationship.

'I'm just going to check on Shelly,' he said vaguely, with no suggestion that she join him, 'and then we'll head off.'

Of course, there was no such thing as just 'heading off' in the outback. An inordinate amount of time was spent checking the cold-boxes, loading them with medicines and vaccinations, before finally Kell did a quick check on the Jeep itself, ensuring the two-way radio was working and there was plenty of water on board.

'How's Shelly and Kate?' Abby asked, attempting to flick a fly and look calm at the same time, determined not to show Kell she was even remotely bothered at the prospect of spending a morning with him.

'They're going really well. Shelly just wasn't positioning her right and only putting her nipple in, so Kate was having trouble latching on.'

'Oh.'

Well, what else could she say? Here was a guy with all the muscles and brawn of a labourer talking about 'nipples' and 'latching on' and not even breaking a blush. Heavens, even the father, a doctor to boot, had had trouble with the subject. Kell Bevan really was a one-off!

'Do you want to get the sandwiches?' Kell suggested as Abby wilted in the already sweltering heat. 'We won't exactly be inundated with burger bars on the way,' he added, noting Abby's rather reluctant stance. 'And a Thermos of coffee wouldn't go amiss,' Kell shouted as Abby stomped back into the clinic.

So she was the tea girl now?

Opening the fridge, Abby's heart sank lower, if that was possible.

Where was the prosciutto, pastrami, sun-dried tomatoes and olives?

Where were the bagels and crusty rolls when you fancied one?

Pulling a loaf out of the bread bin, Abby made do with the provisions to hand.

Peanut butter or Vegemite wasn't exactly going to provide a gourmet picnic but, then, what had she expected?

She was an outback doctor for now.

'What are you doing?'

Kell's presence made the tiny kitchen even smaller and it

wasn't just because of his imposing height either—the very fresh scent of him, the million or so male hormones flying around the air, coupled with the cringe factor of a night of exhausting passion in his very strong brown arms, made buttering a round of Vegemite sandwiches seem suddenly extremely complicated.

'I'm making lunch,' Abby said through slightly gritted teeth. 'Just as you asked.'

'I asked you to *get* the lunch,' Kell said patiently, as if he were talking to a petulant two-year-old, 'not *make* it. Heavens, where would we be if we treated our doctors like that?'

His sarcasm wasn't wasted, and a blushing Abby followed him out of the clinic kitchen into the staffroom where Kell pulled the lid off an esky.

'Fresh damper, cream cheese, roast beef and home-made chutney. There's a bit of room still—I mean, if you're really partial to Vegemite sandwiches.'

'The roast beef will be fine,' Abby said grudgingly, as Kell took two seconds flat to make a Thermos of coffee.

'Be a shame to waste them, though.' Kell winked, grabbing Abby's rather paltry attempt as they went past and somehow managing to look sexy as he ate and walked towards the car.

She sat in the furnace of the Jeep as Kell loaded the esky into the back with her mouth watering. Only then did she realise that, apart from the cheese and crackers she had shared with Kell last night and the meal on the plane, she'd barely eaten a thing in two days.

'Do you want one?' Kell offered, climbing in beside her and turning on the engine.

After a second's hesitation Abby took the wretched Vegemite sandwich, and as the air-conditioning kicked in and the salt of the Vegemite worked its magic, the butterflies that had been present since she had woken in Kell's arms settled a notch.

'Better?' Kell asked after ten minutes or so of driving.

'Much. How far is it?'

'A couple of hours.' He smiled at Abby's rather pained expression. 'Abby...'

The teasing note had gone from his voice and Abby knew what was coming next.

'If you're going to say, "About last night,"' Abby said, staring out of the window and wishing this conversation could be over, 'then don't.'

'I think a few words might be called for.'

Abby didn't want a few words, didn't want a post-mortem as to what could possibly have possessed her to sleep with him. Actually, she didn't need one. As Kell hauled the Jeep over to the side of the red dusty road, the engine still idling to allow the air-conditioning to work, she met those dark eyes for the first time since last night and there and then she answered her own question.

He was divine.

Seriously so.

'I like you, Abby.'

It seemed such a strange thing to say. Not 'I fancy you, Abby' or 'let's pretend last night never happened' or even 'No one will see us out here if you're up for a repeat', and the simpleness of his statement startled her.

'You don't even know me,' was all Abby managed as she picked at one perfectly manicured little fingernail.

'You don't have to know someone to like them,' Kell said seriously. 'You don't have to know their family history and how many sugars they have in their coffee to know how you feel.' When she didn't answer, didn't even manage a half-smile, he carried on. 'I just like you. I like the way that even though you'd never been on a bike before, you got on, I like the way you weren't too intimidated to ask for your computer, that you chatted away to Shelly about getting her whites whiter when I'm sure there was a million and one things you'd rather have been doing...'

That was rewarded with a very grudging smile and Abby was rewarded tenfold with a slightly wider one back.

'I even like the way you stood up to Ross and me this morning. How you put the patient first. It can't have been easy, and I admire you for it.

'Now, on to last night.'

Mortified, Abby resumed her scrutiny of her nail but Kell was having none of it, capturing her chin with one very large but very gentle hand and turning her to face him. 'Hazarding a guess, I'd say last night was completely out of character. I'd be so bold as to suggest that jumping into bed with a male midwife was pretty uncharted territory for you.'

His hint of humour made the whole scorching conversation almost palatable.

'Jumping into bed with anyone is pretty much uncharted territory,' Abby admitted, scarcely able to believe she was prolonging the agony.

'Flowers, meals, chocolates…' Kell suggested as Abby nodded. 'Movies…'

'I hate going to the movies,' Abby said.

'Of course you do.' Kell grinned. 'The theatre, then?'

Again she nodded. 'But I'll settle for a video.'

'And a few kisses, working up to the main event, which would take place somewhere a few months down the track?'

'That just about sums it up,' Abby admitted, flicking her worried brown eyes to his. 'Look, what happened last night simply mustn't happen again.'

'Which relegates it to the one-night stand thing you so obviously abhor,' Kell said with annoying logic.

'P-perhaps, but I'm just not in the m-market for a relationship,' Abby stammered. 'There's just too much going on in my life right now to deal with one, that's why last night should never have happened.'

'Don't say that,' he insisted. 'OK, it was probably too soon, and no doubt if we had our time over we'd have taken things a tad more slowly...' His brow furrowed and he shot her a look that made Abby start as he shook his head. 'I'm sorry, Abby, I've gone over and over it and even with the benefit of hindsight I still wouldn't change a thing. Last night was amazing and wondrous and special so, please, please, don't regret it.'

His words stunned her.

Stunned her.

To hear this six-foot-something would-be cowboy speaking so romantically, for him to somehow have turned her scorching embarrassment around and made everything, if not all right, at least bearable, had Abby dumbstruck.

'I don't regret it.' He watched her blink in surprise at her own admission. 'I know I should, and I guess in some ways I do, but...'

'We were good, weren't we?'

That sexy grin was doing terrible things to Abby now; the butterflies were dancing again, but more in sexual excitement than nervousness.

'Let's start again, huh? Only this time I'm not going to lay a finger on you. Sex is completely off the agenda until we're way past the courting stage. I'll see what I can do on the flowers and chocolate front but the theatre might be a bit of an ask. Still, if there's any local plays on in town I'll be sure to book two of the best seats.'

'You don't have to date me,' Abby said. 'Like I said, a relationship...'

He put his hand up to halt her. 'I'm not going to date you Abby,' Kell corrected her. 'I'm going to woo you, and I'm going to it so damned well that by the time I'm finished with you, a relationship will be exactly what you want!'

She was grateful when Kell ended the conversation and as he flicked the engine back to full life and pulled off the handbrake, Abby realised with a flood of relief that the shame of last night, the utter mortification, had thankfully all been left somewhere on the dusty outskirts of Tennengarrah.

OK, Abby reasoned, last night hadn't been the most sensible thing she had done in her life, but it certainly hadn't been the worst.

In fact, in the scheme of things, Abby mused as the Jeep jolted along the endless red earth, finally accepting the massive Akubra hat Kell offered when the sun was too hot on her dark hair, when she was old and grey and pulling memoires out of a crocheted hat, last night would be right up there, along with her getting her medical degree, her first delivery, her first kiss even.

Stealing a surreptitious look at Kell from under the rim of her hat, a tiny sigh escaped from her lips.

Who was she kidding?

Last night took centre stage.

CHAPTER FIVE

HAD ABBY BEEN in any hospital in Australia, in the world come to that, keeping her mind on the job after such a romantic declaration would have been an impossible feat.

But they weren't in a hospital.

Far from it.

In fact, even Abby's earlier vision of a clinic seemed high-tech as Kell swung down from the Jeep and opened the back door.

'We're a bit early, but we'd best get things ready.'

'Where's the clinic?' Abby asked, looking hopefully at the relatively few buildings dotted around the dusty settlement.

'You're sitting in it,' Kell replied cheerfully, opening boxes as Abby tentatively climbed down.

'We work from the back of a Jeep?'

The note of horror in her voice stopped Kell from whatever it was he was doing and he gave her an almost apologetic smile. 'Once every three months the flying doctors come and we get the luxury of working inside their plane, but that happened a couple of weeks ago, so you'll have to wait a while.'

'Considering my contract's only for twelve weeks, I might not even get to meet them,' Abby said, running her eyes along the boxes Kell was opening.

'You're kidding, aren't you? By the time your stint here is up, you'll be on first-name terms with all of them. We do clinics in various parts most days of the week. There might even be someone here that we need to evacuate today. It doesn't always have to be a high-drama situation to call them out. Nine times out of ten it's an infected wound or unstable asthma, or a complicated pregnancy.'

'What about deliveries?' Abby asked, the drama of yesterday still fresh in her mind. 'Do women in labour come to the clinic?'

'Sort of. I run what could be loosely called an antenatal clinic, and if we anticipate anything other than a straightforward delivery, we'll generally arrange the transfer of the woman to a higher level centre prior to her confinement date. The rest we try to persuade to deliver at the clinic, which can be hard because pregnancy's not really acknowledged in this culture.' Kell grinned at Abby's open-mouthed expression as he carried on explaining. 'But that's becoming less so now. On the whole, the younger people are a lot more open and used to us. You just have to be very wary. What would seem like an obvious remark to make can cause a lot of offence.'

'Such as?' Abby asked. 'I mean, what would you term as an "obvious remark"?'

'When are you due?' Kell responded with a shrug as Abby's mouth dropped another couple of inches. 'Just tread very gently. You'll soon know if you've caused offence because they'll either go all quiet or laugh in embarrassment.'

'So how on earth do you run an antenatal clinic if you can't even acknowledge the fact a woman's pregnant?'

'I've confused you, haven't I?' Kell gave her an apologetic smile. 'Just watch for a while, Abby, you'll soon get the hang of things. As to your question about deliveries, no doubt one afternoon you'll be on your own at the clinic working away and someone will come in in early labour. Now the "normal" thing to do would be to send them away, tell them to come back when they're more advanced, but not so with the local indigenous people. They generally move away from camp when they're labouring and until relatively recently a bush midwife would deal with them.'

'A bush midwife?'

'Unqualified to you, but, believe me, those women have got a lot of experience. Anyway, now we're getting a lot of women come to the clinic, which is great, but again tread warily. If a woman appears in early labour, don't send her home with a cheerful smile and tell her she's got hours to go yet, because if you do you probably won't see her again. Just make her comfortable and probably for the first few times give one of the regulars a buzz.'

'Oh, I'll do that all right!' Abby muttered, shaking her head and feeling more than a touch overwhelmed.

'You'll soon get the hang of it,' Kell said, with far more confidence than Abby felt. 'And here's our very first patient. This will give you a clearer idea, Abby.'

A very thin woman was walking towards them, dressed in a vibrant hot pink dress, carrying a small bundle in her arms.

'Vella,' Kell called as she came closer, his face beaming as he looked at the tiny infant she was carrying. Vella's wary brown eyes looked over at Abby who Kell quickly introduced.

'This is Abby, she's a doctor from Sydney,' he explained, as Vella laid the baby down on the rug in the back of the Jeep.

'When did this happen?' Kell beamed as he gently unwrapped the infant.

'She came too quickly for me to get to you,' Vella said, not answering the question and watching Kell like a hawk as he looked the little girl over.

'She's your fourth, isn't she?' Kell asked. 'Did everything go all right?'

Vella gave a small, embarrassed nod.

'And are *you* feeling OK?'

Again a small nod. 'Just check the baby.'

This was a very new baby, Abby soon realised. The cord was

dry but still in place, and she watched quietly as Kell weighed the infant in the old-fashioned hand sling, practically singing encouragement as he swiftly performed a detailed examination of the tiny girl. Checking her spine, her hips for any signs of congenital dislocation, holding her up and then letting her fall into his hand, checking for the startle reflex.

'Wonderful,' Kell said as he measured the infant's head, his fingers probing her fontanelle. Then, like a magician, he pulled out a lolly stick to check inside the tiny mouth.

'She's perfect,' he said, handing the little girl back before broaching the subject of immunisation, to which Vella seemed hesitant. But Kell for the first time pushed a touch.

'Keep Mulla away,' he said. 'In four weeks' time we can give her the first needle, and bring the other children—they should have them, too.'

Vella didn't look too convinced, but at least she wasn't shaking her head now as Kell got out a yellow folder and started to fill it in. Its familiarity touched Abby. The same yellow folder which was given to newborns born in high-tech delivery rooms was used here as well, and she watched as Kell diligently wrote up his findings before handing it to Vella, who with a shy smile stood up then wandered off back into the bush.

'As casual as that visit looked,' Kell said thoughtfully, 'it's been decades in the making.'

He looked at Abby's non-comprehending expression and gave a small smile. 'A case of east meets west, or west meets south.' Still Abby stared at him quizzically. 'The Aboriginal community has its own way of doing things. They have their own system, their own schooling, law enforcement and their own medical beliefs. It's taken a lot of time and patience from both parties for them to accept our ways, or at least some of them.'

He took a swig of water from a bottle then offered it to Abby who without a second's hesitation took it gratefully.

'We can be a bit pompous.'

'So you've told me.'

'I meant the medical profession in general. Sometimes we seem to forget that penicillin's only been around for a relatively short time yet these people have been living, surviving, thriving in the most hostile of conditions since the beginning of time. The Aboriginal people are arguably the oldest surviving race and it hasn't been by chance. As bizarre as it may seem, their ways really do work.'

Abby looked at him thoughtfully. 'Not that well, Kell,' she pointed out. 'The infant mortality rate is appalling. Take what happened with Shelly yesterday—stuck out here, it wouldn't have taken much for it to have been an entirely different scenario.' She wasn't arguing, just pointing out facts, and it felt good.

So surprisingly good to be sitting with their legs dangling out of the back of a dusty Jeep in the seriously middle of nowhere, sharing a bottle of iced water.

'Which is why it's so good that the two cultures are meeting. Sometimes it's hard to hold your tongue, to not insist that things are done your way. You'll see for yourself what I mean soon enough, but for every time you do, you'll be rewarded tenfold. The fact Vella bought her baby to us, that she's probably going to let her have her immunisations and be monitored, is a huge step forward. OK, I didn't get to do a postnatal check on Vella but she's starting to trust me.'

'She is,' Abby agreed thoughtfully. 'Actually, I can remember reading something about—' She didn't get to finish her sentence as Kell dismissed her words with a swish of his hands.

'Don't do that!' he warned with a grin. 'It's OK with me and Ross, but nothing puts the locals more offside than quoting books at them. And I can see their point. Centuries of culture can't really be summed up in a couple of books, so if you're not sure about something, just ask them. They're only too happy to share if you go about it the right way.'

'Is that a gentle warning?' Abby asked, but Kell didn't answer. 'Are you worried that my acid tongue might wither years of diplomatic relations?'

A smile twitched on the edge of his lips and Abby held her hand out for the drink bottle. 'Well, don't be,' she whispered needlessly, standing up as a few people approached the Jeep, looking at her with wary brown eyes, nudging and giggling each other as Abby forced a nervous smile. 'I'm only mean to my colleagues.

'And, by the way what's Mulla?'

'Evil spirit,' Kell whispered. 'And your best line of defence. Believe me, after three months in this place you'll be glad of that word!'

She should have felt supernumerary, should have felt supremely nervous, watching an efficient Kell effortlessly chat with all the patients, giving needles, pulling off dressings, checking ears and eyes and handing out little tubes and bottles.

But she didn't.

Instead, after a couple of nervous starts Abby found herself joining in. Filling the little yellow child care books in, with her gold-gel penned scrawl, weighing cute babies with the hand sling, checking breasts, prescribing antibiotics, even laughing along with the locals at her appalling attempts at their language.

The sun was hot on her arms and on the back of her legs, her olive skin no match for the scorching heat of the early afternoon sun, and when Kell filled her hat with water then plonked it back on her head, instead of screeching in horror she sighed with relief as the icy rivers of water ran down her neck and back and for five minutes or so Abby remembered what it was like to be cool as she carried on with the work.

'Can I borrow you, Abby?'

Patting a little girl on the head, Abby smiled at her mother and made her way back to the Jeep, where Kell was staring at a nasty-looking wound on a young man's leg.

'This is Mike, the local mujee, or medicine man. He's brought

Jim to see us—reluctantly,' Kell added under his breath. 'Jim didn't want to come. What do you make of this?'

Nodding to Jim, Abby took a closer look at the leg. It was red and swollen and angry-looking, the area around the infection blistering with the tell-tale appearance of cellulitis. 'Is it a bite?'

Kell shook his head. 'He thinks he knocked it on a tree, but never really gave it a thought till it swelled up.'

Abby's mind flicked to the city, to the plan of action she would take there. Order an X-ray, perhaps a small probe in the emergency theatre and some wound swabs, then up to the ward for elevation and IV antibiotics. Kell was obviously thinking along the same lines.

'We could evacuate him.'

'No.' The young man pulled his leg back and with elaborate gestures and a lot of broken English got the message across that his wife was due to have a baby any day now and there was no way he was going in the big plane in the sky.

'You could both go,' Kell suggested gently. 'Lara could have the baby in hospital.'

'No.' Clearly agitated now, he made to go, but Abby put a firm hand on Jim's shoulder.

'Steady, Jim,' Abby said firmly but gently. 'No one's going to make you go anywhere, but I really do need to take a proper look at it.'

Reluctantly he put his leg back down and Abby rummaged through the large metal boxes Kell had dragged onto the floor. 'I thought I saw some magnifying glasses.'

'Here,' Kell pulled them out. 'Do you want an incision pack?'

Abby gave a small nod. It was a tiny procedure, one she did practically every day, but back in Sydney she was in a sterile theatre, and the back of a Jeep didn't even compare, but the thought of Jim heading back into the bush with that nasty infection didn't exactly leave her with a choice.

For a makeshift theatre the Jeep actually sufficed quite well. Hand-washing from a water flask didn't exactly seem sufficient, but with a good rub with alcohol and sterile gloves with about ten times the amount of Betadine she normally would use, Abby felt confident the wound was prepped enough to explore. Gently she administered some local anaesthetic, and even a very stoic Jim let out a murmur of pain despite Abby's best attempts.

'Mulla,' he moaned, holding his thigh and glancing down every now and then.

'No Mulla,' Abby said cheerfully, as the three men present turned to her with slightly startled expressions. 'I think the problem's a bit more simple than that!' Abby's smile was one of satisfaction as her scalpel hit a hard object. The fact there was something embedded in the wound made the prospect of a satisfactory resolution all the more tangible. 'There it is!' she added triumphantly, working a small dark dot out with her forceps until a large jagged-looking thorn was being held up for all to see.

'Steady, mate,' Kell said as a not so stoic Jim lay back on the floor of the Jeep, beads of sweat on his brow. 'The worst is over now.'

'Not quite.' Abby winced on Jim's behalf. 'I just want to get some of the pu—'

'We get the idea,' Kell interrupted with a wink as Abby took the hint and worked on quietly, taking a swab and then irrigating the wound for ages till she was quite sure the job she had done was anything other than makeshift. Quietly pleased with her work, Abby was just about to put a large sterile dressing in place when Mike tapped her on the shoulder.

'Won't be long now,' Abby said in her crisp efficient tone, even flashing a smile as she looked up briefly.

The smile didn't last long.

With something approaching horror she watched as Mike pulled what looked like an old chamois out of his shorts pocket and with hands a world away from Abby's latexed ones smeared a thick oily goo over the painstakingly cleaned wound then nodded for Abby to continue.

She didn't dare look at Kell, didn't dare look at anyone. Instead, Abby gave a small tight nod and, swallowing hard, resisted the urge to pick up her saline swabs and clean the revolting mixture away. Instead, she placed the wad of combine in place and secured it with a large clear waterproof dressing.

'I'd like to give Jim an injection of penicillin, please, Kell.' She looked at his deadpan face but she could see the flash of a smile in his eyes as he solemnly nodded.

'Sure, Doctor.'

'It should be fine now,' Abby said as Kell helped Jim down. 'But if the redness gets worse or if the pain increases...'

'We will come and see Dr Bodey.'

'Or even me,' Abby added pointedly, and even Mike laughed.

'Or you, yes, Doctor, we will come and see you.'

Watching as Jim limped off, Abby heard a gurgle of laughter coming from Kell.

'You were fantastic!' he enthused. 'Absolutely fantastic.'

'I was just doing my job.' Abby shrugged but her pink cheeks told Kell she was pleased. 'Do you think I pushed it too hard at the end when I said he could come and see me?'

'Mike laughed, didn't he? I tell you, Abby, you're in.' For a second he looked at her, only for a second, but enough time for Abby's cheeks to change from a cute pink to a rather unflattering shade of puce. 'I'm sorry about earlier, I should never have tried to lecture you.'

'Hey.' Abby put her hands up. 'I'll take all the advice I can get out here.' Her eyes strayed to the one box that hadn't been opened—the esky—and Kell followed her gaze.

'Ready for lunch.'

'I was about two hours ago,' Abby admitted, licking her lips as Kell pulled the esky down. Taking a rug, Abby fashioned a picnic area and poured two mugs of coffee as Kell played a very good mum, pulling off foil and handing her thick wedges of the best bread Abby had tasted, filled with the thickest slabs of beef and cold fried onions, the home-made chutney adding a delicious tang as Abby chewed in what undoubtedly wasn't the most feminine fashion.

'This is divine,' Abby groaned in pleasure.

'Wait till you taste the vanilla slices.'

'I'm going to go back to Sydney the size of a house at this rate. How often do you do the mobile clinic?'

'Most weekdays,' Kell said, ladling more chutney into one of his rolls and somehow flicking the flies away as he did so. 'This is just one of many. Some take a full morning to get to. Still, at least June packs us a bigger lunch so there are compensations.'

'I'll say. So how on earth did Ross manage?'

'He didn't is the simple answer. There was another doctor, Richard Hoskins, but he'd been trying to retire for the past decade. He only stayed on because he couldn't bear the thought of what would happen otherwise. It's good Ross found us or the clinic would have had to close.'

'What would you have done?'

Kell shrugged. 'There would still have been more than enough work, there are a lot of nurse practitioners in the outback, but having a doctor and a well-stocked clinic just makes it all the more interesting. Shelly's a midwife as well, so we're a level-I centre, which means we can have uncomplicated labours. Now, if we could just persuade an anaesthetist to come on board...'

'Oh, so I'm not good enough?'

'You'll do.' Kell smiled. 'You did really well.'

'I did not,' Abby insisted. 'There was nothing done today that wouldn't have been done without me.'

'That's not true.' Kell shook his head so definitely Abby actually found herself starting to believe him. 'That leg was nasty. I was pretty sure it was just straight cellulitis. I was erring on the side of evacuating him, you've saved a call-out.'

'Hopefully,' Abby said thoughtfully, 'now that the foreign body's out, there's a good chance it will heal nicely.'

'And,' Kell said, the laughter evident in his voice, 'you managed not to scream in horror when Mike put his home brew on your nice irrigated wound.'

'Oh, the scream was there,' Abby said grimly. 'What was that stuff?'

'Billygoat weed, and the most amazing thing of all is it works.'

'I'm sure it does,' Abby said, as Kell gave her a slightly startled look.' I don't have a completely closed mind, you know. In the city they're putting honey on wounds now and it's proving more effective in some cases than the most sophisticated antibiotics and dressings, and only last week the vascular surgeons put leeches on some poor girl's finger after microsurgery, and the most amazing part of all is they've probably saved her from having it amputated. There's a lot to be said for alternative medicine.'

'You're a bit of a dark horse, aren't you, Abby?'

'What's that supposed to mean?' He was looking her in *that* way again, his eyes boring into her, making her blush with the simplest of sentences.

'You come across so brusque, so efficient, so old school, and I don't mind admitting when you stepped off that plane I thought you were about to turn tail and run.'

'I nearly did,' Abby admitted, hiding under the brim of her hat, anything other than meet his eyes.

'And yet here you are now getting down and dirty, mixing with the locals as if you've always been here.'

Abby managed a half-look at him as she bit into her sandwich, but she nearly choked when Kell spoke next.

'What happened, Abby? How come you took up the position when you didn't want to?'

'I told you, if I wanted the consultant's position—'

'That's the formal version,' Kell interrupted. 'Come on, Abby, what's your story?'

Her sandwich was finished so that diversion wasn't open. Reaching for her mug, Abby realised her coffee was down to the dregs. For an age she didn't answer, just stared out at the red dusty view, watching a small wind storm flicking up a few dry leaves and circling them around, little mini-whirlwinds dancing on the plain, and it was only then she turned her troubled eyes back to Kell.

'Why does there have to be another version?'

'Because for all your confidence, for all your brittleness and take-me-or-leave-me attitude, I can't help but think you're a woman with a lot on her mind.'

'You assume one helluva lot,' Abby flared. 'considering we've only just met.'

He didn't say anything, he didn't have to. The truth was, and they both knew it, Kell had in one night got closer to Abby than anyone had in a long time, and the tears she had cried after they had made love hadn't been post-coital bliss, just the sheer overwhelming release of tension.

Her mind flicked back as Abby remembered how he had held her, how good it had felt, how a relative stranger had somehow known how to hold her, what to say.

What not to say.

'Who hurt you, Abby?'

She gave a very short, very false smile, then relented with a shrug. 'No one. I took care of that part all by myself.' When her cryptic words brought no comment Abby carried on talking, her eyes following the dancing leaves, pausing every now and then as the wind dropped, taking the time to regroup, to tell her story as best she could. 'I was going out with another doctor, David. He was junior, one of the residents. When I say going out, it was hardly...' She paused for a moment then cleared her throat. 'We went out for six months. He liked parties, I liked restaurants, he liked pubs, I liked dinner parties.'

'Not the ideal match,' Kell ventured, but Abby shook her head.

'He made me laugh and it felt surprisingly good. I've spent most of my life buried in books, working my way towards being a consultant, it's always been my dream…' Realising she was getting off the track, Abby cleared her throat. 'You know what it's like, there's always some social event you're expected to go to.' She laughed as Kell shook his head. 'Well, there is in the city. Anyway, we went to all the social dos together. I didn't mind when he wandered off with his crowd it was just nice to have someone to go with. Like I say, it wasn't a deep and mean-ingful relationship.' A blush darkened her cheeks. 'You may find this hard to believe after my behaviour last night but we never even slept together.' She waited for a chortle of laughter, a scoff of disbelief, but it never came. It was as if Kell knew how hard this was for Abby, and he just nodded gently. 'Of course, the rest of the hospital thought we were serious, they didn't realise how casual the whole thing was.

'He was in a car crash.'

Despite the intense heat, Abby shivered, visibly paling as Kell watched her. Placing his sandwich down on the rug, he moved across to where she sat alone, putting his arm around her instinctively, knowing there was worse to come.

'Were you on duty?'

'Oh, I was on duty all right and I tried so hard to save him, but I didn't.'

'You couldn't,' Kell suggested, but Abby shook her head and for the third time in their short history he was witness to her tears. Only these weren't tears of elation after a birth or the re-lease of tension after love-making, these were choked, agonis-ing rasps that seemed to convulse her. He sensed her agony, yet he knew she had to go on, knew that in this case out was definitely better than in.

'I didn't,' she sobbed. 'Because I thought I knew him, be-cause I treated him like a friend, not a patient.'

Kell looked at her, his eyes full of questions, and he screwed them closed when Abby spoke again, feeling her pain as he imagined the scene.

'I didn't order a drug tox screen.'

He let her cry for a moment, held her close till the tears abated slightly and she could talk again.

'He had massive head injuries and internal injuries, but I still think that had I known he was on drugs, if I'd only given him Narcan and reversed the opiates, he might have stood a chance, might have lived.'

'What did the coroner say?' Kell's voice was practical, calm and to the point, and Abby took a deep breath.

'That he died from his injuries, that nothing could have been done.' As Kell opened his mouth Abby shook her head. 'I got a rap on the knuckles, I didn't get off completely scot-free. He pointed out the absence of the drug screen, how lucky I was that it ultimately didn't contribute to his death.' Her voice strangled in her throat as she continued. 'Everyone blames me.'

'I'm sure they don't.'

'But they do. I've heard a couple of the nurses talking and you've no idea how many times I walk into a room and the conversation stops, or they suddenly start discussing the appalling hospital coffee.'

'Hospital coffee is appalling,' Kell said. 'I'm sure it's a frequent topic of conversation.'

'I'm not imagining it, Kell.'

'Maybe not, but have you ever considered they're not talking about your part in it? The fact a doctor was on drugs, came into the department and died, well, that's enough to keep most staff rooms going for months.'

'Maybe,' Abby said tentatively. She had never really thought of it like that and she chewed on her bottom lip, barely noticing Kell's arms were still around her. 'Anyway, whether they blame me or not, it's really immaterial. The simple fact is that I blame myself. I should have treated him as just another patient, not assumed that just because I knew him…' Her bottom lip wobbled and a tear slid down her cheek. 'Or thought I knew him.'

'That must be hard as well.'

Abby nodded. 'There are a million questions buzzing in my

head that I'm never going to have the answers to. Why would someone so young, with everything going for them, who knew all the risks...how could he do it to himself, and if he did have problems why couldn't he have spoken to me?'

'Nobody has those sorts of answers, Abby. People mess up their lives for different reasons and, as hard as it is to watch, sometimes there's nothing you can do to help.'

'I don't believe that.' Abby shook her head firmly, wiping angrily at her tears with the back of her hand. 'There's *always* something that can be done. When I get back to Sydney I'm implementing a new system for the addicts that come through the department. At the moment all we do is treat their symptoms and, depending who's on at the time, perhaps make a referral to the drug clinic or hand them a pile of brochures. I want us to have a more structured approach, possibly some trained counsellors on staff. There's a rapid detox clinic within the hospital, so the basics are in place. We just need to utilise the initial contact in Emergency more effectively.'

'Sounds interesting,' Kell said thoughtfully, but Abby hadn't finished yet. 'And I'm trying to arrange a drug awareness course for the staff, not just to alert them what to look for in patients, but in each other—'

'Abby,' Kell broke in, his voice calm and strong, 'it sounds like you're taking a hell of a lot on.'

'Maybe.' Abby shrugged. 'But someone has to do it. Wringing our hands and saying it's just too big isn't going to help.' Her voice softened and Kell had to strain to catch what she was saying. 'I made a promise.'

'To David?'

Her eyes were glistening with a fresh batch of tears as she nodded. 'After he died, I promised him that I wouldn't let his death be in vain.'

'Do you really think you can make a difference?' His questions wasn't derogatory. Instead, there was a note of admiration, of wonder in his voice as Abby gave a determined nod.

'Absolutely.' She gave a wry laugh. 'That is if Reece ever gives me the consultant's position! There's a bit of spadework that needs to be done there. Apparently, since the night David came in, I'm suddenly the queen of investigations.'

Kell's arm tightened a fraction around her shoulders in a friendly sort of squeeze. 'Running too many tests, huh?'

Abby nodded.

'Total body scan for a fractured toe?'

Again she nodded but there was a tiny smile on her lips.

'Full cardiac work-up for a touch of indigestion?'

Her smile was a bit wider now. 'All the time.'

'And I bet every ninety-year-old who clips the kerb with his car gets a full drug screen.'

She managed a laugh but it was laced with tears. 'Every single one. Reece said that I needed to get back to basics, to practise some grass roots medicine without the luxury of a million radiographers and pathologists.'

'Boost your confidence a bit?' Kell ventured.

'Or shatter it altogether.'

'Oh, I don't think so,' Kell said with a sureness that was alien to Abby. 'A breech delivery unaided, a mobile clinic in the middle of nowhere without even one call to the flying doctors—I'd say that's a pretty good start.'

'I can call them?' Abby looked up sharply.

'With the radio in the Jeep.' Kell grinned.

'But I thought that was just for emergencies, or to get in touch with the clinic.'

'Oh, no, nine times out of ten I radio through at least once each clinic to ask advice from one of the doctors. They'll be wondering where I've got to today. I shouldn't have told you that—you'll be on all the time now.'

'No, I won't.' Standing up, she looked at the ants marching purposefully towards Kell's discarded sandwich. 'You're looking at the new, confident Abby Hampton.'

Kell grinned. 'How about I clean up here and we eat the vanilla slices in the back of the Jeep?'

Never had a change of subject been more gratefully received!

Though she'd dug her heels in, though she'd thought she might die without her laptop and an internet connection, that night, when Abby finally set up the computer and took an age to establish a connection, when she finally hit the 'new mail' button, when she tried to describe the past twenty-four hours of her life, the paltry four-line greeting she sent to her family didn't even begin to encompass the roller-coaster of emotion she had set foot on.

Looking out of the massive glass door, the setting sun illuminating the sky a fiery red, silhouetting one single lonely tree in the endless glowing landscape, Abby truly understood the beauty of the vast outback, took solace in the tiny speck she was in the scheme of things and finally managed to look back on the previous night without her heart skittering into shameful palpitations.

CHAPTER SIX

FOR ALL KELL'S promise of wooing her, from the lack of attention he paid her in the ensuing weeks, he had obviously thought better of it!

Not a single flower, chocolate or even so much as a video graced Abby's palm or even merited a mention.

Sure, they worked well together, laughed at each other's jokes and rowed about the patients every now and then and, sure, the air crackled with sexual tension like a balloon rubbed on nylon whenever the two of them were together, but whatever game Kell was playing, a quick chase clearly wasn't on his agenda.

Not even a slow one, come to that.

As the days turned into weeks, a gnawing feeling pitted at Abby's stomach, a sense of time moving on, quickly running out, but curiously coupled with a sense of sheer relief.

What was the point of a romance that couldn't possibly go anywhere?

The outback was in Kell's blood, he'd told her that on their first night.

The city pumped in Abby's veins.

Not that she didn't love Tennengarrah, not that the people weren't wonderful, the work amazing and the scenery literally breathtaking, but it wasn't, neither would it ever be, home.

Maybe Kell was right to hold back, Abby mused late one afternoon while, sitting at her desk exhausted after another mobile clinic, yet reluctant to go home. If one night together could feature so heavily in the jigsaw of her life, imagine three months' worth?

Imagine falling in love, and it would be so easy to do, Abby conceded, only to have to kiss him goodbye.

'Right, I'm done.' Snapping the lid on her gel pen, Abby gave a smile to Kell as she walked past.

'See you, Abby,' Kell called cheerfully, hardly bothering to even look up from what he was doing. And though she knew it was for the best, that there was absolutely no point in pursuing this, she couldn't just leave things there.

'Are you on in the morning?' Abby asked, lingering too long at the door.

'Nope.' Kell smiled. 'I've got four days off now. Not that there's going to be much R and R taking place—there's a pile of jobs waiting for me back home.'

Home.

From the little she knew of him, the house he rented next to hers wasn't Kell's home.

Apparently his real home was a massive sprawling property with a zillion cows and an endless demand on his time.

'Oh, well, enjoy.' Abby smiled though her heart sank. She was officially off at the weekend which meant she wouldn't see Kell till Monday, not that he seemed remotely bothered. 'I'll see you after the weekend, then.'

Kell barely looked up. 'Sure. Catch you later.'

Leaving the clinic, Abby bristled with indignation.

Catch you later.

What was she, one of his blessed cows or something?

The evening stretched on endlessly before her. Checking her emails, Abby listlessly read about parties she hadn't been to, the plays she hadn't seen and the new menus she hadn't sampled.

Heavens, it was hot!

Stripping down to her undies, Abby pulled the ring on a can of beer and rolled her eyes, thinking of the fifty-dollar bottles of wine her colleagues were undoubtedly ordering at this very moment.

'It's Monday, Abby,' she corrected herself. Even her favourite restaurant at Darling Harbour would be quiet.

Even the news was different here—in-depth reports on the drought, the cattle markets, the weather gone into in such detail, when in truth it could have been summed up in one word.

'Hot.'

Or two.

'Stinking hot.'

The T.V. commercials might just as well have been in Japanese, the latest breakthroughs in the eternal problem of female exfoliation barely got a mention when there were worming tablets to be discussed or the latest in water tanks to be sold!

She couldn't even break her diet and ring for a pizza, and sitting in the local watering hole with the locals endlessly talking about Tennengarrah's annual ball preparations wasn't really an option in Abby's current restless mood.

What was the point of a ball when Prince Charming so clearly wasn't interested? When Prince Charming had already fitted the slipper and no doubt moved onto pastures new!

'Hey.'

Prince Charming standing with a rather wilted bunch of flowers and a rapidly melting bar of chocolate was the last thing Abby was expecting. And though her underwear was fabulously expensive and undoubtedly flattering, it wasn't exactly the look she was hoping to achieve when Kell finally deigned to drop by.

'Doesn't anyone knock here?' Abby asked, grabbing a throw and tucking it around herself.

'No.' Kell shrugged, but from the way he couldn't quite meet her eyes Abby was sure he wasn't as cool as he looked.

'What are these for?' she asked rather ungraciously as Kell handed her the flowers.

'You said you liked flowers and chocolates, and there's no movie theatre for a few hundred k's, but I've got a good video lined up.'

She actually laughed. 'Four weeks after the event is stretching it, Kell, even allowing for disconnected phones and a family death.' She looked at his non-comprehending face. 'That's the sort of excuses we women come up with when men don't call. Not that you needed to call, Kell,' Abby rambled on. 'We see each other every day at work.'

'I've been trying to play it cool.'

'Well, you've done an amazing job.'

'I figured that if I laid low long enough, you'd realise what you're missing.'

It had worked!

'Are you doing anything?' Kell pressed. 'Tonight, I mean?'

'Actually, I've got a table booked for eight and there's some clothes I need to pick up from the dry-cleaners before they close, but apart from that...' She looked at his blank face. 'Tell me, Kell, what plans could I possibly have in this backwater?'

Her words were too harsh, too condescending, and Abby regretted them, but Kell turning up like this was the last thing she'd been expecting, and letting him glimpse the effect he was having on her was way too dangerous.

It was easier to play it tough.

'Get dressed,' Kell said, ignoring her sarcasm. 'There's something I want to show you.'

Void of a single witty answer for once, Abby didn't back-chat him.

For once she did as she was told.

Now they'd slept together, now they'd shared a bed, riding on the back of Kell's bike wasn't such a balancing act!

OK, she had no official claim on him, but their rather too distant shared intimacy at least mentally permitted Abby to hold onto Kell's waist as they belted along the dirt roads, the wind whipping the words out of her mouth as she occasionally spoke. With Kell's back now morally accessible to rest her cheek on, Abby finally permitted herself to relax.

Sort of.

The late sun was still hot on her bare thighs, the engine purring between her legs as they tore through the endless distance, the occasional silver windmill glittering by a thirsty dam.

Tennengarrah *was* beautiful, Abby admitted almost reluctantly, for she didn't want to be enamoured of the land. Didn't want to fall in love with its undeniable charms because surely that could only make leaving harder.

She wanted it to be a job, as bland as a concrete building, a line on her résumé, a means to an end.

Not a life-changing experience.

But it entranced her. It had a rugged naked charm not unlike Kell and even that analogy seemed fitting, for the land he was so much a part of was so much a part of him.

But the analogy didn't end there.

She didn't want to love Kell either.

Didn't want to admit that the overwhelming attraction that had propelled them to bed was so much more than skin deep. Didn't want to acknowledge that his smile, his walk, every damn thing about him had her in the palm of his hand.

Love was out of bounds.

Love made you do stupid things, like chuck in eight years of hard work on top of six years of study, made you give up long-held dreams of being an emergency consultant, hold back on a promise you'd made to a friend, made you contemplate a life with a dark-haired charmer and a cattle ball once a year and endless dark-haired, dark-eyed, eternally laid-back children.

She simply mustn't go there.

They rode for ever, up winding rocky paths, over bumpy terrain, the bike allowing them access to places even the Jeep couldn't negotiate. She had no idea where they were going and in truth Abby didn't care. Being with Kell such an unexpected treat, the whys and wherefores could wait a while.

Up they went, the landscape more awe-inspiring by the moment, each blink like the shutter of a camera, revealing a more amazing view, and Abby rued that she hadn't even thought to bring her camera. When they finally stopped Kell switched off the engine, pulling off his helmet and shaking his hair, and Abby did the same.

'We'll have to walk the last bit. Are you up to it?'

His question made her laugh. She wasn't quite that feeble!

'Oh, I think I can manage it.'

But a gentle bush walk wasn't what Kell had in mind.

Pulling a backpack on, he led the way, holding her wrist every now and then as she negotiated a rock, or climbed a none-too-small cliff face until finally she knew they'd reached their journey's end, for nowhere on earth could be more idyllic.

Amidst the dry, unforgiving land she surveyed a true oasis. Two massive billabongs carved into the dark red rock, the water as blue and clear as crystal, beckoning her hot, aching body.

'It's beautiful,' Abby gasped, drinking in the view, her eyes finally resting on Kell who gazed at the scene before him with knowing eyes.

'I know.'

'Does it get busy, I mean with tourists…?'

Kell's eyes found hers. 'I've never seen another soul here.'

'Never?' She ran a nervous tongue over her dry lips.

'Never,' Kell affirmed.

'Any crocodiles?'

'None.'

'You're sure.'

'Positive. Do you reckon we've earned a swim?'

Abby wasted no time with false modestly. To have made a token protest, to have forced a blush or pulled a face would have been pointless. After all, they'd more than seen each other naked and perhaps more to the point, after a long hot dusty bike ride never had water looked more inviting!

As they stripped down, as they ran whooping into the icy water, it wasn't even sexual excitement that made Abby feel suddenly alive, though the sight of Kell naked certainly took care of that. No, it was more the thrill of the child within her, the utter joy of being here, and they duck-dived and swam and splashed and grabbed each other's ankles. Abby found that she wasn't such a bad swimmer after all, nowhere near Kell's standard, of course, but, Abby reasoned, if this was his back-yard pool then he had every reason to practise.

'Come on.' Shivering, her fingers and toes wrinkled, her teeth chattering, Abby dried herself with the small towel Kell offered, then waited as he pulled a rug from his bike box and laid it on the ground.

'I've never brought anyone here before.' Abby was about to laugh, to make some light-hearted comment, but she heard the serious note in Kell's voice and knew it would be out of place.

'No one?' Abby checked.

'No one,' Kell confirmed. 'I've always kept it as my own, somewhere to escape to, somewhere to come and think.' He rolled onto his back, and stared up at the darkening sky.

'What are you thinking now?'

'How nice it is to be here with you...'

Abby lay on her back, smiling into the dusk at the quiet lull of his voice, but her smile faded as Kell carried on talking.

'How I don't want you to go.'

She felt his face jerk towards hers and she lay there rigid, staring unblinkingly at the sky filling with stars. And even though what Kell had said was exactly what Abby had wanted to hear, she wished somehow he could take it back, flick the switch and carry on the game they had been playing, that they were friends, lovers once but really just friends. Not this horrible grown-up version with feelings and beginnings and the inevitable end.

'You've ignored me for the last month.'

'I have not.'

'Oh, you've been lovely to me at work, but—'

'Abby, do you not think I've wanted to see you, not wanted to take you out?'

'Then why didn't you?'

Kell gave a low laugh. 'Because I knew the minute I got you alone I'd be moaning how I don't want you to go, getting heavy, doing all the things I've never done before.'

'Never?'

'Never.'

His honesty scared her, the whole thing scared Abby actually, how one man could have her acting so completely out of character, how one night could have the potential to turn her life around so completely and so irreparably she couldn't even begin to contemplate it. And from the serious look on Kell's face he understood the impossibility of it, too.

'It could never work Kell.' She heard him exhale, saw his eyes close, the tiny shake of his head. 'It couldn't, Kell, and you know that as much as I do. We're just too different.' She let out a low laugh, trying to lighten the suddenly dark, volatile mood. 'Can you imagine me getting excited like Shelly is about the annual Tennengarrah ball? Can you imagine me discussing cattle per hectare and the local craft market with Clara?'

Her voice dropped a shade and she tried to keep the tremor out of it as she continued. 'Can you imagine you in the city, Kell, cooped up in some tiny apartment, catching the train or bus to work when you're used to all this?' He didn't answer and his silence tore through her. 'It could never work,' Abby said more lightly than she felt, the reality of her words delivering an agony she couldn't portray to him.

'I'm not a hick, Abby, I wouldn't be like Crocodile Dundee.'

'I know you wouldn't, but it would be a huge move and the truth is I wouldn't exactly be around to make things run smoothly for you. With this drug programme and everything,

I'm going to be putting in obscene hours.' Realising she was getting nowhere, Abby propped herself on her elbow and dug Kell in the ribs, trying to inject some humour into this awful situation. 'Did you pick up my suit from the cleaners'? We're meeting everyone at the wine bar at seven then on to the theatre, and Reece wants us to meet for eighteen holes of golf on Sunday.'

'Sounds good,' Kell insisted, but Abby shook her head.

'For a holiday perhaps, but you'd end up hating it, Kell, and in turn you'd end up hating me, which I couldn't bear.'

'Don't say that.' He shook his head furiously. 'I could never, ever hate you.'

'Well, maybe hate's too strong a word, but it *would* end up tearing us apart. Tennengarrah's in your blood, Kell, you said it yourself. This is where you belong.'

'But not you?'

Abby shook her head.

'Isn't it worth a try?'

Again she shook her head. 'If it was just about me, Kell, I'd say yes. Even though I've wanted to be an emergency consultant all my life, what's happened between us is so big I actually think I could let it go, give us a genuine try. *That's* how serious I feel about you…'

'But?' Kell's single word was spot on and Abby sat up restlessly. Burying her face in her hands, she massaged her temples as she let out a long, painful sigh.

'All this hot air I've been blowing is starting to take shape.' Looking down, she smiled at his confusion. 'All that tapping away on my computer and firing off emails has finally paid off. My dream's got a name now—EDAP, or Emergency Drug Assessment Programme. Admin's finally come to the party and they're going to allocate funds for one counsellor for a three-month trial. The rapid detox clinic is going to let us have first refusal on a daily bed and I've got more lecturers lined up for the staff than I can count. I can't just walk away now. What sort of message is that going to send?'

'Can't someone else take over?'

She shook her head wearily. 'Oh, Kell, I'm not vain enough to think I'll be the best emergency consultant in the world, that the department's going to collapse if I don't return, but I know for a fact this programme will. Sure, someone might pick up the ball and run with it for a while, but I've called in a lot of favours to get where we are now. If I pull out, how can I blame anyone else for doing the same?'

He didn't say anything and for a while neither did Abby. They just stared into each other's eyes, trying to work out some sort of answer when in truth there wasn't one.

'Anyway...' Abby attempted a grin. 'Given that we've only spent one night together, it might never come to that. Who knows? By the time my contract's up we might be sick of the sight of each other and counting the days until I go!'

Her hollow words didn't even provoke a response, they both knew they were already in way too deep. 'What if you stayed just a bit longer?' The hope in his voice diminished as Abby gently shook her head.

'What would be the point, Kell? The end's still going to be the same. Let's just enjoy what we have for now, huh?'

'A holiday romance, you mean.'

'A working holiday romance,' Abby suggested, with more conviction than she felt.

'I guess it's an improvement on a one-night stand,' Kell said grudgingly as Abby gave a relieved sigh. 'But I don't want us hiding, Abby. I mean it. There's not going to be any pretending we're just colleagues and scuttling around corners like naughty teenagers. We're on or we're off for the next couple of months, not somewhere in between.' He pulled her closer, if that were possible, breathing her in, revelling in her scent, her presence, before he continued. 'That's another reason I've been holding back, Abby. It isn't just the thought of losing you I can't stand, it's the thought of only having half of you.'

'Why do you think I'd want to hide our relationship?'

'Well, you didn't seem exactly thrilled to have slept with a lowly nurse when you woke up on our first morning together.'

'Oh, Kell,' Abby sighed, appalled at his take on things. 'That didn't even come into it. I was mortified at waking up with someone whose surname I didn't even know, someone I'd only met a few hours before. It was never, ever about that.'

'So I'll do?' A cheeky grin played on his lips, crinkling around his eyes, and Abby fell just a little bit deeper as she gazed back at him.

'I guess you'll have to.' Her answer was casual, flip almost, but the utter adoration blazing in her eyes told Kell she was teasing.

'So no hiding, we're riding back into town as a couple.'

'It looks that way.' Still the casual voice remained, but a bubble of excitement welled inside her, the prospect of going public both thrilled and terrified her—that she could spend her nights wrapped in his arms, awake with him in the morning, come home to him at night. Any hope of remaining casual disintegrated as her lips instinctively moved towards his, desperate to confirm the depth of her feelings with a kiss, but Kell hadn't finished talking yet, the soft smile sliding from his lips as his serious eyes held hers for a moment.

'And when your time's up, Abby, what will we do then?'

She didn't want to think about it, didn't want anything to ruin this precious sweet moment, but deep down she knew there was no escaping it, that the inevitable end would hang over them, not just at tender moments like this but every step of their short way, and some sort of answer was needed. 'Look back with love,' Abby ventured as Kell's eyes shuttered closed for a second or two. 'Enjoy our memories.' Abby managed a quick wince. 'That came out like a holiday commercial. Oh, I don't know, how can I say what it's going to be like? Let's not think about it for now, huh? Let's just enjoy the time we've got, Kell.'

The sky was dark now, a deep indigo, yet she could still see his features, the moon a silver-white ball, the stars multiplying every time she looked, like a million jewels winking and blinking, and Abby felt safe beneath nature's canopy as Kell held her close. As he pulled her towards him, the lips she had missed so much sweeter than her vivid memory, the swell of him against her thigh, nudging higher, parting her womanly warmth, so welcome, so wanted, her hands coiling through his damp black locks, her brown legs wrapping around his hips, breasts swollen and full against his solid chest as words faded away and instinct took over.

Their love-making was as unspoilt and natural as the land that cushioned them, primal and vital in the scheme of things yet so much more than a quenching of primitive desires, than the cocktail of hormones that had catapulted them together that first night. And as wondrous as it had been, it paled in comparison to the reverent way he held her now.

As they made blissful love, as Kell caressed her, not just with his hands but with his eyes, his body, his mind, Abby witnessed there and then the sheer and unequivocal privilege of being a woman.

CHAPTER SEVEN

KELL TOOK ABBY home.

To his real home.

A rambling, massive property where Abby met his father, an older version of Kell, with long dark hair greying at the temples, a sun-battered face and a smile that matched his son's. She even forgot to be nervous when Kell held her hand and introduced her to his two brothers, Kane and Rory, whom he clearly adored. And as they all shared a delectable meal Abby bathed in the rosy glow of just being with Kell, learning about him, watching him interact with the family he loved, and the more she glimpsed the more her thirst for knowledge increased, the more she needed to know.

'Can you show me around?' Abby asked as three bikes roared off into the night, a father and two sons, politely choosing tonight to pop down to the local.

No mean feat when it was a half-hour ride!

They drifted outside, following the sound of whinnying horses, hands loosely entwined, and Abby finally worked out why Shelly had laughed at Kell's supposed need for cash. The property reeked of wealth and success and, if it was at all possible, Abby admired Kell more for his nursing work, for caring and sharing his amazing knowledge when he so clearly could live off the land. And though the closest she'd come to a horse had been a donkey ride along Manly beach years previously, despite the fact a horsy person was the last thing Abby would ever be, standing here, the dusty scent of sawdust filling the air, dark faces peering over the fences, excitedly greeting their master, nudging their hands for a treat, for a moment or two Abby almost felt as if she belonged.

'It's beautiful, Kell. Do you use these horses for...?' She gave a helpless look at Kell as she struggled to find the word she was looking for.

'Droving?' Kell replied. 'Not so much these days. A lot of it's done on the bikes now, but for shorter stock routes we still use them. Some of the bigger properties use helicopters.'

'Bigger?' Abby blinked.

'This is nothing compared to some.'

'So do you still go droving?' Abby asked, though really she had no idea what the word even meant.

'Not really. We hire drovers now. The property's doing really well, which inevitably means more paperwork. Kane's still really into it, and Rory heads off more often than not, though he tends to go on ahead and set up camp. Every now and then I get the urge, though, and use up the best part of my annual leave, droving cattle by day and sitting by a campfire at night. Nothing really beats it.'

'I still don't understand what it's for,' Abby said, mystified. 'These stock routes everyone goes on about. What's the purpose of it?'

'To feed the cattle.' Kell patiently explained. 'We move them on to where they can feed. You have to follow the stock routes so they can graze along the way. You should come one time, see it for yourself. Kane often takes tourists out, there's no better way to see the outback.'

She doubted that! An air-conditioned mini-bus sounded a far more comfortable option! Nervously Abby patted one of the more persistent horses, her newfound closeness to nature diminishing rapidly as a pink tongue lolled out, brushing her hand and catapulting Abby back in a fit of nervous giggles. 'I'm not very good at this, am I?'

'You're doing fine,' Kell assured her. 'Though I take it you weren't signed up for the pony club as a child?'

'Afraid not,' Abby admitted. 'I was one of those geeky children who begged her parents to take her to the science museum. Still, it doesn't mean I can't appreciate them.'

'OK, maybe my first suggestion was a bit optimistic, but we really should take a couple of horses out maybe one day this weekend.' He grinned at her startled expression. 'We'd take it gently. I'd really like to show you around the property properly.'

'Maybe,' Abby mumbled. Suddenly thoughts of snakes and spiders were starting to filter in and Kell threw an arm around her as she gave a nervous shiver.

'Come on, you,' he said in that deep, slow voice. 'How about that video I promised?'

'I have to get back,' Abby said reluctantly, as the credits rolled, lingering over a glass of Australian red as Kell lay on the couch beside her, running one lazy hand through her hair. 'I'm on first thing in the morning.'

'Sure.'

She shared his reluctance to leave, felt the coolness on the couch as he stood up. As he pulled on his boots, she glimpsed the domesticity, the sheer luxury of being with him, and shivered at temptation that beckoned.

That with one single word all this could be hers.

A level head was called for, but hard to find, as his bike slid along its dark path, the headlight illuminating fireflies, the night air humming with the wildlife, but this time when they came to Abby's house there were no awkward goodbyes, no nerves at the door, just the delicious feeling of coming home together, the heady excitement as he kissed her, slowly undressed her with his eyes before his hands had even moved, and the slow unhurried pleasure of their love-making.

'Abby, meet me at the clinic!'

The phone had only rung once and in her sleep-fuddled mind Abby struggled to register that it was Shelly speaking on the other end.

'There's been a bus crash. A mini-bus,' she added, and Abby felt momentary relief as the number of potential victims reduced somewhat. 'On the main road into town.'

'How long will it take to get there?' Blinking, she looked at her alarm clock, the numbers flashing three a.m. as Kell jumped up beside her and started to pull on his clothes.

'Half an hour or so. I'm trying to round up Kell—he'll get there more quickly on his bike. Ross is loading up his Jeep and Clara should be just about at the clinic. Jack, the police officer, is going directly to the scene.'

Abby toyed with lying, but only for a second. Lives were at stake and anyway they'd already decided to come out in the open. 'Kell's here,' Abby said, screwing her eyes closed in embarrassment as she held the phone with one hand and pulled on the knickers and shorts Kell was handing her.

'Oh.' The single word said it all, but Abby was saved from saying anything further as Kell grabbed the receiver, enabling Abby to finish getting dressed.

'Ring Ross, tell him to have two emergency back packs waiting. I'll take Abby on the bike with me.'

They roared, literally roared up to the clinic, the adrenaline kicking in, though not enough to completely diminish the cringe factor of Clara's and Ross's open mouths as the new couple so blatantly stepped out.

'How many injuries?'

Ross shook his head, helping Abby on with her massive backpack. 'A truck driver just called through on the radio—at least eight, possibly twelve. The nearest flying doctors are *en route* to Adelaide with a preemie baby so apart from Jack we'll be on our own for a while. I'm going to stay here because the road ambulance is heading out as well so no doubt the victims will start trickling in here soon. Do what you can as first on the scene then get back here. We're going to need everyone on board.'

They fled through the night, the roar of the bike a lonely howl in their mercy dash, and Abby shook with fear, mentally preparing herself for the sight that would greet her, going over and over the basics in her mind. But nothing, *nothing* prepared her for the sight that first greeted them—two massive road trains, their lights blaring and two hulking men flagging them down, their harsh, rough faces choking back tears as they explained that the accident was still a couple of minutes away, their lights a warning to the massive road trains that took this road to slow down, to stop and help...

Because out here a truck driver might be all the help you could get.

The bus was on its side, a gaping, mangled hole displaying the wreck of human life inside, and Abby felt the hot, acid taste of bile in the back of her throat.

Oh, she'd been to numerous accidents, seen more car crashes than she could remember, but she'd arrived *later*, when the firefighters, paramedics and police had secured the area, when her medical brain had been one of many. But nothing on the bike journey had truly prepared her for arriving at this devastating scene an hour after all hell had broken loose...

And being the first medical personnel there.

They bred them tough out here.

Some dad, grandad even, a truck driver, a salt-of-the-earth bloke who should be singing along to the radio or rambling into his CB, was performing CPR on a teenager who should be gossiping, or laughing, or dozing as the mini-bus tore through the endless outback. And Abby knew there and then that the image that greeted her would never ever leave her, would always stay with her as she took in bodies lying strewn on the roadside, moaning, screaming, some sobbing, presumably having dragged themselves out or been pulled out by the truckies who had stopped.

'If they're moaning they're breathing,' Kell called, unstrapping the hard hats from the backpacks and flicking on the torch lights attached to them as he followed some frantic hand signals from Jack and headed for the bus, leaving Abby to make her way over to another truckie still working on the lifeless form beneath him.

As Abby knelt down, hands that should have been shaking were surprisingly steady as she examined the young woman. She held one hand up in the air, the other coming to rest on the truckie's shoulders, feeling the exhaustion, the desperation as he slumped beneath her touch.

'She's dead.'

There was no time for introspection, no time to close the young eyes or offer a prayer, just on to the next one.

On to a life that could maybe be saved.

Kell wasn't waiting for orders.

Kell was in the bus, giving the kiss of life into a young guy a couple of times then securing a collar around his neck.

'Here, mate,' he called to the truck driver who was helping Abby to climb through a gaping, savage tear in the upturned bus. 'We need to get this guy out now! Abby,' he said, his torch flashing through the twisted wreck onto a pale bloodied face, 'I think that one should be next.'

She heard the gurgle, the horrible chilling sound of the death rattle, as Kell's torch flicked away and Abby jerked into response, the ABC ingrained into her coming to the fore. Clambering painfully slowly over the remnants of life and simultaneously trying not to register that fact, she somehow made it to her patient, her outstretched hands lifting the chin that was falling onto its chest. The light on the top of her hard hat shone onto her patient and Abby saw that the face she held in her hands was that of a young woman.

Sweeping the airway with her fingers, the A dealt with, Abby moved on to B. Placing a resuscitation mask over the slack mouth, she blew into it, relief flooding her as she saw her patient's chest move, the lifesaving breath flooding life into the woman she held in her arms.

'Stay still,' Abby ordered firmly, as she started to come to. 'I need you to stay very still,' Abby said more loudly, as the young woman started moaning and thrashing. Abby held the woman's forehead firmly with one hand as she rummaged in her backpack with the other, only able to finally comfort her patient and introduce herself properly when the cervical collar held her patient's neck safely in line. 'I'm Abby, I'm a doctor.'

'Jessica.' The tiny voice was a most welcome sound and she tried not to think how one minute, two at the most, would have rendered this life extinguished.

Despite the darkness, the unfamiliarity of the surroundings, Abby performed a brief examination, the visible injuries in no way accounting for Jessica's pallor, but as she palpated her abdomen and felt Jessica guard against her touch as she let out a moan of pain, Abby knew the damage was internal. Working quickly, she inserted IV access, tearing at the wrappers with her teeth when no other option presented itself. Setting up the IV fluids, she opened them full bore.

'We're going to get you out just as soon as we can, Jessica,' Abby said comfortingly. 'More help's on the way, but I can't move you by myself.' She deliberately didn't mention the weight of metal pinning the young girl to her seat, the jagged precarious journey Jessica would face to escape from these hostile surroundings. As she heard a whimper behind her, however reluctantly, however much she didn't want to leave this sick, frightened young girl, Abby knew she had to move along to the next unlucky victim.

'If they're moaning they're breathing.' Kell's words rang in her ears as Abby's eyes surveyed the mini-bus, her eyes fixing on a young man who stared back at her with agonised, terrified eyes, and though he was moaning Abby knew he needed help and fast! 'We'll get you out very soon,' Abby said assuredly, as she looked over her patient, words of comfort and reassurance spilling from her lips as she assessed her patient, but her heart sank as her eyes moved downwards, knowing with one awful glance that no amount of modern medicine was going to save this young man's leg. Slipping a tourniquet around his dirty, bloodied wrist and setting up IV access in the back of his hand, she gave a generous dose of pethidine along with the IV fluids which she hung on a gnarled twist of metal above them, only vaguely registering that Kell was back working with her now, which gave Abby some hope that the worse was over.

'What have we got?' Abby asked.

It was the first chance to take stock, the first attempt to formalise a plan of attack, yet still there wasn't the luxury of a calm conversation. It took place as Abby did her best to stabilise the young man's leg while Kell and a truckie struggled to move the weight of steel which trapped him.

'One serious head injury. He's in a bad way, Abby, he needs to be intubated. Clara's just arrived and she's going to do that.'

'What else?'

'Mainly leg and chest wounds. How's the young girl?' He gestured over to Jessica who was ominously quiet now.

'Not good. I want to get back over there.'

'Go.' Kell nodded. 'We're nearly free here.'

Oh, she didn't want to leave this patient, she wanted to stay, to help, to comfort, but three pairs of hands on one body was a luxury they simply couldn't afford here. 'It won't be long now,' Abby said to the young man, before she turned to leave. 'And I'll see you outside very soon.'

Through the twisted wreck Abby crawled, her backpack catching every which way, the extra torch she held in her teeth flashing images too painful to contemplate as she inched her way over, her only comfort the sound of the young man being lifted out of the wreck of the bus.

'Jessica.' Abby pulled an eyelid open, blasted the torch into the girl's eyes. 'Jessica!' she said more urgently, feeling for a pulse as mercifully Jessica's eyes flicked open.

'Get me out of here,' Jessica begged.

'We will, just as soon as we can. There's a lot of wreckage pinning you.'

'I'm going to die.' Jessica was crying quietly now and none of the comforting words Abby attempted worked now as she pushed some refrigerated blood through the IV line, the precious resource desperately needed here.

'This was supposed to be a holiday...' Jessica moaned, her weak voice still managing to portray her mounting hysteria, depleting what little energy she had. 'This isn't what it was supposed to be like...'

'What do you need?' Kell was beside her now but Abby didn't even turn to register him.

'I need to get her out,' she said urgently.

More help had obviously arrived and a portable oxygen cylinder was passed through to them and Abby gratefully placed a mask over Jessica's deathly pale lips.

'I don't want to die here.' Jessica's terrified eyes caught Abby's.

'Jessica.' Abby's voice was sharp now, a mental slap to her patient's pale cheek. 'Listen to me. You are *not* going to die because guess what? I'm not going to let you. Got it?' Her eyes held Jessica's, who mercifully seemed to be calming, but the whiteness of her tongue had a chill running down Abby's spine. 'Get another IV line into her,' Abby ordered, 'and push through some more blood.' But before the words were even out, Abby changed her mind. 'No, I'll do that. Kell, go and get some more hands here. I want her out!'

'It's daytime in England,' Jessica sighed, drifting in and out of consciousness.

'I thought I heard an English accent.' Abby smiled. 'Are you here on holiday?'

'I'm taking a year...' Her voice trailed off and this time no amount of calling her name seemed to reach her and Abby knew time was running out fast. Shouting for help, her bare hands pulling at the seat pinning her patient, Abby struggled to free her, to get her out of this hell hole, to keep the promise she had made...

'The flying doctors are about to land,' Kell shouted through the darkness. 'We're setting up flares along the main road, we can get the head injury evacuated...'

'Jessica's going off,' Abby shouted. 'Get Jack and as many pairs of hands as you can so we get her out, and *then* we'll decide who's going first on the plane!'

Whoever Kell got, they were strong, but even with the three of them it took a superhuman effort to force the seat forward to somehow slide Jessica's body through an impossibly small gap. And as was so often the case, as she slipped out from her tomb Jessica's condition deteriorated rapidly.

'What have we got?' Abby almost wept with relief as a concerned face greeted her, the golden wings pinned to the man's very white shirt the most reassuring sight she had ever seen. 'I'm Hall Jells, the senior medical officer. I think we may have spoken on the radio.'

'Abby Hampton,' Abby said breathlessly. 'Emergency Registrar. Her name's Jessica, that's all I've got. Severe abdominal injures, she's just lost consciousness. She's had two units of blood and a litre of Hartmann's solution, but her blood pressure's still dangerously low. She desperately needs Theatre. I've also done a brief assessment on a young male with a serious head injury—'

'I can only take one,' Hal broke in.

'Take Jessica,' Abby said, painfully aware of Kell's frown as he came over and caught the last of the conversation. 'Hospital's her only hope.'

They liaised for a few moments as they loaded her onto the plane, but as she went to run off Abby turned momentarily.

'She's from England.' Such a paltry summing-up of a young woman, but it was all Abby knew, a tiny personal touch, and as Hall gave her a knowing nod she knew he understood.

'We'll do all we can.'

CHAPTER EIGHT

AT SOME POINT, night became day, but no one really noticed.

The clinic resembled a war zone, young people fighting for their lives, their limbs, as all around fought with them.

Ross and Abby, guided by the knowing voices over the two-way radio, performed a lifesaving burr-hole on the young man Kell had wanted to evacuate first, relieving the growing blood clot pressing against his brain and giving him a chance at life.

Shelly, who should have been nursing her daughter, snapped into nurse mode and worked alongside Kell and Clara as if she hadn't missed a day, as friends—who anywhere else in the world would be mere neighbours—tended Matthew and Kate.

The whole town pulled together on this black Tennengarrah day. Cups of tea and welcome glasses of water appeared like magic as endless limbs were secured with temporary plaster of Paris back slabs and wounds cleaned and stitched, chest drains inserted and, more poignantly, tears wiped. The flying doctors swooped down intermittently, relieving them of one or two patients, until finally all that was left was a floor awash with bandages, swabs and blood. The exhausted crew, who had been awoken in the middle of the night, had not even paused for breath since.

'Nice work, guys.' Ross stood in the middle, his arm around his exhausted wife. 'You've all done the clinic proud.'

'Have we heard anything from Adelaide?' Abby asked, taking a long cool drink straight from the tap.

'Hall rang earlier.' Kell's voice made her still and she paused over the tap, dreading what was coming next. 'Jessica had a lacerated liver and a ruptured spleen, along with a perforated bowel. She's in Intensive Care.'

'But she made it out of Theatre.' Hope sparked in her voice and Abby quickly fought to quell it, knowing there was a long, long way to go.

'She made it out of Theatre.' Kell nodded with quiet satisfaction. 'Good call, Abby. I'd have sent the head injury.'

'That would have been a good call, too,' Abby said generously. 'Heaven knows, they both needed help.'

'Well, I for one wouldn't have fancied performing abdominal surgery here. Give me a burr-hole any day of the week.' Ross half laughed.

'If you're so good with a drill,' Shelly jibed, 'how come my shelves are still lying in their boxes on the hall floor?'

'Kell said he'd do them.' Ross gave his wife a playful squeeze around the waist. 'Hey, Abby, are you sure that you don't want to stay a bit longer? Say, a few years?'

There were a few laughs a few 'hear, hear's' but as Abby met Kell's eyes she could see the pain behind his smile, the nonchalance in his actions for once not coming naturally.

'And I thought I was here for a bit of a holiday.' Abby attempted a joke. 'Well, are we going to get this place cleaned up so I can have a long overdue shower?'

'No one's cleaning a thing,' June, who Abby now knew to be the legendary hairdresser's aunt and clinic sandwich maker, said the words with such determination not even Abby would have attempted to argue. 'I'll pull on some gloves and get started, and when you're all rested you can come and finish off. You can't even use the excuse that you've got to restock as you've used all the supplies.'

'Come on.' Kell slung a casual arm around Abby's shoulders. 'I don't know about you, but I'm exhausted.'

Abby's eyes flicked around the room, waiting for a few winks or jeers, but she realised they were all too exhausted to even bother with the latest romance blossoming in Tennengarrah. As tragic as the night's events had been, they'd at least dimmed the spotlight on Abby and Kell.

Almost.

Shelly caught up as Abby wearily signed off the drug book.

'Don't think you're getting off that easily,' Shelly whispered, an impish grin on her usually innocent face. 'I want *all* the details.'

'You bring the wine.' Abby smiled, grateful for the chance of some feminine insight.

'Deal.'

'What are you and Shelly cooking up?' Kell asked as Abby wearily climbed on the back of his bike.

'Girl talk.' Abby shrugged, then smiled as Kell turned around and gave her a quizzical look. 'Whatever that is! I've never really been one for sitting cross-legged on a bed and engaging in a heart-to-heart.'

'Then you don't know what you've been missing!'

'Oh, and you'd know, would you?' Abby grinned, poking a pink tongue out between her lips. 'Being a midwife and everything.'

'So I'm in touch with my feminine side,' Kell said as Abby slapped his back. 'It makes for one helluva lover.'

CHAPTER NINE

FOR A FEW days at least, Tennengarrah was the talk of Australia. Or at least it felt that way.

Every news bulletin was filled with images of distraught relatives in England, Germany, Sweden, shell-shocked and stunned as they boarded jumbos, weeping into the cameras, begging their loved ones to hold on till they got there.

Overdressed reporters, who reminded Abby of herself on her first day in Tennengarrah, talked earnestly into the cameras, trying to ignore the flies that buzzed around their heads and landed unceremoniously on their faces as they spoke of the remoteness, the difficult access, the sheer devastation that had struck these unlucky tourists.

But even with the benefit of a script and hundreds of thousands of dollars' worth of equipment, not one of the reporters managed to truly convey the sheer majesty, the grandeur of a land virtually untouched by human hand. Not one of the news bulletins managed to match the image indelibly etched on Abby's mind, the sight she had witnessed as she'd first neared the scene. Not one of them truly portrayed the antithetical sight of the mini-bus, as out of place in this setting as a plastic bag on a deserted beach, the horror of the tourists scattered like dolls on the roadside, the harrowing sight of the makeshift mortuary, or the impressive, anxiously awaited sight of the flying doctors landing their plane on the dirt road, treating the injured and ferrying the wounded.

Restoring order to chaos.

Even the clinic had its share of news coverage. And the lump in Abby's throat, which felt strangely like pride, welled as she replayed her video tape. Minutes of coverage turned into a couple of hours, a legacy of leaping for the remote and pressing the record button every time the news came on.

There was Ross—blond, stunning, articulate, praising his staff.

There was Shelly, pale from combining breastfeeding with a diet, but managing to look like she'd never left nursing for even a second as she bagged an unconscious patient with one hand and spoke into the telephone with the other.

Clara was there, of course, eternally laid-back, completely unruffled—a true outback nurse by anyone's standards.

She cringed as she saw herself, startled by her golden tan, her face void of make-up, tousled dark hair tossed into the scruffiest of ponytails, a far cry from the sleek city girl she was so familiar with, ruing the fact she even cared that her bottom looked massive in her khaki shorts, when beside her Jessica lay a breath away from death's door.

And, of course, there was Kell.

Abby deserved a callus on her index finger for the amount of times she hit the pause button, freezing his image, pausing him in mid-sentence.

And whatever way she looked, he was beautiful.

'Knock, knock,' Shelly called out as she pushed open Abby's front door—about as formal as an entry got in Tennengarrah. Having learned her lesson on more than one occasion, Abby had stopped wandering around her home dressed only in her underwear. Cotton shorts and a crop top—topped with the Akubra Kell had given her—was a far better look than a blushing, eternally embarrassed doctor!

'I was just coming over to see you.' Abby smiled, simultaneously flicking off the video and pretending to be engrossed in a soap. 'Where's Kate?'

'Asleep, and Matthew's having an afternoon doze so I've left them with June for half an hour.'

'You haven't forgotten it's your six-week postnatal check today, have you?'

'No such luck.' Shelly pulled a face and picked up the magazine Abby had discarded on the coffee-table. 'I don't suppose we could lie and pretend I've had it?' she asked hopefully.

'Not a chance. Do you want to head over to the clinic? Or I could do it here.'

'You don't mind? I know Kell's seen more of me than I can even bear to think about, but smiling at him as I head for the treatment room is something I could do without. A girl's got some pride. It's such bliss having a female doctor here.'

'Come on.' Abby stood up. 'Let's get it over with then I can make a coffee or we can have some iced tea I've made.'

'Now you're talking.'

Abby's bedroom had to suffice, and though she was professional, Abby still reeled at the informality of the outback. Postnatal checks with the neighbours while you spoke about the latest lipstick shades were an entirely new ball game.

'All back to normal.' Abby finished, labelling Shelly's pap smear and sorting out her vast doctor's bag which had tripled in size since she'd first arrived in Tennengarrah.

'Not quite,' Shelly sighed. 'I'm still several kilos heavier than nature intended. I'm restarting my diet tomorrow—it's only four weeks till the ball.'

Hardly a ball, Abby thought but didn't say. A massive barn draped in fairy lights more than likely, but it was all everyone in Tennengarrah seemed to be speaking about these days.

'What will you be wearing?'

Abby shrugged. She hadn't given it a second's thought, well, maybe a second. Apparently the men would all be in formal wear and the thought of glimpsing Kell in a suit did strange things to Abby's equilibrium.

'I bought one nice dress with me—I guess it will have to be that.'

'Show me.'

Popping the sample in a plastic bag, Abby went and washed her hands before returning. 'I'll drop this over to the clinic later, it will go on the run to Adelaide tomorrow.'

'If only Bruce knew what was in that little esky he carries.' Shelly giggled and Abby laughed along with her.

They got on really well.

Shelly still burned with shame when she remembered their meeting, insisting she wasn't obsessed with the washing, and Abby burned for other reasons when she recalled that fateful night. Girly chats weren't something Abby was particularly used to, but Shelly was so insistent and so disarmingly nice, Abby's uptight exterior whittled away to zero when she was around. For the first time in her life Abby had a woman friend, someone she could moan to, someone she could gossip with for hours about absolutely nothing, someone to bemoan PMT and cellulite with.

And she loved it.

'Come on,' Shelly nagged. 'Your dress.'

Pulling a white dress out of her wardrobe, she watched Shelly's face for her reaction.

'I love it.' Shelly bounded over, running her hand along the sheer organza. 'Just look at those ruffles around the bust and those tiny straps.'

'Hopefully they'll survive the night,' Abby said, ever practical, but though her next question sounded casual she held her breath as she awaited the answer. 'Do you think it will be all right, for the ball, I mean?'

'You'll be the most glamorous one there. Kell won't be able to keep his hands off you,' Shelly enthused. 'Ooh, look.' Shelly ran an appreciative eye over Abby's dressing-table. 'Gosh, I miss the city sometimes. A quarterly trip into town isn't any-where near as fun as hitting the shops every weekend, and by the time I've made sure we're stocked up for the next century there isn't exactly time to go make-up shopping.'

'Here.' Pulling open her drawer, Abby tossed a make-up bag to Shelly which she pounced on like an eager puppy. 'It's one of those freebies you get if you spend enough on a bottle of foun-dation or whatever. I haven't even opened it.'

'You haven't opened it?' Shelly asked, aghast, tearing at the zip like a child on Christmas morning, pouring the countless mini-lipsticks and nail varnishes onto the bed and examining each one with relish. 'And you don't mind?'

'Enjoy.' Abby grinned. 'Six weeks from now I'll be swan-ning round a department store, ordering facials and massages and getting my nails done. It's the least I can do.'

'Don't,' Shelly grumbled. 'I don't even want to think about you leaving. Why don't you stay a bit longer? Six months at least.' Following Abby out to the kitchen, she perched on the bench as Abby poured two long glasses of iced tea.

'But there's a new doctor coming to take my place.'

'There could be two new doctors starting and we'd still be short,' Shelly pointed out. 'The clinic's really taking off now. Please, think about it, Abby.'

'I can't.' Abby picked up one of the glasses and handed it to Shelly. 'I've got a job, a life back in the city.'

'But it will still be there if you stay a few more months, and you must admit you're enjoying yourself.'

'I am,' Abby admitted without even having to think about the answer.

'And if I remember rightly, there's not too many men like Kell floating around...'

'Shelly.' Abby's voice had a warning note to it. They spoke about Kell now and then—he wasn't off limits exactly, but the

inevitable end to the blossoming romance most certainly was.
'Leave it, OK?'

'I can't,' Shelly sighed. 'You clearly adore each other. How
can you bear to leave him?'

Fiddling with a lipstick, Abby rouged her lips, determined
not to pursue this painful subject, but the chance to talk about it,
to glean some fellow feminine insight was simply too tempting,
and she gave up on her lips with a low moan. 'Was it hard—for
you, I mean?' Abby asked, turning from the mirror, her troubled eyes meeting Shelly's. 'Did you just say yes straight away
when Ross asked you to come here with him?'

Shelly nodded. 'I didn't even have to think about it.'

'Well, there's your answer,' Abby said cryptically, as Shelly
frowned. 'Maybe Kell and I aren't as serious as you and Ross.
I mean, the fact you didn't even have to think about it surely
means—'

'It doesn't mean a thing.' Shelly said with certainty. 'Look,
Abby, you and I are different. You've got a career.'

'So do you.'

'Not like yours.' Shelly gave a small laugh. 'You're about
to become an emergency consultant, for heaven's sake, and
you've got that blessed drug programme you're always going
on about. I was a reluctant nurse who'd already thrown in her
job to concentrate on Matthew. I wasn't giving up a glamorous
job I was completely dedicated to. All I had to give up was a
whole heap of angst.'

'It's hardly glamorous,' Abby said. 'You should see the department on a Saturday night.' Her smile faded from her face as
she carried on talking. 'I just can't do it, Shelly,' Abby said quietly. 'Kell knows where I stand. I've been straight with him from
the beginning and he's been straight with me. We both know
this relationship isn't going anywhere, so we've just agreed to
enjoy what time we've got together.'

She'd said it so many times Abby almost made it sound convincing, but how many nights had she lain in Kell's arms star-

ing out of her window, counting the endless stars in a bid to beckon sleep and wish that she'd signed for twelve months, six even? But to change her contract now, to extend her stay, would only raise false hope.

For everyone.

Oh, she loved Tennengarrah. It wasn't even a reluctant admission now. Kell had taught her to ride, endless days spent ambling around the bush, picnics by billabongs, listening to the horses whinney as they lay and cooled off in the red dirt, or drank from the water's edge, lying in Kell's arms and trying to hold onto a slice of heaven, trying to pretend it could be for ever.

'I'd best get this over to the clinic.' Putting down her empty glass, Abby effectively ended the conversation, and Shelly gave her a half-smile, concern etched on every feature.

'I'm here, Abby, if you ever need to talk.'

Abby did need to talk, she knew that much. But to whom? Shelly and Kell were hardly objective and her family, when she'd broached the difficult subject on the telephone, had practically choked with laughter at the vaguest prospect of Abby staying in Tennengarrah.

'Thanks,' Abby said lightly, but both women knew it wasn't going to happen. When make-your-mind-up time came, Abby knew she was on her own.

Though obviously thrilled to see her, Kell frowned a bit when she came in. 'Can't you stay away from the place? I thought you were off this afternoon?'

'I'm just dropping a sample off.' Abby shrugged. 'How has it been?'

'Quiet as a mouse. Clara's out on a home visit, then she's going to head straight home and Ross is going out on a mobile clinic. Poor guy. It's a big one today and it will take for ever in this heat.'

'What about you?'

'I'll just twiddle my thumbs here, I guess, in case someone does come by.'

The clinic was supposed to be open till four and though they often worked way past that, sometimes even with inpatients, there was still a measure of guilt in shutting up early, just in case someone was banking on them being open.

'You go with Ross,' Abby offered. 'I can watch things here.'

'You're sure?'

'Of course I'm sure. Anyway, I've got a pile of notes I should have written up ages ago.'

Ross and Kell didn't take much persuading. In ten minutes flat they were out of the door and Abby made herself a coffee, sitting in the air-conditioned comfort of the clinic with her feet up on a stool, actually quite appreciative of a chance to tackle some paperwork.

The silence didn't last long.

'Hi, Abby.' A nervous Martha rapped at the door, then walked in. 'Anyone else about?'

'Sorry.' Abby smiled, putting down her pen. 'Ross is out with Kell, and Clara's gone home early. There's only me here.'

'You're the one I want to see.' Martha perched nervously on the edge of the seat Abby gestured to.

'Trouble with your dad?' Abby asked gently.

'No more than usual. He still refuses to have the operation, still says that he doesn't see the point. Ross came to the house and spoke with him yesterday but Dad's still adamant he doesn't want any surgery and he doesn't want to be resuscitated if anything happens.'

'I heard.' The silence around them lingered for a moment or two as each woman dealt with her own feelings—Martha wondering how she'd cope without her father and Abby wondering how, as a doctor, she could stand by and watch a relatively young man die.

'Anyway, it's me I'm here for.' The words surprised Abby. Though slowly she was being accepted by the locals, a patient actually volunteering to see Abby was a rarity to say the least. 'I know Ross wouldn't say anything, or Kell or Clara, but, well, they're friends, not that you're not nice and everything…' Martha blushed but Abby just laughed away the young woman's awkwardness.

'A bit of distance works wonders sometimes. I know exactly how you feel, Martha. I got the worst case of sunstroke during my first fortnight here and, believe me, coming to on a trolley with Ross and Kell checking me over was just a touch too close to home. Sometimes it's nice just to be a doctor and a patient.'

The ground rules worked out, Martha took a deep breath.

'I'm pregnant.'

Abby didn't say anything, just listened and watched Martha's body language. She was a doctor here, not a friend who leapt around the table and offered congratulations.

'Or at least I think I am. I'm two months late.'

'Have you done a test?' Abby asked, then apologised straight away. 'Silly question. You're not exactly inundated with pharmacies here, are you?'

'That's what got me in trouble in the first place. They sell condoms in the store, but Darlene works there, and Shirley. He could have got some from the pub, but his dad was there.' Her voice was angry and Abby could feel her frustration at living in such a closed community. 'Nothing's private here, but I know that's no excuse for being so careless. I guess you think I'm stupid.'

Abby didn't think that for a second.

Who was she to judge?

After all, Kell's skimpy denim shorts hadn't exactly had room for a tiny foil package and Abby herself hadn't come to Tennengarrah equipped for a night of spontaneous safe sex.

Her period had been anxiously awaited and for once gratefully received!

'My dad's going to kill me, if the shock doesn't kill him

first.' The tears came then and Abby sat quietly, opening a box of tissues and letting Martha cry for a while before she spoke.

'Why don't we do a test first, make sure of the facts before we work out what you're going to do?'

Martha gave a watery nod, and took the specimen jar Abby gave her. Abby set about trying to find the pregnancy testing kits, which proved a bit harder than it first appeared. None of the cupboards or drawers held anything and she was half-tempted to give Shelly a quick buzz, but, bearing in mind Martha would be back any second, she didn't want to upset her patient further. Martha might think Abby was broadcasting the news.

She found the tests eventually—locked in the drug cupboard, of course!

Where else would they be?

'It's positive, isn't it?' Martha's fearful voice broke the tense silence.

Oh, it was positive all right. The blotting paper had barely been dipped before a dark pink cross had appeared!

'It is,' Abby said, peeling off another wad of tissues as the inevitable tears came again. 'But it's not the end of the world.'

'Oh, it is, Abby, it really is. What am I going to do?' Martha wailed. 'What am I going to do?'

'Cope.' The one word stopped the tears in their tracks and Martha looked up sharply.

'You'll cope Martha, because if there's one thing I've learnt in my time here it's that they breed them tough in the out-back. The women here can cope with anything that's thrown at them—snakes, bites, droughts, even pink crosses on pieces of blotting paper. Now, first up I'm going to examine you, check that your dates correspond with your size…'

'And then…'

'We'll do nothing.'

'Nothing?' Martha looked up, aghast.

'We'll let the news sink in for a couple of days. At this stage a few days either way isn't going to make much difference. But

I have to tell you, Martha, that at this stage of pregnancy a couple of days is really all I can—'

'I don't want an abortion.' Martha's voice was the steadiest it had been since she had arrived at the clinic, and Abby gave a small nod.

'Then you won't have one. But when you've calmed down we'll have a long chat and work out exactly what it is that you do want.'

'I want to have the baby, Des does, too.'

'Des is the father,' Abby checked needlessly, the glow in Martha's teary eyes an obvious indicator. 'And you've both discussed it?'

'It's all we've spoken about for the last few weeks. It's just how we're going to tell Dad that's sending us into a spin. Des is a farmhand. Dad even likes him, which is saying something! But it's going to kill him when he finds out. And I'm serious. Dad could have a heart attack when he hears the news. I'm only eighteen, and if Dad dies, how will I manage? How are we going to cope with the farm without Dad? I need him, Abby, especially now, even though I don't want him to know…'

'Martha.' Abby's voice was sharp, but her eyes were still gentle. Bill's reaction to the happy event had flicked through Abby's mind and Martha had a valid point—given the shape Bill's heart was in, a defibrillator on hand when they broke the news might just come in useful!

'I'll come with you,' Abby said immediately, and Martha let out a sigh of sheer relief. 'I'll even tell your father for you if that will help, but all that is a while away. For now all I want you to do is calm down and for you and Des to get used to the idea that you definitely *are* pregnant, then I want you to come and see me and we'll go through everything from antenatal care to how to tell your father.'

And with that Martha had to make do. As good a doctor as Abby was, there was no magic wand she could wave, no handkerchief to pull out of the hat or puff of smoke that would make the endless problem, faced by women the world over, disappear.

By the time Abby had examined Martha, a cuppa or two shared and the best part of a box of tissues used up, Martha was finally ready to face the world and go home. Abby at last had a chance to tackle her notes, though her mind wasn't really on the job, and she happily put down her pen again as Kell and Ross stomped through the clinic, downing a jug of iced water before they even graced her with a greeting.

'Sorry about that.' Kell grinned, managing to look hot and bothered and sexy all at the same time as he refilled the jug from the tap then banged ice cubes from the tray into it. 'It's boiling out there.'

Kell made way as Ross splashed his face with cold water then went the whole hog and put his blond mop of hair under the jet. 'He's right,' Ross moaned, filling yet another glass. 'I'd better head off and see how Shelly's coping. I gave Kate her immunisations today, and it's hardly the best weather for a febrile baby. I bet the air-conditioner's struggling to keep up. Any problems while we were out?'

'None.' Abby smiled.

'Any patients?' Ross checked.

'None,' Abby lied, deliberately omitting Martha's visit. 'Just me and my notes.'

'Well, why don't you head off?' Ross suggested. 'Kell can lock up, and if anyone comes they can buzz me at the house. And, by the way, thanks for this afternoon—it made a helluva difference, having Kell there.'

Now *that* Abby didn't need to be told!

Ross was out of the clinic in double time, anxious to get back to his beloved Shelly, and Abby fiddled hopelessly with her notes, all too aware that she and Kell were alone.

'Go,' he said, as he picked up files and pushed trolleys against the walls. 'I'll just make sure everything's set up for the morn-

ing, or if Ross needs to open up during the night. You can start
the shower running!'

His lazy smile had her stomach in knots, and if it hadn't
been over forty degrees outside Abby would have run all the
way home!

CHAPTER TEN

ABBY NEEDN'T HAVE rushed.

In fact, by the time she had showered—slowly—dressed—
slowly—and stretched out on the sofa, Kell still hadn't arrived.
She didn't meant to fall asleep but only when she heard someone
banging around in the kitchen did she open her eyes to the delicious sight of Kell, with a welcome glass of water in one hand.

'What time is it?' Abby asked as the ball of his thumb
brushed a piece of sleep out of the corner of her eye.

'Seven.'

'Seven!' Sitting bolt upright, Abby looked around the darkening room.

'Why on earth didn't you wake me?'

'You looked tired,' Kell said easily. 'I thought I'd let you
sleep. I've fixed dinner.'

Indeed he had.

A tray laden with huge slices of smoked salmon salad was
carried through, followed by crusty damper and a massive jug
of lemonade. 'Looks delicious,' Abby murmured, licking her
lips appreciatively. 'You spoil me, you know.'

'You deserve it.'

They ate, but for once the silence between them wasn't like

the silence of so many carefree, lazy evenings they'd spent together. She could feel Kell's eyes on her, almost taste the tension as he refilled her jug and every now and then opened his mouth to speak.

'What is it, Kell?' Abby asked finally, when she'd chased the last caper around her plate with her bread and drained the last of the lemonade from her glass.

'What?'

'Something's wrong,' Abby said bravely, more bravely than she felt. Her departure was only a few short weeks away now and serious, in-depth discussions were proving far too painful.

'Nothing's wrong, Abby. In fact, everything's perfect—too perfect, I guess.'

Here it came. Levering herself up, Abby moved from the floor to the sofa, but there was no solace from his gaze there so she rose and padded over to the window, watching the one dark tree on her horizon, the fire of the sunset revving up for its nightly show. She'd seen it, heard it all before and simply couldn't go through it all again.

'Is it so impossible to envision us being together?' Kell asked as Abby let out a slow long sigh. 'I know I'm probably not what you expected in a partner, I know I'm not exactly highbrow, but, Abby…'

She turned, her eyes wide, appalled at what she was hearing, appalled that Kell could even consider the problem was him. 'It's not you, Kell. Hell, you've accused me of being a snob before but surely you don't really think that I'm that shallow?'

'Of course not,' He stood up, walking over to the window to join her, but for once there was nothing confident in his walk, and the hands he laid on her shoulders were loaded with uncertainty.

'Kell, we've spoken about this,' Abby said wearily. 'You know I hate the thought of leaving just as much as you do, but we agreed to just leave it, to just enjoy our time together.'

'That was before.' His black, unreadable eyes met hers then and she felt his hands tighten on her shoulders.

'Before what?'

'Why didn't you tell me, Abby?' Kell rasped. 'You know we can work things out.'

He'd lost her now. Abby stared at him with confused eyes, the conversation truly leaving her behind now, her bewilderment only deepening as Kell took a deep breath and carried on talking. 'I found the test.'

'What test?'

'The pregnancy test. I wasn't snooping or anything like that, but when I was clearing up I saw it as I emptied the bin.'

'It wasn't mine...'

'Well, it wasn't mine or Ross's! Oh, come on, Abby, you said there had been no patients. Look...' His voice trailed off as she started to laugh.

'So this is what the evening doze was in aid of, and making my supper? You thought I was pregnant! Oh, Kell...'

But Kell didn't join in with her laughter, his hurt, confused eyes meeting hers as he checked and checked again that Abby really wasn't pregnant. 'You're sure you're not hiding anything from me?'

'Of course I'm not, so you don't have to worry. Nothing's changed.'

A look she couldn't read flashed over his face—relief, disappointment, she truly didn't know—but as she stood there Abby knew how hollow her words were. She could scream from the rafters that nothing had changed but for an hour or two Kell had glimpsed the possibility of a future, a future that could never be, and losing it was only going to hurt.

She forced a giggle, a bright smile. 'Nothing's changed,' Abby insisted, and as the ringing phone shrilled it was a laughing Abby that picked it up.

She wasn't smiling as she put it down.

'Bill's on his way in—he sounds bad.'

They ran over to the clinic, an anxious Ross meeting them at the door as he fumbled with the large lock. Pushing in the security numbers on the alarm panel, he briefed them.

'Martha rang. She said that the GTN spray wasn't working, so I told her to stay there, that I was on my way, but, par for the course, Bill insisted that she bring him in.'

Kell was turning on the lights as Abby pulled up some drugs and turned on the oxygen.

'She's only a couple of minutes away. She just rang and said he'd got worse, he's barely breathing.' Tyres screeched outside and the trio rushed to the doors, but Ross put a warning hand on Abby's shoulder. 'No heroics, Abby, just the basics, remember. He doesn't want Intensive Care and he doesn't want to be resuscitated.'

Thank heavens for brute strength.

It took every inch of brawn to carry a limp grey Bill from his vehicle through the clinic as Abby waited with red dots and oxygen mask in hand. Martha was screaming, completely distraught, one look at her father enough to convey the gravity of the situation.

That this was surely the end.

'Don't let him die,' she intoned, clutching at Abby who slipped the mask over Bill's slack jaw, knowing with a sinking heart that his minimal respiratory effort wasn't going to hold out for much longer.

'Please, Abby, don't let him die, not without him knowing.'

Abby's long fingers probed the clammy neck but almost as soon as she located the flickering pulse there she lost it again, and as Bill sank further back onto the trolley Abby looked up urgently. 'He's arrested.'

His chest was so wet with perspiration the red dots wouldn't take, and Abby had to rub his chest with alcohol swabs to enable them to stick.

'Abby.' Ross's voice was sharp. 'Bill didn't want this.'

Looking over at the monitor, Abby saw the wavy irregular line of ventricular fibrillation. A single shock from the defibrillator could make it revert it to normal. A possible miracle was in her hands and Ross was saying no.

'Please, Abby!' Martha was pleading now. 'Do something!'

'Charge the defibrillator.' It took a second to realise that she'd spoken, that the firm, crisp order had actually come from her own mouth, but as Ross shook his head angrily Abby knew that indeed she had, and that, what's more, she was on her own.

'Abby.' It was Kell speaking now, Kell shaking his head as he wrapped an arm around a hysterical Martha. 'Bill knew this would happen.'

'Fine,' Abby said through gritted teeth, flicking the charge switch and placing the gel pads on Bill's chest. 'I'll do it myself. If it's the nurses' board you're worried about facing, Kell,' Abby added, with a slightly bitter note as she carried on with cardiac massage while waiting for the machine to charge, 'I'll take full responsibility.'

She knew she was out of line, knew Kell's reluctance had nothing to do with legalities, but as she shocked Bill, the predicted miracle didn't transpire, and it took three further shocks and a couple of lonely attempts at cardiac massage before Kell reluctantly joined her.

'You don't have to take all the flak, Abby,' he said, placing an ambu-bag over Bill's mouth and pushing oxygen into his lungs. 'We'll share it.'

Ross stood back, his face set in a grim line before he, too, joined them, pulling up drugs and joining in, but from the furious look on his face Abby knew she was in for it.

'I'll explain later,' Abby said, catching his eye for a split second.

'Oh, you can bet on it, Abby,' Ross snarled.

They worked in steely silence, only the harrowing sound of Martha's sobs breaking the bleeps of the monitors, the hiss of the oxygen, the short, sharp, orders from Abby, and when finally the wavy line reverted to a slow but regular rhythm, when Bill's chest rose and fell without the aid of Kell, they all stood back for a moment and watched as Bill started to breathe unaided, watched as he started to slowly come to.

But there was no jubilation, no nods of appreciation or congratulations on a job well done, just the cold morning-after feeling of facing the consequences. As Abby checked Bill's blood pressure, her shaking hand for once couldn't be blamed on adrenaline, just the appalling but unfortunately all-too-regular fear of a passionate decision being dissected in the sterile surroundings of a courtroom.

'My office.'

Abby almost smiled. Ross didn't have an office, just a regular seat in the staffroom, but it was hardly the time to point it out.

'I need to talk—'

'You've got that right at least,' Ross interrupted furiously.

'To Martha.' Abby's voice was surprisingly even as she looked her colleague in the eye then turned to her patient's daughter.

'Thank you,' Martha sobbed, as Abby put a comforting arm around her and guided her away from the trolley where her father lay to the nurses' station, dragging up two chairs and handing Martha a wad of tissues.

'I don't know that your father's going to say the same,' Abby said gently. 'Bill's wishes were very clear, and going against them…'

'I'm his next of kin,' Martha said fiercely, in a surprising show of strength. 'It was me insisted that you resuscitate him, I didn't leave you with any choice.'

Abby shrugged. Litigation was a worry but not a relevant one for the moment. Her problem right now was how to handle Martha, Bill and the jumble that was their lives in whatever time was left. 'What I'm trying to say, Martha, is that at any moment what just happened to your father could happen again. At any moment,' she added, her words hitting the mark the second time around. 'And even if we do attempt to resuscitate your father, this time around we mightn't get him back. If you really do want him to know that you're pregnant, it has to be now.'

'Now?' Martha asked, aghast, and Abby gave a small but definite nod.

'Now, Martha.'

'But it could kill him.'

Abby took a deep breath. Her hands reaching over, she squeezed the icy ones of Martha, trying somehow to inject strength, hope, and then berating herself because maybe there wasn't any to be had.

'Then again, this news might be just what your father needs to hold on.'

Kell gave a small smile as they approached, moving to the head of the trolley to make room for Martha.

'Can he hear?' Martha asked, her eyes darting anxiously to Kell, who nodded.

'He just spoke,' Kell said gently. 'He was asking for you.'

'I'm here, Dad.'

Suddenly Martha looked so much younger than eighteen. She looked like a wary ten-year-old as she grasped her father's hand and struggled not to cry. Abby didn't fare so well, tears quietly slipping onto her cheeks as she watched a child who had lost her mother take the biggest gamble of her life and try to save her father.

'I know you don't want to live, Dad, I know how hard it is for you, but I need you, especially now' Her voice broke and she glanced up at Abby, who nodded for her to go on. 'I'm having a baby.'

For a second Abby doubted whether Martha's words had registered, but as Bill's heart rate picked up and grey eyes that were begging to be permanently closed flicked open, Abby knew that Martha's admission had hit home.

'And I can't do it without you. Des loves me and I love him

and we really want this to work, but if I lose you now, if you go and leave me, I don't know how we'll manage...'

Abby placed her hands on the heaving shoulders as Bill's eyes closed again. 'Let him rest now, Martha, he's exhausted.'

'Martha?'

The tiny voice stilled them all but Bill didn't say anything else, just squeezed his daughter's hand tight, and it was Kell who found a chair and placed it at the bedside. 'Abby's right. He needs to rest. Maybe he'll do it better with you sitting beside him, huh?'

'What did Ross say?

Kell found Abby, oh, so much later, sipping coffee in the staffroom and staring vacantly out of the window.

'He made me a coffee then said he'd back me all the way.' Abby gave a small laugh. 'He's great, isn't he?'

'He is,' Kell agreed. 'But I'd give him up for you.' When even that didn't raise a smile he closed the door quietly behind him. 'It was Martha's pregnancy test, wasn't it?'

Abby gave a small nod. 'She didn't want anyone else to know just yet.'

'I understand.' Kell sat down on the sofa beside her, but instead of it comforting her suddenly all Abby wanted to do was cry. 'It was nice, though,' Kell said, his voice pensive, his four little words not needing the further explanation that came. 'Thinking it could be us for a while.'

How did he know?

How could he have known that she'd been sitting there thinking exactly the same thing?

That Abby Hampton, city doctor, almost a consultant, was sitting staring out of a window dreaming of a little scrap of blotting paper turning pink, trying to imagine a life where careers didn't matter, where sleepless nights had nothing to do with the road death toll and everything to do with your own little bundle of love.

They'd make beautiful babies, Abby mused.

An almost consultant and an almost cowboy.

CHAPTER ELEVEN

'I HAVE TO go.' Kell's deep voice merged with her dreams and Abby stretched languorously beside him as he brushed her shoulder with his lips. 'Do you want me to set the alarm?'

'Too many questions,' Abby mumbled, pulling his arm back over her and nestling herself back into the curve of his body, feeling the early morning swell of him nudging against the soft inner curve of her thigh. But instead of wrapping his arms tighter around her, edging his body nearer and waking her in the most intimate of ways, he moved, kicking back the sheet and climbing out of bed. Abby found herself frowning into the pillow. 'Where are you rushing off to?'

'I've just got to go.'

He didn't mumble exactly, didn't jump out of bed and pull on his jeans with barely a glance, but the emotional distancing Abby had felt in the past couple of weeks was blatantly evident, and for a while, as she pulled the sheet tighter around her and stared blankly into the grey shadows of the dawn, Abby felt the abyss she had tried to ignore for so long now deepen as Kell stood to go.

'Where?' She held her breath as she said the single word,

knowing she had crossed the invisible line they had created between them.

They were two independent people, two stars colliding perhaps, but they both knew their explosion was transient.

Kell belonged here, Abby there, and never the twain should meet.

That was what she wanted, what she had insisted upon, so why was she crossing the line now? Abby tried to fathom as she turned on her side and hit him with the full weight of her question, her hair cascading on the pillow, one glorious pale bosom spilling over the sheet, a stark contrast to the golden shimmer of her arms. 'Where do you have to go? You're not on duty for a couple of hours.'

His eyes couldn't meet hers and Abby chewed her bottom lip as she watched him fumble with the fly on his jeans. 'I just need some space, that's all.'

'Kell.'

Her single word stopped him in his tracks and she watched him hesitate in mid-motion, watched the arms that had been holding her through the night stiffen as he paused, his T-shirt in mid-air, and she waited, waited for him to grin, to catch her eyes and smile that lazy smile, to say 'to hell with it' and climb back into the warm bed beside her and kiss away all the horrible doubts that seemed to be flitting into her mind lately with alarming regularity.

But he didn't.

'What do you want from me, Abby?' Not for a second did he raise his voice, not for a moment did she feel threatened, but so ominous was his tone that for the first time since meeting him Abby felt the sting of his disapproval, the dearth of pain in his voice and she gulped as she tried to answer, but Kell was too quick for her. 'Two weeks from now, you're out of here.' His hand slapped against his thighs and his eyes bored into her as she lay on the bed, naked against this unexpected onslaught. 'Two weeks from now, according to you, I might add, you're going to be right back where you belong. So what's with all the questions, Abby? What's with the sudden need to know my every movement when this time in a fortnight you'll be picking up the pictures and smiling at the memories?' Pulling on his boots, he tossed her an angry glare as she lay there, her eyes wide, reeling from his words.

'Kell?' The question in her voice was evident but the hand that reached out for his was quickly rebuffed.

'What, Abby?' he snarled, but just as quickly as his anger had blown in it seemed to dissipate and she watched as he sat hunched on the end of the bed, his body so loaded with sadness, rejection, despair it made her want to weep. 'I just don't think I can do this any more, Abby,' Kell said in a low hoarse voice. 'I can't just lie next to you and pretend the end isn't going to happen.'

Work was awful.

All Abby wanted to do was to speak to Kell in the privacy of her home, to finish whatever Kell had so unexpectedly started.

Correcting herself, Abby pushed open the clinic door and walked inside. Kell's outburst hadn't been that unexpected. Since the night Bill had become so ill, since the night a baby that hadn't even existed had entered their fragile equation, they had been walking on eggshells, pretending time wasn't racing by, that her departure wasn't imminent…

But, as they knew only too well, ignoring things didn't make them go away. Soon her flight would be waiting, not only waiting but departing from the gate in ten minutes, and could a Doctor Abby Hampton please make her way to the departure lounge as soon as possible.

Ross as usual was in great spirits. 'C'mon, Abby, you've got a mobile clinic this morning. If you want to go to the ladies, make it snappy.'

Feeling like a two-year-old Abby took his advice. Too many times she'd been caught out, and asking Kell or Ross to stop the

Jeep wasn't the only indignity one had to suffer in the outback. Thoughts of spiders and snakes and mozzies who seemed to have taken a liking to her were enough incentive to dutifully head off to the ladies' room as Kell moodily loaded up the Jeep.

'How's Bill?' Abby asked Clara as she picked up her bag.

'The same.' Clara shrugged. 'Martha's coming in this afternoon after her ultrasound so hopefully that will cheer him up a bit. I've been trying to get him to talk all night but he's not even attempting to be polite now. Hopefully Ross will have more luck.'

'Let's hope so.' Abby looked over at her patient who met her gaze momentarily, his disinterested eyes flicking away to the bland curtain beside him, and though it hadn't been her intention, though the anger that boiled inside her wasn't aimed at Bill, Abby made her way over.

'So Martha's having her ultrasound today,' Abby said enthusiastically. 'Is she going to find out what she's having?'

So lethargic was his effort it barely merited a shrug but Abby carried on her chatter, refusing to be dismissed, flicking through Bill's notes at the end of the bed as she spoke. 'Your blood work's looking good, Bill. You should be thinking about going home in the next couple of days.'

'I'm too sick.' His eyes didn't even attempt to meet hers and for a moment or two Abby said nothing.

'Then you need to be in a proper hospital, Bill.'

'This is as good as any hospital.' Bill shrugged. 'I get all the care I need here.'

'No, Bill, you don't.' Abby's voice was firm, sharp even, and out of the corner of her eye she saw both Ross and Clara jerk their eyes towards her.

'This is a clinic, an excellent clinic maybe, but it's not a specialist unit. We're here as a holding base, a chance to stabilise patients before they're moved. Neither Ross nor I are cardiac specialists and right now that's what you need.'

'I'm not leaving Tennengarrah.' It was the most emotion

Abby had heard from him in days but, as sorry as she felt for Bill, as awful as his plight was, Abby felt angry. Angry that such a young man, with so much to live for, with a daughter that loved him, with a grandchild on the way, could let it all go.

'Bill.' Abby moved closer and though she felt, rather than saw Kell enter she didn't look over, her mind too focussed on this important conversation to let her personal life interfere. 'I'm sorry to say this but, like it or not, you're leaving Tennengarrah.' Taking a deep breath, Abby continued. 'Now, you can leave here on a plane with one helluva lot of hope and a family waiting for you when you get back, or...' The silence around them built for a moment then Abby gave a brief shrug. 'I'm sure I don't have to spell out the other option to you.'

'I'm not going to have an operation.'

'And you're sure, quite sure, that you know what you're saying? Ross has asked me to speak to you again. He says that you're still adamant you don't want to be resuscitated and I have to respect that, so if you want me to countersign his findings then today's the day, Bill. If that's what you really want, then that's what I'm going to do.' Though her pen was poised over Bill's notes she watched her patient closely, registering his muscles quilted around his mouth, a slightly nervous swallow. And though Abby had no intention of signing the papers under these circumstances, Bill wasn't to know that. 'Your daughter needs you, Bill.' She'd said it before, they'd all said it, but this time, for the first time, the words seemed to hit their mark.

'Why would she need me?' Struggling to sit, Bill was the most animated Abby had seen him, but though her heart was in her mouth Abby kept her stance impassive, allowing her patient to continue, knowing it was Bill who needed to speak if ever they were going to get anywhere. 'Why would she need me when all I can do is sit and watch the farm go to pot? If I'm gone she and Des can do something, build it up, make a decent life. I'm better out of the way.'

'He's good, then?'

She watched Bill frown, his eyes confused. 'Who?'

'Des. He's good around the farm?'

Bill shrugged. 'Well, he's a hard worker. Thinks he knows it all, of course.' Realising he'd said too much, Bill lay back on his pillow, but Abby wasn't missing her chance.

'I was like that,' she said, her voice gentler, perching herself on the side of the bed but making sure she didn't get too close. 'I thought I knew it all, too. You saw what I was like yourself when I got here. A city doctor who'd seen it all, sure there was nothing this backwater could teach me. Not that I said it, of course, but I'm sure everyone got the message.

'It's not like that out here, though, is it?' Abby said softly. 'It's beautiful, inspiring, wonderful, but it's a tough old land, and though I've learnt so, so much in the past months I haven't even scratched the surface. It's people like Kell and Clara who teach people like Ross and me, who show us how this land works, how to work with it and sometimes even cheat it.

'They need you, Bill.'

'I'm scared.' A thin, bony hand reached out and Abby took it in hers. 'Scared that if I have the operation I won't wake up. I know it doesn't make sense, I know I need it...' Tears were trickling down his cheeks and he didn't move to wipe them. 'I'm just so scared.'

'I know, Bill,' Abby said gently. 'And I can't give you any guarantees. But if you have the operation at least you've got a chance, and by all the statistics a good one. Bypasses have come on even since you had your first one five years ago. They'll have you walking a few steps within twelve hours, you'll be back here within a couple of weeks. But even without guarantees, it is a chance, Bill, and more importantly it's your only one.'

As Bill slumped back on his pillow, Abby knew better than to push things. Taking on a more authoritarian tone, she stood up. 'I'm not going to sign the order because I think we both know that's not what you really want, but you have to make a choice and soon, or it will be out of both our hands.'

* * *

'You did a good job back there.'

It was the first words Kell had spoken to her in the two-hour journey, apart from the odd comment about 'bloody mozzies' or 'stupid cows' that wandered into the path of the Jeep, making the long journey ever longer as Kell, rather less patiently than usual, would get out and give them a hefty slap, moving them on as Abby sat there, wishing this awful morning would end, that she could think of something witty or at least relevant to say.

Something that didn't sound like small talk.

Staring out of the window, aimlessly drinking in each lonely windmill, each thirsty dam Abby wondered how she could bear to leave, and if she couldn't, how she could possibly bear to stay. 'I know how Bill feels,' she said softly. 'I've only been here a while, but I know how hard it is to leave, to think that I'm probably seeing all of this for the last time.'

The silence seemed to go on for ever and Kell didn't even look over, just changed gear for something to do and fiddled a bit more with the air-conditioning, but even as he finally opened his mouth Abby knew what was coming next.

'Bill doesn't have a choice Abby. You do.'

She opened her mouth to speak but Kell beat her to it. 'I'm not asking you to live here for ever, Abby. Hell, I understand about the drug clinic, about your career, but surely we're worth a few more months. Surely what we've had together merits you spending a little bit longer here.'

Oh, it did.

Tenfold, a hundredfold.

But how could she possibly tell him her fears, that another six months beside him, waking with him each morning, falling asleep with him at night, could only make it harder? Make leaving impossible.

'I just can't,' Abby said hopelessly, a paltry return to such a heartfelt statement, and she heard Kell's low sigh of disbelief as he shook his head. 'It's better this way, Kell.'

Thankfully they were professional enough and, perhaps more pointedly, busy enough to put their personal feelings to one side as the clinic got under way. Even though she had only been here a handful of times, already Abby felt accepted, recognising a few familiar faces amongst the patients, working methodically as Kell ran the post- and antenatal clinics alongside her.

'That's looking a lot better.' Smiling as he removed the bandage on Jim's leg, Abby checked the wound thoroughly but there were no signs of infection or inflammation. In fact, the wound had healed way beyond Abby's expectations. 'Maybe Jim can spare me the recipe before I head back to the city because whatever he put on your leg certainly worked.'

As Kell saw his last patient, Abby started to pack up and pulled out the esky, but even the sight of lunch did nothing to whet her appetite, remembering so poignantly their first lunch together, right here in this very spot. Opening up to each other, telling Kell the real reason she was here.

It was hard to believe it was over so soon.

'Abby.' Kell's voice had a ring to it Abby had never heard before, and even before she had looked up her adrenaline was starting to kick in. Between them they had seen some sights over the past months but never had Kell sounded anything other than his usual laid-back self.

It took only a second to realise the cause of his concern. Kell was standing beside a woman and in her arms lay an infant, or at least that was what Abby first thought, but on closer inspection the child lying limp and exhausted in the woman's arms would have been around two, his large dark eyes were sunk in his head, his mouth drooling as he struggled with each breath. As Abby recognized Vella, Kell's arms reached out to take the child from its mother's arms and Abby found her voice.

'Leave him with Vella.' Her words were firm, decisive, and Kell instantly put his arms by his side, a questioning look on his face as he turned to Abby. But there wasn't time to explain. Guiding the woman to the Jeep, Abby felt rivers of sweat running down her back and between her breasts as the direness of the situation hit home.

'Is this your little boy?'

Vella nodded, clutching her child closer, her eyes watching Abby's every movement. 'His name's Billy. He can't breathe.'

'Do you want me to put in an IV?' Kell was pulling emergency trays out, snapping into action, but Abby shook her head.

'No. I want you to get on the radio and get the flying doctors here, a.s.a.p. Kell, tell them we've got a suspected case of epiglottitis.'

She watched as the word registered with Kell, and for a second she was sure he paled beneath his tan, but even before she nodded a confirmation, Kell was onto it, back to the calm efficient bush nurse he was.

'Help him?' Vella's eyes looked pleadingly at Abby and she sensed her impatience.

'Vella, I think your son…' Abby started, but her voice trailed off. There was no place for long words here, their different languages, barely allowing for the briefest of exchanges let alone medical terminology. Vella simply wouldn't understand that one false move, one fright and her child's throat would spasm, blocking off his airway so tightly that even with medical intervention the chance of intubating him would be remote at best. 'Billy is sick,' Abby said slowly. 'We mustn't move him or upset him.'

'They're mobilising.' Kell approached softly, placing one heavy yet reassuring hand on Abby's shoulder. 'Dr Hiller's on the line.'

'Thanks.' Though desperate for advice, Abby stood slowly so as not to upset the child.

'Try not to disturb him,' Abby warned—needlessly, she realised. Now Kell knew the diagnosis he was standing back, letting Vella do all the reassuring. 'Explain to Vella that he needs to be kept calm, that there's a reason why we're not doing anything for him.'

'Sure.'

Their eyes locked for the tiniest of instances and as Kell flashed a reassuring smile Abby was eternally grateful, grateful not just that Kell was here with her but for the blessed fact that today was the day of the mobile clinic, that medical help was actually on hand.

That this little boy stood a chance.

'Have you done any anaesthetics?'

Dr Hiller was straight to the point and Abby was relieved at the absence of small talk instantly, warming to the wise, reassuring voice on the radio.

'I have,' Abby started, 'but not on a child with epiglottitis. The couple of cases I've seen have been with an anaesthetist in the room.'

She was telling the truth. Epiglottitis struck the same fear into doctors as meningitis did into mothers everywhere. Rarely seen now with immunisation, it still popped up every now and then, and Abby, not for the first time, realised the enormity of the work here in the outback, that the massive net they tried to cast was shot with gaping, awful holes, how the very immunisations Vella had reluctantly accepted for her newborn had been missed by this child.

'Don't move him.' Dr Hiller's voice was crisp over the radio. 'Don't distress him with the portable oxygen or by putting needles into him. Just sit tight and let the mother do all the comforting. It's her you'll need to keep calm, but Kell will be onto that.'

'What if...?' Abby's voice trailed off, knowing the awful answer to her question before Dr Hiller even responded.

'If he stops breathing, his airway will be so swollen it will make intubation almost impossible. Give it one go and if there's no luck move straight to a needle cricothyrotomy or tracheostomy.'

Abby winced into the receiver she held in her hand. A cricothyrotomy or tracheostomy involved making an incision into the patient's throat and establishing an artificial airway, but in a child as sick as this a happy result was definitely not guaranteed.

And though, as an emergency registrar, Abby had performed her share of this lifesaving procedure, they had all been done in a well-stocked resuscitation room with relatives safely tucked away and an anaesthetist hot-footing it down the corridor, a world away from this dusty desert and their limited equipment with the child's mother watching her every move...witnessing the last-ditch attempt to save her child's life.

'How long till help arrives?'

The crackling of the radio didn't diminish the direness of the answer.

'An hour.' There was a slight pause as Abby felt the abyss of solitude. 'Give or take, we hold clinics there, so there's no trouble getting in and they're already on their way. Just set everything up as best you can, and if he stops breathing you'll be ready.'

Kell had been busy while Abby had been away. He hadn't put an oxygen mask on the child, but he had placed the tubing over Vella's shoulder, unnoticed by the babe in her arms, and Vella was holding it near her child, hopefully raising the concentration of oxygen he was breathing.

Mike, the mujee, had appeared as if from nowhere, and sat with Vella, patiently talking to her, and Abby was grateful for his presence, knowing that right now he was what Vella needed.

They worked on, only sharing the occasional murmur between them as they opened packs and checked their equipment, but the glance they shared as Abby check the tracheostomy pack was one of pure dread, the outlook, if it came to that, too dire to contemplate.

But for all their internal fears, Vella was only ever the recipient of gentle words of reassurance as they took it in turns to fan her and her child. Billy was leaning forward, his body sagging with each noisy breath, and never had Abby felt more useless, her years of study and practice counting for nothing against this harsh, unforgiving land, waiting with ears on elastic for the low hum of the plane, the only chance Billy really had.

It was the longest hour of her life, the wait interminable, Abby could only liken it to watching some awful documentary, watching a child dying in some remote foreign land and knowing there was nothing you could do. But this wasn't on the screen, this was real life, this was Australia in the twenty-first century, for heaven's sake!

For once even the flies didn't bother her. She barely bothered to flick them away as she took her turn to fan Vella and Billy.

'It's coming.' Mike gave her a reassuring nod as Abby cocked her head.

'I can't hear anything.'

'You won't yet.' He pointed to some birds flying overhead and Abby frowned. 'They know before us.'

Another seemingly tiny snippet, yet again it floored her, all the knowledge, the generations of learning, secrets passed down, ever down. Abby heard the distant hum of the plane, her mouth opening in admiration as she offered up a silent prayer of thanks.

Maybe it was the movement, the sudden lift in tension, but just as they all relaxed, as an end to this torturous time seemed in sight, Abby saw the child lie back a fraction in his mother's arms. Vella simultaneously let out a low moan of terror. Billy's colour, never particularly good, seemed to be grey now, the life force draining out of his tiny body. Abby rued the second she had relaxed and Kell, in one movement, took the limp body from Vella, laying the toddler on the rug at the back of the Jeep as Mike took the weeping woman to one side, his dark, knowing eyes catching Abby's. She felt the weight of modern medicine fall to her shoulders as she felt the tiny lifeless form beneath her hands.

Kell deftly slapped the back of Billy's hands to bring up the veins, finally getting IV access into the child, pushing in the antibiotics they had already pulled up and connecting a flask of fluids as Abby placed an ambu-bag over Billy's slack mouth and tried to push oxygen into his lungs.

They had both set up for this moment, formed a plan of attack should the worst happen, but the resistance in the bag told her she wasn't getting anywhere, and with a frantic shake of her head she looked over at Kell who passed her the laryngoscope—the curved torch that would act as a guide to the tube Billy so desperately needed to help him breathe.

'I can't see anything.' Abby's voice trembled as she peered into the child's throat, trying to visualise the vocal cords, but Billy's throat was too swollen, making any hope of passing the tube impossible.

The seconds that had ticked by so slowly for the past hour were suddenly whizzing past at an alarming rate, every second moving them unwillingly closer to the three-minute mark that would mean this little boy would suffer irreversible brain damage.

'They're coming.' Mike's voice was jubilant, hopeful, but both Abby and Kell knew his hope was false, that even if they ran like Olympic sprinters from the plane they would be too late.

Resuming the bagging Abby shook her head as she saw his rapidly decreasing oxygen saturations on the portable monitor. 'I'm going to do a cricothyrotomy. Pass me the twelve-gauge needle.' Abby's firm voice belied the appalling sense of dread in every fibre of her being, her one last shot at getting vital oxygen into the little boy.

Vella's screams multiplied as she watched Abby prepare the neck with a swift swab of Betadine, the pitiful wails causing a flurry of activity in the trees around them, startled birds flitting away, but it all went unnoticed by Abby, every cell in her being focussing on the little boy before her as she felt for the correct area in his neck, felt her way with trembling fingers and then held her breath as she pushed the needle in, dissecting the swollen tissue, the tiny space the needle created allowing a hiss to escape as Abby let out the hot air she had been holding in her own lungs.

'Come on, Kell,' she snapped, as he pushed together the connections, the harshness in her voice not even meriting a glance. No criticism intended and none taken, just a desperate attempt to save a life. He connected the tiny airway she had created, no wider than an intravenous needle, to the oxygen tubing, and this time, when Abby squeezed the ambu-bag gently, she watched with sheer relief as Billy's chest moved, colour slowly returning with each gentle push of the bag.

'His oxygen saturation is coming up,' Abby said, glancing at the tiny portable monitor. 'This will at least hold him until...' She didn't finish the sentence, the sight of the flying doctor team descending upon them the sweetest she had ever seen.

'We meet again' was the only greeting Dr Hall gave as he set to work, checking his patient, listening to Abby's handover as his nurse worked alongside him, passing him the equipment he needed as they secured Abby's handiwork, stabilizing the little boy before moving him to the plane.

'Dr Abby?' Mike came over, his face almost obliterated by a huge bushy beard, but there was no mistaking the gratitude in his eyes as he shook her hand. 'This is your last clinic?'

'Yes,' Abby said simply, not quite ready for the first round of goodbyes yet knowing they had to be faced.

'Thank you.' His hand reached into his pocket and, pulling out a glass jar, he handed it to Abby, his dark hands closing around Abby's for a moment, the significance of his gesture bringing tears to Abby's eyes as she looked at the muddy lotion in the bottle.

'Billygoat weed.' Abby smiled through her brimming eyes. 'I'll use it wisely. And thank you, too, Mike. I've learnt a lot from you.'

And then he was gone, back to where ever he'd come from, and Abby stood there, holding the treasured glass jar in her hand. She was barely able to answer as Kell broke into her thoughts with a slightly gruff voice, the inevitable farewells undoubtedly painful for him, too. 'Dr Hall's ready to move Billy.

'We've taken bloods and given him his first dose of antibiotic,' Kell said to Dr Hall, his voice resuming its more usual nonchalant tones as the team gently moved Billy onto a stretcher. Abby carried the IV flask as they headed for the plane, with Kell relaying all the drugs that had been given as if he were reading off a shopping list, the emotion gone from his voice now, back to the unflappable bush nurse Abby knew.

Loved.

Now order was restored, now a life wasn't balancing on a knife edge, that word popped into her consciousness again, knocking her sideways with its impact, taunting her with the impossibility of the match.

'You did pretty damn good there, Dr Hampton.' They were both shielding their eyes, watching the white plane winging its way through the blue sky, carrying its precious load. 'And without a radiographer or path lab in sight. You saved his life,' Kell said more insistently when Abby didn't respond, wrapping an arm around her and pulling her towards him.

'We did,' Abby corrected, but Kell wasn't having a bar of it.

'No, Abby, you did. The second you saw him, you knew what was happening. It was you who told me to leave him with his mum, not to touch him, not to upset him.'

His words hit home and it was then Abby realised how far she had come, how right Reece had been to send her, that Tennengarrah had been a learning curve she had needed to explore.

'Let's get you home, huh?'

Home.

Climbing into the Jeep, Abby rested her head against the passenger window, and this time as she gazed out of the window it wasn't aimlessly. This time she tried to capture each image, to relish it, to save it, to hold it in her heart for ever and wondered why she had to feel this way.

Why the word 'home' couldn't conjure up for her endless red earth dotted with white weatherboard houses, why it didn't signify tired, lonely windmills working woefully empty dams.

A career was there for the taking, one where she could make a real difference.

And for the hundredth time in as many minutes she wondered what was wrong with her. Why the sterile anonymity of a concrete hospital and the pressures of dealing with drug addicts held more charm than the medicine she was practising here. Why the creamy sails of the Opera House seemingly billowing across the harbour filled her mind when she thought about home. Why walking unnoticed along a crowded street with shops and cafés held more charm than the life she could lead here...

If only she would stay.

Kell sensed her pensive mood and drove along in silence, idly humming along to his favourite CD. Even when they pulled up at the clinic, laboriously restocked the boxes and refuelled the Jeep, filled in Ross on the day's events and headed for home, there was no idle chit-chat, just a loaded sadness as she pushed open her front door.

'I'll say goodnight, then.' She heard the uncertainty in Kell's deep voice as her eyes shot up, startled.

'Where are you going?'

Soft lips met hers briefly, the scratch of his cheeks brushing against hers as he pulled away. 'I know this is hard for you, Abby, it's hard for me, too. I can understand if you need some space. Anyway, I've got to be up early.'

'You're not on duty tomorrow.'

Kell shrugged. 'I'm hitching a ride with Bruce. I've got a few things to do in town.'

'Oh, Kell.' Her eyes sparkled with tears and she squeezed them closed. The thought of one night apart from him sent her into a spin of uncertainty, yet here she was checking out for good, signing up for a life without him. 'I don't want you to go, that's not what this quiet mood's about.'

'You don't?' Hope sparked in his eyes, that lazy, familiar smile spilling onto his face and Abby didn't even try to resist the urge to reach out and touch him, to somehow capture his smile in the palm of her hand.

'I don't,' she said, her word muffled by the weight of his kiss.

But even as they drifted towards the bedroom, even as he laid her down and kissed her as only Kell could, as their bodies mingled with the infinite desire they ignited, the tears still sparkled in her eyes.

The weight of his body as he lay on top of her, the silhouette of his shoulders as he moved inside her, the feel of that dark tousled hair beneath her fingers, the scratchy maleness of his thighs as they moved against her were all captured in the glistening pools of her eyes, as something deep inside told her to treasure this memory.

And later, as he held her, snuggled into her and slipped one arm under her then cupped his other hand over her breast as he drifted off to sleep, the tears that had threatened all day fell, sliding into her hair as she recalled the bitter-sweet memory of their love-making.

Sweet in its perfection.

Bitter in its finality.

CHAPTER TWELVE

'COME ON, LAZYBONES!'

Peering around her front door, Abby blinked a few times at Shelly, running a sleepy hand through her tousled hair. 'What time is it?'

'Ten a.m.,' Shelly said in a matter-of-fact voice, pushing open the door and marching inside leaving Abby to wince at the bright sunlight, close the door and follow her through to the kitchen.

'Is there a problem at the clinic?' Abby asked, perching on a barstool and trying desperately to wake up properly. 'Only Kell left at the crack of dawn, so if you're looking for him...'

'No,' Shelly answered cheerfully, depositing a large bag and simultaneously filling the kettle. 'It's you I'm after. In fact, I've even got a bit of gossip, but it's the ball tonight that I'm really here about. We've got to go to the hairdresser's.'

'Now?' Abby protested. 'But it's the crack of dawn.'

'Hardly!'

'Believe me,' Abby mumbled, 'on my day off, ten a.m.'s the crack of dawn.'

'Well, we were lucky to get in. There are about one hundred and fifty women all wanting their hair done today. It took a hell of a lot of sweet-talking to get an appointment. She's even going to do your nails.'

Abby glanced down at her hand, weakening at the thought of a manicure. The French polish she had arrived with had long since depleted.

'So how did you get her to agree?' Abby asked, half yawning and wishing the kettle would hurry up.

'Never you mind,' she said lightly as Abby's eyebrows furrowed. Shelly was up to mischief, Abby just knew it. 'Let's just say I've got contacts. Now all we have to worry about is looking beautiful. I just wish I'd taken my diet a bit more seriously.'

'Don't be ridiculous,' Abby admonished. 'You look great.'

'Exactly,' Shelly sighed.

'I meant you look wonderful.' Abby grinned. 'For someone who had a baby ten weeks ago you're looking amazing.'

'Amazing's the word,' Shelly moaned, depositing a steaming mug in front of Abby. 'Did you know you can actually get stretch marks on top of your old stretch marks? My rear end looks like a map of Australia.'

'And we all know how patriotic Ross is.' Abby winked, perking up as she took a few sips of coffee. 'So, what's the gossip?'

'Your replacement's arrived!'

'My replacement?' Suddenly Abby didn't feel so perky any more. Instead, she felt twitchy and threatened, but she kept her smile in place as Shelly continued.

'He's two weeks early. Apparently he ran out of money in Coober Pedey, though how anyone can break the bank there beats me! You're supposed to make your fortune there fossicking for opals. Heaven only knows what he spent it on.'

'What's he like?'

Shelly gave a small sigh. 'English, very English. His name's Timothy, not Tim or Timmy but Timothy, and even though I'm an exceptionally happily married woman, I have to admit he's gorgeous.' Shelly let out a shriek of laughter. 'And the best bit is, I'm not the only one who thinks so.'

'You've lost me,' Abby admitted.

'You should have seen Clara blushing. I'm serious!' she exclaimed as Abby gave her a disbelieving look. 'Ross can't believe it either. I mean, Clara's just Clara, salt of the earth, never in a flap, but she was blushing to her roots and dropping things all over the place when Ross showed Tim around this morning.'

'Timothy,' Abby corrected, standing up and draining the last of her coffee. 'So who's going to look after the clinic tonight? Bill's still hanging in there, I assume.'

Shelly nodded, but again Abby found herself frowning, sure she had seen a tiny blush grace Shelly's cheeks. 'Ross really thought you'd hit home with your pep talk but I'm afraid he's still staring at the curtains and sinking further and further downhill. Anyway, Ross has asked Noelene Barton to fill in for tonight. I doubt you'll have met her, she's not exactly sociable, but she's a registered nurse and every now and then, at Christmas and the like, she does a couple of shifts to keep her registration up. She's going to babysit the clinic.'

'And who have you got lined up—for Matthew and Kate, I mean?'

'No one.' Shelly grinned. 'That's the best bit about this place. I'll bring the kids and I probably won't see them all night, there'll be a million and one women clucking over them like broody hens. And the best bit of all…' She gave a cheeky wink. 'By the time we get home, they'll both be so exhausted they'll sleep the entire night through.'

'You scarlet woman, you.' Abby grinned.

Whatever clout Shelly had by being Tennengarrah's loyal doctor's wife, she'd certainly used it today. June's house was a hive of activity but all the grey roller-haired ladies parted as Abby and Shelly walked in, and instead of protests they smiled affectionately as Abby's hair was curled around yellow and pink foams. Not even the slightest murmur of disapproval went up as Abby was privy to the one and only manicure of the day.

'I can't fit you in again this afternoon so you'll have to do the rest yourself. I need you to take the curlers out an hour before the ball,' Anna the hairdresser instructed in such a serious voice Abby wondered if she was about to be asked to sign a consent form! 'But you mustn't brush your hair, that will make it all go frizzy. Just put a dash of the serum I gave onto your hands, work it through your fingers and run it through the curls. They should fall beautifully.'

'Th-thank you,' Abby stammered as the whole room looked on.

'And try and let your nails dry for at least an hour before you do anything. You don't want any dints in your varnish.'

'Of course not.'

Only then did it dawn on her, looking around the smiling faces, the nudging going on behind the occasional magazine, that her preferential treatment had nothing to do with being the locum doctor, nothing to do with Shelly and her 'contacts'.

It had everything to do with Kell.

His early morning dash with Bruce was starting to make sense now, and as they paid and left Abby couldn't wait to get Shelly alone and confront her.

'Where's Kell gone today, Shelly?'

'How should I know?' Shelly strode on, the blush on her cheeks only confirming Abby's suspicions.

'Because the whole of Tennengarrah does,' Abby snapped, as Shelly finally slowed down. 'That's what this is all about, isn't it—the hair, the nails, Kell disappearing to "pick up supplies"? What on earth was he thinking?'

'It's not Kell's fault.' Shelly swung around, a sight for sore eyes in massive rollers. 'He hasn't said a word. It was Bruce who mentioned...' Her voice trailed off but Abby wasn't going to let her leave things there.

'What exactly did Bruce mention? Come on, Shelly, I need to know.'

'Kell went into town a couple of weeks ago. Bruce saw him in the jeweller's, that's all, and Kell asked to go back today.

Bruce thinks it's to pick up a ring. It's all hearsay, Abby, but it doesn't take much for word to get around here.'

'He's going to ask me to marry him.' The shiver in her voice was one of pure amazement. Even though she had suspected it, saying it felt completely different.

'He loves you, Abby.' Shelly took a couple of anxious breaths, 'This surely can't come as that much of a surprise,' she said. 'Please, please, don't let on I've said anything.'

'Just so long as you don't say anything else.' Abby's mind was whirring, the need to be alone, to think things through overriding politeness for now. 'I mean it, Shelly, don't say a single word to anyone.'

Anna had been right. Her hair did fall beautifully, but as Abby stared into the mirror, her snaky dark ringlets hanging over her shoulders, the white ruffles of her dress accentuating her tan, Abby barely recognised herself.

But it wasn't the coiffed woman staring back at her that was so unrecognisable, it was the very fact she was actually seriously considering staying, breaking her promise to David, throwing every professional dream she had held dear for so long now away in the name of love.

A whole afternoon wrestling with her soul had made the picture no clearer, and as Abby walked past the clinic the weight of indecision made her linger a moment, peering into the windows and trying to picture herself there. The sight of Ross, dressed to the nines in a dinner suit, though, wasn't one Abby was expecting!

Pushing the clinic door open, Abby made her way to the small ward, a questioning look on her face as she walked over. 'What are you doing here?'

'I could ask you the same.'

Abby gave a small shrug. 'Kell rang. He got held up with Bruce, but he's on his way back. He said he'd meet me there. What's your excuse?'

'Your pep talk with Bill worked. He's decided to have the

operation, so I called the hospital and they want him there to-night—there's been a cancellation and there's space on the the-atre list on Monday. We've been waiting all day for the flying doctors but they just rang through and should be here within the hour.'

So Shelly had been lying! 'Can't Noelene deal with it? I thought she was looking after the place tonight.'

Ross gave a tight smile. 'She's making a cuppa. And Bill needs to be handed over properly. It's not fair to land it all on Noelene.'

'Or Shelly,' Abby exclaimed. 'Shouldn't you be over there admiring her new dress, telling her how fabulous she looks?'

'Don't make me feel worse,' Ross groaned. 'Hopefully they should be here soon. Shelly's putting on a brave face but I know she's been looking forward to tonight.'

'Go,' Abby said as Ross gave her a wide-eyed look. 'I mean it, Ross. Shelly's been looking forward to tonight for ages. I can take care of Bill.'

'But what about you? What about Kell's...'

Abby shook her head as Ross's voice trailed off.

'Kell's plans for tonight,' Abby ventured as Ross winced in embarrassment. 'Don't worry, Ross, I had already worked it out for myself.'

'So why are you putting your hand up for an extra shift?' Ross asked perceptively, his grin disappearing as Shelly an-swered, her voice was thick with emotion, black, mascara-laced tears slipping down her cheeks as she rummaged in her bag for a tissue.

'Here.' Ross pulled a wad from the box on the desk, a startled note in his voice as he watched his crisp, efficient colleague dissolve into a mass of tears. 'I'm sorry, Abby. I was only jok-ing, I didn't realise there was a problem.'

'There shouldn't be,' Abby sniffed. 'We love each other, I know that more than I know anything.'

'So what are you so scared of?'

Abby took a deep breath, her eyes finally dragging up to Ross's, who waited patiently as she struggled to answer. 'I'm scared that when Kell asks me to marry him, I'm going to let my heart rule my head and say yes.' Ross looked at her bemused as Abby cried harder. 'It could never work, Ross, it's just all too hard. Kell's not going to leave here, he told me the first night we met he couldn't even consider it, that Tennengarrah's in his blood...'

'But not yours,' Ross finished for her gently.

'Not mine,' Abby said sadly. 'Oh, I've grown to love it. I love the people, the work. If anything, I've enjoyed practising medicine here more than I ever have in the past, but I just can't stay here for ever. I've got commitments in the city, promises that need to be kept, and if I agree to marry Kell I'll be letting so many people down.'

'Yourself included?' Ross asked gently.

'Myself included.' Abby nodded. 'Look, I know the work I do in the city isn't everyone's cup of tea but, Ross, it's something I really feel I have to do. If I let it go now, some time in the future I know I'm going to regret it.'

Ross looked at her thoughtfully for a moment before speaking, his knowing eyes surprisingly understanding. 'Which is no way to start a marriage.'

Abby nodded glumly as Ross continued gently. 'Sometimes you can think about things too much, Abby. Shelly had a home, a life, a family in Melbourne, a special needs child and an ex-husband to boot. If we'd really sat down and thought about the logistics of packing up and moving here, we'd probably never have made it.'

'So why did you?' Abby asked. 'What made you do it in the end?'

'I loved her,' Ross said simply. 'And I loved Matthew and I loved Tennengarrah, so I really hit the jackpot when I got all three wishes granted.'

'You did,' Abby said softly. 'But, then, you knew what you

wanted, Ross. If a genie popped out of a lamp now, I don't know what my three wishes would be.'

'Some space,' Ross suggested gently, and after a moment's deep thought Abby nodded slowly, scarcely able to believe her ears as Ross offered her an out. 'There's a plane landing soon and it's heading for Adelaide. Maybe they can make room for a doctor on board, a doctor heading for home.' As Abby swallowed hard, Ross continued, passing endless reams of tissues as he did so. 'You can get a connection to Sydney when you're there, even if you have to sleep on the airport sofas for a while. Look, I'm not one for goodbyes, either, Abby, and with the whole town watching you two tonight, waiting and watching Kell's every move, I can imagine the pressure you're under. If you want to go now, I'll understand.'

'But my contract—'

'Timothy's here now, and he's more than happy to start working.'

'What will you tell Kell?'

'That Bill needed a doctor escort. I'll tell him the truth when the ball's over.'

'Shelly will kill you,' Abby warned, but Ross begged to differ.

'Shelly will understand.'

But still Abby didn't get it. 'Why would you do this for me, Ross? Why would you take all this on?'

'You delivered my daughter, Abby,' Ross said slowly. 'A breech birth in the middle of nowhere. We both know how awful that could have been. You're an amazing doctor and, given the chance, you'd have been an amazing friend to Shelly and me. I reckon I owe you at least this.'

It didn't take long to pack, Tennengarrah wasn't exactly lined with shops and Shelly had lightened her of every last scrap of make-up. Abby's case snapped closed with surprising ease. The only extra thing she took was the rather battered dusty old hat Kell had given her, and as she pulled it on her head, Abby heard the buzz of the plane, the lights filling her empty living room for a second and as it swooped in for landing, she screwed her eyes closed and mentally begged for Kell's understanding, for him to know that even if she was taking the supposedly easy way out, every last step was loaded with agony.

'All ready?' Ross met her outside the clinic, took her computer and wheeled the suitcase the last few steps as Abby struggled to hold back the tears.

'Where's Martha?' Abby gulped, looking around through tear-laden eyes as they loaded Bill onto the plane.

'She can't go, that's one of the reasons Bill found it so hard to make the decision. It's a long, lonely day in hospital when you know you're not going to get any visitors. But Martha needs to stay and look after the farm and in the long run that will give Bill more peace of mind. They were both getting too upset saying goodbye, so Dr Hall suggested that she race home and put on all the lights. They're going to fly low over his property so he can see it again.'

Any chance of a controlled goodbye dissolved there and then as a new batch of tears burst forth, and for a moment or two Abby struggled to catch her breath.

'Come on, Abby.' Dr Hall's voice was kind but firm. 'Ross has got a ball to get to.'

'You've got your first wish.' Ross gave her a quick hug and as she stepped onto the plane Abby turned.

'When I've worked out what my second one is, I'll let you know.'

'You can do a ward round when we get to Adelaide,' Dr Hall grinned as he sat down next to her and clipped on his seat belt. 'There are a couple of patients doing very nicely there, thanks to you.'

'Jessica?' Abby asked, and Hall nodded warmly.

'She'll be going home in a couple of days. Well, not to England, but her parents have flown over to be with her and they're going to have a nice gentle family holiday before they all head back. And the little tacker with the epiglottitis is doing well. He's off the ventilator and they're trying to wean him off his tracheostomy.

'You've been an asset,' he added warmly. 'We're sorry to lose you.' He busied himself then, politely not noticing her tears as he concentrated on his notes in front of him as they flew out of Tennengarrah, the plane flying even lower as they passed over Bill's property. Abby held his thin hand tightly as he leant back on the stretcher gazing out of the window into the darkness, the lights blazing their goodbyes down below. Holding back her tears was the hardest feat Abby had ever undertaken, but this was Bill's goodbye, not hers. And when the last light had disappeared, when just the endless night sky surrounded the windows, he leant back further on his pillow, his scared, sad eyes meeting Abby's.

'I'll see it again, won't I?' His weak voice was barely audible over the engine, the oxygen mask over his face forcing Abby to lean forward to catch his words. 'This isn't the last time, is it?'

Smiling bravely, Abby leant forward, squeezing his hand ever tighter. Her voice was so positive, so assured and full of hope, even Abby wondered where it was coming from. 'You're doing the right thing and you *will* see it again, Bill. This isn't goodbye.'

Comforted, reassured, his anxious eyes closed for the bliss of sleep as Abby sat dry-eyed beside him, not even attempting small talk with the busy, efficient staff and wishing, wishing more than she ever had before, that someone, anyone, could say the same words to her.

CHAPTER THIRTEEN

'THIS COFFEE'S DISGUSTING.'

As Abby walked into the staffroom she looked at the gathered night staff, grabbing a quick drink before the Saturday night shift started and she managed a rueful smile. Gone were her insecurities, the paranoia that the conversation shifted each and every time she entered the room.

The coffee here *was* disgusting and, as Kell had pointed out, it really was all that was on the nurses' minds.

'Then it's just as well I've been shopping,' Abby said, pulling a massive jar of the most expensive instant out of her bag. She pulled a marker pen off the whiteboard. 'That should keep the hordes off,' she said as she placed it on the coffee-table.

'It will, too.' Jane, the night charge nurse, grinned as she read Abby's bold writing. '"Hands off! Abby Hampton, Consultant." Present company excepted, I hope?'

'Absolutely,' Abby said as she checked in her pigeonhole and pulled out a few manila envelopes. 'Finally,' she groaned, as her new name badge fell into her hands. Clipping it on, the one she'd waited so long for, Abby accepted the trickle of applause that went around the room.

'So it's finally official,' Jane cheered. 'Our Abby really is a consultant.'

'So it says here.' Peering down at her white coat, the sense of anticlimax surprised even Abby.

She'd been back a fortnight now. Visited the Opera House, taken a ferry across the harbour and lain on Manly beach, walked around the Botanical Gardens, slipping off her shoes and revelling in the soft damp grass beneath her feet. Been to the theatre, eaten authentic Thai Tom Yum and Japanese Tepanyaki Beef on various nights with the best of them as her colleagues had toasted her success, shopped till she'd dropped and had more than her share of facials and massages.

Everything she'd missed, everything she'd wanted, there for the taking now.

And it didn't mean a thing.

Only work was her salvation, the one real pleasure she had. Nothing, not even a tourist bus crash, or a child with epiglottitis in the middle of nowhere, quite made up for the thrill of promise that filled city emergency rooms the world over as they prepared for a Saturday night.

It was either there or it wasn't.

You either got it or you didn't.

But as she pulled her stethoscope around her neck, clipped her pager in her pocket and walked through the already steaming waiting room, past the 'Staff Only' doors and into the pulsing hub of activity on the other side, Abby knew that work alone wasn't enough.

That love had won.

Oh, she wasn't about to down tools and leave, the drug programme was too precious to abandon at this fragile stage, but, then, so was her relationship with Kell. Abby's hand dug into her pocket, her fingers closing around the half-finished letter she had written. Hopefully she'd get the time to complete it on her break tonight, that she could somehow translate the jumble of thoughts in her brain into a semblance of a letter. That she was sorry she had left, but not sorry she'd come back. Sorry for the pain she had caused. But could she ask for a favour?

Was a year too long to ask Kell to wait? A year to get the programme running, a year to see things through...

'We're down two staff,' Jane said briskly, handing Abby a mountain of patient files. 'We've only got one nurse really qualified for resus at the moment.'

'What about you?'

Jane gave small shrug. 'I'm in charge, so officially I don't count, but, of course, if something comes in I'll just have to split myself in two, or three,' she muttered as the emergency bell went.

'No.' Abby shook her head firmly. 'Get me the supervisor on the phone and I'll have a word.'

'Done,' Jane barked as she shooed out a couple of drunks who had wandered through. 'There's not a nurse on the wards prepared to come down, so they've agreed to send an agency nurse.'

'Great,' Abby muttered.

'Don't shoot the messenger.' Jane grinned. 'Who knows? The agency might get it right for once and send someone who's actually done emergency and not a poor woman who's spent the last decade nursing geriatrics!

'It looks like you're wanted,' Jane sighed, relieving Abby of the notes and gesturing towards resus. 'Roll on seven a.m.'

'Wanted' was an understatement. A grad nurse was attempting to stop an elderly man strapped to a cardiac monitor from climbing over the cot sides of his gurney as Haley, the sister down for resus, set up a bed and started to pull up drugs.

'What's coming in?' Abby asked, getting straight to the point as she pulled on some latex gloves.

'Query heroin overdose,' Haley said, filling up a syringe from a vial. 'Security just alerted us. His so-called friends just dumped him in the car park. Uh-oh.' Jane's face at the door didn't bode well.

'Ambulance Control just radioed through. They're bringing in a motorcyclist with major head injuries. I've paged the trauma team and they're on the way.'

'How about that extra nurse?' Abby called to her departing back.

'She's on her way, too!'

'You, set up for the cyclist,' Abby ordered Haley, as the orthopaedic registrar flew through the door. 'I'll deal with the OD. Hopefully the security officers will stay and help!'

She wasn't joking! Making sure she had everything else to hand, Abby rechecked the drug Haley had drawn up, knowing that if this was indeed a heroin overdose, the man being carried in grey and lifeless by Security could very well turn into one angry young man indeed when his overdose was reversed.

'It's Pete,' Abby said as the young man was placed on the trolley beside her.

'I really thought he'd turned his life around after the last scare.'

'Ever the optimist,' Haley sighed as the orthopaedic registrar made his way over.

'My motorcyclist hasn't arrived yet, how about I lend a hand?'

He bagged the patient with essential oxygen as Abby struggled to find a vein in Pete's thin bruised arms. 'Got one,' she said finally on her third attempt. 'And not a moment too soon. It looks like your motorcyclist is here,' she commented as the blue lights of the ambulance flashed past the window. 'I'll be over to help when I can.' Picking up the syringe, Abby gave a thin smile to the two burly security guards. 'Ready, guys.'

The drug worked in seconds.

The young man, who only seconds before had been deeply unconscious and barely breathing, precariously close to death, suddenly attempted to sit up, cursing and swearing angrily, furious with the world.

'Hi, Pete,' Abby said in a resigned voice as the vile language continued. 'So you've come back to see us again.'

Even with their combined strength, the security officers were struggling to hold the young man down, and Abby stood back slightly as she spoke to him. 'You nearly died, Pete.'

'I'd have been fine.'

'No,' Abby said sharply. 'A couple of minutes more and you'd have been brain damaged, and a couple of minutes more than that and you'd have been dead. Now, I want you to calm down, and when you have, you and I are going to have a long talk.'

'You're wasting your time,' Pete shouted, struggling to sit up. 'What would you know?'

'Too much,' Abby said, meeting his eyes full on. 'I lost a dear friend because of drugs and I lose more patients than I can even bear to think about due to them, so I know plenty. Now, like it or not, Pete, I'm on your back, and for once you're going to listen to me.'

'Get lost,' Pete sneered.

'Settle down, mate.'

The calmest, most easygoing of voices, so out of place in an emergency room, suddenly filled the air and Abby stared, just stared at the muscular, tanned forearm that was pushing Pete back down onto the trolley.

'I'd suggest you lie there and do what the doctor says, huh? It can't hurt to listen.'

Still her eyes didn't dare move. Instead, they stayed trained on Kell's arms, scrutinising every dark hair, the veins on the back of his hand, the neat white nails, terrified that if she moved if she blinked, if she even breathed, he might somehow disappear.

'What are you doing here?' She finally croaked, confused, overwhelmed but utterly, utterly delighted.

'Didn't the agency say I was coming?' Kell winked.

'*You're* the agency nurse?'

'A word, Abby, please?' Jane's none-too-dulcet tones wouldn't wait and with a bemused shake of her head Abby made to go, but her legs just wouldn't move.

'Go,' Kell said gently. 'We'll still be here when you get back, won't we, Pete?'

'I'm so sorry.' Jane grimaced as Abby came over. 'I never thought he'd just march in.'

'Who?'

'Kelvin. The agency's really overstretched the mark this time. He's a bush nurse—a bush nurse!' Jane repeated, shaking her head in disbelief. 'I told him there's no snakes here, young man, and I said he could try and make himself useful tidying the pan room and running a few patients up to the ward.'

'And what did he say?' Abby asked, a markedly absent smile forming on her lips.

'Well, that's just it. He just shrugged and carried right on over to resus, I honestly don't think he's the full ticket, and he's certainly not what I ordered from the agency.'

'His name's Kell, Jane, not Kelvin, and he's exactly what you ordered.'

'What do you mean?'

Abby was smiling now, really smiling as Jane stared at her, bemused. 'You need to loosen up a bit Jane. He's *everything* this department needs.'

He was, too.

On they worked, through this busy Saturday night, and nothing, not a single thing, fazed him. Flirting gently with the old ladies, chatting amicably with the drunks, making tea and toast for the down-and-outs one minute, performing cardiac massage on a teenager the next. Even the sex workers who trickled in tired and weary in the small hours of the morning perked up a bit when they saw Kell writing his notes at the nurses' station.

'Where did *that* come from?' Gloria, one of the regular sex workers, asked as Abby finished stitching her hand, gaping in open-mouthed admiration as Kell breezed into the theatre to check a drug with Jane.

'He's from the bush,' Jane said once Kell had gone, snipping

Abby's suture, her voice growing more gushing by the minute. 'And despite my earlier doubts, he's an absolute treasure.'

'That'll be right,' Gloria muttered. 'They don't make men like that in the city.' Sitting up, she straightened her red boob tube and patted her curls. 'I could give him my card on the way out.' With a saucy wink she fished in her purse. 'I might even offer him a discount.'

'That won't be necessary, Gloria.' A distinctly proprietorial note came to Abby's voice as she pulled off her gloves and tossed them in the bin.

'What are you getting so uppity about?' Jane teased good-naturedly as a wide grin split Gloria's face.

'I'd say your doctor is in love, Sister.' Gloria laughed, stepping down off the trolley and attempting to straighten her inch of skirt. 'And if she's got any sense, she'd better do something about it!'

Abby found Kell in the staffroom, boots on the table, lounging on the sofa as if he came here every night.

'They really weren't talking about you, Abby,' he said with a smile as she came in. 'This coffee is seriously bad.'

'There's a jar of decent stuff in the kitchen.'

'I saw, but it also said it was the property of Abby Hampton and hands off.'

'Since when did that stop you?'

The joking was over now, the small talk had run out and Abby stood utterly still as he came over and put his arms around her, burying his head in her hair, breathing in the sweet smell as if it was the life force he depended upon.

'God, I've missed you. Don't ever, ever leave me like that again.'

'Oh, Kell.' She held him, held him so close, his skin, his smell, everything she missed, everything she needed. 'I just couldn't see how—'

'Hey.' He pulled her chin up gently. 'No getting upset. I'm

here, aren't I? And Jane's already offered me a whole fortnight of shifts.'

'Don't, Kell.' She shook her head fiercely, determined to get in first, to counter his temporary solution with a permanent one. 'You told me the first night we met you could never leave Tennengarrah, and I can't be cross at you because I felt the same. You'll end up resenting me—'

'Abby.' His voice broke in, that lazy, lazy smile halting her in her tracks. 'That was the first night I met you—before I'd held you, tasted you, made love to you. You can't hold me accountable for what I said then.'

'You love it there, Kell. I can't ask you to leave.'

'You haven't,' Kell pointed out. 'I've made that choice all by myself. You running away like that has taken me to hell and back, but in other ways it's been exactly what I needed. Tennengarrah's got its charms and I love it, yes, but without you, Abby, it just felt empty. Maybe I needed that time without you to realise that I *could* leave, to see what really mattered to me.' He let his words sink in, staring down at her with love blazing from his eyes as his voice imbued her with long-forgotten hope. 'You know when they say, "Love will find a way." Have you ever stopped to think what that means?'

'It's all I've thought about,' she admitted, one shaking hand retrieving the letter, watching his face for a reaction as he read it, watching the wonder in his eyes when he finally looked up.

'You'd give it all up for me?'

She nodded slowly but with absolute certainty. 'You don't have to leave, Kell. All I'm asking is that you wait a year for me.'

'No.' Her eyes shot up at his answer, confusion turning to wonder as Kell carried on talking. 'We don't have to wait, Abby. I'm not letting you out of my sight ever again. I'm coming to live here, with no hang-ups, no resentment, because, quite simply, I love you. You're a consultant, for heaven's sake, a consultant with a crazy dream about saving the world, and the most amazing part of it is that I'm starting to think you could do it.'

'I'm hardly going to save the world,' Abby countered. 'This programme will barely scratch the surface.'

'It's a start, though,' Kell said gently. 'And who knows where it will lead? This is where you belong, Abby. I'm not going to punish you for that. I just want to be with you.'

Hope flared deep inside and she waited, waited for it to be doused, for the ifs or buts that would surely come, a demand, a condition, a time span that would surely render the problem insurmountable. But black eyes just kept on smiling, and those strong arms moved around her as he fumbled in his pocket and pulled out the ring she'd been so scared to glimpse.

'It's an Argyle diamond,' Kell said as she stared in wonder at the massive pink diamond glinting back at her, set high on a delicate gold band. 'I know you're probably not one for pink, but I saw the stone and I just fell in love with it—rare and unique like you, and from the heart of Australia like me.' He slipped it onto her shaking hand as she stared at it in bemused wonder.

'Are you sure, Kell, I mean, really sure? This is such a huge step, Tennengarrah's in your blood...' The last question slipped out of her mouth, needing to be voiced and, more importantly, needing to be answered.

'Tennengarrah's in my blood,' he interrupted, then planted the softest, gentlest of kisses on her mouth before he finished, before it was Kell's turn to put the world to rights...

'But you, Abby, you're in my heart.'

* * * * *

The Doctor's
Outback Baby

Helen, David, Ryan, William and Amy Browne,
with love.

PROLOGUE

'I HATE TO ASK.'

Clara gritted her teeth as Shelly came through the clinic doors brandishing the off-duty book. Everyone always 'hated to ask', but it certainly didn't seem to stop them from doing exactly that!

'I just don't see how we can ask Irene to prepare Bill for the flight and give the Flying Doctors a handover—she was only supposed to be babysitting the clinic.'

'She *is* a registered nurse,' Clara pointed out.

'Who barely practises.' Shelly had a point, Clara could see that much. Bill Nash, after weeks of deliberation, had chosen today to finally agree to the cardiac bypass surgery he desperately needed. And as luck would have it, the surgeons in Adelaide had a theatre cancellation on Monday, which hopefully wouldn't give Bill too much opportunity to change his mind.

Which was great and everything. But today also happened to be the one day in the year when something actually happened in the remote outback town of Tennengarrah. She'd requested the night off months ago. As soon as the ball committee had decided on the date Clara had penciled her request into the roster. She'd even booked a hair appointment, hoping that for one night at least her rather thin, impossibly straight, short red hair could be somehow transformed. And now here was Shelly, who also happened to be a registered nurse, asking her, yet again, if she would mind saving the day.

'Surely there's someone else,' Clara mumbled, hoping Shelly would take the hint but knowing it was futile. It wouldn't even enter Shelly's head to put her hand up.

Why bother when there was good old Clara?

'There isn't,' Shelly sighed. 'Kell's the only other nurse and as he's on a day off I can't get hold of him. We might not even need anyone. The Flying Doctors could come at any time, they might even be here this morning and then tonight's off duty won't even be an issue. But when they do come they're going to want a thorough handover, it's just not fair to ask Irene to do it when she's barely looked after him. Look, Clara, I'd do it myself, it's just…' Her voice trailed off, and Clara knew she was waiting for her to jump in, knew Shelly was waiting for her to let out an incredulous laugh and say, no, don't worry. She knew how much Shelly was looking forward to the ball, knew Shelly had been on a post-pregnancy diet for weeks and was looking forward to finally having a romantic night with her husband Ross, Tennengarrah's resident doctor, and that of course Clara wasn't suggesting that she actually work tonight.

But for the first time in living memory Clara stood firm. Tonight was just too important to her.

'What about Abby?' Clara suggested hopefully, and not with entirely innocent intentions either. Abby Hampton, an efficient doctor from the city who was nearing the end of her three-month stint in the outback, had been the thorn in Clara's side for weeks now and the prospect of Tennengarrah's ball without the stunning Dr Hampton present was extremely appealing. Even so, Clara blushed guiltily as she pressed the point, knowing her motives weren't entirely pure. 'I know she's a doctor, but we all pitch in with things like this, and she's not exactly enamoured of the place. I'm sure Abby wouldn't mind holding the fort.'

'I can't ask Abby.' Shelly shook her head, but an excited smile was starting to form on her lips as she looked around to check that the coast was clear. 'Honestly, Clara, I just can't.'

'What's going on?' Clara asked. 'Come on, Shelly, tell me. There's only Bill here and he's asleep. Why can't you ask Abby?'

'You have to promise not to breathe a word.' Shelly's eyes were wide. She was grinning broadly now and Clara found herself reluctantly smiling back, her annoyance with Shelly's thoughtlessness evaporating at the chance of a piece of gossip.

'I promise. Come on, Shelly, don't keep me in suspense. Has she finally decided to head off back to Sydney to her beloved emergency department?' Clara asked, rather too hopefully.

'Oh, it's better than that,' Shelly said excitedly, perching herself on the edge of the desk and beckoning Clara closer. 'And if you let it slip I'll never—'

'Get on with it.' Clara laughed, sitting back on her seat and waiting to hear what Shelly was so excited about.

'I can't ask Abby to work tonight, because I have it on excellent authority that someone else wants to ask her something.'

'I'm not with you.' Clara shook her head, bemused.

'You really don't have a clue, do you? Where have you been hiding the last week or so, Clara? The bush telegraph's been working overtime,' Shelly whispered excitedly. 'Guess where Kell is?'

'On a day off.'

'Yes, but guess what he's doing?'

'He said he was going into town,' Clara shrugged. 'Bruce was going to fly him there.'

'Which he did a couple of weeks ago, and Bruce saw him going into a jeweller's!' When Clara still didn't catch on Shelly thumped her playfully on the arm, jumping off the desk with an excited whoop as for Clara reality finally dawned. 'Kell's going to ask Abby to marry him, Clara! I'm on my way over to Abby's now. I've managed to squeeze her in to get her hair and nails done, though she's absolutely no idea what Kell's got planned. I can't possibly tell her that Bill's finally decided to have the op or she'll be over in a flash, that's why I'm bending over backwards to sort out the roster and make sure everything goes smoothly. Nothing must spoil tonight for them. Can you believe Kell's actually going to propose?'

Clara couldn't.

For a moment the world stopped. She could hear Shelly laughing and talking in the background, was vaguely aware even of Ross and some other guy walking in, but for that moment in time her heart felt as if it wasn't beating any more. Clutching Bill's pile of notes to her chest as if it were some sort of shield, she sat there as the news washed over her.

Kell Bevan was going to propose.

After all these years Kell had finally got off his blue-jeaned backside and made a flight into town to pick up a ring on the day of the Tennengarrah ball.

It was just how she'd imagined it.

Just how she'd secretly dreamed it would be. The barn alight with fairy-lights, tea-candles burning on the tables, the scent of white gardenias filling the night air, the stars twinkling endlessly above as Kell finally proposed.

Maybe she hadn't prayed hard enough.

Perhaps when she'd made the mental bargain with the powers that be she hadn't been specific enough, had forgotten to point out what should have been so blazingly obvious.

Kell should have been asking her.

CHAPTER ONE

'AND THIS IS Clara, who knows more about Tennengarrah than the whole lot of us put together, don't you?'

'Sorry?' Realising that not only was she being spoken to but that a response was very much the order of the day, Clara turned her slightly startled expression to Ross.

'I was just telling Timothy here how much we all depend on you, and that if he needs anything he only has to ask.' Ross Bodey's rather strained smile left Clara in no doubt she'd been daydreaming too long and it hadn't gone unnoticed.

'He's the new doctor,' Shelly mumbled in an undertone, pushing Clara forward to shake Timothy's outstretched hand. 'From England.'

'But you're not due for a couple of weeks yet.'

It wasn't the most welcoming of greetings—in fact, on a rating of one to ten it would barely have scored—but, given the bombshell Shelly had just been dropped, Clara was amazed she could actually speak, and what was more her voice even sounded vaguely familiar!

'I ran out of cash.'

His admission startled her out of her confusion momentarily. Shifting the pile of notes into one arm, Clara accepted the outstretched hand and found herself looking into two smiling green eyes, even managing a rather forced smile back as thankfully he went over the formalities she had clearly missed.

'Timothy Morgan. It's a pleasure to meet you.'

'Clara Watts,' she mumbled, stealing a closer look. He certainly didn't look like someone who would run out of cash. His clothes, though casual, were certainly top notch and he had a very English, rather upper-crust accent, his thick curly brown hair was superbly cut but, more importantly, there was a slightly unassuming air about him, a refreshing openness to the smile he easily imparted as he shook her hand firmly. 'So you're from England. Are you here on a working holiday?'

'That's right,' Timothy answered cheerfully. 'Though I've been away for nearly a year now, working and trying to fit in all the touristy things.'

Lord, he could talk. She'd only asked a question to be polite! All Clara really wanted to do was dash off to the loo, bury her head in her hands and go over the news Shelly had so happily imparted. But instead she had to stand and make polite noises as Dr Timothy Morgan took her on an impromptu virtual tour of Australia, pulling photos out of his pocket like a magician as he told her how he'd bought a cheap ute, worked his way down the east coast of Australia and was now working his way up the middle.

'I was hoping to make my fortune in Coober Pedey,' Timothy chattered on easily. 'I read in my guide book that some tourists make enough to fund their entire trip, only in my case I spent three weeks fossicking in the dirt for opals and ended up spending a fortune having the two tiny stones I found mounted, which wasn't exactly the plan, so I'm hoping to start here early.'

'How early?' Shelly asked hopefully, peering at the roster as Ross started to laugh.

'You can't ask the poor guy to work on his first night here— he should be over at the ball, getting to know all the locals in one swoop. What's the problem?'

'I can't get anyone to work tonight.'

'But I thought Irene was coming.'

'She is, but she made it very clear she doesn't want to hand over to the Flying Doctors. So if they don't get here before seven, one of us is going to have to be here, and I can hardly ask Kell or Abby.'

'And you can't ask Clara,' Ross said firmly. 'She's on the ball committee, for goodness' sake, they've been planning this for months.'

'No, you can't ask Clara.'

The conversation that had been taking place ended abruptly, every eye turning as the new guy in town put in his ten cents' worth to a problem that clearly wasn't his.

'Because I intend to ask her to dance.'

It was an unfortunate moment to drop the pile of notes Clara had been precariously balancing.

Unfortunate, because from the look that flashed between Ross and Shelly they clearly thought Timothy's rather vocal intentions had caused her lapse in concentration.

Unfortunate, because Shelly, an eternal romantic at the best of times, would be for ever on her case now about the gorgeous new doctor and why didn't she make a bit of effort with him.

And unfortunate, because there was nothing dignified about scrabbling on the floor, trying to pick up endless reams of blood results and ECG printouts scattered over a seemingly ten-mile radius, with a heart that was bleeding inside.

Kell was going to propose.

It was like an awful mantra resounding in her head. Biting on her bottom lip to fight the sting of tears, Clara could feel her face reddening with the effort of not crying. She wished they'd all just leave her alone. Go and do whatever needed to be done on a Saturday morning and let her get on with her day.

Let her get on with her life.

A life without Kell.

'If the Flying Doctors haven't come by the time the balls starts, Irene can still watch him and give me a call when they get here. We'll hear the plane coming in anyway. It will only take half an hour or so to hand over.'

'But, Ross...' Shelly protested.

They were all on the floor, kneeling down and pretending not to notice Clara's red face and shaking hands.

'No buts,' Ross said firmly, standing up and shuffling the mass of papers into a pile that would take for ever to sort out. 'Have you told Bill's daughter the news?'

Clara shook her head, grateful for the change of subject. 'I've been ringing all morning but I can't get through.'

'No doubt she's out on the farm. It's probably best someone tells her face to face, given that she's pregnant and everything. I might head over now. Do you want to come, Timothy?'

'Where do they live?'

'Just out of town.'

Timothy gave a small grimace. 'Which in the outback means a couple of hours' drive. Sorry, Ross, would it be a terrible career move if I turned you down, given that I've just spent the last twenty-four hours bumping along in my ute to get here?'

'Of course not.' Ross laughed. 'I just feel guilty, leaving you on your own on your first morning here. Shelly's got a hairdresser's appointment, Kell and Abby are off duty...'

'I'll be fine,' Timothy said assuredly. 'A shower and a sleep are top of my list at the moment. Still...' those green eyes turned to Clara, who was attempting to fashion Bill's notes into some sort of order '... I wouldn't say no to a quick guided tour of the clinic, if Clara doesn't mind. I'd hate for something to happen and not have a clue where anything's kept.'

'Good idea,' Ross said enthusiastically, obviously thrilled to have Timothy on board. 'You don't mind, do you, Clara?'

There it was again, the automatic assumption that she'd come good. 'You don't mind' was up there with 'I hate to ask' and Clara's personal favourite, 'Oh, Clara will do it'.

Well, she did mind.

Right now she wanted some peace, wanted to sort out Bill's

notes, wanted some time to gather her thoughts and figure out what on earth she was going to do, not hold yet another new doctor's hand and show another fleeting visitor the ropes, only to have them leave again.

Of course she didn't say as much. Instead, she nodded, her clear blue eyes briefly meeting Timothy's. 'Sure, I'd be happy to.'

'Great.'

'Sorry about this,' Timothy ventured once they were alone. 'I'm sure you've got a million and one things to do without taking me around. It's just that I went for an interview at a bush hospital up in Queensland when I first came to Australia. I got there early, as you do for interviews, and a patient went and had a cardiac arrest while I was sitting outside the interview room.'

Clara was only half listening as she pushed open the coffee-room doors and pointed in the vague direction of the staff kitchen before heading towards the main work area. Timothy's backpacking stories really held no interest for her.

'Anyway, it turns out I was so early the doctor interviewing me wasn't in the hospital yet.'

'Really?' Clara said distractedly, turning up the volume on Bill's cardiac monitor before she crossed the room as Timothy hovered annoyingly over her right shoulder, watching her every move. 'I'll take you though to our treatment room.'

'So there I was, going over my interview technique, the ink on my medical certificate barely dry, and this nurse came running up.'

'Two beds,' Clara said, pushing open the heavy back swing doors as Timothy carried on nattering. 'This sometimes doubles as a second resuscitation area if we get a major incident...' Her voice trailed off in mid-sentence and she turned around sharply. 'You were the only doctor in the hospital?'

'Barely a doctor, really.' Timothy nodded as Clara's mouth fell open. 'I came to Australia as soon as I finished med school—I hadn't even had my new cheque books delivered.'

He watched a frown pucker her freckled face. 'One of life's better moments.' Timothy smiled. 'Ringing up the bank and asking them to change the Mr to Dr. You'd be amazed how that surly voice on the other end of the phone changes when they realise your rather shaky bank balance is in for some serious improvement.'

'But you're too…' Snapping her mouth closed, Clara didn't finish her sentence, but Timothy had already got the gist.

'Too old to be an intern?' he finished for her with a grin. 'I was a mature student. In fact, a student's practically all I've ever been. I spent three years at uni fiddling around doing a business and finance degree, then two months out in the big wide world made me realise the family business just wasn't for me. They're financial planners.' Timothy grimaced. 'My parents get the same thrill watching the stock market that I get watching a cardiac monitor.'

Clara laughed, actually laughed. 'Sounds as if you could use some financial planning yourself.'

But Timothy just shook his head. 'Heaven forbid. Sure, I could ring them up and ask them to wire me some money but I wouldn't give them the satisfaction.' He gave a grim smile. 'There's the rest of my life to worry about mortgage payments and retirement funds. When I get back to England I'm hoping to study to become a surgeon so there's years of being sensible ahead, but for now I intend to enjoy myself, despite my parents' objections.'

Clara sensed the edge of his voice but chose not to push. 'So what happened?' She registered his frown. 'At your interview in Queensland?'

'Oh, that!' Timothy grinned, his easy smile back in place now. 'Well, this nurse comes rushing up and tells me that Mr Forbes in bed four has gone into a cardiac arrest.'

'So what did you do?' There was impatience to her voice, which Timothy seemed not to notice.

'Well, for starters I asked just where bed four was, and while she was at it would she mind telling me who the hell Mr Forbes was and, perhaps more pointedly, if there was another doctor in the house.'

'But what did you do with the patient?' Clara pushed, genuinely enthralled now, as any nurse would have been at such a story. 'What on earth happened?'

'I took a crash course in crash calls.' He laughed. 'Thank heavens I watch *ER*. I was giving out orders, calling out to charge the defibrillator, massaging Mr Forbes's chest. I even intubated him.'

'Really?' Clara asked, suitably impressed, but Timothy shrugged modestly.

'I'd had a few goes in Theatre.'

'But still,' Clara enthused. 'There's a big difference between the controlled setting of Theatre with an anaesthetist over your shoulder and running your first cardiac arrest on your own. You did really well.'

'Not that well,' Timothy groaned. 'The patient died.'

'Ouch.'

'And I didn't get the job.'

'But why?' Clara protested. 'That's so unfair.'

'That's life.' Timothy shrugged. 'Someone smarter, with more experience, got in first.'

'I know the feeling,' Clara muttered.

'Sorry?'

'It doesn't matter. Come on, I'll show you around properly, though hopefully there won't be any repeats.' They walked around the theatre, Clara pointing things out, flicking machines on and off and taking Timothy through the resuscitation trolley, even surprising herself by pursuing a conversation with him.

'So, which hospital did you end up in?'

'Adelaide.'

'But that's the other end of the country,' Clara pointed out.

'And I took my time getting there, let me tell you.'

'Maybe later.' Clara grinned. 'I do actually have some work to do.'

'Sorry, I tend to go on a bit, but despite my poverty I've just about saved up enough money to head back to Queensland when I'm finished here and do the next level diving course.'

'You've already done one?'

'Two,' Timothy replied. 'It was amazing. You should see some of the photos I've taken of the barrier reef—I'll show you some time. Have you been there?'

Clara shook her head. 'I haven't been anywhere. Apart from three years in Adelaide to study nursing, I've never been away from here. It sounds wonderful, though. I've heard it's stunning.'

'Oh, it is and nothing beats seeing it at first hand. Our diving instructor gave us some food to take down. The fish actually come and feed out of your hands—I even saw a shark not six feet away.'

'Don't,' Clara yelped. 'I'd die.'

'I nearly did,' Timothy responded, his eyes widening in fear just at the memory. 'Apparently if you ignore them they'll ignore you, but I must have used up half my air tank I was hyperventilating so much. You should do it some day, take off and backpack around this amazing land. It's been the best year of my life.'

'I'd love to,' Clara admitted, 'but I can't see it happening. I can barely get a night off to go to the ball. Can you imagine Ross and Shelly if I asked for a whole year?'

'Don't ask.' Timothy shrugged. 'Just do it.'

'Easier said than done.' Looking up, she realised Timothy was waiting for her to elaborate. 'The clinic used to be tiny, just one room and one theatre, when I started. But since Ross and Shelly came last year it's really grown. Ross is totally committed to the place, he's for ever lobbying for more staff and more funds and for the most part it's worked. The closed-off area is yet another extension and when that's completed we're going to be upgraded from a clinic to a bush hospital. There's going to be two wards and a proper delivery suite, which will be great, of course, but the trouble is the staff ratio hasn't exactly kept up with the patients so far. Kell and I do most of it between us, Shelly pitches in when she can, but she's got a new baby and a three-year-old to take care of. She wants to be at home with her babies and, frankly, I don't blame her. Matthew, her three-year-old, has got Down's syndrome,' Clara explained, but Timothy just nodded.

'I know.'

'So her hands are full already, without taking on a load of extra shifts.'

'So it all falls on you?'

'And Kell,' Clara said quickly, but when Timothy just stared back at her she let out a low sigh. 'Mainly me at the moment,' she admitted. They were in the storeroom now, out of earshot of Bill, so Clara was able to be honest. 'We don't normally have inpatients, at least not for more than a couple of nights, but Bill didn't want to be transferred and he was too sick to go home...'

'And, of course, Kell was busy with Abby,' Timothy said perceptively. 'So it all came down to you. You are allowed to have a life, too, you know.'

'It's not that bad,' Clara protested. 'It's just been a bit full on these past few weeks.'

'You should take some time off, I bet you've got heaps owing. Go and see this magical land of yours. I know that's what I'll be doing once I've done my three-month stint here. When I've got my advanced diver's certificate I'll be able to take tourists out to the reef myself. I've got a two-year working holiday visa and I intend to use every last day of it. Diving's great.'

'There's not much ocean in Tennengarrah,' Clara needlessly pointed out.

'Then I'll just have to stick to medicine while I'm here, I guess.' He was smiling at her and, what was more amazing given her mood only twenty minutes earlier, Clara was smiling back, only this time it wasn't forced or awkward. This time it seemed the most natural thing in the world. 'Thanks for the tour and by the way…' He was walking out now, heading for the door as Clara turned back to Bill's notes. 'I still want that dance.'

'So Cinderella shall go to the ball after all.'

The sound of Bill's voice filling the silence made Clara jump. Crossing the room, she smiled at her patient as she wrapped the blood-pressure cuff around his arm.

'You were supposed to be asleep.'

'Everyone would have stopped talking if I'd opened my eyes. It's nice to hear a bit of a gossip.'

Bill had been lying in a state of lethargic depression for weeks now, and Clara was so relieved to see his familiar, kind eyes with a bit of sparkle back in them that her own worries flew out of the window. After checking his obs, she perched on the edge of his bed for a little chat.

'It's good to have you back, Bill.'

'It's good to be back. Now that I've finally decided to go ahead and have the bypass I feel better.'

'You'll feel even better when you've had the operation. Not at first, of course, but after a month or two you'll be a new man, Bill. I'm sure you've made the right choice.'

'I hope so.' She could see the glimmer of fear in his eyes and instinctively Clara put her hand over his and gave it a small squeeze. 'You're a good girl, Clara,' Bill said as he gripped her hand back. 'Ross, Kell, Shelly, Abby, they're all great and everything, but you're one in a million, do you know that?'

'Stop getting maudlin.' Clara blushed, but Bill wouldn't let up.

'I remember when your parents died. One of Tennengarrah's blackest days it was. We were all so worried about you, wondering what would become of you. Just fifteen years old and with no one to take care of you…'

'I had loads of people,' Clara broke in. 'Everyone helped.'

'Still, a lot of fifteen-year-olds would have gone off the rails. But not you. You put your head down and got on with it, didn't you? Really made something of yourself. The whole town's so proud of you, Clara. You're a true Tennengarrah girl.'

'So is Kell,' Clara pointed out, trying not to linger on his name too long, trying to have a normal conversation without betraying the agony in her heart. It wasn't too hard to do. After all, she'd been hiding her feelings where Kell was concerned for years, it came almost as naturally as breathing. 'He's a guy, of course, but he's a local, too.'

'For how long, though?'

On any other day and under any other circumstance she'd have managed a shrug or a smile, managed to carry on talking as if she didn't have a care in the world, as if Kell Bevan was just another friend and colleague. Only today she couldn't do it.

Today as Clara sat in the still, quiet ward with her one and only patient, something that felt suspiciously like a tear pricked her eye as Bill carried on talking.

'This is hard on you, isn't it, Clara?'

'What do you mean?' Confused, she shook her head, went to pull her hand away, but Bill gripped it tighter and those kind eyes stared back at her thoughtfully.

'Kell's a bit more than just a friend to you, isn't he?'

Aghast, Clara's eyes widened, her mouth opening to let out a small wail of protest, but Bill moved quickly to reassure her.

'No one knows, so don't be embarrassed. I've known you all your life, you're like a second daughter to me, but even I didn't have a clue. You've always just been Kell and Clara, two school kids, two mates and later two nurses. I never even realised until a couple of weeks ago how you felt. But watching the two of you working together, how your whole face lights up when he comes in the room, how difficult it's been for you when Abby's around, well, I guess something just clicked in my head. You do care for him, don't you?'

It was pointless denying it, pointless when tears were streaming down her face as her old mate Bill gently held her hand.

Bill wasn't just a patient—he was friend, a surrogate uncle.

Endless nights had been spent in the cosy womb of his kitchen after her parents had died. Bill and his beloved wife had taken her under their wing, the whole town had, in fact, ensuring she'd always felt loved. Cheering her on through her school exams then later welcoming her back with open arms when finally she'd got her nursing degree.

Lying to Bill wasn't an option.

'I was going to tell him how I felt tonight,' Clara whispered. 'I knew he was seeing Abby, but I really didn't think it was that serious. I thought she was just another girlfriend, that she'd move on in a couple of weeks and things would be back to normal, and now it would seem that they're getting engaged.'

'She hasn't said yes yet,' Bill pointed out.

'Oh, she will,' Clara said ruefully. 'And deep down I know that it's right. They love each other, they're really well suited. It's just so hard to take it all in…'

'Oh, Clara.' Bill lay back on his pillow as she struggled to hold it together.

'I'm sorry, Bill, I'm supposed to be cheering you up, not landing all of this on you.'

'I wouldn't have it any other way,' Bill said gently. 'Things will get better for you Clara. When my Raelene died I thought my life was over. I never thought I'd be happy again, didn't care if I lived or died. And now look at me. I've got a grandchild on the way, I'm having an operation that will give me another decade. And you know what? I reckon once this op is over, once I'm back home, on a good day I'll even be able to say that I'm truly happy, and you'll be able to say it one day, too. It won't always hurt this much.'

'I know,' Clara said bravely, then changed her mind. 'Actually, I don't know, but I really hope so, Bill.'

'Hey, there's plenty more fish in the sea…'

'Bill…' Clara let out a rueful laugh. 'As I just said to Timothy, there's no ocean for miles here, there's really not that many fish to choose from in Tennengarrah.'

'What about the *Carry On* guy?'

'Who?'

'*Carry On Doctor*, the one with the posh voice who killed his first patient.'

'What are you talking about?'

'The one he was talking about—the guy who had the heart attack at his interview in Queensland! Like I said, I was only pretending to be asleep.'

'He didn't kill him, Bill.' Clara grinned through her tears. 'It wasn't Timothy's fault he couldn't save him—it actually sounds as if he did really well. There's not many junior doctors that could intubate a patient under those sorts of circumstances. At least the patient was given every chance.'

'I guess.' Bill gave Clara a small wink. 'I had a quick peek when he came in and he's a good-looking guy, that Timothy.'

'Don't go there, Bill,' Clara warned, but he carried on anyway.

'Why ever not? He's already lined you up for a dance. Maybe tonight won't be such a disaster after all.'

'Forget it. Tonight's already a disaster.' Standing up, Clara gave her favourite patient the benefit of a very nice smile. 'How about a cuppa?

'And some toast and Vegemite?' Bill asked hopefully. 'I'm not nil by mouth yet.'

'Give me ten minutes to sort out your notes and I'll make us both a round of toast. I could use some comfort food right now,' Clara said warmly, thrilled that Bill's appetite was finally returning.

And not just his appetite, Clara realised happily. Bill was flicking through the TV guide with more than passing interest.

'There's your favourite soap opera starting soon, Clara. Why don't you pull up a chair and have your lunch-break here? I promise not to mention Kell.'

'It's a deal.' Heading for the desk, Clara turned briefly, back in control now but still just a little shy at having finally revealed her secret. 'You come back to us safe, Bill.'

'I hope so.'

'I know so.'

CHAPTER TWO

BECAUSE IT DIDN'T matter any more, because it mattered not a jot how well she did her make-up or how well her fine red hair behaved, tonight of all nights everything worked.

The subtle blonde foils Clara had reluctantly agreed to at Anna the hairdresser's insistence lifted her short, practical hairstyle into a pretty gamine crop, accentuating her clear blue eyes and high freckled cheekbones. She hadn't used the green foundation, though. She'd had it in her drawer for weeks, had bought it on an occasional trip to town, won over by the sophisticated shop assistant who'd sworn it would neutralise even the deepest blush.

Oh, and how she would have blushed.

Blinking back a fresh crop of tears, Clara tried to beat back the image of finally telling Kell how she felt. How she'd planned to take him outside, away from Abby, away from the prying eyes of the locals, and tell him that he wasn't or ever had been just a friend…

Shaking her head firmly, Clara took a deep breath, refusing to go down that track, refusing to indulge herself in wasted dreams. Instead, she eyed herself critically in the mirror, pleased despite herself with her efforts. Even the rather shakily applied mascara and neutral lipstick for once didn't look like a little girl had practised with her mother's make-up. The antithesis of vain, she didn't even possess a full-length mirror, so the only way to view her dress was by standing precariously on the toilet lid, which, Clara realised, didn't really give the full effect when your head was chopped off from view.

Oh, lord!

Swallowing nervously, she stared at the sleek black-stockinged legs that seemed to go on for ever, a massive expanse of unfamiliar thigh slimmed down by the high heels she was wearing, but even the occasional appearance of her legs didn't jolt her as much as the sight of her breasts, jacked up in a strapless bra, wriggling and jumping in excitement at their first taste of freedom from her practical sports bra.

It was too much, way, way too much! Everyone would fall off their chairs laughing when she walked in.

Glancing at her watch, Clara bit back a surge of panic. It was already ten past seven, she was supposed to be setting up the food table now, the band would be waiting for their pay cheque before they started and if she didn't go now…

Picking up a massive tray of egg and chutney sandwiches, Clara headed for the door, then changed her mind midway. Dumping the tray in the hallway, she dashed back into her bedroom and drenched herself in perfume, then ran around the house in a manic frenzy, trying to remove every lingering trace of the beastly three dozen eggs she'd hard-boiled before heading outside and walking down the high street towards the barn and wondering why the hell she'd even bothered.

She'd be coming home alone.

Nobody laughed.

Oh, there were a few whistles and cat calls when she walked in, blushing furiously and wishing she wasn't carrying a pile of sandwiches so she could hitch down her dress a bit, and a couple of the guys slapped her on the back as if they were bringing up her wind and reminded Clara that if she had any trouble tonight she only had to ask.

As if she'd run into any trouble, Clara sighed, adding her tray to the heaving table. As if she was going to have to beat off a stream of admirers with a stick.

'You look fabulous, Clara!' Shelly made a beeline for her. 'Your dress is divine, you look just wonderful.'

'So do you.' Clara smiled. 'Where's Ross?'

'I was about to ask you the same. He "popped" over to the clinic an hour ago. You didn't see the Flying Doctors' plane there when you went past by any chance?'

Clara shook her head. 'He's probably just writing up the transfer letter. Bill's case is pretty complicated.' The frown on Shelly's face told Clara she wasn't appeased. 'He'll be here soon. Anyway, the night's still young, the band's booked until one—speaking of which, I'd better go and pay them.'

'Well, hurry back,' Shelly whispered loudly. 'There's no Ross, no Kell and no Abby. Even Timothy hasn't made his way over. Apart from me and the kids, our table's the emptiest one in the barn.'

She would have hurried back—in fact, Clara would have loved to have sat down and had a glass of punch or champagne, but instead Hamo, Jim and Mitch all decided to get their duty dances out of the way early and the next twenty minutes or so were spent being twirled around the floor by various colours of checked shirts as the band sang about shearing sheep, billy tea and all the things Australians held dear after a few cans of beer. Arriving back at the table, her face flushed, giggling at one of Hamo's more lewd jokes, her smile instantly faded as several strained faces turned to greet her.

'What's wrong?'

'Nothing,' Ross said too brightly.

'Where's Abby?'

'The Flying Doctors came,' Kell replied, without looking up. 'They needed a doctor escort.'

'Why?' Clara asked immediately. The Flying Doctors were exactly that, and Bill wasn't that sick at the moment. She couldn't think of one possible reason why Abby would have needed to go. 'Who was the doctor?'

'Hall Jells. He just thought it would be safer if the clinic provided an escort,' Ross responded, without meeting her eyes, and from the pained look Shelly was flashing at her Clara decided not to pursue it, instead taking a glass of champagne from Bruce, the local pilot who was doubling as a waiter, and trying to ignore just how divine Kell looked tonight.

'So this is where all the action is.' The appearance of Timothy lifted the mood somewhat. Everyone fell on him as if he were a long-lost friend, obviously grateful for the diversion, and Clara found herself frowning. She felt as if she'd turned on her favourite soap only to realise she'd missed an important episode. Everyone was talking normally, smiling and cheerful, but something wasn't right.

Something was definitely going on.

'I fell asleep,' Timothy explained needlessly, and, choosing the chair next to Clara's, he sat down and gave her the benefit of a very nice smile. 'It was supposed to be a fifteen-minute power nap.' He glanced at his watch. 'But that was about four hours ago.'

'Well, I'm glad you made it.' It was merely a polite comment, just as she would have given to any newcomer, but Timothy caught her eye and suddenly the massive barn seemed to shrink.

'Really?' Timothy asked, as if it really mattered.

Taking a nervous sip of her champagne, Clara held it in her mouth for a second or two before swallowing, wishing she had used that blessed green foundation after all.

'Really,' she said finally, the admission surprising even herself.

Clean-shaven and freshly showered, Timothy was pretty easy on the eye, but it wasn't just his undeniable good looks that were working their charm here. There was something about his smile that told Clara it was just for her.

'You look wonderful,' Timothy said very slowly and very deliberately, and for all the world he sounded as if he really meant it. 'Your hair looks nice, different.' Green eyes raked over her and Clara could feel her pulse flickering in her neck as he scrutinised her slowly.

'I—I had foils,' she stammered. 'Just a couple...'

'I've no idea what foils are.' Timothy grinned.

'A few blonde tips.'

Timothy nodded. 'Looks great, although I love red hair.'

'That's because you haven't got red hair,' Clara countered, blushing ever deeper. And even though the conversation flowed easily, even though they were only talking about foils and hair and oversleeping, she felt as if she were caught in a rip, seemingly following the tide of a normal conversation as a throbbing undercurrent pulled her in an opposite, unfamiliar and definitely dangerous direction.

'I'll go and get another round. Clara, do you want to give me a hand?' Kell asked, standing up. Instead of falling over her chair to help him as was usually the case, for the first time in living memory, Kell actually had to repeat himself as she laughed at something Timothy had said. 'Clara, do you want to give me a hand with the drinks?'

'I'm fine.' Clara smiled, deliberately missing the point, gesturing to her half-full glass as Kell shrugged and turned to go.

'I'll help!' Matthew jumped up, determined to impress his big buddy Kell. 'We can play—'

'Hide and seek,' Kell groaned, but his face broke into a smile as he took little Matthew's hand. 'We'll have one more game of hide and seek and then I'll get that beer.'

'How about that dance?' Timothy pushed, but Clara shook her head, turning briefly to check Kell really was out of earshot.

'How about someone telling me what's going on,' Clara said

sharply to her friends gathered around the table. 'Why on earth has Abby gone to Adelaide as a doctor escort?'

'Tell her, Ross,' Shelly choked, her voice unusually angry. 'Tell Clara the mess you've made of things.'

Clara almost spilt her drink in surprise. Never in all the time she's known Shelly and Ross had they been anything other than devoted to each other. She'd never heard so much as a cross word pass between them and now here they were practically rowing at the table in front of everyone. Something was wrong, seriously wrong, and Clara stared from one to the other with her mouth gaping open.

'Come on, Ross!' Timothy grinned eagerly and then shut up when every one turned and shushed him.

'Abby's gone,' Ross started slowly, as Clara's mouth dropped ever further. 'She's leaving tonight with the Flying Doctors. She found out Kell was going to propose and she simply couldn't face it. She didn't want to leave like this, but on the other hand she didn't know how to say goodbye.'

'Does Kell know?' Clara's voice was barely a croak. She wished she'd used the green foundation now. Her face must surely be as red as a beetroot as she struggled with the news, relief flooding her veins intermingled with a horrible surge of guilt as she glanced over to the bar where Kell stood.

'No!' It was Shelly speaking now, the bitterness in her voice clearly evident. 'Ross is going to tell him that little gem later, once the ball's over, though I'm sure he knows something's up. The poor guy's walking around with an engagement ring in his pocket and he doesn't even know that Abby's bolted!' She turned her teary face to her husband. 'Well, you can leave me out of it, Ross. I just can't bear to see his face when you tell him what you've done.'

'I didn't do anything,' Ross said through gritted teeth. 'You were the one who had to go and spill the beans to Abby. If you'd just stayed out of it we wouldn't be in this mess.'

'So it's my fault now.'

'It isn't anyone's fault,' Ross relented, putting a hand over Shelly's. 'It's just the way things have turned out. Abby didn't want to hurt Kell when she said no. She was beside herself and she didn't know what else to do.'

'But why?' Clara asked, utterly bemused that anyone could run out on Kell. 'Why would she leave when he was going to propose and everything?'

'She just couldn't deal with it,' Ross said, tight-lipped. 'She belongs in the city—'

'He's coming back,' Timothy interrupted, 'so now might be a good time to change the subject.'

An awful silence followed as every one struggled to come up with something, until the baleful eyes that had silenced Timothy earlier begged him for help as Kell returned with a tray of beers.

'We have pints in England!' Timothy started, and Clara groaned into her wine at his dreadful efforts at conversation, but, as it turned out, Timothy was spot on. A lengthy discussion ensued between Kell and Timothy on the merits of pints versus schooners, warm versus icy cold and the alcohol content of either, giving the collective table enough time to exhale their held breaths and at least look as if a bombshell hadn't been dropped.

It was a great evening.

People often wonder what committees do, how one little ball could take so many months of preparation. But all their work, all the painstaking attention to detail paid off a hundredfold as midnight struck and the lights dimmed a further notch, the bush music slowing to love ballads matching the mellower mood of the crowd.

'What's going on, Clara?' Kell mumbled into his beer. 'The Flying Doctors wouldn't have needed an escort for Bill—you know that as well as I do. I've been trying to get you on your own all night to find out what's happening. Please, Clara, I need to know.'

Blinking rapidly, trying to choose her words carefully, Clara put a tentative hand across the table, opening her mouth to speak and praying she'd say the right thing.

'Time for that dance, I think.' Never had Timothy's timing been more appalling. Turning her angry eyes to him, she shook her head.

'Not now, Timothy,' she said, the irritation in her voice evident. Couldn't he see this was a private conversation?

'No excuses,' Timothy responded cheerfully, pulling her reluctantly to her feet as Clara turned and gave an apologetic shrug to Kell.

'Hold on a second.' Making her way back to the table, ignoring Timothy's obvious impatience, she met Kell's eyes. 'I'll speak to you outside after this dance.'

'What was that about?' Timothy asked once they were on the dance floor.

'Nothing.' Clara shrugged, grateful the dance floor was so packed and she could bury her flaming cheeks in Timothy's chest. She really was a useless liar.

'Because it really wouldn't be very sensible to tell Kell tonight.'

Startled, she looked up, surprised that he knew her secret.

'It would probably sound better coming from Ross.'

Relief flooded her veins, pleased that he didn't know her ulterior motives, but her relief was short-lived, turning instead into anger. She damned well wasn't about to take advice from Timothy, he hadn't even been in Tennengarrah a night yet. As if he knew what was best for Kell!

'Just leave it, Timothy,' she snapped. 'You don't know all that's gone on.'

'Keep your hair on.'

Rolling her eyes, Clara prayed the music would stop. OK, he was good-looking, funny at times and, yes, she admitted reluctantly he was a great dancer, but she hadn't heard the saying 'keep your hair on' since high school and she certainly wasn't going to let this overgrown teenager thwart her one stab at happiness tonight.

Abby had gone. Kell was devastated.

Why shouldn't he hear the news from someone who cared?

'Looks like they've made up,' Timothy commented as Ross and Shelly floated by. Shelly's eyes closed as she rested her head on Ross's shoulder, a dreamy smile on her face as they drifted along out of time with the music.

'It's the first time I've heard a cross word between them,' Clara admitted. 'Mind you, Shelly was pretty excited about tonight, she wants the world to be as happy in love as she is.'

'That's a nice thing to want.'

Clara didn't respond. Instead, she leant against Timothy, letting him lead, and perhaps for the first time that night she actually relaxed and enjoyed the fruits of the nine months of preparation that the ball had taken as she ambled along in time with the music, just enjoying the moment, enjoying the heavy throb of the bass and even revelling for a moment in the delicious spicy spell of his aftershave.

Timothy really was a good dancer, she thought almost reluctantly as the music stopped and they stood apart.

'I love this song.' Timothy smiled as the band started up again. 'Can I persuade you to join me for a second dance?'

Clara hesitated. She loved this song, too, and if truth be known she'd actually enjoyed dancing with Timothy. It hadn't been awkward like it was with some of the guys, hadn't been the duty dance every man in Tennengarrah felt compelled to have with the trusty Clara. Timothy had actually made her feel like a woman, not some annoying little sister, but she'd promised to meet Kell.

'Better not,' Clara said, the reluctance in her voice surprising even herself. 'But thanks, that was nice.'

Making her way across the room, she longed to dart into the toilet, desperate to check that she looked OK, to be sure she looked her best for the most difficult conversation of her life.

Gulping the night air into her lungs, she stared out into the darkness. The throb of music coming from the barn sounded a mile away as she stared up at the twinkling stars and begged for inspiration, her heart rate rising alarmingly as she heard heavy footsteps. Turning expectantly, forcing a smile, she stared into the darkness as he approached, not quite ready but determined not to miss her moment.

'Timothy!' The shock in her voice was evident. 'What are you doing here?'

'Getting some fresh air.' He shrugged. 'The same as you.'

Clara raked her mind. She didn't want to be rude, didn't want to be obvious, and she definitely didn't want to explain to Timothy why it was so important he left right now, but really he was leaving her with very little choice.

'Please, Timothy,' she started, her eyes turning frantically to the barn, her ears straining at the sound of approaching footsteps that she knew this time were definitely Kell's. 'I really need you to go.'

'Why?'

'I just do,' Clara whispered loudly. 'I really need to be on my own right now.'

'No, you don't.'

Aghast, she watched as he folded his arms and eyed her thoughtfully.

'In fact, I'd say the best thing you could do right now is get yourself inside and have that other dance with me.'

'Timothy, please, you don't understand...' she begged.

'Oh, but I do,' Timothy replied, and for the first time since she'd met him his voice was serious and there wasn't a glimmer of humour in his green eyes. 'You like Kell, don't you?'

'Of course I like Kell,' Clara spluttered. 'I've known him for—'

'I don't mean as a friend, Clara. You like Kell and you're hoping that when you tell him about Abby, he's going to realise just how much he actually likes you!'

Her shocked expression only confirmed his diagnosis.

'You're looking at a guy whose best friend was the captain of the rugby team,' he offered by way of explanation. 'I've spent more time than I care to remember watching other people's relationships flourish from the sidelines of my beer glass.'

'You've got it all wrong,' Clara insisted. Kell was practically on top of them. Any moment now he'd see them together and she needed to be alone for this.

'I don't think so,' Timothy responded, moving forward. 'Now, I'm going to apologise in advance for what I'm about to do, and though you probably won't realise it now, though you're probably going to hate me for it, I'm about to stop you from making the biggest mistake of your life.'

'What on earth—?'

She didn't get to finish, didn't get to say another word. Suddenly a hot wedge of flesh was pressing against her, pinning her up against the barn wall as she struggled furiously, her automatic scream hushed by the weight of his lips, her arms clamped against his chest with absolutely no room for manoeuvre.

Yet for all the shock, for all the adrenaline pumping through her veins, fear didn't enter into it. She knew Timothy's infuriating intentions, knew the sight of her stockinged legs hadn't catapulted him into a sexual frenzy. This was a duty kiss, she realised as she wrestled to get away, a duty kiss of the worst possible magnitude. And worse, far worse, despite struggling like a cat being dipped in water, despite her internal fury at her misdirected assailant, for the tiniest second, for a smidgen of time so small it was barely there, the fighting stopped, the resistance in her slipping away as other, rather more disturbing thoughts flitted into her mind.

Irrational thoughts that really shouldn't be given any credence...

The tangy aftershave that had assailed her on the dance floor, stronger now at such close proximity, his heavy ragged breathing as his chest moved against hers, the feel of her breasts pushed against the cool cotton of his shirt, and the faint tang of whisky as his lips moved against hers.

'Clara?' She could hear Kell's voice in the darkness, hear him closing in on them, and she made a last agonised struggle to escape. But Timothy was having none of it, his grip tightening on her more, if that was possible, as Kell approached.

'Oh!' She heard the surprise in Kell's voice, the muffled cough as he backed away. 'Sorry, guys.'

Only when Kell had gone, only when he was sure they were alone did Timothy pull away, his arms on the wall either side of her now like a temporary cage as he met her furious, glittering eyes.

'How dare you?' she started, her voice breathless, legs trembling with fury and something else that she would have died before admitting to. A great kisser he might be but she certainly wasn't going to let this over-inflated, pompous Englishman know that two minutes up close and personal with him had had the slightest effect in the romance stakes. She was furious.

That was all.

'How dare you?' she repeated, her voice a touch stronger now but no match for Timothy who broke in before she could even get started.

'Tonight's not the night, Clara. It's better coming from Ross.'

She shook her head incredulously, straightening up but still no match for his height even in her stilettos. 'How would you know? You haven't even been here a full day and you think you know what Kell needs. What, is it better coming from a guy? Better that a doctor breaks the news?'

Timothy shook his head, opening his mouth to speak, but nothing was stopping Clara now. Her voice finally found, she let it rip.

'Ross has only been here a year. I've known Kell all my life, so I don't need Ross to tell me when I can and can't talk to a friend, and I most certainly don't need to hear it from you. He has every right to know, every right to hear it—'

'I agree.'

'You do?' Confused, her voice stalled momentarily, the fire dying in her voice as she turned her questioning eyes to him.

'Of course he should know about Abby, but that's all. You can deny it all you like, but I'm sure there was more you were going to tell him and kissing you was the only thing I could think of to stop you from making the biggest mistake of your life.' Her burning anger was replaced with scorching shame, the glittering, defiant eyes sparkling with embarrassed tears as Timothy carried on gently, even smoothing a stray tendril of hair back behind her ear as she stood there, mortified.

'And if you told Kell you loved him, that's exactly what it would have been.'

'Hey, Clara, is everything all right?'

Hamo's none-too-dulcet tones made them both jump, Clara because she wasn't expecting it and Timothy because from the look on Hamo's face anything other than a positive reply wasn't going to be pretty.

She could have said no, could have burst into tears and landed Timothy right in it, but instead she forced a bright voice as the heavy weight approached. 'Everything's fine, Hamo.'

'You're sure?' he checked, eyeing Timothy in anything other than a friendly fashion. 'Because if you need anything you only have to give us a call.'

'I'm fine, Hamo, really.'

They both stood in strained silence as Hamo shrugged and wandered back to the barn.

'Thanks.' Timothy's smile was one of pure relief, but it changed midway when he caught sight of Clara's face.

If she'd been angry before she was furious now, the brief pause enough to reinflate her sails. Pushing his arms away, she faced him angrily.

'I didn't do it to save your skin,' she snapped. 'The fact is I hate violence or perhaps more to the point no doubt I'd have been the one who ended up suturing you and stuck in the obs ward for the next forty-eight hours feeding you through a straw.'

'So we both got lucky.' Timothy grinned, totally unfazed by her anger. 'Can we go back to being friends now?'

'We never were friends,' Clara retorted. 'I'd hardly even class you as a brief acquaintance.'

'Oh, and I suppose you go around kissing all your brief acquaintances like that?'

His humour, if you could call it that, was so appalling Clara could scarcely believe the tiny laugh that escaped her lips, but somewhere in mid-laugh it changed to a sob, and as a tell-tale tear worked its way out Timothy politely pretended not to notice.

'Is there somewhere we can sit down? Preferably on something that isn't made of hay, or I'll be sneezing all night.' She was in no position to answer, tears were choking her now, and when Timothy took her by the hand and led her to a wooden bench she followed him without resistance, sitting on the edge and digging in her bag for a tissue.

'You're supposed to have a silk handkerchief,' Clara sniffed, producing a huge ream of toilet paper.

'I dropped it when I heard Hamo coming.'

They sat in silence for a moment or two, Timothy looking up at the endless stars, one hand loosely over the back of the bench behind her as Clara wept quietly on, blowing her nose and wishing he'd just go away then changing her mind when his hand reached for her shoulder and pulled her in. He let her cry without words, just patting her shoulder and waiting patiently till she'd reached the gulping stage before finally she spoke.

'How did you know I liked him in that way? Is it that obvious?'

'Only to me.' She felt him shrug beneath her cheek. 'I know I'm good-looking and everything, I know women swoon whenever I approach.' He laughed and caught her wrist when she playfully thumped his chest. 'But when you dropped those notes I knew it wasn't because of my devilish charm. I figured Shelly had said something to upset you, and when I heard about Kell and Abby getting engaged, well, it seemed to fit.

'I know you don't believe me, I know you think I'm interfering, but it really would have been a bad move to tell him.'

'Maybe not,' she argued. 'Maybe if he—'

'Clara.' Timothy pulled her face up. Cupping her chin with his hand, he gazed into her tear-filled eyes. 'You look adorable tonight, Kell's had too much to drink and once he finds out that Abby's done a runner he's going to be devastated. It doesn't take Einstein to work out where it would all end up.'

Clara blinked back at him, her forehead furrowing, positive his lips were twitching as he stared back at her.

'Bed,' Timothy said patiently.

'Maybe that's what I wanted,' Clara said defiantly, but Timothy just shook his head, any hint of a laugh fading as he stared back at her.

'No, it isn't, Clara. You think that's what you wanted, but you know deep down that you'd have hated yourself in the morning. And worse, far worse, you'd have lost Kell as a friend.'

'How do you know?' The anger was back in her voice now. Pushing his hand away, she stood up, half expecting him to grab her, to pull her back beside him, but Timothy sat unmoved. 'Maybe bed's exactly where I wanted it to end up. And if you hadn't decided to play the moral majority maybe bed's where I'd be heading right now. And I tell you this much, Timothy, right now it sounds like a far better option than this!'

'Go on, then, go back in there, go and tell him how you're feeling, but half a bottle of wine and a broken heart really doesn't put you in the best position to make rational decisions. Take it from someone who knows.'

She stood for a moment, torn with indecision, knowing Timothy to be right yet praying he was wrong.

'We've all made mistakes,' Timothy ventured, sensing weakness. 'We've all had our hearts stomped on,'

'Please.' Clara flashed a tear-filled glare at him. 'What would a good-looking doctor know about a broken heart?'

'Plenty.' He smiled. 'I've only been a good-looking doctor for a year, remember. Eighteen months ago I fell hook, line and sinker for one of the RNs on a surgical ward, and when I say I was besotted by her I mean I was seriously besotted. I had the ring picked out before I'd even plucked up the courage to ask her on a date. She was seriously stunning. The only trouble was, I was working as a nurse's aide...'

'You were a nurse's aide?'

'I had to pay my bills. Anyway it was good experience, taught me how to actually speak to patients, which is something even the best medical schools don't even touch. Anyway, Rhonda never even glanced in my direction, not even once, until we were at a party. You know the type—a load of doctors, nurses and med students and way too much booze and suddenly she was all over me.' He gave a cheeky grin. 'It was the best night of my life. I'll spare you the details, but I'm sure you get the picture. She was on an early shift and I told her I'd see her later that day at work and we'd go out for dinner, maybe go and see a band or something.'

'Sounds nice,' Clara commented.

'It would have been,' Timothy agreed. 'Only, when she saw me on the ward the next day in my nurse's aide uniform her face dropped a mile and she told me that she couldn't possibly meet me later, that something had come up. And that was that.'

'She dumped you for that?'

Timothy winced and nodded. 'Of course, I should have told her I was really a medical student, that one day she'd get the doctor she so clearly wanted.'

'Why didn't you?'

Timothy shrugged. 'Too much false pride, I guess. I wanted her to want me for me.'

'Fair enough.'

After a moment's thought she sat down beside him.

'The story doesn't end there, though.' His arm slid behind her in what should have comforting brotherly sort of way but suddenly Clara was having terrible trouble breathing. 'There's going to be a huge postscript.'

When Clara didn't respond he carried on regardless. 'After I finish here I'm going to do my diving course and I'm going to walk back onto that surgical ward with a white coat on, tanned as brown as a conker, and...'

'And what?'

'I don't know.' Timothy frowned. 'The fantasy gets a bit hazy there. Either we'll walk off into the sunset and live happily ever after, or I'll be terribly cruel and pretend I don't even remember her name and totally ignore her relentless advances. I haven't quite worked the ending out yet, but when I do I'll let you know.'

'Revenge is a dish best eaten cold,' Clara said with more than a trace of bitterness, smiling when she saw Timothy's startled expression.

'It's an Arabic saying,' she explained. 'I have the same sort of fantasies, I think it's because I watch too many soaps.'

'What's your favourite?'

'My favourite soap or my favourite fantasy?' Clara sighed. 'OK, you asked for it. I dream that maybe one day Kell will wake up and realise how much he adores me, realise that he simply can't live without me, and when he tells me I'll just shrug and say he's too late, that I've moved on, that...' Her voice trailed off, the tears starting again as she realised the futility behind so many wasted dreams.

'What do I do now, Timothy?' The indecision in her voice was so alien that for a moment there even she didn't recognise it. She was a bush nurse, for heaven's sake, used to thinking on her feet, used to making life-and-death decisions completely unaided, but right here, right now she'd never felt more unsure in her life.

'Go home,' Timothy said gently.

'I can't.' Clara shook her head. As appealing as his suggestion was, there were a million and one jobs to be done tonight and most had Clara's name on them. 'There are the chairs to be stacked, the barn to be—'

'You'd have left it for Kell,' Timothy pointed out, 'so why not let someone else do it?' He had her hand now and was leading her away from the barn, away from Kell and a half a life's worth of dreams. And after only a moment's hesitation, after only a tiny glance backwards, Clara realised, to her own amazement, that she was meekly walking away with Timothy taking the lead.

Walking away with barely a backward glance.

CHAPTER THREE

'MORNING!' EVER CHEERFUL, rubbing his hands against the crisp morning air, Timothy breezed into the clinic as Clara concentrated rather too intently on the pile of surgical gloves and suture equipment she was faithfully stocking. 'Where is everyone?'

'They should be along soon,' Clara mumbled, blushing to the roots of her foiled tips, shy and utterly unable to meet his eyes.

'The staff or the patients?'

'Both,' Clara answered weakly. 'Ross has been here since the crack of dawn, admitting a labouring woman who's in room one. He's just raced home to grab some breakfast, he shouldn't be much longer.'

'Do you want me to hold the fort?'

'Sorry?'

'If you need to go in with her, I can watch here.'

Clara shook her head, finally realising where Timothy was coming from. 'She's fine. Her mother's with her. The aboriginal women generally prefer to be left to themselves when they're in labour.'

Surprisingly Timothy nodded. 'It was the same in Adelaide.' He gave a wry laugh. 'Personally I'd be screaming from the rafters and demanding every intervention known to mankind.'

'Me, too.' Still she couldn't meet his eyes, but such was her relief at the near normality of their conversation Clara even managed a small smile. 'Still, it's good that they trust us enough to come to the clinic. It's important we respect their wishes, so I've made sure she's comfortable and if she needs anything they'll let us know. I'm just stocking up. Go and grab yourself a coffee.'

'Sounds good. Do you want one?'

'I'm fine, thanks.'

Only when he had ducked into the kitchen did she managed to string two breaths together. Yesterday had been spent cringing under her duvet cover, mortified at how close she had come to confronting Kell and reeling in horror at the lengths to which Timothy had had to go to stop her. She'd prayed to be struck down by something horribly contagious so she could hide from the world for a fortnight or so.

All to no avail.

'Did Ross tell Kell?'

He was back, talking in a theatrical whisper and grinning like an eager puppy as he awaited the latest instalment, utterly oblivious to Clara's discomfort.

'I assume so.' Clara shrugged, realigning the boxes of gloves for the umpteenth time. 'I only saw Ross for two minutes this morning, just long enough to get a quick handover, and apart from that I haven't seen anyone since…' Her voice trailed off as her blush deepened. 'Since I left you.'

'Me neither,' Timothy said.

The silence was awful and, putting her bravest foot forward, Clara turned around tentatively. She stared somewhere in the location of his left cheek, completely unable to meet his eyes, grateful that Timothy didn't make a comment about her heavy, swollen, red eyelids.

'Thank you.' When Timothy raised a quizzical eyebrow she elaborated further. 'You were right to stop me from saying anything and I'm only sorry—'

'Forget it.' Timothy broke in, waving his hand dismissively, his easy smile staying firmly in place. 'I'm just relieved we're talking. I've actually been psyching myself to come over for the last hour or so. I was terrified of the reception you'd give me.'

'Me?' Clara asked, startled.

'Yes, you.' Timothy grinned. 'I was half expecting to get a slap on the cheek or something. If I'd known the number of the clinic I'd have been tempted to ring in sick!'

'You didn't look very nervous,' Clara pointed out, grinning in spite of herself.

'I'm a good actor. Look, I probably had no right to interfere, no right to step in the way I did and mess up your plans. I just can't help myself sometimes.'

'Well, I'm glad you did.'

'And I'm glad you're glad, if that makes sense. Shall we start again? Forget everything that's happened and start over.'

Accepting his handshake, Clara gave a small nod and finally managed to look at him, not for long, just for a second or two, but long enough to know that, as good as Timothy's offer sounded, as much as ten minutes ago she'd have given everything she possessed to wipe the slate clean, to obliterate Saturday night's disaster from living memory and banish it from both their minds. Right here, right now, staring into those smiling green eyes, looking up at that open honest face, Clara knew that it simply wasn't going to happen.

Somewhere in mid-handshake, life became terribly complicated all of a sudden.

Somewhere along the way she caught the scent of his aftershave, remembered how it felt to be held by those hands, the weight of his lips on hers, the scorching kiss that she had forcibly pushed from her mind, a moment in time she'd been too embarrassed to relive…

Until now.

Now the events of Saturday night were rushing back in to her consciousness, playing over and over in her mind with glaring clarity, but her near miss with Kell barely got a look in, and judging by the slightly questioning look in Timothy's eyes, from the subtle increase in his breathing and a nervous tongue running over his lips, Timothy was remembering it, too.

'Friends?' she croaked, forgetting to pull her hand back, barely managing to get the single word out.

'Friends,' Timothy agreed. If anything, his voice was even less steady than Clara's. His warm hand was still on hers, green eyes practically obliterated by his dilating pupils as the world seemed to stop for a moment. Only the untimely appearance of Ross snapped them both to attention, causing a flurry of nervous coughing as their hands shot back and those surgical gloves came under another barrage of scrutiny, this time from both a doctor and a nurse.

'Hi, guys.' Oblivious to the simmering tension, Ross came and parked himself on the nurse's desk as Clara gratefully headed for the kitchen.

'Do you want a coffee, Ross? I was just going to make one.'

'In a bit.' Ross's voice was grim and when Clara actually looked at him she realised Ross wasn't his usual sunny self.

'What's up, Ross?'

'Plenty.' He flashed a wry grin at Timothy. 'Sorry to leave you on your own yesterday but a few things came up.'

'No problem,' Timothy said easily, the silence growing as they waited for Ross to fill it.

'How's Mary doing?'

'Very well.' Clara smiled. 'The contractions are full on now, but Louanna said again that they just wanted to be left alone as much as possible and that she'd call if they wanted anything.'

With business out of the way, Ross had no choice but to break the news.

'Kell's leaving.' For a moment he didn't elaborate, just let the news sink in as Clara stood there, stunned. She could feel Ross's eyes on her, Timothy's, too, and knew they were both expecting some sort of reaction.

'I'm sorry, Clara,' Ross said gently. 'I know this is going to be hard, on you especially.' Startled she looked from Ross to Timothy. Surely he hadn't told him! But her confusion turned to relief as Ross continued. 'I've already put the vacancy on every nursing agency in the phone book, but it might be a while before we get someone.'

'When is he going?' Clara asked, expecting a fortnight, a month even, but nothing prepared her for Ross's answer.

'At the end of the week. But we had a long talk about things yesterday and the upshot is that Kell's finished working at the clinic as of now. He's going to spend the rest of the week packing and sorting out his paperwork.'

'Doesn't he have to serve his notice?' Timothy asked, his practical questions such a contrast to the emotions that were coursing through Clara.

'He offered to,' Ross sighed. 'The thing is, Timothy, that's not how we run things here. Over the years Kell's put in way above what his contract dictates. Everyone chips in here, and at the end of the day that's how somehow we manage to run a clinic with limited staff and resources that's stuck in the middle of nowhere. It's time to pay Kell back for all he's given to Tennengarrah. He wants to go after Abby and I think we owe it to him to support his decision. He's going to move into a flat and find work before he looks her up, so he's got a lot to sort out before he leaves...' He gave a small shrug. 'People have to want to be here.' Ross stood up and seeing Clara's shocked expression mercifully misinterpreted it. 'Shelly said she'll help out as much as she can. She didn't want to come back to work so soon after having Kate.' He gave a wry laugh. 'Actually, she didn't want to come back to nursing, full stop, but it's not as if there's much choice at the moment. I'm sorry, Clara. I can see you're upset. I really will try and get more help.'

'It's not that.' Clara forced a smile. 'I don't mind the extra work. I'll just miss him, that's all.'

'We all will.' Ross agreed. 'You more than most, no doubt. You've been friends and colleagues for ages.'

Clara nodded, the lump in her throat not really permitting much else, but thankfully Timothy managed to fill the awful gap that followed.

'I don't mind pitching in. I know I'm not a nurse, but when I was a medical student I worked nights as a nurse aide, so I'm more than happy to wear two caps—not literally of course.' He laughed. 'We can't have Clara running herself ragged.'

'Thanks,' Ross said warmly. 'It's just as well you turned up early. How do you fancy being thrown in at the deep end?'

Timothy grinned. 'It's my favourite pastime. Mind you, I normally have an air tank.'

'Timothy dives,' Clara explained, finally managing to resume the conversation, but her heart really wasn't in it.

'Well, Kell was supposed to be doing a mobile clinic this morning...'

'I don't mind,' Clara volunteered, more than happy to be out on the road, but Ross shook his head. 'Kell finally persuaded Jim to have that testicular lump looked at, and it's probably not very politically correct but, given that this is the bush, I think it would be better if a guy went along.'

'I'd need a map,' Timothy said hesitantly, 'and a quick read up on testicular lumps before I head off.'

'We're not that cruel.' Ross laughed. 'I wouldn't send you out on your own on your first day here! You can go to a mobile clinic with Clara later in the week—they take a bit of getting used to so it's best if you just watch the first few times. I'll do the mobile clinic today if you don't mind staying here and running the morning surgery. Normally Monday mornings are pretty much routine, sore throat and ears, a few stitches perhaps. If you don't know how anything works, just ask Clara.'

Oh, she tried, she really tried not to roll her eyes, but as both men turned to her she did exactly that. 'We'll be fine, Ross,' Clara sighed. 'You go on ahead.'

'How are you doing?'

It was the emptiest the clinic had been all morning. The second Ross had driven off, the floodgates had opened and every ailment that had been put on hold in preparation for the ball had chosen today to surface. Given Timothy's relative inexperience, Clara braced herself for endless questions, but apart from the occasional prompt as to where things were kept Timothy had pretty much rolled his sleeves up and got on with the job. The older locals had been fine, chatting easily to the new doctor, offering to 'shout' him a beer even, but some of the younger guys hadn't been overly friendly with Timothy, taking it upon themselves to act like a collective group of protective older brothers and returning his attempts at small talk with the most suspicious stares and surly remarks. Not that Timothy seemed bothered. He just got right on with the job in hand, happy to ask Clara's opinion every now and then or to advise the patient to come back for a follow-up visit when Ross returned when he felt a more experienced physician's opinion might be called for. To Clara's pleasant surprise, the morning clinic passed smoothly.

'I'll just finish these stitches and then we should be able to grab a coffee.'

'Sounds good to me.' Timothy peered over her shoulder, smiling at the young man who eyed him suspiciously. 'Make sure you take all the antibiotics, Mitch, and come back if there are any problems.' Lowering his voice for Clara's ears only, Timothy moved in over her shoulder. 'I'm sorry if I've been a real pain this morning.'

'You haven't,' Clara conceded, feeling guilty for her eye-rolling earlier. 'You've done really well. Before you put the kettle on, could you put your head into Mary's room? Tell her I'll be along soon. I just gave her some pethidine before I started this, so hopefully it will be taking effect.'

'Done.' He turned to go then changed his mind. 'Can I watch—I mean when Mary has the baby? If it causes her any embarrassment then, of course, I won't...'

'That'll be fine,' Clara smiled warmly. 'Hopefully it won't be too much longer now.'

'I'll see about that coffee.'

Famous last words!

Settling back to work, Clara snipped the last of the stitches then placed a wad of Melanin and a neat bandage over Mitch's hand, but just as she was sure a well-earned break was finally imminent a commotion brewing outside forced a low sigh to escape from behind her mask.

'Sounds like Hamo's not at his sunniest,' Mitch volunteered, as a few loud expletives winged their way into Theatre. 'Do you need a hand? I can usually calm him down.'

'Better not,' Clara sighed. 'He's usually pretty good for me.' Securing the bandage with tape, she handed Mitch the antibiotics, hating to rush her patient but knowing she was needed elsewhere. 'Make sure you do as Timothy says, and if there's any problems come straight back.'

Jumping off her stool, she discarded all the sharps then followed the noise to the nurse's desk, hoping Hamo wasn't going to take his obvious bad mood out on Timothy. Aggression in the workplace was unfortunately par for the course these days, whatever part of the world you lived in, but as trained as the staff were to deal with it, it was hardly a great first day welcome for Timothy. Hamo occasionally turned up at the clinic the worst for wear, needing stitches or whatever, but one look at him and Clara knew that in this instance more was going to be called for. His face was tinged grey and he was clutching his stomach with one fist, the other dividing its time between holding onto the desk at the nurses' station and punching in the air as he cursed the world at large and Timothy in particular.

'Hamo, what's wrong?' Clara asked, making sure she didn't get too close.

'I need some painkillers and the so-called doctor here won't give them to me.'

'I didn't say that, Hamo.' Timothy's voice was calm, laid back even, much to Clara's relief. With Hamo in this volatile mood even the slightest hint of confrontation could turn things ugly, but Timothy seemed to know exactly what he was doing. His stance, though confident, was non-confrontational and Clara listened as he carried on talking, all the time watching Hamo. 'I can see that you're in a great deal of pain, but before I can give you anything I need to examine you.'

'I just need an injection,' Hamo snarled through gritted teeth, staggering towards them, and Clara realised with a surge of nervousness that his short fuse had really snapped this time. But Timothy had obviously read the situation the same way and in one swift motion he pulled Clara out of the way and moved himself forward, effectively standing between her and the patient.

'Why don't you go and check on Mary?' Timothy suggested, as Hamo doubled over again. And though Timothy's voice was calm, friendly even, Clara knew it was an order and not a request, though she had no intention of following it. Hamo was a tricky customer at the best of times but Clara had always been positive he would never lift a finger to her.

She wasn't so sure that courtesy would be extended to Timothy.

'I'd rather stay here,' Clara said firmly, but Timothy shook his head.

'We'll be fine, won't we, Hamo?' For the first time he looked at Clara. 'Once I've explained to him that we've a young woman here about to give birth, he'll settle down. He's hardly going to knock out the only doctor for miles and put a woman and her baby's life at risk.' Turning back to the patient, he gave him a smile. 'Right, let's have a look at you, then,' he said. Deliberately ignoring Hamo's reluctance and taking his elbow, he guided him to the trolley. 'That's the man,' Timothy said matter-of-factly. 'Up on the trolley so I can have a look at you and then we'll see about pain control.'

Suitably impressed, Clara undressed Hamo and tried to take a set of obs as Timothy slipped an oxygen mask over his face and attempted to get a history. 'What's been happening, Hamo?'

'I just want an injection.'

'Not until I know what's wrong with you. How about you tell me when this pain started?'

'How about you give me a needle?' Hamo was getting agitated again and Clara took over.

'Hamo, enough. Let the doctor have a look at you and answer his questions. And I need you to stay still so that I can run a set of obs on you.'

But Hamo was having none of it. Pulling off his mask, he tried to lever himself off the trolley, which wasn't a good move as the brakes weren't on and the trolley lurched forward, unfortunately clipping Clara none too gently on the hip.

'Hamo.' Pushing on the brakes with his foot, Timothy's voice for the first time wasn't quite so laid back. 'Lie down. You're not going anywhere because you're not well enough. Now the quicker you answer my questions the quicker I can make a diagnosis, but I *cannot* give you an injection until I'm sure what's going on.' His eyes met Clara's but the annoyance in his voice didn't abate. 'Now, Clara, can you, please, check on Mary?'

'Can I have a quick word, Timothy?' Widening her eyes for Timothy's benefit, Clara kept her voice even. 'About Mary.'

He gave a brief nod then turned his attention back to his patient.

'I'm not going to fight you, Hamo. If you want my help you can have it, but that has to be your call. Now, lie there for a moment and decide whether or not you're prepared to co-operate. I'll be back shortly.'

Only when they were out of earshot did they speak.

'I assume this isn't about Mary?'

Clara nodded. 'I know Hamo's being obnoxious, but the truth is, Timothy, in all the time I've known him he's never been aggressive towards me. I just wanted you to be clear on that. And he's never once asked for an injection—it normally takes a supreme effort to get him to take even the mildest painkiller. It isn't drugs that he's after, I'm sure of that. He must be in a lot of pain to be acting this way.'

'I don't doubt that he is,' Timothy said thoughtfully. 'Thanks, Clara, I'll take it on board. I'm actually seriously concerned about him. I'll have to examine him, of course, but I'm pretty sure he's going to need more care than we can offer here.'

'Do you want me to get the Flying Doctors on the line?' Clara offered.

'I'll just have a look first—hopefully he's calmed down a bit by now. Oh, and, Clara.' Turning, she paused, expecting a quick question, but from the look on Timothy's face she realised he wasn't best pleased. 'Next time there's a violent situation and I ask you to leave, please, don't argue the point.'

'I wasn't arguing.' Clara flushed. 'Like I said, I've known Hamo all my life. I'm sure he'd never hurt me.'

'Sure's not good enough,' Timothy said grimly. 'Suppose he'd lashed out in pain or tried to hit me and missed, suppose he'd ended up blacking your eye.'

'I'd have been all right,' Clara answered quickly, but from the look on his face it was clearly the wrong answer.

'Maybe you would have been, but how do you think Hamo would have felt afterwards and how would the rest of the town have dealt with him when word got out? You come with a lot of surrogate brothers, Clara, I saw that for myself on Saturday night. And while I'm not excusing violence, sometimes the lines get blurred when a patient's in pain. Sometimes we have to save them from themselves.'

She'd never thought of it like that and, suitably chastised, Clara turned away. 'I'll just check on Mary,' she murmured, but only as she walked off did she realise the full horror of the situation Timothy had just averted and her hands were shaking slightly as she knocked on the door of the side room and walked in.

'How are things?'

'Better.' Louanna looked up from her daughter. 'What was all the noise about outside?'

'One of the patients got a bit upset,' Clara said tactfully, 'but it's all sorted now. I'm sorry if it upset Mary.'

'She didn't hear a thing,' Louanna said softly. 'That injection really helped. She's even managed to doze off. Things seem to be slowing down—the labour won't just stop, will it?'

'I'll just have a little look. I'll try and not disturb her,' Clara said, moving quietly and checking the baby's heart rate with the foetal monitor then standing with her hand on Mary's stomach for a few moments. 'The baby's heart rate is good and strong. I'm not going to wake her and do an internal. I'm sure things are moving on just as they should.'

'So why have the pains stopped?'

'That's mother nature giving Mary a chance to catch her breath before the real hard work of pushing starts,' Clara said assuredly. 'Just let her rest and when she wakes, or if you need anything at all, just come and let me know.'

Timothy had been busy while she had been away. IV fluids had been run through a line and were hung beside the gurney on a pole as he inserted an IV bung. Hamo was still in obvious pain, but the aggression of previously seemed to have subsided. He was even keeping on his oxygen mask.

'How is she?' Timothy asked, without looking up, taking a large syringe of blood from the IV bung as Clara hovered with the IV line.

'Resting. How's Hamo?'

'Still in pain, but more compliant now. He let me take a set of obs.' The worried grimace Timothy pulled was for Clara's eyes only and he nodded appreciatively as he pulled out the syringe and Clara immediately connected the IV fluids, securing the access with tape while Timothy filled various vials with the blood he had collected. 'Give him a two-hundred-millilitre bolus of fluid, then run the flask over four hours,' Timothy instructed Clara, then turned to Hamo. 'I'm just going to have a word with Clara, Hamo, and then I'll be back with that injection.'

'What do you think is going on?' Clara asked, once they were out of earshot.

'He's got an acute abdomen,' Timothy replied. 'He's in a lot of pain and he's been vomiting since the early hours of the morning.'

'Any blood in it?' Clara asked, but Timothy shook his head.

'None. I've asked him about his alcohol intake...'

'I bet that went down well.' Clara grimaced.

'Actually, when I explained to him why I need to know, he was quite open. He drinks regularly, but even Hamo admits that he excelled himself at the ball on Saturday night. I think he's got acute pancreatitis, and if that's the case he's going to need to be transferred.'

Clara nodded. Pancreatitis was sometimes caused by excessive alcohol consumption and although the treatment was fairly conservative—careful monitoring of IV fluid intake and urine output, along with strict pain control—there were many possible complications, some of which could be life-threatening.

'We haven't got the facilities to do the blood tests for pancreatitis here, but they can be sent of with him when the Flying Doctors come,' Clara said, gesturing to the tubes in the kidney dish Timothy was holding. 'But we've got the urinary test strips that'll do the job. I'll see if he can give us a specimen.'

'I've already asked,' Timothy said grimly. 'And he flatly refused.'

'Well, if it is pancreatitis, he's going to need a catheter. We could get a specimen that way.'

But Timothy shook his head. 'Again, he refuses. Until I give him some pain control I don't think we're going to get much further with him.' He glanced at his watch. 'How much longer do you think Ross will be?'

'An hour, maybe two. Do you want me to try and contact him? Mind you, if he's running the clinic he mightn't hear the radio, and there's no satellite coverage where Ross is so I can't even get him on his mobile.'

Timothy shook his head. 'I might as well talk to the Flying Doctors. It's obvious he needs to be transferred and the quicker we get things moving the better. If you can get the Flying Doctors on the line for me that would be great.'

'What about pain control?' Clara asked, knowing her question wasn't an easy one to answer. Acute abdomens were notoriously difficult to diagnose, and woe betide any junior doctor who gave analgesia without a concrete diagnosis. Once the symptoms were masked by analgesia it would make the surgeon's job of an accurate diagnosis that much harder and could, in fact, prove life-threatening.

'I'll talk to the Flying Doctors first, but the truth is I can't leave him in pain till they arrive.' For a second or two he chewed on his bottom lip then he gave a brief shake of his head, his slightly hesitant stance changing. 'No, I'm confident of my diagnosis. He's got upper abdominal pain after a large drinking episode, he's tachycardic with low blood pressure and his temperature's up, frequent vomiting and he's got a positive Cullen's sign.'

Clara had kept up with Timothy's findings until then, but her slight frown didn't go unnoticed.

'Discoloration around the umbilicus,' Timothy explained. 'This great surgeon in Adelaide pointed it out to me once, and Hamo has got the same thing. Still, I'd feel a lot happier giving him an injection with a positive urine test to back me up. You get the Flying Doctors on the line for me, and while you're taking care of that I'll have another go at persuading Hamo to provide a specimen.'

All to no avail, though.

Timothy had to relay his findings to the very experienced Dr Hall Jells, or Dr Hall as the locals all knew him, and Clara cringed for Timothy, knowing Hall's questions would be brutal. Leaving him for a second, she made a last-ditch attempt to persuade Hamo, but it was a waste of time and she shook her head as she returned, while Timothy rolled his eyes and carried on talking into the telephone.

'I'm fairly confident of my diagnosis.' She watched as he grimaced and held the receiver back an inch from his ear. 'I'm actually very confident,' he said more forcefully, 'and once I've given him an injection I'm sure he'll be far more compliant.' Replacing the receiver, Timothy gave her a tight smile. 'He said to give him 10 mg of morphine.'

'Hall's a great doctor,' Clara soothed. 'If he didn't think you sounded confident, he'd have told you to hold off.'

'Let's just hope I'm right.'

The morphine had the desired effect, Hamo settled markedly, but his observations remained erratic. His heart beating alarmingly fast and his blood pressure dropped more than could be put down to the effects of the morphine.

'Dr Hall wants a catheter in,' Clara said firmly. 'I know you're embarrassed, Hamo, but it really is necessary.'

A weary nod was the only response she got and Clara gave Timothy a worried look as alarms started going off. 'Lay him flat and give him another two-hundred-millilitre bolus and open up the IV full bore,' Timothy said quickly as he set to work inserting the catheter. 'And turn his oxygen up to ten litres.' Clara did as Timothy ordered, expecting Hamo to protest to being laid down, for the pain in his abdomen to make this movement uncomfortable, but as Hamo meekly lay back on the gurney Clara's panic mode upped a notch.

'I think I preferred him angry,' Timothy muttered. 'Right, I've got a specimen.' He handed the small jar to Clara who tested it as Timothy inserted a second IV line into Hamo's other arm to enable them to give him more fluids. 'We have to watch that we don't overload him, though. With pancreatitis they can tip into pulmonary oedema quickly. What does his urine test show?'

'It's positive,' Clara said, holding the dipstick up to the colour chart on the bottle and holding it up for Timothy to see. 'Your diagnosis was spot on.'

There was no sigh of relief, no smug smile on Timothy's face as his difficult diagnosis was confirmed, just a worried frown as he worked on his patient. 'At least we know what we're dealing with. What's his blood pressure doing now?'

'It's coming up,' Clara responded. 'Ninety on forty. Could this be from the morphine?'

Timothy shook his head, flashing a light into Hamo's eyes as he did so. 'I don't think so. His pupils are still dilated and his breathing rate's high. It's the pancreatitis that's causing his collapse. Young men often compensate for a while then drop their blood pressure suddenly, but it's coming up now,' he added with quiet satisfaction.

Hamo started to move around, pulling again at the mask. He was still deathly pale but at least there was a bit of fight back in him now, but even before he started to retch, many years of nursing told Clara what was coming next and she deftly raised the head of the trolley while simultaneously reaching for a kidney dish.

'Do you want an NG tube in?' Clara asked. A nasogastric tube was a soft rubber tube that was passed through the patient's nose and into their stomach. Though the procedure was uncomfortable at the time, once in the tube enabled the stomach contents to be emptied and generally the patient felt a lot more settled.

'Can you do it?' Timothy asked. 'I've only put a couple in before and if he carries on picking up I don't think he'll let me have more than one go and I don't want to cause him more discomfort than necessary.'

'Sure,' Clara agreed, blinking in surprise at Timothy's openness and his overriding concern for the patient's comfort. Most doctors would have battled on, refusing to admit they couldn't do it, more than happy to have a go in the name of experience. But instead Timothy was putting not only the patient's welfare but his comfort first.

It was as refreshing as it was welcome.

Now that Hamo's observations were more stable, now that the crisis had been swiftly and skilfully diverted, the tension in the room subsided a notch. But only a notch. Hamo was still gravely ill and any variance could see him sinking back rapidly into a critical condition.

'Hamo,' Clara said gently, 'I'm going to pass a small tube through your nose and into your stomach. Once it's in you'll feel a lot more comfortable, but it's not very pleasant while I pass it, you might start retching or gagging, but it's very important that you don't pull it out.'

Hamo nodded but as Clara started to insert the tube his good intentions evaporated as his hand instinctively reached to pull it back up. But Timothy was too quick for him, grabbing his arms and clamping them down firmly. Unfortunately, Hamo jerked his head back and the tube came up, which meant Clara would have to start again.

'Come on, Hamo, don't fight me,' Clara said firmly. 'You really need this tube.'

'Sister?' Louanna was at the door, her face concerned. 'I think Mary needs to be seen. She says that she wants to push.'

'You go,' Clara said to Timothy, her mind working ten to the dozen. Second-stage labour in a first baby normally took a while and they really needed to get this tube down. 'Do a set of obs on Mary and the baby. I'll get this tube in and then we'll swap over.' Her eyes locked on Hamo. 'Mary's having her baby, so you need to stay still for me, Hamo. Timothy has to go.'

'Go,' Hamo agreed bravely, gripping the sides of the trolley with his hands and taking a deep breath as Timothy sped off.

Hamo tried, he really did, but as the tube reached the back of his throat again his hands shot up. Thankfully, help was at hand. As he entered the clinic Ross instantly read the situation and sped over to the trolley, gripping Hamo's hands tightly without a word as Clara finished the uncomfortable procedure. Only when the tube was firmly strapped in place did she address her boss.

'Thanks for that.'

'What's been going on?'

They moved out of earshot and Clara gave Ross a brief run-down.

'Hamo came in at the end of clinic with severe abdo pain. He was pretty aggressive, but thankfully he settled with some morphine. The Flying Doctors have been mobilised.'

'What's the diagnosis?'

'Pancreatitis.'

'And that's been confirmed?'

Clara nodded. 'Eventually.' When Ross frowned Clara elaborated, noting his grim face as she explained how Timothy had called in the Flying Doctors and given morphine without the benefit of Hamo's urine test. 'He was great,' she concluded. 'I mean that, Ross. Hamo dropped his blood pressure just before you arrived and it was touch and go for a moment or two, so the last thing he needs is a lecture. I think a pat on the back might be more appropriate.'

'So, do you think we should keep him?' Ross grinned, making his way back to Hamo's bedside. 'Where is he, by the way?'

'Oh, lord,' Clara groaned, casting an anxious eye towards Mary's room. 'I told him I'd be straight in.'

'I'll watch Hamo.' Ross smiled. 'You'd better go where you're most needed.'

She wasn't needed.

In fact, not a single head turned Clara's way as she gently pushed open the door.

Not Mary's, her eyes closed in deep concentration as she bore down, pushing her newborn into the darkened, hushed room.

Not Louanna's, who held her daughter's shoulders, supporting her and staring on in wonder at the unfolding miracle.

And not Timothy's.

The deliciously awkward, eager-to-please young man had vanished. In his place was now a calm and extremely competent doctor, his sleeves rolled up, two large gloved hands holding the infant's head as its shoulders rotated, murmuring words of encouragement in low, confident tones that epitomised the calm feeling in the room.

It was truly a privilege to be there and Clara closed the door quietly, moving in closer—not to interfere, just to observe the beauty of a miracle that never ceased to amaze her, marvelling not only at the wonder of nature but at Timothy's quiet compassion, the love and empathy that seemed to fill the room, giving what could have been just another routine birth the status it deserved.

Even the baby, as it slipped into the world, as Timothy delivered him safely into his mother's outstretched arms, barely let out a cry of protest. Moving quietly closer, Clara watched the unfolding scene, the big dark eyes of the infant blinking at the world around him, his little mouth turning to his mother's breast as she held him ever closer, oblivious to the blankets Clara tucked around them as Timothy worked on, delivering the placenta, quietly unobtrusive but comfortingly there.

'He's all right?'

They were the first words that had been spoken, the almost reverent silence broken by Mary as she dragged her eyes from her newborn and sought Timothy's reassuring ones.

'He's perfect.' Pulling the swaddle of blankets away, Timothy did a very rudimentary check of the newborn. 'I'll check him over properly later, but for now everything's just fine.'

'He hardly cried.'

'He had a gentle welcome,' Clara said softly, just as the baby lost the nipple he was feeding on and the loud wail of protest he made had them all smiling. 'We'll leave you to it now. I'll bring you in a light snack in a just a bit.'

'Thank you,' Mary murmured, turning her eyes back to her newborn as they turned to leave the room. 'Doctor?'

As Timothy turned, she said it again, only this time it was loaded with gratitude, and meaning.

'Thank you.'

* * *

The Flying Doctors always cut a dash.

And as laid back as Clara was at work, she never failed to be impressed when they arrived. She watched out of the window as the white plane touched down, trailing a red haze of dust behind it as it sped along the clinic's runway. The crew made its way speedily over to the clinic, smart in their white and navy uniforms, but however much the scene moved her she knew it didn't come close to what Timothy was feeling, witnessing it for the first time.

The Flying Doctors were an enigma. You didn't have to be Australian to know about the team of men and women who faced the harsh Australian elements daily, the white plane that swooped out of the sky and bought medical technology, knowledge and hope to the most remote of communities, but seeing it for the first time, witnessing a legend close up, was overwhelming to say the least, and Clara smiled to herself as Timothy nervously ran through his handover to Hall, justified his diagnosis and outlined his course of treatment, his Adam's apple bobbing up and down as Hall skimmed through the notes.

'You did a good job, mate.'

It was all Timothy was going to get, but from Hall it was strong praise indeed and Clara caught his eye as Timothy gave a small satisfied nod, a smile on the edge of his lips as he stepped back and let the team take over.

'Look after yourself, Hamo.' Clara smiled as everyone fluttered around, changing over monitors, setting up equipment, moving in the stretcher. Now that his blood pressure had stabilised and the painkillers had kicked in, Hamo was back to his rather gruff self, but the aggression of earlier had gone, leaving him rather shamefaced and subdued.

'I can take care of myself.' He gave a small shrug. 'I'm sorry about before.'

'Let's just forget it, shall we?' Clara said gently. 'You were in pain…'

'It's no excuse.'

'No, it isn't, Hamo,' Clara said thoughtfully, 'but maybe a couple of weeks in hospital will give you some time to think about things.'

'My drinking?'

Clara nodded but didn't say anything. Hamo knew the score—the next move had to be up to him.

'I need to cut down.' When Clara still didn't respond Hamo lay back on the pillow. 'I need to stop, don't I?'

'I think you already know the answer.'

He gave a thin smile then looked up. 'Hey, it's not just me you need to worry about, Clara. I can take care of myself. I'm not so sure that you can, though.'

'What are you talking about, Hamo?' Clara frowned.

'You and the new guy. I saw what happened on Saturday, remember? Just watch yourself. He'll be gone in a few weeks like all the other doctors that drift in and out of Tennengarrah. Look at that Abby Hampton, she didn't even do the full three months.'

'Hamo,' Clara said patiently, 'I'm well aware Timothy's only here for a while, and what you saw on Saturday night…well, it wasn't exactly how it looked. That's all you need to know,' she added quickly, as Hamo started to protest. 'Now, I know you all mean well, I know you guys all think it's your duty to protect me, but I'm pushing thirty now, I'm more than able to look after myself, so if you and your friends can stop giving Timothy the evil eye, it would be much appreciated.'

Hamo gave a reluctant shrug. 'What sort of a name's Timothy anyway? What's wrong with Tim or—'

'Timo?' Clara grinned as Hall made his way back over, ready to move. Hamo finally joined her in a smile. 'You just concentrate on looking after yourself, Hamo. I'll be fine.'

'That birth was beautiful.' They were in the kitchen now, Clara pouring water into two massive mugs as Timothy set to work on the biscuit barrel.

'It was great,' Timothy agreed. 'Look, I hope I haven't put you offside, not coming to get you. It's just when I put my head in she was practically having it, there really wasn't—'

'Timothy,' Clara interrupted, 'Let's stop apologising to each other, shall we? You're a doctor, for heaven's sake, you don't need my permission to deliver a baby.'

'I am, aren't I?' Timothy winked. 'Heavens, I wish I felt more like one.'

'But you've been great this morning,' Clara enthused. 'Hall's not exactly gushing, but he was pretty pleased with your work and I know for a fact Ross was impressed. And as for the delivery...' Clara gestured in the vague direction of Mary's room. 'You were great in there. You couldn't have been better!

'You've no idea how many doctors, I've seen, nurses too come to that, rushing in, lights blazing, taking over, when all most women want is to do it for themselves. You've made this morning very special for Mary.'

'I think the baby took care of that,' Timothy said modestly, but Clara shook her head.

'Mary wasn't even sure she wanted to come to the clinic to have her baby. Now she's going to go back to her people and tell them how well it went, which can only be a good thing. Word of mouth can be our greatest asset but it can have its downsides, too. Hopefully Mary might persuade some of the other women to give the clinic a go now and that can only benefit us all. Have you done many deliveries?'

'Three, though I've seen loads more. I was always begging to be let in, I love the labour room.'

'Me, too.'

'Still,' Timothy admitted, 'it helped that you were only a call away. I don't think I'd have felt quite so confident if I'd been there on my own. That baby really did come quickly at the end—I wasn't trying to play the hero or anything.'

Arranging a tray for Mary, Clara stopped in mid-motion, a teacup in mid-air as a smile ghosted across her lips.

'I don't think you have to try, Timothy.' Her back was to him so her voice so soft he probably didn't even hear it. 'I've a feeling playing the hero just comes naturally to you.'

CHAPTER FOUR

NORMALLY CLARA LOVED the mobile clinic.

Loved being out on the road, alone with her thoughts and the treat of a picnic lunch before heading back, driving the Jeep along the endless red roads, assured of a warm welcome from the patients she had nursed over the years.

But not this morning.

This morning, she had been relegated to passenger. Timothy, keen to get his bearings, bumped the clinic's Jeep along, grinding gears and attempting small talk as Clara responded in monosyllables.

But her aloofness had nothing to do with the fact that yet again she was playing nursemaid to a new doctor, or the fact that the prospect of four hours alone with Timothy had her stomach twisting into strange excited knots...

Instead, it had everything to do with the house call they were making *en route*.

Pulling out her next patient's notes, she attempted to read them impassively but failed miserably. Her eyes blurred as she read the hospital doctor's covering letter.

Some days she hated her job.

Looking up from the notes, Clara realised that they'd missed their turning about two minutes ago. 'You were supposed to turn left back there,' she mumbled, fishing in her pocket for a tissue and blowing her nose loudly.

'When?' Slamming on the brakes, Timothy craned his neck as he shot the Jeep into reverse. 'You didn't say.'

'I did,' Clara said through gritted teeth, massaging her neck which had been positively whiplashed as the vehicle had growled in protest. 'I told you to take the next left.'

'Half an hour ago,' Timothy pointed out, clearly as irritated as Clara. 'A reminder wouldn't have gone amiss.'

'You were the one who wanted to get a feel for the area,' Clara snarled. 'Do I look like a talking map?'

They bumped backwards in angry silence, finally locating the turning which, Clara realised, unless you knew it existed, didn't exactly stand out.

Well, she wasn't going to apologise!

'Do you want a quick look at the notes?' Clara offered instead, but Timothy shook his head.

'I had a read before we came and Ross bought me up to scratch. This is the lady with breast cancer and cerebral metastases who doesn't want any further treatment, right? She's having trouble sleeping and I'm to—'

'No!' The force behind her voice came as a surprise to them both and Clara took a couple of deep breaths before she carried on talking. 'This is Eileen Benton, happily married, mother of two wonderful children, who dabbles in ceramics and also happens to have breast cancer.'

'Hey, Clara!' Slamming on the brakes again, Timothy pulled the handbrake on and turned to face her. 'What's your problem this morning?'

'I don't have a problem,' Clara retorted. 'I'm just pointing out that Eileen isn't merely another diagnosis. She also happens to be a beautiful young woman—'

'I'm sure she is,' Timothy broke in, 'and no doubt I'll find that out for myself in a few minutes. Is that what this is about?

Do you not think that I'm qualified enough to be treating your precious patients?'

'What are you talking about?'

'Here.' Pulling out his prescription pad, he scribbled furiously on it. 'Temazepam 10 mg—that's what she needs isn't it? Ross said she was having trouble sleeping. As you clearly think I've little to contribute, why don't you go on ahead and see her? And I'll wait in the car.'

'Timothy?' Swallowing hard, Clara realised she'd gone too far, that she'd taken her rather pensive mood out on him when it simply wasn't his fault and an explanation was called for. 'It's not you I'm upset with.'

'Isn't it? You've made it blatantly clear you don't want me along this morning. I've been trying to talk to you the whole way here and you've completely ignored me, which is fine. If that's how you want to work then that's your right, but when it comes to the patients' care don't take your bad mood out on me. I was merely attempting to check I'd got a handle on her diagnosis before I walk in there. Now, if I'm not quite up on all the patients marital statuses and pastimes it has nothing to do with me being an unfeeling bastard and everything to do with the fact I've been in this town less than a week.'

'She's a friend.' The catch in her voice took the wind out his sails for a moment. She heard his sharp intake of breath, saw his knuckles loosen their grip slightly on the steering-wheel. 'I know practically everyone in this town, but Eileen really is a good friend. I was a bridesmaid at her wedding, I delivered her babies…' Swallowing hard, Clara fought back her tears—the last thing she wanted was for Eileen to see her with red glassy eyes. 'That's why I've been quiet in the car.' She gave a small shrug. 'Rude even. I just really don't want to do this.'

'Did you tell Ross?' he asked gently. 'Maybe Shelly should be the one to look after her.'

'I asked Ross if he'd mind sending Shelly, but apparently

she got upset when she heard that Eileen was refusing any further treatment...'

'So did you,' Timothy pointed out, but Clara just gave a wry laugh.

'Ah, but I don't have children that are around the same age. Apparently it makes it worse.' Leaning over, she checked her reflection in the rear-view mirror, then blew her nose again. 'I'm probably being a bit unfair. I'm sure if I'd reminded Ross just how close Eileen and I are he wouldn't have sent me. I should have stood up for myself a bit more.'

'Do you want me to go in,' Timothy offered, 'by myself? I could walk to the house from here and say that I got a bit lost. She won't even know you're here.'

Clara shook her head. 'I'm fine now.' Jumping out, she pulled out her bag and waited as Timothy got out, a shy smile on her lips as he walked over. 'And I'm sorry about earlier. I'm actually really glad you're here.'

'Clara! I'm so glad it's you.'

Stepping inside, Clara's misgivings were instantly dispelled. The warmth of Eileen's welcome, the obvious delight that she was there, told Clara there and then that the pain of nursing Eileen would be worth it. Nursing mightn't be the most glamorous job in the world but the relationships forged with patients were always special and none more so when they were friends.

Agony though this journey they were embarking on would undoubtedly be, Clara vowed at that moment that they would travel it together with dignity and affection, strengthening their friendship as they faced the unknown together.

'Happy birthday!'

'Eileen!' Clara let out a small moan of embarrassed protest as a brightly coloured package was thrust at her. 'You shouldn't have.'

'Why on earth not? It's your birthday after all. So, what else did you get—anything nice?'

Clara gave a small shrug. 'Nothing yet,' she mumbled,

quickly changing the subject. 'Eileen, this is Timothy Morgan, he's the new doctor in Tennengarrah,'

She waited as they shook hands but Eileen hadn't finished embarrassing her yet. 'Are you trying to tell me that no one even remembered your birthday? What about Bill, Ross and Shelly, Kell—'

'I hate a fuss, you know that,' Clara broke in. 'Ross and Shelly will do something tonight, no doubt, at Kell's leaving do, he's got his head in the clouds—I'll fill you in on all that later. And Bill's hardly in a position to go shopping. Did you hear he had the operation in the end? He's doing very well apparently.'

'Is that a lecture I can feel coming on?' Eileen's smile never faltered, but there was a notable tension in the room as Clara fumbled with the wrapping paper. 'I know you, Clara, and I also know where you're leading. Bill changed his mind and just look how well it's all worked out.'

'I'm not here to lecture you, Eileen,' Clara said softly, staring at the small bowl covered in bright ceramic pieces, a glorious picture of the sun and the moon and hundreds of tiny silver stars. It would have taken for ever to make and, given Eileen's fragile health, it made it all the more special. 'This is beautiful, I'll treasure it.'

She'd sworn to herself that she wouldn't cry, sworn that she'd get through this without even a hint of a tear, but looking up at her friend Clara realised she wasn't alone with her tears as Eileen sobbed quietly. She wished she could go over there, put her arms around her friend and tell her she thought she was doing the right thing, but she couldn't.

Couldn't watch Eileen give up on her life with hardly a fight.

'You've been having trouble sleeping since the metastases were diagnosed?'

It was Timothy who spoke, his voice so strong and clear that for a moment it sounded as if it didn't belong and Clara felt a stirring of anger for his apparent callousness, which she quickly fought to check, reminding herself that it was the diagnosis that was callous, not Timothy.

'I slept well at the hospital,' Eileen gulped. 'In fact, that's just about all that I did! It's just since I've come home that I've been having trouble. I get all worked out about silly things. I'm fine during the day, I just get on with things…'

'No doubt you're busy.' Timothy gestured to the pile of toys in the corner. 'How old are your children?'

'Seven and four. Rhiannon's at school, Heidi's having a nap at the moment—you'll see her soon, no doubt. Like I said, during the day I'm fine…' Her voice trailed off and Clara ached to fill it, didn't want Timothy to push yet she knew he had to.

'But at night?' Timothy said gently as Eileen buried her face in her hands, the weight of the horrible cloud that hung over her too heavy for her thin tired shoulders.

'I make lists.' Eileen's voice was a strangled whisper. Pulling a piece of paper from the coffee-table, she held it in the air and a strangled sob followed. Clara felt like joining in, but she sat quietly as Timothy made his way over, joining Eileen on the settee, not remotely awkward, not uncomfortable, just tender and gentle and infinitely patient as he took the paper and read it quietly.

'Rhiannon loves cucumber in her sandwiches, but she doesn't like the skin,' Eileen said softly as Timothy carried on reading. 'And Heidi can only sleep if she has her favourite blanket. Jerry knows that, of course, but she doesn't just like it over her, she likes the top part tucked under her cheek, and even though she says she doesn't want apple juice in the morning, she wants it really.' Her voice was shaking, her hands too as she took the list back from Timothy. 'It probably seems stupid. I know they're all going to be fine, that they'll be well looked after. I know I can't put everything down on paper, can't sum up their little personalities in a few pages. It's just…' Her voice trembled. 'It's just that…'

'Maybe you're not ready to hand them over yet?' Timothy

suggested softly, as Clara held her breath, watching in awe as Timothy gently pushed further. 'Are you having second thoughts about cancelling the treatment?'

'I don't know.' Eileen's voice was almost angry. 'I just don't know if I can go through it all again, and more to the point I don't know if I can put Jerry and the kids through it again. The last lot of chemo was hell on earth, but at the time I figured it was worth it. That I'd beat the cancer and get on with the rest of my life. Now I'm being told I need radiation treatment, possibly surgery and if I'm very lucky I might even get a follow-up round of chemo to top the whole lot off. And for what? A few more months?'

'It might be a lot more than that,' Timothy said, but seeing Eileen shake her head he looked at her thoughtfully for a moment before changing tack. 'Suppose you're right, suppose that the worst-case scenario comes to fruition and all you get out of this is a few more months, what would that give you?'

Eileen looked up at him puzzled.

'Where will six months see your family?'

'Heidi would be at school,' Eileen whispered.

'I don't have children,' Timothy volunteered, 'but, from what I've heard, that makes a big difference. Once they're off at school during the day things get a bit easier, don't they?'

Eileen nodded. 'If the worst does happen, even though Jerry says he'll manage, I know that at least if both the girls were at school it would make things easier for him.'

'For the girls, too, perhaps,' Timothy suggested. 'Routine can be very comforting. What else?'

Eileen gave a small teary smile. 'Rhiannon's eighth birthday, our tenth wedding anniversary.'

'Worth fighting for?'

Eileen nodded, but her face was lined with indecision. 'Is it fair on them, though? I'd have to go to Adelaide for all the treatment—a half-hour appointment is a three-day round trip.'

Clara saw Timothy frown and broke in. 'The air ambulance

only takes patients while they're unwell. When Eileen has her radiation treatment she'll qualify, but if it's just a follow-up visit or a regular consultation she has to take the bus. That's a day there and a day back for a half-hour appointment.'

Eileen nodded. 'And if it doesn't work, that's time I could have spent with them.'

Retrieving the list, Timothy read it again closely, not answering her question at first. 'You're wrong, Eileen, there's nothing stupid about this list, I happen to think it's beautiful. This is the type of thing the children will treasure one day. One look at this and they'll know how much you love them, and hopefully you'll be around to read it with them. They need you, Eileen, and you need them.' His voice changed. Snapping back into doctor mode, he handed her over the bottle of pills. 'One at bedtime. Only take one, mind, because if you wake up in the night and can't get back to sleep you can take another one. They're pretty short-acting and won't leave you feeling groggy the next day, but I've a feeling you won't be needing them once you make up your mind. Do you want me to get Ross to speak to the specialists in Adelaide?'

When Eileen didn't answer straight away, he carried on talking. 'Just because you start treatment, it doesn't mean you can't change your mind later. You're still in control here and Clara and I will support you in whatever you decide.' Looking over, he smiled as Clara stepped forward.

'Why don't you talk it over with Jerry? I'll call back tomorrow,' Clara suggested gently, holding back the sigh of relief as Eileen finally nodded.

They didn't talk about it in the Jeep. He seemed to sense she was just too raw to go over things, but far from the strained journey earlier this time, when Timothy made small talk, Clara responded warmly, even managing a laugh or two at his appalling jokes. And later, as they ran the mobile clinic, as she watched him interact with the locals. Not once did she need to interrupt, not once did she take him to one side and warn him the way things were done out here.

A strange well of pride, a flutter of excitement grew in her stomach as she watched him work. A junior doctor he might be, but Clara knew that it was only a matter of time before he found his feet and the world would be all the richer for having him. Timothy was a true doctor in every sense of the word. He had it all—tenderness, compassion, wisdom and all topped with that generous smile, and Clara wondered how she could ever have thought him awkward.

Timothy Morgan was going to be one helluva doctor.

They lay on the rug, laughing immoderately at Timothy's silly jokes, and Clara didn't mind for a moment having the new guy along with her, didn't mind sharing her picnic lunch or the quiet time she normally adored.

In fact, she relished it.

'That would have to be the best picnic I've ever tasted,' Timothy groaned. 'Did you make it?'

Clara shook her head. 'I know I moan how much work I get, but Shelly hasn't lumbered me with the lunch duties and cleaning the clinic yet. June takes care of all that, you'll meet her soon enough.

'You did great with Eileen.' Her change of subject went unacknowledged for a moment or two, Timothy sensing this was hard for her. Flinging some crumbs, they watched for a moment as the ever-hungry galahs who had been hungrily watching them bravely swooped out of the trees and devoured their impromptu feast.

'Look how close they come,' Timothy sighed. 'I wish I'd brought my camera.'

'They're practically tame,' Clara said, 'I feed them all the time.' Her voice grew serious. 'I meant what I said about Eileen—I mean, I don't think I could have changed her mind and I know Ross has tried...'

'Look, thanks for the vote of confidence,' Timothy said modestly, 'but I really don't think her change of heart had anything to with me. It was more a timing thing.'

'Perhaps,' Clara admitted, 'but you really were great with her.'

'Because I'm not close to her, it makes it a lot easier to be objective. And don't put yourself down. It was you she wanted to see and I don't doubt for a second it will be you doing most of the legwork if she does go ahead with the treatment.'

Clara nodded. 'I know she'll have to go to Adelaide for the radiation treatment and the surgery but Ross says that she can have the chemo at home this time—it will make all the difference.'

'It's a lot of work for you, though.'

Clara shrugged. 'I'm used to it. And it really isn't that much extra work. I just have to go and set it up. It's a small syringe driver that delivers the drug in a measured dose, so she can have it strapped to her and she can walk around with it, do the housework, whatever. I just hope she doesn't get so sick this time. That's if she decides to go ahead.'

'Let's just wait and see, huh?' The galahs had finished feeding now, fluttering back to the treetops and eyeing the visitors suspiciously. 'People and emotions I can deal with,' Timothy sighed. 'I'm just dreading a big emergency, especially somewhere like here…'

'You'd be fine,' Clara said assuredly, but Timothy just let out a long sigh.

'Doesn't anything scare you, Clara? You just seem so calm about everything. I sometimes wonder if I'll ever be that assured.'

'Of course you will be. It's just experience. Mind you, I still go cold when there's a car crash. We had a big one here a few weeks back.'

'The bus crash?' Timothy checked as Clara nodded. 'I saw it on the news.'

'It was awful.' Taking a sip of her water, she fiddled with the water bottle for a moment or two before carrying on. 'That's how my parents were killed.'

The silence around them was loaded. She could feel his eyes on her, knew that he was waiting for her to elaborate.

'Their injuries weren't that bad?' Looking up, she registered the confusion in his eyes. 'If medical help had been nearby, they'd both have lived. Mum had a pneumothorax, a chest tube would have saved her, and Dad had internal bleeding. By the time the Flying Doctors arrived it was too late.'

'Is that why you went into nursing?'

Clara nodded. 'Not for a few years after the event, though. I was only fifteen when it happened but, as Mum said, I was always going on forty.' Clara grinned, but her eyes were shining with tears as she explained. 'I was always a really sensible kid, so it wasn't hard to buckle down and concentrate on my schoolwork to get the grades for uni.'

'Who looked after you after they died?' Timothy asked. 'Have you got a lot of family?'

Clara shook her head. 'There was only me. I've got an aunt in Melbourne who said I could stay with her, she's got loads of kids and she said that one more wouldn't make a difference— in the nicest possible way,' she added, registering Timothy's taken-aback expression. 'But I couldn't bear the thought of leaving everyone and everything I knew, so I decided to stay here.'

'On your own?' He couldn't keep the shock from his voice but Clara just shook her head.

'I wasn't on my own for five minutes.' Clara smiled. 'It's like one big extended family here. I stayed with Bill and his wife for a while after it first happened and they were great, they always have been. Then when I was ready I moved back home, but I was never left alone, everyone pitched in.' She gave a soft laugh. 'I don't think I cooked a single dinner for two years.' Standing, she shook out the rug, the conversation definitely over, but Timothy knew there was a lot of hurt there, a lot more to be said.

He didn't push it.

* * *

'I've come for the empties!' A rather shrill voice pierced the clinic as Clara finished the restock.

'Thanks, June.' Clara smiled, handing the elderly lady the empty Esky. 'Lunch was lovely. I've left a note on the fridge for next week's mobile clinic roster. And a word of advice—if you see Timothy's name down, make an extra round of sandwiches, he eats like a horse.'

'Who eats like a horse?' Timothy grinned, a bar of chocolate and a can of cola in hand as he made his way over.

'Timothy, this is June.' Clara introduced them, expecting Timothy to impart a brief nod or a quick handshake. 'June makes the lunches and cleans the clinic.'

'The magic fairy that comes in at night?' Timothy said, putting down his can and shaking June's hand warmly. 'I was saying to Clara today that that was the best picnic I've ever tasted.'

'He was, too,' Clara agreed, smiling to herself as June blushed and patted her heavily sprayed curls.

'What was that relish in the sandwiches?' Timothy continued, food clearly one of his favourite topics.

'My own onion jam.' June gave a conspiratory wink. 'It just adds that little something extra.'

'It certainly does,' Timothy agreed.

'The recipe's been passed down in my family for generations,' June gushed. 'But I'm sure I could rustle up a jar just for you, Doctor, seeing as you're so partial to it.'

'That would be great.' Timothy grinned. 'And none of this "Doctor" business, it's Timothy.'

'Timothy,' June purred, tying on her pinny. 'Right, then, I'd better get started.'

'Did I hear right?' Ross's jaw was practically on the floor as he made his way over. 'You've managed to score a whole jar of June's onion jam? Shelly and I have been dropping hints for months. How about you, Clara?'

'Same here.' Clara grinned. 'I'll have to come over to yours for dinner one night, Timothy, if you've got your own stock of the contraband.'

'Any time.' For a tiny second their eyes locked, and June's blush paled into insignificance as Clara turned purple.

'About five o'clock, then.' Ross smiled as a suddenly confused Clara fumbled for her bag and headed for the door. 'Kell doesn't want a big fuss, just a few steaks on the barby at ours is all I could get him to agree to.'

'Sure.' Clara nodded, glancing at her watch and racing towards the door, determined to catch the last ten minutes of her soap. 'I've just told Shelly that I'll bring the dessert, but remind her of that, Ross, when she's panicking later—she always does way too much food.'

'We'll see you there?' Ross checked with Timothy, as Shelly came over, smothering a yawn as she pulled out the keys ready to lock up on another day.

'Great.' Heading for the door, Timothy turned around. 'How much should I put in?' As Ross frowned Timothy elaborated. 'For the present.'

'Oh, no.' Ross's frown faded as he waved him off. 'You've barely met the guy, so we don't expect you to chip in for his leaving present.'

But Timothy wasn't going anywhere.

His eyes narrowing, he eyed Ross for a moment or two before continuing. 'I meant for Clara's birthday present.' Those green eyes weren't smiling as he took in their horrified expressions. 'I thought as much—you really have forgotten, haven't you? Do you realise that Eileen Benton remembered? She's been diagnosed with secondary cancer yet she still managed to make a present and wrap it up and remembered to wish Clara happy birthday!'

His eyes moved to the window, to Clara hurrying past, her red hair bright in the afternoon sun, and a smile softened his unusually harsh features as Ross and Shelly stood there, shamed

by their own thoughtlessness and stunned at the emotional outburst from the happy-go-lucky new doctor!

'You know, guys, what attracted me to this place when I saw
the advert for the job was the *supposed* "close knit community."
Well here's a bit of free advice—drop that stitch and the whole
place will unravel.'

Turning to go, Timothy changed his mind. 'And while I'm
making myself unpopular, I might as well get everything off
of my chest. Do you know there's nothing more annoying than
being told that just because you don't have children you can't
possibly know how much life hurts? Eileen Benton is Clara's
best friend. Clara was her bridesmaid, she delivered her babies,
and nursing her is hurting Clara like you wouldn't believe. But
then again, how would you guys know? I'm sure you never
thought to ask.'

The knocking on her front door didn't come as any surprise.

People always knocked at Clara's door. Whether it was for a
cup of sugar or a wound dressing change because the clinic was
closed, Clara was used to hearing a quick rap on her front door
before it was pushed open and the familiar Australian greeting
'G'day' echoed down the hall.

Only this time the heavy knocking on the door wasn't followed up with footsteps, just a long pause before it started again.

'It's open,' Clara shouted loudly, her hair still dripping from
her shower, a baggy T-shirt skimming her thighs as she eyed the
mountain of clothes that lay in a higgledy-piggledy pile on her
bed. She wished that the jumble of T-shirts and shorts and occasional shirt could somehow transform themselves into something that looked even remotely sexy.

'In here,' Clara called again as the knocking continued. Picking up a rather sheer lilac top she had bought eons ago, she hastily shoved it under her pillow. Sexy it might be—she'd bought
it from a mail-order catalogue in a fit of madness—but there

wasn't exactly much call for see-through lilac organza in Tennengarrah.

Realising she was actually going to have to answer the blessed door, Clara let out a small sigh, tore herself away from her rather limited wardrobe and padded barefoot along the polished floorboards of her hallway

The knocking on the door mightn't have been a surprise but the sight of Timothy Morgan standing in her doorway, hand poised ready to knock again, most certainly was.

'Didn't you hear me?' Clara remonstrated, blushing furiously as she pulled her oversized T-shirt down over her oversized bottom and gestured him to come in. 'I said it was open.'

'I heard you,' Timothy mumbled, and if Clara hadn't known better she could have sworn that he, too, was blushing as he followed her through to the lounge. 'But it didn't seem right just to barge in. I thought perhaps you were expecting someone. I didn't want to startle you.'

'You didn't,' Clara lied, waiting for Timothy to tell her what he wanted, to explain why he was here, but when nothing was forthcoming, ever practical, Clara got straight to the point.

'What can I help you with?'

'Help me with?' Timothy gave her a slightly startled look. 'Nothing. I just came to walk you over to the barby.'

'Oh.'

'I thought it might make things a bit easier for you if you had someone to go with.'

'Oh.' Not the wittiest of responses but it was the best she could do. 'I'm just getting dressed. Can I get you a drink or anything?'

'No, thanks.' He gave a nervous smile. 'I'll just wait here, shall I?'

Clara nodded, her smile equally nervous. 'I shan't be long. Make yourself at home.'

Sitting himself on the edge of the sofa, Timothy looked around, taking in the heavy wooden furniture, the clutter of framed photos on every available surface, the worn rug on the wooden floorboards. It didn't look like an independent, just on thirty, woman's home and if he hadn't known better he wouldn't have been surprised if Mr and Mrs Watts had strolled into the lounge to assess Clara's escort for the evening!

But despite the fact it was clearly a family home, neither was it a shrine to her parents. A few bright cushions broke the rather bland colour scheme, a DVD and impressive music system filled the entertainment cabinet and a pile of glossy magazines littered the coffee-table.

It was just too big.

Too big for her to be alone in.

A lump in his throat expanded like bread in water as he imagined Clara at fifteen, here in this very lounge, confused and alone, struggling to comprehend the cruel hand the world had dealt her.

'You didn't have to sit staring at the wall,' Clara admonished as she walked in. 'You should have put the television on or some music or something.' She was moving quickly, straightening magazines and trying desperately not to meet his eyes, awkward and exposed as the lilac organza made its first debut, not quite meeting the waistband or hipband or whatever it was you called it on the way too skimpy denim shorts that Clara was positive she was way too old for.

'You look fabulous,' Timothy enthused, catching her wrist as she rushed past and standing up beside her. 'Is this a last-ditch effort to make Kell realise what he could be missing out on?'

She started to laugh, even opened her mouth to lightheartedly agree, but somewhere midway she changed her mind. His hand was hot and dry around her wrist, she could feel her radial pulse flickering against the fleshy nub of his thumb, and as her eyes met his the confusion that flickered could easily have been misinterpreted for something that looked suspiciously like lust.

'No,' she said slowly, her voice coming out more breathlessly than she'd intended. She cleared her throat as she retrieved her

wrist before heading off to the kitchen to collect the dessert she
had promised Shelly. Resting her burning cheeks against the
cool white kitchen tiles, she ran a steadying hand across her
rarely exposed midriff, concentrating on slowing her breathing
down as she contemplated the shift in her feelings, the revelation that utterly astounded her.

'I'm doing this for me.'

CHAPTER FIVE

IT SHOULD HAVE been the worst day of her life.

Should have been hell on earth, saying goodbye to Kell and to all her secretly harboured dreams.

But somehow, with Timothy by her side, with his arm slung casually over her shoulders as they sidled up to the barby and handed over a bottle of wine and the huge Pavlova Clara had made, it wasn't as agonising as she had thought it would be.

It wasn't agony at all, in fact.

Ross and Shelly fell on her the second she arrived, plying her with some champagne as a cake appeared with rather too many candles twinkling away.

'You didn't have to do all this,' Clara said shyly, as everyone crowded around and belted out 'Happy Birthday.' 'It's no big deal.'

'It's a very big deal,' Shelly said, thrusting a massive bottle of perfume into her hands and giving her a kiss on the cheek, her sparkling eyes guiltily catching Timothy's for a small second.

Even when Kell took her to one side and told her she was the best friend a guy could wish for and gave her a glimpse of the engagement ring. Clara managed a genuine smile and a kiss on the cheek for luck, and actually meant it when she wished him well, wished him and Abby all the love in the world.

'It's all right,' Clara mumbled, as she made her way back to Timothy who was trying to look as if wasn't watching. 'I didn't say anything out of place—you don't have to slam me up against a wall and start kissing me again.'

'Shame.' Timothy laughed, 'I rather enjoyed that.' His voice grew more serious. 'How was it?'

'It was OK, believe it or not.' Clara blinked. 'Mind you, I think it helped that I didn't like the ring he'd chosen—Argyle diamonds really aren't my thing.'

'You didn't tell him that?' Timothy yelped.

'Of course not. I told him it was beautiful, that Abby would love it, all the sort of things that a good friend would say.' The slight break in her voice didn't go unnoticed and Timothy eyed her with concern.

'Time we were out of here, I think.'

'It will look rude,' Clara protested. 'I should offer to help Shelly clear up afterwards.' But it was a half-hearted effort and when Timothy started on the round of goodbyes she joined in, grateful for his foresight as tears grew alarmingly close at the final hurdle and Kell pulled her in for a final goodbye hug.

'Come on, you,' Timothy said when finally it was over. 'Let's get you home.'

They walked back in silence. Shooting a look sideways at him, she watched as Timothy pretended to be intrigued with the miles of empty road ahead and a smile played on the edge of her lips.

'I'm all right,' she ventured. 'You are allowed to talk to me, you know.'

'I was trying to give you some space.'

'Well, you don't have to,' Clara replied. 'I'm fine. More than fine, in fact, I'm not even crying.'

'You did really well.'

'It wasn't all that hard in the end,' Clara admitted. 'I guess at the end of the day I'm happy for him.'

'Still hurts, though.' They were at her door now, and Clara turned to face him.

'Not that much, at least not as much as it would have if I'd made a complete fool of myself on Saturday night.'

'You wouldn't have made a fool of yourself,' Timothy argued, and Clara let out an incredulous laugh.

'Oh, come on, Timothy, of course I would have. That's why you stopped me, remember?'

He stared at her then, really stared, his mouth opening to speak then closing again, but Clara filled the gap for him.

'I'd have looked like an idiot… I'd have looked…'

'Clara.' Something in his voice stilled her, and when she looked up something in his eyes told her he meant business. 'I stopped you from telling Kell how you felt because I could see how awkwardly things might have ended up. But never, not even for a moment did I think that you'd have looked silly.' One hand cupped her cheek and she found herself staring back at him, her eyes trapped like those of a rabbit caught in the headlights. 'You would never have looked like a fool,' he said more forcibly, 'because any guy in their right mind would be glad to hear it from someone as gorgeous as you. I just didn't want to see you get hurt.'

He was fumbling in his pocket now and Clara couldn't be positive but she was sure she could see the beginning of a blush darken his cheeks as he pulled out a small box from his shorts. 'They're not quite Argyle diamonds, I'm afraid.'

Bemused, she opened the small navy box he offered, staring dumbly at the two small earrings twinkling back at her.

'They're opals,' he offered needlessly, when Clara didn't say anything. 'If you get out a magnifying glass, of course. I found them when I was fossicking in Coober Pedy, and I had them made into earrings.'

'They're beautiful,' Clara murmured, snapping the small box closed and handing them back.

'They're yours,' Timothy said shyly. 'Happy birthday, Clara.'

'Don't be ridiculous.' Her hand was outstretched but Timothy wouldn't take them back. 'I can't take them, Timothy. We both know that you had these made for your blonde nurse... Rhonda, isn't it?'

'It is and I did,' Timothy said slowly, 'but I'd say you're rather more deserving, and anyway I've got an ulterior motive.' He gave her the benefit of his lovely smile. 'Their colour changes, depending on the mood of the wearer. So next time I think you're furious with me I can sneak a look at the stones and know that you're just premenstrual or whatever.' He watched a smile creep across her face, watched as she opened the box again, her eyes staring in wonder at the small opals glittering back at her. 'What colour are they now?'

'Turquoise,' Clara said breathlessly, 'with tiny flashes of red.'

'You know what that means, don't you?' he whispered, his lips moving towards hers for the second time since their recent first meeting. 'Maybe you do like me after all.' Only this time his movements were unhurried, this time she had every chance to escape, every chance to call things off. There was no barn wall to lean against, nothing holding her up other than an arm that moved around her waist, steadily pulling her in, and even though this kiss was a world away from the one they had shared, even though this kiss was loaded with emotion and tenderness, there was a heady familiarity about it, a delicious sense of rightness as she revisited that unique masculine smell, the quiet strength of arms that held her, the rough scratch of his jaw mingling with the soft sweet fruit of his lips and the cool heady feel of his tongue. And somewhere in mid-kiss, somewhere mid-breath, her eyes opened, realisation dawning, and she pulled away startled, but still he smiled, still he held her, still he adored her with his eyes.

'I'm sorry.'

'I thought we were going to stop apologising.'

'I—I am, w-we are,' she stammered, her eyes darting over his shoulder and catching sight of the gathered crowd in the distance at Ross and Shelly's, terrified how much she had enjoyed kissing Timothy and feeling strangely disloyal to the adoration she had, till so recently, felt for Kell.

'Don't look at Kell,' he whispered, pulling her hand up to his chest, 'Here, feel, I'm real Clara. Not some fantasy, not some distant dream you've got into your head.'

'It just seems wrong.' She turned her troubled eyes to him. 'Yesterday—'

'Forget yesterday.' Timothy implored. 'Clara, we both know we're attracted to each other.'

She nodded slowly. It would have been stupid to deny it with a heart rate topping a hundred and lips still tingling from his kiss.

'But what if you're a rebound? What if—?'

'We'll be each other's rebounds,' Timothy whispered. 'We'll massage each other's bruised egos and have three delicious months together, spoiling each other and inflating each others egos till we both think we're gorgeous.'

'I'm scared,' Clara admitted, 'scared of being hurt again.'

'No one's going to get hurt,' Timothy whispered, 'because we know the rules from the start. I'm going to be gone in three months, you're going to stay here. And that's OK. We've both got different goals, different lives to lead. But we can still make this the best three months of our lives, still make each day count.'

'It's not that easy,' Clara argued. 'Look at Abby and Kell, look how hard it's been for them.'

'OK, then.' Timothy shrugged. 'We can work alongside each other in a state of pent-up frustration, say goodbye at the clinic each evening and carry on being lonely.'

She stared back at him, the warmth the strength he radiated seeping into her, filling her with a fresh surge of confidence and a rare glimpse at a future that might just be OK.

'Just because it isn't for ever, it doesn't mean it can't be wonderful.'

He made it sound so straightforward, made the world seem

surprisingly simple all of a sudden. Live for today, to hell with the consequences, just lean on each other for however much time they had. As she pushed her front door open and he followed her inside, Clara was assailed by a sudden sense of freedom, an empowering surge of adrenaline as for the first time in her adult life she acted on impulse and let her heart lead the way and finally lived for the moment.

'No regrets in the morning,' Timothy checked as Clara shook her head.

'No regrets.'

'You're gorgeous,' he enthused, barely closing the door as he ravaged her again. He made her feel beautiful, made her feel every bit as sexy as one of the stunning models in a magazine, as divine as one of the blonde seductive soap stars that graced her television every evening. The way he kissed her, held her, adored her, rippled through her dented pride, soothing away the hurt, the pain she had learnt to live with for so long now. Only when they made it to the bedroom did she start to panic.

Somehow she had expected some restraint, for the infamous English reserve to rear its head, but despite his impeccable manners at work, despite his usual politeness to all and sundry, in the bedroom it would seem Timothy didn't possess even an ounce of modesty. Instead, he was undressing with lightning speed, almost falling over as he pulled off his boots such was his haste to get back to her.

More worrying than that, though, was the fact that naked he was gorgeous.

Seriously gorgeous.

Which would have been a bonus, of course, if she didn't feel like a beached whale in comparison!

Some men really are better undressed and, as divine as he looked with clothes on, seeing him in all his naked glory had Clara's confidence plummeting like a lift with the cable snapped. His body was perfectly toned, the honey brown hair only applied to his head. His legs, arms and chest were gently brushed with golden blonde, courtesy of the hot Australian sun. And the only bit the sun hadn't seen wasn't being particularly shy either, begging her to come closer, transfixing her to the spot as she eyed his delicious length. And Clara wished like she had never wished before that she were a tenth as beautiful as Timothy. Wished the sun didn't ravish her body with a million freckles, wished she'd stuck to every diet and done a million sit-ups each morning. Slowly, cringing with embarrassment, she pulled off her T-shirt, wishing her sports bra wasn't quite so sensible, wishing her breasts weren't quite so big and the soft mound of hair as he pulled at her panties wasn't quite so, well, ginger! But she could hardly ask the hairdresser for foils down there and, given the fact it was still only seven p.m. and the lights weren't even on to switch off, all she could do was pray they'd somehow make it to bed somehow conjoined...

But Timothy was having none of it.

'I want to see you,' he murmured, moving back, peeling her reluctant hand away as she tried fruitlessly to cover herself. 'Oh, Clara...'

His moan was so thick with desire, his eyes so blazing with lust that for a second she almost believed him, for a moment, as he ran his approving eyes over her body, she actually believed she was beautiful. But nerves caught up as his scrutiny became more intense, as his hands touched one gloriously ripe breast and he lowered his head to kiss it.

'I'm too fat,' she mumbled, her hands moving to cover herself, wishing it was night-time, wishing the shutters on her window could shut out just a bit more of the bright evening light.

'Never hide yourself.' Timothy shook his head, peeling her hands away again and slowly, slowly bending to kiss one aching pink nipple as his hand slipped between her legs, parting the golden amber until Clara moaned in pleasure, the heat of his touch, the utter admiration in his eyes finally hitting the mark until under his skilful touch she felt truly beautiful.

Slowly he laid her on the bed, kissing every last freckle, chasing away every last doubt until all she needed, wanted, craved even, was for him to fill her, so close to surrender as with one thrust he entered her, her legs coiling around his back like a reflex action, her ankles entwining as she pulled him closer, moved with him, gasped with him, gave in to him, gave in to her body, answered his urgent demands with needs of her own as they exploded together, her buttocks rising off the bed as he moved her higher, longer, deeper than Clara had ever thought possible, the blessed release of her orgasm a cleansing renewal, an unexpected but delicious liberation from the ties that had bound her for so long.

Lying in his arms, naked and spent, not even caring that the sheet lay in a crumpled heap on the floor, Clara was scarcely able to believe that her heart, which had felt so wounded, so broken, so bleeding, actually felt whole again.

Turning to face him, she frowned at the troubled expression on his face. 'W-what's wrong?' she stammered, sitting up abruptly and grabbing for the sheet, feeling twitchy and exposed all of a sudden, so sure that the bubble as usual was about to burst. 'I thought you said no regrets.'

'I did, didn't I?' Grabbing her wrist, he pulled her back beside him, her frown fading into a gurgle of laughter as Timothy carried on talking.

'I'm just worried what Hamo's going to have to say when he finds out about us.'

CHAPTER SIX

'WHAT DID SHE have?' Squinting at the alarm clock, Clara struggled to come to as Timothy made his way none too quietly into the bedroom, pulling off his shorts and boots in that order and wondering why he nearly toppled over.

'Both.' He grinned into the darkness as, kneeling up on the bed, Clara rubbed his tired shoulders. 'My first set of twins. Ross stayed but I did it all myself. A little boy first, he took for ever to come but the second one was over in fifteen minutes. She was breech, but there wasn't a problem.'

'I bet Rick was over the moon,' Clara commented. 'Even though he said he didn't care, I know he wanted a boy.'

'Well, he struck the jackpot with both. I'm surprised they didn't find out.'

The dizzy excitement had gone from his voice now, replaced instead with deep low tones as he relaxed under Clara's gentle touch.

'I guess when you've tried so hard to have a baby the sex doesn't really matter,' Clara said softly. 'They've been on IVF for years, which is no mean feat out here.'

'How come you weren't there?' Timothy asked. 'For the delivery, I mean. You've been so involved—I thought you'd want to see it through.'

'You've built a good rapport with Rick and Emma and they had Ross there as well. I know how exciting delivering twins is, I figured you deserved a go.'

'And a breech to boot!'

'A night for firsts.' Clara smiled, carrying on the massage and enjoying it every bit as much as Timothy clearly was. The feel of his skin beneath her fingers, the tense balls of muscle softening as she worked them gently, moving in ever-decreasing circles along his shoulders as he rolled his neck and breathed out slowly.

'Lord, it felt good, Clara. So good, in fact, I might even give up on surgery and change to obstetrics.'

'You say that after every delivery.' Clara laughed. 'But I know what you mean. There's nothing quite like it, is there? Watching that tiny little bundle come into the world, it still gets me even after all these years.'

'It was amazing. Hey.' Reaching over, Timothy picked up a bottle. 'Look what Rick gave me—a bottle of champagne and a cigar. How about it?'

'Yes to the champagne.' Clara smiled, enjoying his euphoria. 'But if you light up in here, you're sleeping alone.'

'Fair enough.' He popped the cork in a second, didn't even bother to get glasses, and never had the world seemed so great, lying in bed sipping icy champagne out of the bottle with a man as divine as Timothy. 'Do you know what I fancy?' Timothy asked, handing her the bottle. 'The biggest slab of pizza.'

'We're not in London,' Clara pointed out, levering herself out of the bed. 'The nearest I can come up with is some cheese on toast and if you're lucky a slice or two of tomato.'

'I'd rather have you.' His hand reached over and pulled her back. 'Would you find out?'

'Find out what?' Clara asked, settling back into the crook of his arm, shivering with expectancy as he ran a lazy hand along her waist.

'What you were having—if you were pregnant, I mean.'

She stilled in his arms. 'I've never really thought about it.' So deep was her blush that despite the darkness Clara was sure he must feel it radiating from her like a furnace.

She hadn't thought about it.

At least not until recently.

With Kell the fantasy had stopped at the barn. Tea lights and gardenias had been as far as she'd got, but since she'd been with Timothy suddenly all sort of ridiculous thoughts were popping into her consciousness at the most inappropriate of times.

Like now.

Imaging herself pregnant.

Imagining Timothy's euphoria.

Gurgling babies with his deep green eyes, or perhaps her blue ones topped with toffee-brown curly hair…

But not ginger.

The fantasy always pulled up short there.

'I think about it.' His clear voice filled the darkness. His honesty almost scared her. 'I think about it all the time.'

If ever there was a time when life for Clara was pretty near perfect, those first couple of months with Timothy were just about it.

He adored her.

Not just in bed, but in everything she did. And it was nice, so refreshingly nice to be a part of a couple. To have someone to come home to or someone to wait up for. To have someone ask about her day and actually listen as she rattled on about how busy the clinic was, how appallingly long the mobile clinic had taken without Kell, how insufferable it was, for all intents and purposes, to be the only nurse in an expanding clinic. Even a fleeting bout of gastro was bearable with Timothy clucking over her like a broody hen, ringing in sick for her and policing the telephone whenever Shelly rang to enquire how she was doing. Even the agony of nursing Eileen, watching her hair disappear along with her spirit, was made slightly more bearable with Timothy beside her, letting her rant about the injustice of the world or simply holding her when she wept, when it all became too much.

'Ross asked me my plans yesterday,' Timothy ventured one morning, as they waited for the third snooze alarm to finally force them out of bed. Staring into the semi-darkness, Clara didn't say anything, just pulled back the sheet and made to get up as a grumbling Timothy pulled her back to the cosy warmth of the bed.

'Come on, Clara, five more minutes—there's no rush.'

'Oh, yes, there is.' Pushing the sheet back, Clara lay for a moment willing her legs to move from the cosy warmth of Timothy's embrace. 'If I don't get a move on, I'm going to be late and so will you.'

'Doesn't matter.' Timothy grinned. 'Ross told me he's already written my reference.'

It was a joke, a tiny little light-hearted comment, but not for the first time Clara felt her heart sink further at the inevitability of Timothy's departure. Three months had stretched before them like an eternity at the start, like the beginning of the school holidays when she had been a child. Endless weeks stretching ahead, an endless summer that would surely last for ever. But it was almost over now, like the uniforms being taken out, pencil cases checked, books being labelled. A glimpse of what lay ahead had her heart sinking at the prospect...

'Just five more minutes,' Timothy grumbled. 'I'm trying to talk to you.'

'It's seven o'clock, Timothy.' Clara gestured to her small alarm clock. 'I'm supposed to be there in half an hour and I'm supposed to be doing a house call on Eileen this morning.'

'She's going to get better,' Timothy said gently, as Clara listlessly pushed the sheet back, dreading the house call she had pencilled into her diary for later that day.

'You don't know that,' Clara snarled, terrified to believe him. 'I thought doctors were supposed to err on the side of caution, be guarded in their outlooks. You can't just sit there and say she'll get better just like that. What's the point of false hope?'

'No point at all,' Timothy said evenly, refusing to rise to her outburst. 'But there is still hope for Eileen. Chemo does this, Clara, you know that better than anyone. The cure can be worse than the disease, you've got to stay positive for as long as Eileen needs you to and not a day longer.'

'So you're a psychiatrist as well as an oncologist now, are you?'

Her bitter words were so out of character with her usual gentle nature that for a moment or two they both just stared at each other, until Timothy broke the strained silence.

'Don't shut me out, Clara. I'm here for you.'

She gave a low laugh. 'But for how long, Timothy? It's all very well for you to be positive, to have encouraged Eileen to take the treatment, to offer to be there, but you're not going to be, are you? It's me that will be left holding her hand, it's me that has to witness the kids watching their mother slowly dying. You'll be up in Queensland with your underwater camera, snapping away at the reef, so don't lie there and tell me not to shut you out when we both know that you're going anyway.'

Standing under the shower, Clara massaged shampoo into her hair, trying to ignore the memory of Timothy's hurt expression when she had left the bed.

He was only trying to help, only trying to comfort her, she knew that deep down, but therein lay the problem.

Soon he would be gone, out of her life and on to pastures new—and what then?

She'd always been independent, self-reliant, but Timothy had crept into her heart with alarming stealth, had become the rock she leant on, her hope, her sounding-board, and all too soon it was going to be taken away.

Of course she wanted him to stay, she wanted that more than anything else in the world, but she was scared, scared of telling him just how much she wanted it. Terrified of a needy note creeping into her voice, terrified of betraying to him just how much she needed him, that he was so very much more than a rebound.

They walked over to the clinic together, for once the silence between them unusually strained.

'Do you want me to talk to Ross—about staying on, I mean?'

'You do what's right for you, Timothy.'

'What about us?'

They were at the clinic door now, hardly the best place for an in-depth discussion, but Clara did her best. 'I want you to stay on. It's just…'

'Just what?'

Clara took a deep breath. 'Well, you're going to go one day, aren't you?' When he didn't say anything Clara pushed a bit harder. 'Aren't you?'

'You know I have to.'

Clara gave a small nod, not trusting herself to speak.

'There's nothing to stop you coming with me, though.'

'So my job doesn't count? I'm only a nurse all of a sudden.' She turned hurt eyes to him. 'It didn't take long for you to start pulling rank, did it?'

'That's not what I meant and you know it,' Timothy flared, but Clara refused to back down.

'I'm the only nurse here, Timothy.'

'There's Shelly.'

That didn't even merit a response. 'If I walk away now, what's going to happen? Who's going to take care of people like Eileen?'

'Ross will have to find someone else,' Timothy said evenly, and Clara gave a scoffing laugh.

'Oh, come on, Timothy, we've got a permanent ad in all the papers, we're registered with every agency in the land and still we never get anyone for more than a few months. I can't just walk away. This is my family, I have a duty to them.'

'What about your duty to yourself, Clara?' Timothy pushed, refusing to get it. 'Don't you deserve to have a life, to be happy? You don't owe Tennengarrah anything.'

But Clara refused to be swayed. The anger faded from her voice and she managed a wobbly brave smile. 'This is my home,' she said softly. 'I'm an outback girl and you're an up-and-coming surgeon. Timothy, what we've had, what we've got, it's great, but we both know...' Swallowing hard, she looked up at him. 'That this was never for ever.'

'And that's the way you want it?'

Oh, it wasn't, but it was the way it had to be so instead of speaking the truth she forced a smile. 'You've got that blonde charge nurse to get back to.'

'Oh, come on, Clara.' Timothy pulled at her hand. 'I haven't even given her a thought. What about you?'

Confused by his question, she didn't respond.

'Do you still think about Kell?

There was something in his voice she couldn't interpret, a wariness she was scared to explore.

'Clara?' His voice was sterner now, demanding a response, but Clara simply couldn't give one. Instead she pulled her hand away and walked inside. Finding shelter in the ladies' loo, she buried her face in her hands with a low moan. Screwing her eyes closed on stubborn tears, she dragged a deep breath into her body.

Kell hadn't entered her head for weeks now. It was Timothy she thought about, Timothy who demanded every second of her mind, but was that what he wanted to hear? That the rebound had misfired? That the love and devotion she had felt for Kell didn't come close to the feelings she had for him?

And suppose she did tell him, suppose she took the biggest gamble of her life and laid it all on the line, where could it possibly lead? He might adore her, want her, but he certainly didn't need her.

Timothy was going to be a surgeon while she was a true Tennengarrah girl. The rules had been laid down at the start—it was she who had broken them.

For a second she wavered. Toyed with the idea of going with him, exploring Australia, taking a diving course, following her heart...

Prolonging the agony.

And it would be agony, Clara realised, pulling off a wad of loo roll and blowing her nose loudly. Because one day his visa would run out, one day the dream would have to end, and far worse than the hurt she felt now, far worse than the confusion in his eyes she had witnessed this morning, would be the pity.

The pity in his eyes when she told him she loved him.

'Where's Ross?' Walking out of the loo, she looked around the empty clinic, frowning at Timothy's bemused expression.

'I don't know.' Timothy shrugged. 'There's no one here.'

'But he has to be here.' Pushing open the staffroom door, Clara peered inside as Timothy caught up with her.

'He isn't. I've checked everywhere.'

'The door was open.' Clara frowned. 'Ross would never leave it unlocked, never.'

'Maybe there was an emergency,' Timothy suggested, but Clara shook her head firmly, a gnawing bubble of panic starting to well inside her throat.

'There's often an emergency,' Clara countered, her heat skittering into a gallop as she eyed the clinic again, pushing doors open and calling out his name before turning back to Timothy. 'But Ross always locks up behind himself, it's second nature.' Running over to the drug cupboard, she fumbled with her keys and wrenched it open, shaking her head at the neat boxes staring back at her, everything in its place just as it should be. 'We haven't been robbed.'

'Maybe he got a call-out, maybe—' The sound of footsteps running towards them had them both letting out a mutual sighs of relief, grins appearing as Ross bounded into the clinic.

But their relief was short-lived.

One look at his grey, angst-ridden face had Clara's heart spinning into free fall, her usually steady hands trembling as she reached out to her colleague, her voice shaking. 'Ross, what on earth's happened?'

Oh, she tried to stay impassive, tried to put on her best calm expression as Ross's terrified eyes met hers, but even before he'd finished speaking a small wail of horror escaped Clara's lips.

'It's Matthew.' She could hear the terror in his voice as he said his son's name, the fear, the panic all rolled into one as this normal weekday suddenly exploded into a nightmare, as everything safe and good was swept from under them. 'He's gone missing.'

CHAPTER SEVEN

STRANGE WHO PERFORMED in a crisis.

Such an irrelevant thought, but as Clara stood there, momentarily stunned, as Ross physically crumpled, she watched in grateful awe as Timothy took over. The most junior, the most inexperienced of all of them snapped into leader mode in an instant. His friendly, open face strong, his steps purposeful as he walked over to Ross and in clear uncompromising tones demanded answers to the questions he rapidly fired.

'When did you last see him?'

'Midnight.' Ross was sobbing openly now. 'We checked them before we went to bed. Normally Shelly goes in before her shower but Abby rang this morning—'

'Forget that.' Timothy dragged him away from irrelevancies. 'When did you realise he was missing?'

'Shelly rang.' Ross balled his fists into his eyes, forcing deep breaths into his lungs in an effort to hold it all together. 'Maybe ten, fifteen minutes ago.'

'Have you called the police?'

Ross nodded, but the panic in his voice reached hysterical proportions as he continued. 'But Jack's two hours away, there's some campers trespassing over at Winnycreek...'

'He's coming, though,' Timothy checked, almost shaking

Ross as he forced his attention. 'And did he say he was calling in help?' A small nod was the only answer Timothy got, but he turned his attention to June, who had burst through the doors, a wide smile on her face as she saw her permanently hungry young doctor coming towards her.

'June.' Timothy's voice was incredibly calm. Taking the bemused woman's hands, he spoke in low tones. 'Matthew has gone missing.' As she started to whimper he gripped her hands tighter and Clara watched as he gave the terrified woman instructions. 'I need you to stay calm, I need you to go and knock on every door you can think of and get someone to do a ring around. I want everyone who can help at the clinic, CFA members, anyone with a Jeep, a plane—do you understand?' He didn't wait for an answer and as June scuttled off he addressed Ross.

'Go back to the house.'

'I have to look—'

'Look again through the house and the garden,' Timothy broke in. 'Look in every cupboard, under every bed, every shed—he's likely to be close by. And then report back here in half an hour. But you have to keep looking. Is there anywhere you can think he might have wandered to, anywhere?' Ross shook his head, fear turning to anger as hopelessness took over, as Timothy pushed harder. 'Come on, Ross. Is there anywhere you can think of?'

'He doesn't go anywhere on his own. For heaven's sake, he's three years old, he's got Down's syndrome, he wouldn't know how to cross a road!'

'Ross.' Finally Clara found her voice, and on legs that felt like jelly she led Ross to the clinic door. 'Do what Timothy's saying, go and look with Shelly.'

As Ross raced towards the house Clara ran a shaking hand through her hair, willing herself to stay calm, to think, to form some sort of plan.

'We're going to find him.'

'Oh, and you know that too, do you?' Her tear-streaked face turned to him. 'It's going to be forty degrees today, Timothy. A little boy on his own in the outback won't last a morning. There's dingoes, snakes, dams—that's if the heat doesn't kill him first.'

'We're going to find him.' Not for a second did his voice waver, the optimism in his voice so strong Clara almost believed him. 'But we have to all pull together.'

And pull together they did.

The whole of Tennengarrah poured into the high street, all determined to play their parts, all determined to bring a special little boy home. Bruce setting off in his plane before the first trestle table had been hoisted up, clipboards appearing, maps spread out, the CFA volunteers pulling on their orange uniforms as they pored over the maps, chewing on cigarettes as they formed a plan, shouted orders, organised groups and gave out whistles.

Timothy was in charge for now, and every one knew it. Mike, the aboriginal medicine man, appeared with a group of his men, ready to share their knowledge of the bush, to utilise their tracking skills and search for clues in their own unique way. And though Timothy had only been there a relative five minutes, though his knowledge of the land was minuscule, it was him they all deferred to, him they all ran their plans by. A leader was needed and Timothy filled the part, his crisp English accent authoritative, his manners impeccable as he thanked everyone profusely, no matter how small their contribution— even the cup of tea a tearful June pressed into his hands got the same polite, grateful response. Even Hamo, Timothy's unofficial arch-enemy, bordered on approachable as he handed Timothy a fluorescent jacket and told him to put on the hard red hat. Timothy did so without comment, but the gesture didn't go unnoticed by Clara who chose that moment to slip back to the clinic.

'Where have you been?' Timothy pulled her aside the second she emerged again. 'Everyone's ready to head off.'

'I've just set up a bed for him, turned up the ice machine, set up some fans…' Registering his frown, Clara realised that, despite his air of authority, despite the leadership he was showing, this was uncharted territory for Timothy and she patiently explained her movements. 'Unless he's found in the next hour or so, Matthew's likely to be suffering from heat exhaustion. A couple of degrees centigrade either way will be the difference between survival and death, between walking away unscathed or brain damage. Our first priority will be to cool him. I was just making sure everything was ready.'

She watched as Timothy put his hands up to shield his eyes, squinting at the morning sun only just starting to show its bite, and almost felt the surge of fear that engulfed him, registered a nervous swallow as he turned to the gathered crowd.

'Let's get moving,' Timothy called above the anxious chatter, demanding attention, which he respectfully received. 'Now, remember, only search the area you've been allocated. When you're sure it's clear, come back and Hamo will brief you again. We have to keep in touch.'

'Ross is coming.' The hope in Clara's voice faded as his ashen face came into view.

'You go to Shelly,' Timothy said firmly.

'I should be searching,' Clara argued. 'I know the land like the back of my hand.'

'So do most of the locals,' Timothy pointed out. 'But Shelly needs you now. You need to keep her calm, let her ramble if she wants to, but anything she says, no matter how small, if you think there's a clue there, let me know.'

Clara nodded. Turning to go, she swung back around and for a second, despite the hub of activity, despite the crowd that surrounded them, it was as if only the two of them were there. 'He'll be OK, won't he?' As contrary as her words sounded, as furious as she'd been at him for his blind optimism, suddenly it was everything Clara needed, hope to cling to as she faced

Matthew's mother, strength to feed from as she dealt with the agony ahead.

A tiny smile softened his features for a second.

'He's going to be fine,' Timothy said softly, before turning back to the crowd, back to the search teams he had organised, back to the people who also needed his quiet strength.

Shelly didn't even look up as Clara slipped quietly inside. Trapped in her own private hell, she sat on the edge of the sofa, staring unblinkingly at a tattered book she held in her hands as Clara sat beside her.

There was silence for a moment or two before Shelly finally spoke.

'It's his favorite book.' Shelly ran her finger over the cover. 'You've no idea how many times I've read it to him. He gave it to Kate when she was born, but he still sneaks it out of her bookcase every night for me to read, then he insists that I put it back.

'He's going to be OK, isn't he, Clara? They'll find him, won't they?'

And though she had seen Ross's agony, though she had seen fear and pain in more patients than she could truthfully remember, as Shelly dragged her eyes to Clara, Clara witnessed there and then the utter devastation of her friend, and she felt grateful, so grateful for Timothy's optimism, for the ray of hope she could offer. Even if it was a false promise, even though the answer couldn't possibly be known, now wasn't the time to take hope away.

'He's going to all right.' Clara took one of Shelly's cold hands and held it tightly. 'Everyone's out there, looking for him, and they're going to find him, Shelly.'

'I should have looked in on him first thing. I always do,' Shelly sobbed. 'But Abby rang, and I was just so grateful the kids were still asleep so I could have a proper chat, and all that time—'

'You did nothing wrong,' Clara said firmly. 'This isn't your fault.'

'Oh, it is.' Shelly was inconsolable. Used to grief, Clara let her talk, let Shelly voice her fears as she herself sat quietly holding Shelly's hand.

'His whole little world has changed since Kate came along. He's so much more clingy and jealous, and I tried to give him more time, tried to be there for him, but there was always something going on, always a shift that needed to be filled...'

'Oh, Shelly.' Tears brimmed in Clara's eyes as she watched her friend and colleague struggle just to remember to breathe, and only then did Clara realise that Shelly's supposed insensitivity at times had nothing to do with her. Shelly was another mum battling to do it all, to somehow find enough hours in the day. 'I'm sorry. If I'd known, I'd have done more.'

'You couldn't have done any more.' Shelly shook her head. 'You do too much already. Abby rang this morning, she said she had some great news and she sounded so happy, so excited that for a second I thought they were coming back, that we'd finally have more staff and I could stay home with the kids. But she told me they were getting married and instead of being happy for them I was disappointed. What sort of person does that make me?'

'Normal.' Clara wrapped her arm around Shelly's heaving shoulders. 'Everyone misses them, and though we're thrilled they're happy it doesn't mean we can't be disappointed that they're gone.'

'Matthew misses Kell.' Shelly gave a soft laugh. 'He used to make Matthew laugh, called him "big guy" and played hide and seek with him. Kell would know where to look, he'd know what to do.' Her voice was rising, panic overriding sense now.

It was the longest morning of her life.

Like a pendulum Shelly swung between hopelessness and despair, bursts of manic laughter as she recalled some of Matthew's more endearing traits countered almost immediately with rasping, desperate hopeless tears as Clara fought to comfort her, to somehow be a friend and a professional, to hold out hope yet attempt to face the truth. The minutes that had dragged by suddenly started to gallop, the cool crisp morning evaporating. She tried to ignore the searing heat and its effect on a three-year-old boy dressed in a pair of pyjama bottoms.

'We should ring Kell.' Shelly's voice was firm. Standing, she started to pace as Clara sat quietly on the sofa. 'He might know what to do, where to look.' Shelly's eyes were wide. She was grasping at straws perhaps, but a shred of hope was better than none at all. 'We have to ring Kell.'

Clara hesitated, momentarily torn, not wanting to head down the wrong path, indulge Shelly's whims only to see her dejected and spent when deep down she was sure Kell could offer no better solutions than the ones already in better in place. And yet…

Kell had been close to Matthew, Clara realised with mounting excitement. During the last few weeks of Shelly's pregnancy Kell had often turned up at the clinic with Matthew, giving him a few crayons to draw with as he himself got on with the work, taking him for walks during his breaks. Hope started to flare. Clara rushed into the hall. Maybe Kell could offer some insight, could perhaps suggest something they hadn't already thought of.

With Shelly watching like a hawk, wringing her hands with frustration, begging her to hurry up, Clara rang the number, cursing inwardly at the recorded message.

'It's an answering-machine,' Clara said helplessly. 'He must be at work.'

She left a brief message, urging him to ring the second he returned. Shelly started pulling out phone books, frantically searching for numbers.

'Ring him at the hospital—I'm sure he's working with Abby.'

It took an age to get through, the switchboard messing up the connection, the emergency ward redirecting her twice, and if the answering-machine message had been cold and impersonal it was nothing compared to the haughty voice Clara encountered that told her Kell Bevan couldn't possibly come to the telephone right now.

'You don't understand,' Clara begged. 'This is an emergency.'

'Which is exactly what Mr Bevan is dealing with,' came the impassive response. 'I'll pass on your message as soon as he's available.'

Shelly was inconsolable. As fruitless as the call might have been, it had offered her hope, something to cling to, something to focus on, and now that it was gone. Now there really was nothing she could do she seemed to crumple before Clara's eyes. Even though she knew emotion was good, that it was better out than in, as Shelly's screams echoed through the house, as baby Kate awoke demanding attention, oblivious to the hell around her, Clara toyed with the idea of sedating Shelly just to restore some sense of order. Instead, she left her momentarily, picking up Kate, hot and angry at having been left so long, and changing her nappy, praying Shelly might settle, would hold it together for just a little bit longer.

'She's hungry.' Clara bought the wailing infant through to the lounge, deliberately ignoring Shelly's agitation, determinedly talking normally. 'She needs to be fed.'

With infinite relief she watched as Shelly checked herself, and though Clara's heart ached for Shelly she kept her voice matter-of-fact. 'Sit down, Shelly, and feed her.'

Mercifully she obeyed, little Kate latching on and sucking hungrily as Shelly kissed the soft blonde down of her baby's head, breathing in her sweet baby scent as if it was the life force she depended on, the one life raft she could cling to in this awful turbulent time.

'I forgot your birthday.' Looking down at her baby, Shelly's voice was a tiny whisper, and though it was so irrelevant, Clara followed her thread, irrelevance far more palatable than the hell they were facing. 'You're being so nice and I've been so awful. If it hadn't been for Timothy…'

'It doesn't matter,' Clara said gently, sitting on the sofa beside her. 'You probably did me a favour—it turned out to be the best birthday ever.' Fingering the tiny opals in her ears, she finally understood. 'Shelly, stop beating yourself up. You've done nothing wrong, nothing wrong at all. I'm here for you.'

'You always have been.'

The ringing of telephone caught them both unawares. Clara jumped up first, fixing Shelly with her best version of a firm glare. 'I'll get it. You carry on feeding Kate.'

Only when she picked up the telephone did Clara realise the tension that had engulfed her. Hearing Kell's voice, so normal, so utterly oblivious to the hell on the other end of the line, had Clara momentarily lost for words. Leaning against the hall wall, she let out a long low moan, tears trickling down her cheeks when finally she spoke.

'Oh, Kell.' If only she'd turned at that moment, if only she'd registered Timothy pushing open the fly door, walking in un-announced, maybe she'd have changed her tone, rephrased her words somehow. 'If ever I needed you, it's now.'

Looking up, seeing the agony on Timothy's face, for a sec-ond she thought the worse had happened, that he was coming with bad news.

'Where's Shelly?' Timothy's voice was barely a croak.

'Feeding Kate.'

'I'm here.' Pale and trembling, Shelly stepped forward, Kate in her arms as her terrified eyes turned to Timothy. 'Have you found him?'

So devastated was his expression that when Timothy shook his head Clara almost dropped the telephone in relief, so sure had she been that the worst possible outcome had actually trans-pired. 'It's Kell.' Handing the phone to Shelly, she took Kate and walked through to the lounge, Timothy following a step behind.

'What you just heard,' Clara ventured as Timothy stood there, his face rigid, his eyes guarded, 'wasn't what it sounded like. Shelly was hysterical. She got it into her head that Kell might know where Matthew had gone. I was in two minds whether to sedate her—'

'It doesn't matter.' Timothy shrugged off the hand on his arm and shook his head, but then seemed to change his mind, his guarded eyes flashing with anger, 'You really think Kell's going to save the day, don't you, Clara, that Kell's going to come through for you? Well, guess what? I'm here and I'm real, not some fantasy you've got locked in your head. I'm the one dressed in fluorescent orange waterproofs when it's thirty-five degrees outside, I'm the one rallying the troops and organising search parties. Where's Kell now?' His lips snarled around the words. 'Where's Kell when you need him, Clara?'

CHAPTER EIGHT

IT WAS PROBABLY a matter of seconds but it felt like hours. Clara bit back a smart reply as Timothy suddenly relented, dragging a hand through his sodden, sweat-dampened hair as he shook his head. 'Now's not the time.' Clenching his fists, he took a deep breath. 'I'm sorry, that was uncalled-for.'

It had been uncalled-for and now most definitely wasn't the time, but as she looked at him she ached physically ached to put her hand to his taut, exhausted cheek to somehow put him right, but all that mattered here was Matthew. There would be time for that later.

'Is Jack here yet?'

Timothy nodded wearily. 'Everyone's here. The Flying Doctors just came in, Hall's checked the bed you set up and he's happy everything's ready. June's even icing sheets and boxing them up in Eskys to wrap him in the second he's found. People are coming in from all over, just wanting to help, to do something, anything. I've never seen anything like it, never seen people pull together in that way.' Sitting down, he rested his head in his hands as Clara started to pour a glass of iced water from the jug. Realising the waste in energy, she just handed him the jug which he took without comment, downing the water in one, not even wiping away the rivers that spilled onto him. Clara quietly watched, sensing his weariness, knowing the force of the harsh Australian sun while simultaneously trying not to imagine a little boy out there alone with the elements.

'Take your jacket off.'

'I have to get back.'

'Two minutes,' Clara implored, pulling the heavy jacket off as Timothy took a tiny, much-needed break. 'What does Jack say?'

'That he has to be near.' For the first time since sitting down he looked up and Clara felt like weeping when she saw the devastation in his eyes, the hopelessness of the message he imparted. 'They're bringing in the police divers, they're going to search the dams.'

'No.' She shook her head fiercely. 'He's hiding somewhere. He's just a baby, for heaven's sake, and he's going to be fine.'

'Clara.' His eyes couldn't meet hers. Instead, he stared at the empty jug in his hands, and she truly couldn't tell if it was sweat or tears that ran down his exhausted face. 'He is just a baby and this is the outback.' She watched his Adam's apple bob up and down, heard the tremor in his voice and she wanted him to take it back, to some how snap back into the wonderful optimist she'd berated before, for hope to impinge on hopelessness, but again he shook his head, 'The police are asking questions, you know the sort of questions as well as I do.'

She shook her head fiercely. 'Well, they're wrong and it's a waste of time even going through it. Their time would be better spent looking for him than heading up that path.'

But Timothy hadn't finished. 'They want to know if Shelly suffered any postnatal depression, if there's any family dynamics, any history that might point to—?'

'No.' Screwing her eyes closed, Clara took a mental swipe at him, or maybe her hands made contact. No matter how many times afterwards she relived the moment she could never be sure, but suddenly Timothy was beside her, holding her heaving shoulders and begging her to stay strong.

'We have to do this, Clara. Yes, Ross and Shelly are friends, yes, we're all close, but at the end of the day you're the nurse and I'm the doctor. When the tough talk comes, it's going to be us.'

'But it's not like that,' Clara said forcefully. 'Ross and Shelly adore him.'

Timothy nodded. 'We know that, but the police don't. They're not pointing the finger, it's just the system.'

'The system?' Jumping back, she stared at him, eyes wide, almost deranged with the preposterousness of the world. 'What does the "system" know about love, what does the "system" know about devotion? Ross isn't Matthew's biological father.' She watched as Timothy flinched. 'Can you imagine the "system's" response to that? I can just imagine the press with that little gem, just imagine the innuendoes, the snide little remarks, when the truth is that Ross loves Matthew more than his biological father. Ross would die before harming a hair on that child's head, so don't you stand there and tell me to be professional, don't you stand there and expect me to ask the tough questions because I won't do it, Timothy, I just won't.' Her voice trailed off as Shelly returned, but there was a determined edge to it as she turned to meet her friend. 'I'll resign here and now before I go there, Timothy. I simply won't do it.'

'Kell doesn't know where he could be.' Shelly's voice trembled as she walked towards them and Clara instinctively took Kate from her arms, sensing the desolation before them. 'They went for walks, but only along the main street. He took him to the park, to the milk bar, but apart from that he can't think of anything. They played peek-a-boo...'

'The barn.'

Timothy's voice forced their attention.

'The barn,' Timothy said again, breaking into a run.

Clara quelled the adrenaline that surged inside her and resisted running after him. Instead, she handed Kate to Shelly and forced an air of authority as her pulse pounded in her temples and instinct told her to follow.

'Shelly, wait here.'

The air was hot in her lungs, too hot to run, but nothing could have stalled her, nothing could have made her stay put as she pounded the red earth on legs that felt like jelly, her chest exploding as she followed Timothy through the town, the locals parting as they blazed a trail through the centre, oblivious of Hamo as he shouted behind them.

'We've already checked it. He isn't there.'

'He has to be here.' She watched with mounting despair as he turned over hay bales, shouting Matthews's name, prodding into the dark, damp mounds in a fruitless, hopeless last effort. 'He was playing hide and seek with Kell at the ball, climbing into empty beer kegs.'

'There are some more kegs out the back.' Hamo frantically beat on the door, wrenching the wooden plank that barred the back entrance as Timothy raced through, the searing heat of the morning sun harsher now after the relative cool of the barn.

'Matthew.'

Something in his voice stilled her.

Something told Clara it wasn't false hope that surged inside her.

'Matthew!'

But jubilation was short-lived, joy had its downside as Timothy pulled the flushed, limp body from an upturned keg. Hamo rushed to smother him with one of June's iced sheets as Timothy barely paused for breath, pulling the cool cotton around the limp little boy and running towards the clinic as if his own life depended upon it. Cheers went up as the gathered locals parted to let them through.

And Clara followed, perfecting her mental plan of attack as she ran. Running through the town, she begged an answer, prayed to a God that must surely be listening that there must be a reason, some sense to it all. That, yes, he was three, and he had Down's syndrome. But the fact he still used a bottle at night and had wandered off with his bottle of juice in his hand might just have saved him.

Professionalism took over then, emotions put aside as they laid the limp body on a gurney. Jack pulled Ross outside and Clara, Hall and Timothy worked together. Hall, the most senior, took the head of the gurney, calling orders in his thick Australian accent.

'What's his temp?'

'Forty point five degrees,' Clara answered, not even looking up as she placed ice bags around Matthew's head, in his groin and under his arms, then filled a burette with fluid as Timothy slapped Matthew's veins, slipped a needle in and enabled the lifesaving fluids to enter his system to hydrate the tiny body that lay on the gurney. 'But cooling started a few minutes ago, he would have been warmer when we found him.'

'Aim to cool him at point two degrees a minute,' Hall ordered.

They worked on almost in silence, Hall occasionally requesting something, but the words were barely out before his requests were met. Clara, ever efficient, the consummate professional, despite her fraught emotions, sprayed the little boy with tepid water, aiming the fans over his body.

'What about a cool bath?' Timothy asked, answering his own questions as he worked diligently on. 'Or would that be too much of a shock?'

'Evaporative cooling is the best,' Hall answered knowledgeably. 'This is the best way to get to this little tacker's temp down. Let's get some blood gases on him, Clara. Timothy, put a catheter in—we need to monitor his renal function.'

On and on they worked, trying to ignore Shelly's screams in the background, Ross's fruitless attempts to be let inside.

'What's his blood sugar?'

'Four.' Clara looked up, perhaps for the first time.

'Temp?'

'Thirty-nine point two.' For the first time she remembered to breathe again properly, watching as the tachycardia signs on the monitor over them became slightly more even, the little dry red face of Matthew grimacing as he pulled at the oxygen mask over his face, scared blue eyes opening momentarily, a fat little hand pulling at the drip in his arm, his eyebrows furrowing as he struggled to focus.

'Looks like we're winning.'

It had to be sweat. Hall was the most experienced, the most laid-back doctor Clara had even had the privilege to work with, but for just a second as Matthew tugged at the oxygen mask and four little limbs moved the way four little limbs should, as Matthew's parched, cracked lips attempted to form a word, Clara could have sworn a tear trickled down the side of Hall's sun-battered cheeks.

'Kell?' The single word was the sweetest they had ever heard, the blue eyes that gazed at Timothy like two precious jewels as Timothy shook his head, gently stroking the little boy's face as he stared down at him.

'Sorry, buddy, you'll just have to make do with me.' He made a pretty good attempt at a calm voice as he called out, 'Let Shelly and Ross in.'

But for all his strength, for all the optimism and hope he had imbued, Clara knew Timothy wouldn't come out of this turbulent time unscathed, and as she led Ross and Shelly in, as they gazed in wonder at the life that had so nearly been taken, she looked up and realised that it was the first time she had seen Timothy cry.

'He needs intensive care.' Hall's voice was gruff but there was gentleness behind it as he addressed Matthew's parents, deliberately ignoring the fact that Ross was a doctor and Shelly a nurse, knowing that now more than ever a terrified mum and dad were all they wanted to be. 'His temperature was very high when he came to us, which can cause a lot of problems, but thankfully he seems to have avoided any serious damage. Neurologically he's responding well and he's putting out urine, which are good signs. Still, I'd be happier to have him at a major centre.'

Ross looked up helplessly and Timothy responded without prompting. 'We'll manage fine, Ross—just go.'

'You'll stay at the house?' Ross checked. 'There's an emergency bell on the clinic door, it rings directly through to the house. If you leave a note people might not be able to read—'

'We'll stay at the house,' Timothy said firmly. 'Don't worry about the clinic—you just concentrate on your family, for as long as it takes. We'll be fine.'

Slinging a weary arm around Clara as the stretcher was gently loaded onto the plane, Timothy pulled her nearer. 'Won't we?'

'I hate being a grown-up,' Timothy moaned as, fed, showered and changed, he finally collapsed on Ross and Shelly's sofa. 'I've just had the most terrifying day of my life and I can't even relax with a glass of wine in case that bloody bell goes off.'

'It kind of makes you realise what Ross and Shelly have to put up with each and every night, doesn't it?' Clara said, listlessly picking up toys from the floor and piling them into a massive wooden box.

'You've changed your tune.' Timothy teased, half-heartedly pinching her on the bottom as Clara retrieved the umpteenth piece of Lego, locating a dusty toast crust along the way. 'I thought *you* were the misunderstood one.'

'I thought I was, too,' Clara admitted, giving in to the mess and plonking herself down on the sofa beside him. 'Today kind of puts things into perspective, doesn't it? I mean, dramas happen here often, and as much as I moan about the hours I put in at least when I go home I can switch off. For Ross and Shelly it's twenty-four seven. Throw in breastfeeding and a special needs child and you can see why Shelly asks me to work over—'

'Doesn't make it right, though,' Timothy said loyally, but Clara just shrugged.

'But it makes sense.'

'Things will change now.' Stretching and yawning, Clara had to wait for him to elaborate. 'I know he was beside himself, I know it was fear talking, but from the way Ross was ranting, the health department wants to watch itself. He's all for closing the clinic down unless they come to the party and organise more staff.'

'Ross would never let this place close,' Clara said assuredly, but her conviction wavered as she turned to Timothy. 'Do you really think it could come to that?'

'Who knows?' Timothy yawned. 'But Ross nearly lost his son today and Shelly's got every reason not to want to fill in shifts any more. You can't do it all yourself, Clara. It's either a part-time clinic or a hospital, not somewhere in between, and I think today might just be the catalyst. Anyway, enough. I need my bed.'

She stood first, made a half-hearted effort to haul him off the sofa.

'Carry me,' Timothy grumbled.

'Carry *me*,' Clara moaned, and then as Timothy gestured to do so she blushed furiously and changed her mind. 'Don't be daft,' she mumbled, purposefully heading for the guest bedroom. 'You'd rupture yourself.'

Sleeping in Ross and Shelly's guest room was rather like being in a hotel, without the luxury of a chocolate on the pillow and a bar fridge, of course. Climbing into bed, they plumped the pillows, admired the counterpane then lay there awkward and rigid, staring at the white ceiling and wishing the curtains closed enough to stop the annoying chink of moonlight that was filtering through.

'It won't ring,' Clara whispered, sensing Timothy's tension, though why she was keeping her voice down was anyone's guess. 'Everyone knows Ross is away. It will only go off if there's an emergency.'

'Which is exactly what I'm afraid of,' Timothy mumbled, lying rigid beside her, staring into the darkness with a tension that was palpable. Cuddling in beside him, she moved slightly to make room for the arm he clamped firmly around her, closing her eyes against the soft down of his chest and running her hand tentatively down the flat plane of his stomach, acknowledging the slight increase in his breathing, a low, almost inaudible moan as her hand moved ever lower.

A woman of the twenty-first century Clara certainly wasn't. Oh, she knew her own mind, was independent, but when it came to sex there was still a refreshing naïvety about her. She'd read all the glossies, devoured television soaps as easily as a box of chocolates and she knew deep down that women could make the first move.

She just never had before.

It had always been Timothy who'd instigated their love-making with Clara still in a state of perpetual surprise that anyone could fancy her so much, that someone so divine could actually want her.

But tonight she knew he needed her.

Needed the sweet release their love-making brought, needed to escape from the horrors of the day, however fleetingly.

Capturing his swollen warmth in her hand, she held it for a moment, revelling in its beauty, thrilled and terrified and excited all at the same time as it sprang to life in her hands, as it responded to her gentle, tentative touch. And his obvious delight in her boldness made her brave, guided her on as her touch became firmer, her lips dusting its length as he gasped beneath her.

'Make love to me, Clara,' he urged softly.

He knew this was hard for her, knew it was uncharted territory, and as she slowly climbed over and lowered herself onto him he registered the nervousness in her eyes, could almost feel the endearing embarrassed blush as she stared down at him, bracing herself for rejection yet knowing she was wanted.

'Clara, you're beautiful.'

And on any other day, at any other moment, she would have brushed aside his compliment, flicked it away with a scornful response, but seeing the adoration that blazed in his eyes, feeling the reverent way he held her, she accepted it with the grace and confidence of a woman in love, believing, almost, that maybe she was all the wonderful things he whispered.

Leaning forward, she heard his moan of approval as he buried his face in her splendid bosom holding her soft bottom, moving her, guiding her as she rocked above him, bringing them both to the sweet release they so badly needed. Sex for sex's sake perhaps, a primal need that had to be fulfilled, an escape from the reality of the harsh day they had shared, but it was so loaded with love and caring it could never have been called gratuitous.

'Clara?' She heard the question in his voice as they lay spent and entwined, gazing into the darkness, the hazy hormonal rush of their orgasm working its balmy magic. 'What I said today—about Kell, I mean…'

'Don't.' Squeezing her eyes closed, she rushed to stop him. She simply couldn't go there now, couldn't spoil this post-coital peace by revealing the depth of her need for the man that lay beside her, sure it wasn't what he needed to hear tonight of all nights.

'It still hurts, then?' Timothy said softly, kissing her shoulder and pulling her back close as a salty tear slid down her cheek.

Oh, it hurt all right, Clara thought as Timothy's breathing evened out, as the arm that held her tightly gently loosened its grip.

Only her pain had nothing to do with Kell.

CHAPTER NINE

'THESE WILL BE GREAT.' Smiling, Shelly peered over Clara's shoulder at the pile of photographs that lay scattered over the table. 'Abby's going to be thrilled.'

'It's a good idea,' Clara commented, trying to choose between a picture of Kell on a bike and one of Kell on a horse and finally choosing both. 'I mean, I know it's only going to be a tiny wedding, but Kell and his family will be thrilled when they see all of these. If they can't have the wedding in Tennengarrah then why not bring a bit of Tennengarrah to the city?'

'You haven't said anything?' Shelly checked. 'To his dad, I mean. This picture board is supposed to be a surprise.'

'I haven't said a word,' Clara assured her.

'Kell!' Matthew's excited squeak as he grabbed a photo had them both smiling as Clara retrieved it from his jammy fingers.

'It certainly is.' Ruffling his hair, she held it up for all to see. 'Look at this one—we have to include it.'

Both women laughed as they stared at the photo—Kell Bevan at twenty-one years of age, not quite fresh-faced but awkward in his new nursing uniform, standing proudly outside the clinic. But even though she laughed, even though it was fun wading through old photos in such a good cause, Clara's lack of emotion surprised even herself.

Oh, she missed Kell, missed their chats, missed having another nurse to share the load, missed him as a friend—but that was it.

She didn't love him.

'What are you doing tonight?' Shelly broke into her thoughts and Clara gave a small shrug, trying to keep her voice light.

'Meeting Timothy at the pub.'

'Any special reason?'

Clara looked up, a wry smile on the edge of her lips. 'You tell me, Shelly. Surely Ross must have said something.'

But Shelly shook her head. 'He honestly hasn't, Clara. I know as much as you—he's going to speak to him about it this afternoon when Timothy's finished the clinic.'

'That's honestly all you know?'

Shelly nodded. 'It's my fault. I can't blame Ross. I've told him too many times over the last couple of weeks that I don't want to hear about all the dramas over the staff at the clinic, and now that I actually want to hear the gossip he's torturing me by keeping quiet.'

Clara believed her. Over the last couple of weeks they'd grown closer. Clara had known that even though Matthew was safe now, there would still be some emotional baggage for Shelly to deal with and she had taken it upon herself to be there for her—to ring Shelly and tell her to come over for a coffee and a chat with the kids—and the effort had been worth it tenfold. Finally Clara understood just what Shelly was up against, and in turn Shelly seemed to understand just how much Clara had done for the clinic, how hard it must have been to have relative strangers burst into town and seemingly take things over, and finally a true friendship had been forged…

'So there are two new doctors starting?' Clara checked. 'And possibly a couple more nurses?'

'All I know…' Shelly blew her red curls skyward, searching her mind for a snippet she mightn't have shared '…is that the two doctors are a married couple. He's an anaesthetist, she's a GP, and they're semi-retiring.'

'Has Ross told them there's no such thing as semi-retirement here?' Clara grinned.

'Don't be stupid.' Shelly laughed. 'And scare them off altogether? As for the nurses, they're coming from the agency. I hope they're a bit keener than the one they've already sent. Ross is tearing his hair out!'

'I don't care.' Clara gave a cheeky grin. 'This is my first afternoon off in months and I refuse to feel guilty. Still, it's good that we're finally getting some staff.'

Shelly nodded. 'Ross read the Riot Act and said that until there's more nursing staff we're only going run a skeleton clinic, and finally they seem to have taken notice. But, honestly, Clara, he hasn't said a word about whether he'll be asking Timothy to stay on. Haven't you two spoken about it?'

'There didn't seem much point,' Clara admitted. 'Until we know if there's actually a job for him, it seemed silly to discuss it.'

'Even with two more doctors, there will still be heaps of work,' Shelly said assuredly, but Clara just shook her head.

'I don't doubt that, but what about the budget? Still...' Smiling brightly, Clara stood up, grabbing her bag from the sofa and swinging it over her shoulder. 'With these extra nurses I could take some annual leave. I must have about two years owing by now. Come on, let's head over to the pub.'

'You could join Timothy on his blessed diving course.' Shelly laughed, scooping Kate into her stroller and following her out.

Clara smiled quietly to herself as she walked along, holding Matthew's hand and her breath at the same time.

She'd been thinking exactly the same thing.

One look at Timothy's face and Clara knew it was over.

Knew that the dreams she'd tentatively built in the sand were crashing back into the sea. But she managed a smile, a brave face as Shelly made herself scarce and Timothy came back from the bar, two orange juices in hand and a look she couldn't read on his face.

'I thought you were never coming.' Taking a sip of her drink, she concentrated on keeping her voice light, ignoring her impulse to pick up her bag and run back to her house, to somehow avoid this horrible grown-up conversation that she knew was heading her way.

'You know what Ross can be like when he gets talking.' Timothy shrugged, forcing his own smile but utterly unable to meet her eyes.

'Did he offer to extend your contract?' Her question was brave, the antithesis of how she felt, but the suspense was killing her.

'He did.' For a while he didn't elaborate, just picked up his beer mat between his index finger and thumb and tapped it on the table a few times before setting it down and carefully placing his drink on it. Clara watched—not because it was interesting but, hell, any distraction was welcome, anything was better than having her heart ripped out of her chest without an anaesthetic. 'I'm leaving, Clara.'

Still he didn't look at her—not that Clara was complaining. The chair seemed to be sliding away from beneath her, the world shifting out of focus for a second or two as she struggled to take the finality of his words in. She waited with a growing sense of futility for Timothy to elaborate, to shyly smile and ask her to come on his travels with him, but he didn't. Instead, he picked up his drink and the blessed beer mat as the pub carried on around them, as the world kept right on turning even though for Clara it might just as well stop now.

'I'm not what Tennengarrah needs,' he said in low, subdued tones. 'They've got two new doctors starting—one's an anaesthetist, for heaven's sake. If Ross is serious about upgrading the clinic then surely the most sensible thing would be to employ a surgeon, not blow a shaky budget on a very junior doctor.'

'Where's he going to find a surgeon?' Clara pointed out. 'It's taken months to get this far. Surely you can stay until he finds someone.'

'Ross said the same.'

'Then why don't you?'

Finally he looked at her, those beautiful green eyes unusually guarded, that beautiful open face so lined with tension it was as if she were looking at a stranger, the harshness in his voice alien to her ears.

'I don't want to be a fill in, Clara. I don't want to be second best. Call me conceited, call me what you will, but I happen to think I deserve better than that. If I'm staying here it has to because I'm needed, because it's me and me alone that's wanted, and a junior doctor just isn't on the top of the wish list here. I've worked hard to get my medical degree. I know I'm not the best doctor in the world but I am a good doctor and I need to do more training, need to get back out there and be all I know I can be…' His wrist caught her hand, forcing her attention, forcing her to look back at him. 'Can you understand that?'

She could.

Oh, she didn't have to like it, but put like that she could understand it, and there and then she berated herself for her optimism, for her stupid wasted dreams of a future beside Timothy. Why would someone with his knowledge, with his passion end his career before it had even begun? Why would someone as beautiful and as wondrous as Timothy throw it all in for someone like her?

'When will you go?'

'I've already packed up the ute.' Aghast, she whipped her face up to him, but he just shook his head. 'I can't settle for being second best, Clara.'

'Then don't.' She registered his frown, knew that she had confused him, and she used the brief pause to clear her throat, to somehow fashion a response. And because she loved him, because this was how they'd both agreed it would end, because she'd do anything to make things easier for him, she did the hardest, bravest thing she'd ever done in her life. 'You're right to move on. Of course I'd love you to stay longer, we both know that. But as good as it's been, we both knew it was never going to be for ever.'

'What about you?' Timothy said gently. 'Will you be all right?'

'I'll be just fine.' Clara swallowed hard, even managed a semblance of a smile. 'I promise not to get drunk and try to declare undying love to you outside the barn. But I will miss you, Timothy.'

She watched as he stood up, drained his drink and offered her his arm. 'I know. Come on, let's get out of here.'

'You go.' Her voice was curiously high. 'We both know I'm lousy at goodbyes.'

'So that's it?' Timothy rasped, but Clara refused to be drawn. 'That's all we're worth. What? Am I supposed to shake your hand or something? Do you want me to say I'll send a postcard?'

'You're the one leaving, Timothy,' Clara pointed out, sarcasm uncharacteristically dripping off her tongue as she continued. 'If you'd given me a bit more notice, I could maybe have rustled up something a bit grander, a cake perhaps or a—'

'Don't.' He closed his eyes but not quickly enough to hide the pain there. Clara finally relented, holding onto his hand as he quietly said goodbye to Ross and a teary Shelly, holding it together as they walked hand in hand towards his dusty and not particularly trusty ute with a heart that didn't feel as if it was beating any more. She closed her eyes for a final goodbye kiss, staring for an age as his ute pulled off into the darkness and stared at the rear lights disappearing along with her soul mate.

Wandering back into the house, she didn't even cry, didn't throw herself on the bed or break down in hysterics—just stared at her house, empty now without Timothy's clutter, his boots gone from the hall, the ton of mess he so effortlessly generated.

Sitting down at the table, she buried her face in her hands.

Kell's images stared back at her and she gazed unseeingly at the photographs, scarcely able to believe that she'd thought she'd loved him.

Hardly able to believe the pain she had thought she had felt when Kell had left, because nothing compared to the loss she felt now, nothing at all.

It was as if she had lost her soul.

CHAPTER TEN

LIFE FOR CLARA continued on autopilot.

A numb state of shock as the days dragged on endlessly and the nights seemed to last for ever.

Even her once busy schedule dwindled with the arrival of fresh faces, so she didn't even have the saving grace of burying herself in her work.

Time was on her hands when she needed it least.

Dressing listlessly one morning, she stared at her empty bed, missing that smiling face on the pillow, sighing wearily as a button flew off her blouse. Since Timothy had left, routine had gone to pot. The mess he generated had been replaced by Clara's now. Normally meticulous, her ironing basket groaned under its own weight, every last work blouse a crumpled mess that would take for ever to iron. She located a needle but finding the thread took a bit longer, hell, even stitching on a button these days required a massive effort of concentration. But finally the job was done and Clara slipped on her blouse, grimacing when she saw the clock and realised that for the first time in her nursing career she was going to be late.

Only when the second button rolled onto the floor did the penny start to drop.

OK, being a seamstress wasn't up there on her list of talents but even *she* knew how to sew on a button. Looking down at her blouse, Clara knew there and then that nothing short of metal wiring was going to hold her blouse together. Her breasts, always large, seemed to have taken on a life of their own.

Fingering her waistband, Clara knew she wasn't imagining things. She'd been the same size for ever, now all of a sudden those smart navy culottes were definitely tight on her.

Definitely.

Under any other circumstances the knowledge would have sent her into a spin, but nothing seemed to matter any more. Since Timothy had gone she'd felt as if she were on beta-blockers, as if she were taking a cardiac drug that permanently steadied her heart rate, kept her blood pressure even.

Nothing seemed to matter.

Slipping off her skirt, she lay back on the bed, moving her hands down her soft white stomach, fingers gently probing until…

Clara had felt more stomachs than she could count, knew what a fundus felt like, the soft regular shape of the tip of the uterus as it bobbed out of the pelvic brim, a tiny life pushing the womb upwards as it grew inside. Suddenly the metaphorical beta-blockers must have worn off, because her heart rate was picking up, her blood pressure crashing through the roof as her body spoke for itself.

Rolling onto her side, she clung onto the pillow for comfort, closing her eyes in an attempt to block out the obvious truth.

'Oh, no,' she whispered, her hands moving down to her stomach again. 'What have I done?'

'Sixteen weeks.' Ross didn't look over, just stared at the screen as he clicked away taking measurements, his voice matter-of-fact, ever the professional, but Clara could hear the kindness behind it.

'I can't be, Ross.' Clara shook her head against the white-papered pillow. 'I've had periods.'

'When?'

Her eyebrows furrowed as she forced her mind to think. 'I've never been particularly regular but I know I've had them…' Her eyes opened wide. 'I had one last month, just after Timothy left. I can remember thinking, Great, that's all I need now. So you see…'

'It wasn't a period,' Ross said gently. 'Some women get bleeding in the first trimester when their periods would have been due…'

'But I'm on the Pill.' She knew her argument was futile, that the image staring back at her from the screen was irrefutable evidence if ever she'd needed it, but still she begged, stabbed at the chance to change the inevitable. 'I take it every morning. I've never missed, Ross, not even once.'

'You had gastro a while back,' Ross reminded her gently, 'when Timothy first started. I remember because Shelly had to fill in for you.'

'But we were careful.'

'Sometimes the damage is already done,' Ross said gently. 'Maybe the Pill you took before you got sick wasn't properly absorbed and if the timing was right, if you'd just ovulated and…' His voice trailed off. 'I'm sure you don't need a biology lesson, Clara. These things just happen sometimes.'

'But sixteen weeks,' Clara begged. 'How could I not have known?'

'It's too small for you to feel it move yet, and I guess with Timothy gone you've had your mind on other things.'

Ross was right on that count, but at just the mention of his name Clara felt her eyes fill up, the true horror of her situation starting to dawn.

'He's a nice guy,' Ross said softly. 'I'm sure he'll stand by you.'

'I don't want him to stand by me,' Clara sniffed, accepting the tissue Ross offered.

'It's going to be long, lonely pregnancy without him,' Ross

pushed. 'Even taking into account the sixteen weeks you've managed to get through unwittingly. He'd want to be there.'

But Clara shook her head. 'To hold my hands during antenatal classes?' She gave a low laugh. 'I'm the one who gives the classes, Ross. I know what pregnancy involves, I know what I'm up against...'

'For the next few months perhaps,' Ross's voice remained even. 'But once that baby comes along, everything changes, Clara. It doesn't matter what your qualifications are, how well you think you're prepared. At the end of the day a baby will turn your world around.' He gave a wry smile. 'If Timothy were here, he'd tell me off now for assuming that just because I've got children I think I know it all.'

Clara gave a puzzled frown as Ross continued.

'He read me the Riot Act his first week here when I insisted that you take care of Eileen. He'd stand by you, Clara.'

'Exactly.' She blinked. 'And the very last thing I'll need is a reluctant partner.'

'He has to be told.'

'No, he doesn't,' Clara responded fiercely. 'Lots of women bring up children on their own these days. There's lots of single mums. Shelly managed on her own.'

'Shelly managed,' Ross said gently, 'but *managed* just about sums it up. There was no time to enjoy motherhood, no one to share Matthew's milestones with—just endless responsibility and angst. Shelly will tell you the same herself. It would be so much easier for you to share this with someone.'

'Not if he doesn't love me,' Clara responded. 'I know he's a nice guy, so nice that no doubt he'll do the right thing, give up all of his dreams of being a surgeon and come back and support me, but I can't live like that, Ross. Timothy said on the day he left that he didn't want to settle for second best and, frankly, neither do I. If he didn't love me enough to stay, I don't want to force him to come back.'

'I'm sorry, Clara,' Ross sighed. 'I really tried to change his mind. When I first offered him the job I thought he was going to take it. He raced back to the house, said he was going to talk things over with you. I had a bottle of champagne ready, I really thought he was staying, then suddenly he changed his mind. Said the outback wasn't for him.'

'That's not what Timothy said.' Clara frowned. 'He made it sound as if you didn't really want him, as if you were just offering him a job because you felt you had to.'

'Clara!' Ross's eyes were wide. 'I'd have given anything to keep Timothy here. He's going to be a great doctor. I even explained that once the clinic moved up a stage and we had a few more doctors on board, he could do a formal rotation here or we'd second him to go the city and get some more courses under his belt. I'd have given anything to keep him.'

'So would I,' Clara managed, turning her face to the wall, eternally grateful when Ross flicked off the machine and pulled the curtain quietly around her, leaving her alone with her thoughts and a little black-and-white photo of the life inside her which she stared at for an age.

'So would I,' she sobbed.

CHAPTER ELEVEN

'YOU'RE SUPPOSED TO be putting on weight,' Shelly admonished gently as Clara stepped off the scales. 'Not losing it.'

Clara gave a tired shrug. 'And you're supposed to be at home with your children, Shelly. I feel awful dragging you out. One of the others could have seen me.'

'Oh, come on, Clara, you're my one and only patient, I'm hardly slaving away. Anyway, I wouldn't miss this for the world.' When Clara didn't smile back Shelly steered her to the small examination couch. 'Ross wants to come and talk to you, Clara.'

'Is something wrong?'

'He's concerned that you're doing too much and, frankly, so am I. You're twenty-eight weeks now, it's time to be cutting down your workload.'

'I've cut right back,' Clara argued. 'I only see a handful of patients now.'

'All the difficult ones,' Shelly pointed out. 'Look, Clara, the baby's a nice size, all your obs are fine, your urine's as clear as a bell, but it doesn't take a nursing degree to know that a pregnant woman's weight is supposed to go upwards. You haven't put an ounce on for four weeks now. You have to learn to delegate a bit more, let the new staff take over some of the load.

In a few short weeks you're going to be on maternity leave and, as much as you don't believe me now, this little one is going to take up every last piece of what's left of your brain.'

'I can't stop seeing Eileen now,' Clara moaned. 'She's just finished her last round of chemo and you know how rough it's been for her. She's got an MRI next week and she's terrified.'

'Then go and see her with a cake instead of your nurse's bag. Just because you're not working, it doesn't mean you can't be her friend.'

But Clara shook her head. 'I promised I'd be there for her. I'm heading over there after here.' Seeing Shelly frown, Clara got in first. 'OK, I'll talk to her,' she sighed. 'Maybe Jenny could take over, she seems really nice.'

'She *is* really nice,' Shelly said firmly. 'Anyway, with a bit of luck Eileen will get the all-clear and then you really won't have an excuse not to put your feet up.

'You still haven't heard from Timothy, I take it?'

'Nothing,' Clara sighed. She slipped up her top and Shelly gently probed her abdomen.

'It's only been a couple of weeks since you wrote and it's not as if you've got an address. If Timothy's having his mail redirected, it could take ages for him to get the letter.'

'Has Ross had any luck?' Clara asked hopefully, but Shelly shook her head.

'We've only got his parents' address and phone number in England. Maybe you should ring them. We've tried every diving school in the phone book and got nowhere. Perhaps he headed home after all.'

'Perhaps.' Clara shrugged, swallowing back the familiar lump in her throat as Shelly pulled down the maternity top then perched herself on the couch beside her. 'But from the little Timothy told me, he's not exactly on great terms with his parents. I don't want to make things more awkward for him and I'm sure a pregnant ex-girlfriend isn't the kind of holiday memento he was hoping to collect. I'd rather try and find him myself before I resort to getting his parents involved.'

'Ross could ring them.' Shelly grinned. 'Say we've under-paid him, that there's this huge cheque here with his name on it—that should get a result.' When that didn't even raise a smile Shelly's voice softened as she pushed a touch further. 'How come you changed your mind, Clara? You were so adamant you didn't want him involved before.'

'I'd love him to be involved,' Clara corrected, 'but only if that was what he really wanted.' Taking a deep breath, she stared down at the mound of her abdomen and ran a hand over it. 'I was lying in the bath and suddenly the baby moved. Not just a little bit, mind, my whole stomach seemed to flip over...'

'Amazing, isn't it?'

Clara nodded. 'I just lay there watching it, and for the first time I actually realised there was a person in there, not just a baby, not just my bump, but a person. And I figured Timothy deserved to know about it.'

'He does,' Shelly said softly. 'You know Ross isn't Matthew's real father?' She gave a soft laugh. 'Or rather you know that Ross isn't Matthew's biological father?'

Clara nodded.

'Neil, my ex-husband, didn't want to know about Matthew, figured a special needs child was just too dammed hard for the life he'd lined up. Now Matthew will never know any different, he adores Ross and that's enough for him.' Her hands moved to Clara's bump, resting her hands there softly for a moment. 'God willing, this little one won't have any of Matthew's prob-lems. God willing, this little person will grow up to be a nosy, inquisitive, intelligent child and you're going to have to answer some difficult questions. Imagine how hard it would be to look this *person* in the eye and say you didn't even tell their father they existed. It's easy to make choices now but eventually you'll have to face them.'

'I know,' Clara gulped. 'And if I don't hear from him in the next week I'll ring his family.' Accepting Shelly's hand, she hauled herself of the couch, blowing her nose loudly on a tissue before turning to face her friend.

'Thanks, Shelly.'

'I haven't finished yet. Our house at six. Roast and veggies and extra-thick gravy.'

'It's forty degrees outside,' Clara moaned.

'I don't care. You need some calories. I might even make a chocolate cake if you're lucky.'

'With custard?' Clara checked, her glittering, tear-filled eyes all the thanks Shelly needed.

'*Chocolate* custard.' Shelly smiled. 'And if I have a glass of wine I might even ring Timothy's parents myself!'

Pulling the Jeep to a halt outside Eileen's, Clara reached over to the passenger seat for her bag, her mind totally focused on the meeting ahead, mentally preparing herself, the sight of Eileen's bald head, her painfully thin, emaciated body still a shock after all this time.

The strength of the contraction that gripped her was another shock.

Breathing out through her mouth, leaning back on the driver's seat, Clara waited for it to pass, her hands instinctively moving to her stomach, feeling the firm mass of her uterus tight against her palms, her eyes flicking to the dashboard clock, counting the seconds then breathing a sigh of relief when it ended.

Braxton-Hicks' contractions.

With a rueful laugh she scooped up her bag and climbed out of the Jeep, the hot midday sun scorching the back of her neck as she walked towards Eileen's home. How many first-time mums had rung her, terrified they were about to go into labour, sure that the irregular false contractions they were experiencing were the real thing?

'When you're toes are curling it's the real thing,' Clara had always said, popping them on to the CTG monitor to prove beyond doubt that all they'd been feeling had been mother nature's warm-up run. Even as she walked she closed her eyes for a second. One day in the not too distant future her toes *would* be curling, her baby—*their* baby—would be coming into the world, and not for the first time Clara felt a wave of panic at the inevitability of it all. The journey she had unwittingly embarked on, one that until now she had chosen to travel alone. But as the weeks had passed into months, reality had started to hit, and now more than ever she needed Timothy beside her, needed him with her.

Missed him so much.

'Only me.'

The days of knocking and politely waiting on the doorstep had long since gone. Instead, Clara pushed open the fly screen as she called out and made her way straight through to the living room, smiling at her friend who lay supported by a mountain of pillows on the sofa, a brightly coloured scarf wrapped around her head, a splash of lipstick out of place on her thin, pale face, but Clara was thrilled to see it all the same. Thrilled that Eileen was making an effort, taking a pride in her appearance.

Still hanging in there.

'I've done my fingernails.' Eileen smiled, replacing the lid on her bottle of nail varnish and holding up her hand as Clara admired her handiwork. 'But I haven't the energy to do my toenails.'

'I know the feeling,' Clara groaned, 'though in my case I can barely reach them. I can do them for you.' Settling herself down, she undid the lid and set to work, glad for the small distraction, the chance to talk without her words sounding horribly rehearsed. 'So, how are you doing?'

'What version do you want to hear?' Eileen sighed.

'The truth will do,' Clara said, without looking up. 'Are you scared about next week?'

'Terrified,' Eileen admitted. 'Last night I took one of those sleeping tablets that Timothy prescribed me. I hadn't taken even one before, the bottle's just been sitting there in the medicine cupboard along with the hundred others.'

'That's what they were prescribed for,' Clara responded matter-of-factly, but even the mention of Timothy's name had a tiny blush dusting her cheeks. 'It's important that you get your rest after all you've been through.'

'I know,' Eileen sighed. 'I just wish it was this time next week, wish I knew if all this treatment had worked.' She gave a low laugh. 'Then again maybe I don't.'

With ten toes painted Clara finally looked up. 'Let's just wait and see, shall we? Whatever the results, we'll cross that bridge when we come to it. Focus on the positives.'

'What positives?'

'Heidi's at school,' Clara said gently, 'and, as hellish as the treatments been, you've had six more months.'

'I want more.' Eileen's voice was hoarse and her request was so basic, so much her entitlement, Clara simply didn't know what to say.

'I'd better do your bloods,' she said instead, reaching down to her bag. 'The results will come to Ross, but they'll also go to your oncologist in Adelaide in time for your appointment next—'

'Are you all right, Clara?'

She didn't answer straight away. Bent over her bag, she stilled for a moment, and then looked up, smiling assuredly. 'Next time an anxious mum rings me about Braxton-Hicks' contractions I won't be so blasé. They're actually quite strong, *aren't they*?'

Eileen gave a small frown. The question in Clara's voice hadn't gone unnoticed. The slight shift in tone told her that Clara was asking for reassurance, but Eileen wasn't sure she could give it. 'They can be strong,' Eileen started slowly, 'but I don't think they should stop you talking!' She gave a nervous laugh. 'Mind you, it could just be me. Nothing ever stopped me talking, not even childbirth. I was roaring at Jerry the whole way

through. Even after two rounds of chemo I was still cursing
loudly, albeit with my head down the toilet…' Her voice trailed
off as Clara sat back in the sofa, her hand moving protectively
to her bump, her eyes closing as another spasm gripped her.
'Do you want me to ring Ross?'

Eileen waited, waited for Clara to look up, to smile reassur-
ingly and say 'Don't be daft', but when her troubled blue eyes
finally opened, when Clara gave a small, nervous nod, her stiff
upper lip actually trembling, Eileen pulled herself up.

'Tell him to come straight away.' Her voice was trembling
as she spoke. 'Tell him to bring Shelly and the emergency delivery pack. Tell them to ring the Flying—'

'They'll know what to do,' Eileen said bravely. 'You just stay
there and try to stay calm.' She patted Clara's shoulders, ignoring her aching body's protests she raced into the hall, returning
moments later and joining Clara on the sofa, where she put her
arms around her. And suddenly it wasn't a nurse and patient
any more, it wasn't even about two friends.

Just two scared women, staring out of the window as they
held each other.

Two women, quite simply praying for time.

CHAPTER TWELVE

'THREE CENTIMETRES DILATED.' Ross fixed Clara with a reassuring smile as Shelly pulled the duvet back around her. 'That's good.'

'No, it isn't,' Clara sobbed. 'It's way too soon...'

'Three centimetres,' Ross carried on over her, 'and your membranes are intact and the contractions seem to be easing off a bit by themselves. We might be able to stop the labour at this stage. Even if we can delay it for twelve hours, that will mean the steroids I'll give you will have time to take effect, they'll help to mature the baby's lungs, but with a bit of luck we'll be able to stop the labour altogether. Now, I'm going to radio through this information and see what the Flying Doctors say. They should be here soon, but it's probably better that we get these drugs started.' He gave a thin smile and Clara knew what was coming.

'You'll need an IV and a catheter.'

'I'll do it.' Shelly shooed him out. 'You get on the radio.'

'Thanks for both of you coming,' Clara said when they were alone. 'Are the kids outside with Eileen?'

'They're back at the house,' Shelly said lightly—too lightly, Clara realised. 'June's watching them for me.'

Lying back on the pillow, Clara knew then that she was loved.

Neither Matthew nor Kate had been more than two feet away from Shelly since Matthew's disappearing act, and the fact she had jumped into the Jeep and raced to get here for her told Clara the true depth of their friendship.

Shelly was very gentle as she inserted the catheter, talking away to take away the sting of embarrassment, and also very professional, but Clara could see the sparkle of tears in her eyes as she flushed the IV.

'This isn't your fault, Shelly,' Clara said gently. 'You know as well as I do that these things happen sometimes. I was fine earlier, not even a twinge, there was nothing to suggest—'

'I know,' Shelly sniffed, 'but two can play at that game, so if it isn't my fault it most certainly isn't yours. I don't want you beating yourself up, wondering if there was something you could have done to prevent this.'

'I'll try,' Clara sighed. 'You've no idea how many women I've said the same thing to, but it's not so easy to be objective when it's your own baby.

'Shelly.'

Something in Clara's voice made Shelly look up.

'Ross told me Timothy had a go at you both once, that he said just because someone doesn't have children it didn't mean they didn't get upset.'

Shelly nodded. 'He was right to say something. I used to get annoyed about the same thing when I worked on the children's ward before Matthew came along. Other nurses would bang on, saying I didn't know how the parents felt because I'd never had my own. It was the same when I did my midwifery, as if I couldn't possibly know what I was talking about because I'd never had a baby.

'I was being selfish,' Shelly finished.

'You were being truthful,' Clara said softly. 'I've never been more scared in my life, never really knew what it was all about until now. I love this baby and I can understand where you were coming from. Timothy shouldn't have said anything.'

Shelly said simply, 'He was just sticking up for you.'

But there was no time for introspection because suddenly the room was filled with personnel and equipment. Dr Hall strolled in, managing to roll his eyes and wink at the same time as he saw Clara lying pale and terrified on the bed.

'My wife's going to love you,' he joked. 'She's after a new kitchen and this one will push me into overtime.' His voice softened as he parked his huge frame on the bed beside her, one rough yet tender hand gently on her stomach as he quietly studied his watch. 'The old way's the best way.' He looked up and held her terrified eyes. 'The medication we're giving you will hopefully slow things down. Now, Ross has already examined you and taken swabs so I'm not going to disturb things while they're quiet as, no doubt, they'll want to check you again at the hospital.'

Clara nodded. Hall's explanations were kept simple and she was grateful, her mind not really up to lengthy explanations. And though she knew all the answers, though she'd been through the scenario before, now she was at the receiving end all her training seemed to have flown out of the window. 'What if I deliver on the way, Hall? Twenty-eight weeks is just too early.'

'We've seen smaller, though, haven't we, Clara?' Pulling her top back down, he gave her a reassuring smile. 'If you do deliver then we've got everything on the plane, but I reckon this little tacker's going to stay put at least till we get to Adelaide, for what it's worth.'

Oh, it was worth so much.

Hall's quiet words of encouragement were everything she needed right now.

Clara managed a brave smile as he stood up, gave the signal to get things moving, until finally, with tubes coming out everywhere, machines strapped to most of her body, she knew it was time to go.

'I'm going with her.' Shelly's voice was firm, but Clara heard the emotion behind it.

'Shelly, I'll be fine,' Clara said quickly, but Shelly was res-olute.

'You're not facing this on your own.' Her voice trembled slightly as she took Clara's hand. 'Ross can take a couple of days off and watch the children. You're not going to Adelaide without someone beside you.'

'Do you want to have that word with Clara, Ross?' Hall's words didn't make sense and both Shelly and Clara looked up in surprise as Ross gave a small tentative nod.

'Two minutes,' Hall said to Ross, and then smiled down at his patient. 'I'll just make sure the plane's ready.'

Clara knew the plane was ready, knew he was just being po-lite, but as she turned her inquisitive eyes to Ross, her curios-ity turned to nervousness as he asked Shelly to wait outside.

'What is it, Ross?' she ventured when they were finally alone. 'What's happened? Is it the baby?'

'The baby's fine.' Ross was quick to reassure her. 'For the moment anyway. The contractions are slowing down now. It's not the baby I need to talk to you about.'

'Then what?' She'd never seen Ross so lost for words and his evasiveness scared her. 'Come on, Ross, tell me.'

'Clara, you know you have to stay calm—you know that, don't you?' he checked as she nodded, bewildered. 'I really didn't want to tell you now, but I don't think I have a choice. I've discussed it with Hall—'

'You're scaring me, Ross,' Clara broke in.

'I'm sorry.' Taking her hands, he looked her straight in the eye. 'Timothy rang this morning.' When Clara didn't respond he carried on gently, 'He didn't say much. He'd tried to phone you at home, and then he rang the clinic. When I said you were out on a visit he said he'd ring back tonight.'

'Has he got my letter?'

Ross gave a small shrug. 'I don't think so, Clara. Like I said, he didn't say much, but my take on it was that he just missed you, that he wanted to talk to you.'

'Did you tell him?' Clara asked, her eyes filling up. 'About the baby, I mean? I promise I won't be cross. In some ways I hope you have...'

'I didn't tell him,' Ross said slowly. 'I didn't know then there was a problem, but even if he rings now, unless you want me to tell him I still can't. Do you understand that?'

She nodded, and as the news sank in so the questions started. 'Is he doing his diving course?'

Ross shook his head.

'He's moved back to England, then?'

She sensed his hesitancy, and she moved to reassure him. 'You can tell me, Ross, I've prepared myself for it.'

Oh, no, she hadn't. As Ross looked up, as his hands tightened around hers, as he started to speak, she finally understood his nervousness, why he had begged her to stay calm.

'Timothy's in Adelaide,' he said slowly, and Clara's eyes widened, the air catching in her throat as she struggled to take a deep breath, to force herself to stay calm as her handle on the world jolted into overdrive. 'He's doing a rotation at the hospital you're going to, Clara. Do you see now why I had to tell you?'

She didn't answer, just lay back on the hard stretcher as the news sank in, the next contraction barely meriting a comment. Ross's words had been like a hand grenade thrown into her brain, scrambling everything, blowing every preconceived idea she'd had about how to tell Timothy, the impact of his words ricocheting through every cell in her body. But as the shock abated, as reality filtered back in, far from desolation, far from the cold fingers of fear that had gripped as her labour had taken hold, Clara was left with a curious sense of calm, a small sense that all was right.

In a couple of hours or so she would see Timothy again.

'Do you want me to ring the hospital?' Ross broke into the smoldering aftermath that used to be her brain, concern etched on every feature as he awaited her reaction. 'I can tell him, if that's what you want. It might give him some time to get his head around the idea before you arrive.'

Clara thought for a moment before answering. Under any other circumstances she would have told him herself, his reaction to the news something she wanted—no, needed—to witness. But there was the baby to think of, a baby too small for this world, and emotional confrontations had to be avoided at all costs.

'Tell him I'm sorry,' Clara said softly. 'Tell him that I never wanted him to find out like this.'

'Of course.' As Hall tapped softly at the door Ross stood up. 'I had to tell Hall. I couldn't really just jump in and tell you without him being aware of what was going on, and we all know how nosy Timothy is. A chopper landing is just the sort of thing that would fuel his curiosity. I didn't fancy him wandering in for a sticky beak, only to see you lying on the stretcher. But apart from that, it's between you and I.'

'You can tell Shelly.' Clara smiled, noting the relieved look that washed over his face. 'I know she'd make your life hell otherwise.'

Ross smiled. 'She and Eileen probably have her stethoscope to the wall as we speak. I'm only kidding. Shelly would never—'

'I know.'

'You're taking this very well,' Ross murmured, as Hall made his presence known again. 'If you want Shelly to come with you, the offer's there.'

'I'll be fine.' Clara smiled as the stretcher moved down the hallway, her hand wrapped around her stomach. 'I mean *we'll* be fine.'

'One out, two in,' Eileen said tearfully as they carefully lifted the stretcher down the front steps. 'Warn the hospital to expect lots of calls!'

Clara didn't remember much about the flight, just lay back and tried to stay calm, to focus on the tiny life within in her and not be too greedy with her prayers.

Twelve more weeks would be pushing it, Clara admitted as she listened to the blips on the monitor beside her. She'd even settle for twelve more days, knowing every day *in utero* was the best chance her baby had.

Twelve hours even…

'Another one?' Hall's hand was back on her stomach, his other one reaching for Clara's as she willed the contraction to end, willed the pain to subside. But it seemed to go on for ever and she gripped Hall's hand harder, moaning in terror as she felt her own toes curl now, knew however much she didn't want to admit it that things were starting to move.

'My back hurts,' she sobbed, retching into a bowl the nurse quickly held out as the activity on the plane started to lift, the anaesthetist pulling up drugs, the nurse calmly opening packs. But her nonchalance didn't fool Clara for a minute.

'How long till we get there, Hall?'

'Another fifteen minutes or so, but if we don't make it, it doesn't matter. We've got everything we need here, Clara.' His words didn't comfort her and she shook her head, her eyes imploring him to stop, to listen and to act.

'I have to get there,' she sobbed, doubling over as another contraction engulfed her, the straps of the stretcher biting into her legs as she sought some comfort, desperate to kneel up, to rock back on her heels, to give in to her body and let the baby come. But still she fought it, willing herself to stay calm, breathing though the pain till it blissfully subsided. 'I have to get to Adelaide, Hall.' He gave a tight nod, pushing drugs through the IV line as the nurse slipped an oxygen mask over her face.

'We're doing everything we can, Clara.' He was fiddling with the IV pump as the anaesthetist passed him another spring. 'Just try and relax, give the medication a chance to work…'

She did as she was told, lying back on the pillow, listening to the pilot radioing through her progress, imagining the scene at the other end, the nurses and doctors waiting, the delivery ward being set up. And Timothy confused and bewildered, the news still sinking in, racing out to the landing strip as the efficient staff waited for the landing. Imagining how hard it must be for him to make sense of it all, trying to tell the waiting crowd that this was *his* child they were expecting...

It didn't look like Timothy.

As the stretcher was moved swiftly from the plane she scanned the faces, Timothy's the only one that mattered now, and as their eyes locked she knew his pain surely equalled hers.

Lines she had never seen before seemed to be grooved into his face. Those smiling eyes were alien now, hurt, bewildered and utterly terrified as he ran along beside the stretcher, unfamiliar in a suit and tie, his white coat flapping behind him as he raced alongside her, squeezing himself into the lift and impatiently turning off his pager, which was bleeping noisily, adding to the fraught confusion that surrounded her.

'I'm sorry,' she started, pulling off the oxygen mask as the lift doors closed, but he shook his head, replacing the mask with shaking hands, his voice gruff and thick with emotion.

'Keep it on,' he said. 'The baby needs it.' His eyes dragged to the portable monitors that surrounded her. 'You need it, too.'

'But—'

'Not now, Clara,' he said firmly. 'We'll talk later.'

And with that she had to make do.

Hall stayed, relaying his treatment to the attending doctors and midwives as they changed over the machines to the delivery ward's own. A cast of thousands seemed to be crammed into the room, separate teams for Clara and the baby, preparing the resuscitation cot and talking in the low urgent voices Clara knew only too well.

'It sounded as if you were having it.' Timothy's voice was a croak.

'When did Ross ring?' She couldn't look at him and it would seem Timothy was having the same problem as his eyes were fixed on the monitor, watching the baby's heart rate and the strength of Clara's contractions.

'An hour or so ago.' He glanced at his watch. 'A bit more maybe. Everyone seemed pretty laid-back, but just as you were due in they radioed through that they were expecting you to deliver *en route*, and the whole place went crazy.'

'It was the same on board.' Clara lay back, closing her eyes as another contraction came, but it was mercifully short and the pain she'd anticipated didn't eventuate.

'I said I'd get you here.' Hall smiled, coming over.

'Thank you so much,' Clara whispered, but Hall just shook his head.

'No. Thank *you*. It makes cleaning up and restocking so much easier,' he said, but the humour didn't quite cover up the emotion in his voice. 'You're in the right place now,' he added softly, 'and the drugs seem to be kicking in a bit. Hopefully this little tacker will stay put a while longer.'

Timothy hovered as the bustle in the room carried on, the drama of an impending birth receding as Clara's contractions died down. And finally, when every last test known had been performed, when surely her haemoglobin must now be in its boots from the amount of blood that had been taken, with wires and monitors coming from everywhere, Casey, the midwife, gave her a slow but optimistic smile.

'Get some sleep,' she suggested. 'I'll put the lights down and let you rest.' She looked over at Timothy, who stood awkwardly at the foot of the bed. 'You, too,' she added, pulling up a chair and gesturing for him to sit. 'You could both be in for a long night—you should try and conserve a bit of energy.'

But sleep would have to wait a while. Left alone in the semi-darkness, they listened to the regular bleeps of the monitors for what seemed like an age until finally Clara broke the strained silence.

'I'm sorry,' she started again. 'It must have been awful to find out this way.'

'Leave it, Clara,' Timothy said in a tight voice. 'Do what the midwife said and get some rest.'

'I can't rest, though,' she responded tearfully. 'I can't just lie back and close my eyes when you're—'

'Do you want me to leave?' Timothy offered. 'If it will make things easier, I can wait outside.'

But Clara shook her head. The thought of him leaving her now brought no peace at all. 'I don't want to fight, but I also know that there's a lot of things that need to be said, and until we at least talk I can't rest. If we can just get it over with—'

'Get it over with?' His voice was incredulous and he struggled to control it. 'Believe me, Clara, this won't be over with in a matter of minutes. Don't lie on the bed like some sort of martyr asking me for absolution, because I can't give it now. That's my baby you're carrying and you let me leave without even telling me it existed.'

'I didn't know,' she said quickly as he gave an unbelieving snort. 'I honestly didn't, not till about a month after you'd left. I thought I was having periods. Remember when I ran out of...?' Her voice trailed off but her words seemed to have reached him and finally he sat down, his face not exactly friendly but, hell, she'd settle for any improvement right now. 'I found out at sixteen weeks.'

'Excuse my maths, Clara, but if I'm not mistaken sixteen from twenty-eight makes twelve. That's twelve weeks you've had to let me know I was about to become a father. If you hadn't come here, if it hadn't been inevitable I'd find out, would I still be in the dark? Was this baby going to grow up not knowing I existed?'

'I wrote.'

'So we're blaming the postman now?' Sarcasm didn't suit him and he changed tack quickly. The delivery ward was no place for a row. 'All I ever did was love you, Clara.'

'You left,' she pointed out, and Timothy raked a shaking hand though his hair. 'It didn't look like love to me.'

'Do you blame me?' His voice was a raw whisper. 'Did you expect me just to live in Kell's shadow? Hell, a second-rate doctor I could just about have swallowed, but a second-rate lover?'

'You were never second rate,' Clara said. 'I was scared to tell you how much you meant to me, scared of being a burden.'

Confused eyes met hers and Timothy stood up slowly. 'We can't do this now, Clara, there's just too much hurt there. I can't go over it all and be expected to stay calm, and neither can you. For now we just have to put it all to one side and get through this any way we can. We've got the baby to think of.

'Our baby,' he added softly, his hand tentatively moving to the ripe mound of her stomach. 'Can I?'

She nodded, watching his face as his hand met her skin, watching his eyes squeeze tightly on tears as a tiny foot or hand made its presence felt, greeting the very new father-to-be with a deft little jab. And as beautiful as the moment was, it was laced for Clara with regret, regret for all Timothy had missed out on.

Casey popped her head around the door, smiling as she came over. 'Hop on if you like,' she suggested, pulling down the side of the bed as Timothy stood there awkwardly. 'If it helps Clara to relax then it's all in a good cause.'

'Will it help?' His eyes searched Clara's face and she nodded slowly, moving over a touch as Timothy climbed on top of the sheet, both awkward and shy as Casey pulled up the side rail.

'We don't want you both toppling out. Reading the monitors, she quietly wrote down Clara's and the baby's obs before turning. 'We'll be in and out all night, but just buzz if you need anything.'

Timothy held her, his movements awkward at first as Clara lay there, rigid and nervous and wondering if it was such a good idea, but as his hand rested on her bump, as he pulled her in just a little bit tighter, their stage fright vanished, many nights holding each other the best dress rehearsal of all.

'Clara?' She heard the anxiety in his voice as she pulled herself up, the monitors going crazy as the lights flooded on, nurses appearing from everywhere as they pulled down the side of the bed and Timothy jumped off, sleepy and dazed at first but snapping to attention in a matter of seconds.

'I can't breathe,' she gasped, her hand clutching the mask over her face, every breath an effort as her heart seemed to gallop inside her chest.

'It's OK, Clara.' Casey's voice was reassuring above the confusion. 'I've turned up the oxygen. Just take some nice slow deep breaths—the doctor's on his way.'

'What's happening?' Timothy's hand gripped hers tightly as she whispered the words, too tired to look up, too exhausted to do anything other than try and breathe.

'She's having trouble breathing.' Casey's words reached her from a distance and Clara realised she was addressing Timothy.

'I can see that,' Timothy responded, the anxiety clear in his voice. 'What I want to know is what's happening?'

'It could be the magnesium sulphate. Although it can stop premature labour, it can also have some worrying side effects,' Casey responded calmly. 'I've turned it off. Clara,' she addressed her patient, 'your lungs are filling up with fluid—that's why you're having so much trouble breathing, Dr Rhodes is coming directly.'

'I'm here.'

Never had she felt more helpless. She couldn't even respond to his endless questions, just struggled to get the air into her lungs as Timothy looked on anxiously. If ever she knew she had been wrong not to tell him, it was confirmed then.

It wasn't just the baby whose life was on the line but her own.

Her child, *their* child, could be left without a mother. Timothy should have been told and nothing would ever change that fact. She could only pray that one day he might understand.

'The baby,' Clara started, but Dr Rhodes just patted her hand.

'Things will start settling now, Clara,' he said confidently. 'We've given you some drugs to reverse the effects and your observations are settling. When things have calmed down I'll examine you—'

'The baby,' Clara gasped, and Dr Rhodes nodded gently, his tone almost patronising.

'It's you we're concerned with at the moment, Clara. The baby's doing just fine.'

But it wasn't what she was trying to say. Her agonised eyes swivelled to Timothy's as she struggled to make herself heard, struggled to make them understand.

'I think my waters just broke.'

It was on for young and old then. Emergency bells were pushed, monitors and IV poles swapped over for portable versions, the operating theatre being alerted, Theatre the safest place to deliver such a tiny infant in case Clara needed an emergency Caesarean. Dr Rhodes examined her as Casey waited with her foot poised, ready to snap the brakes off the bed and move her.

'Fully dilated.' Dr Rhodes looked up at the nurse. 'Let's move.'

Move they did, but only as far as the door.

'It's coming,' Clara gasped.

'Don't push,' Casey said firmly, lifting the sheet, but as impassive as her voice was Clara knew what was happening, knew that this really was it. 'Let's get to the delivery room.'

It took just a matter of seconds. The earlier contractions had done their job, despite the best of modern medicine, and a tiny baby slipped into the world, coming, ready or not, as staff appeared from everywhere. The overhead chimes summoning the neonatal intensive care team to the delivery ward as Clara sobbed in Timothy's arms, scared to look yet terrified not to as her baby entered the world. There was no sound, no crying, but this wasn't the peaceful silence she had witnessed when Timothy had delivered Mary's baby. This was an awful void that seemed to go on for ever, just the briefest glimpse of her pale, limp babe, a glimmer of red hair visible as the tiny bundle was wrapped up and moved swiftly out.

Time was of the essence now.

'A little girl,' Clara said, as the NICU nurse dashed off. 'She's not crying.'

'They've taken her next door,' Casey said gently. 'They're all ready for her. They'll be giving her oxygen and getting her started.'

'Go with her,' Clara begged, as Timothy stood there torn, staring at Clara so pale, so very ill as his daughter's life also hung in the balance. 'Go with her,' Clara sobbed again as Casey pushed her back on the pillow and tightened the oxygen mask around her face.

'Take it easy, Clara. You're not well yourself.'

'Please, Timothy, go with her, stay with her. She's so tiny, she'll be so scared.'

It was the longest night of Clara's life.

Nurses popped in and out, giving her updates, the neonatologist came and gently guided Clara through her daughter's status, her treatment, her chances. And though the news was cautiously optimistic, nothing would calm Clara until she saw her daughter for herself, her anxiety mounting with each laboured breath until finally Casey gave her a sleeping tablet, insisting she get some rest.

'When can I see her?'

'When you're well enough' was the best Casey could offer. 'And the sooner you get some sleep, the sooner that will happen.'

It was the only reason she complied.

CHAPTER THIRTEEN

'Hey, you.'

Opening her eyes, for a second or two the world seemed OK, but it didn't last long.

There was Timothy smiling down at her, those green eyes gentle now, but Clara knew there had been tears and she dreaded what was coming next.

'Is she—?'

'She's beautiful,' Timothy said softly. 'Little stick arms and legs, and she's so tiny it terrifies me, Clara, but she's a fighter.' He picked up a handful of Polaroids and passed them to her. 'She's got your red hair.'

He stared at the picture a moment longer. 'The neonatologist thinks she's behaving as if she might even be twenty-nine weeks gestation.'

'Another thing I got wrong,' Clara mumbled.

'Another week's good,' Timothy said gently. 'And despite how you're feeling, you did really well, Clara. You hung in there long enough to give the steroids a chance to work. I'm so proud of you.'

She waited, waited for a 'but', waited for some recrimination, but it never came.

'I should have told you.'

'Yes,' he said slowly, 'you should have, but I know now that you tried.' Pulling an envelope out of his pocket, he laid it on the bed. 'This was in my pigeonhole in the doctors' mess. Why did you wait so long, Clara? Did you think I'd be angry or something, that I wouldn't stand by you?'

'I knew that you would stand by me,' Clara said cryptically. 'And that was the bit that worried me.' She looked up at his non-comprehending face. 'I don't want to have one of those marriages where people stay together for the sake of the children.'

'And that's what you think it would be?'

She didn't answer, just stared at her hands as he sat on the bed and let out a long weary sigh.

'Casey's called the porters and they're going to wheel you down to see our baby soon, but before we go there's one thing we have to agree on.' She looked up at his glittering eyes and knew that he was close to tears, but his voice was firm. 'Like it or not, I know now about the baby and whether you want me in her life is immaterial. I'm her father and nothing's going to change that fact.'

She gave a small nod but still she couldn't look at him.

'We need to talk, that much is clear. But not today. Today's about meeting our daughter, and if marriage isn't what you want, if a united front is the best we can manage for her, then it has to start here and now.'

A tiny frown puckered her brow, her red-rimmed eyes jerking up. 'You're the one who left, Timothy. You're the one who didn't want me.'

He didn't get a chance to answer as a midwife appeared with two porters hovering behind her and a huge smile on her face.

'Ready to meet your little lady?'

And even though there was so much to be said, so much that needed to be cleared up, Timothy was right. Now wasn't the time.

Someone else came first now.

'Now, you know what to expect,' the midwife checked as she kicked off the brakes. 'I explained about all the tubes—'

'I'm ready,' Clara broke in, wiping her face with backs of her hands, excited and scared all at once as the bed slid down the hall.

It took for ever to wash her hands, for the bell in the neonatal unit to be answered and the door to swing open, but finally she was being wheeled through and even though there must have been twenty cots, her eyes fixed only on one, tiny little tufts of red hair coming into focus as they pushed the bed up beside her.

'She's beautiful.' The staff had moved the equipment enough so the bed could be pushed alongside the incubator. Leaning over, Clara was able to put her hand in, and never had something felt so sweet, so soft, so pure. Tiny little fingers that curled around Clara's, her little chest moving up and down so fast, the soft down that covered her frowning forehead as her tiny closed eyelids moved rapidly.

'Mummy's here…' Clara whispered gently. And even though it felt strange to say it, to believe that after all the babies she'd delivered, all the newborns she'd held, this little one was actually hers. But the word came naturally from her lips, the gush of maternal love flowing so strong it made her catch her breath. Timothy's hand was on her shoulders, holding her tight as she gazed on and on, and even though she couldn't see him she could feel the love that emanated from him as he gazed upon his tiny daughter. 'Daddy's here, too,' she added, as Timothy's hand tightened on her shoulder. 'And we both love you so very much.'

'Have you chosen a name?' the nurse asked as Clara gazed on, overwhelmed, terrified, exhausted but utterly devoted, and it was Timothy who spoke, his voice thick with emotion, breaking every now and then.

'Not yet. We're just getting used to the fact she's here.'

'It's a lot to take in,' the nurse said gently, moving into the background but constantly present, the baby just too tiny to allow for anything else.

It *was* a lot to take in.

And for a few days their relationship, or what was left of it, was put on the back burner as they concentrated instead on their daughter. Feeling every needle, every tube and every grimace as she struggled to hold on, to stay with a world she had joined too early.

'I want to hold her.' Clara's dry eyes were no indicator of the pain behind her words and Timothy pulled her in closer, a cuddle all he could offer as the days ticked by into weeks.

'Tomorrow perhaps,' he said hopefully.

'They said that yesterday.' She could hear the mistrust in her voice, the gnawing panic that seemed to constantly snap at her, and she struggled to quash it.

They were living in a tiny flat attached to the neonatal unit. Although living might be a slight exaggeration—existing perhaps a more apt word.

Existing between visits to the unit, and long, long heart-stopping nights, praying for the phone not to ring...

Dying a bit inside when it did.

And no one could know, unless they had been there, the agony of those calls, the dash to the unit, washing your hands because you had to as staff rushed around behind those glass doors and struggled to get your baby through one more night. The lack of elation when the panic was over, just the cold fingers of fear as you wondered how much a tiny body could take, how long till this roller-coaster ride ended.

'They know what they're doing, Clara, you have to trust them.'

'I know.'

'And we have to start trusting each other.'

Clara jerked her eyes up and shook her head. She had known this day was coming, knew there was so much to sort out, but she simply couldn't deal with it now, her emotions so raw she simply couldn't take any more pain and be expected to function.

'We need to talk,' Timothy said softly. 'And if that's too hard, then I'll talk and you can listen.'

Wearily she nodded, bracing herself for the impact as she stared down at her hands.

'I can see why you don't want to get married, and if you'd bothered to talk to me about it you'd have found out that I actually agree with you. I had a miserable childhood, endless silences followed by endless rows followed my endless silences. It never ended and to this day it still goes on. My parents only stayed together "for the sake of the children," and frankly I wish they hadn't bothered.' She heard the quotation marks around his words, heard the pain behind them, and tears filled her eyes for what he must have been through. 'The saddest part is, now that the children have finally grown up and left home, they're still stuck with each other, too bitter and jaded to pluck up the courage to leave. So you see, Clara, I do understand where you're coming from. I promised myself before I even knew what it really meant that if ever I married it would be the real thing, that if it wasn't what we both wanted then it wasn't worth doing.'

He knelt down beside her, taking her pale shaking hands in his. 'Even if we're not together, though, it doesn't mean I won't be there for you both, it doesn't mean I'm not going to be the best father I can be.'

He was right, she knew that deep down, knew there was no point in living together if he didn't really love her, but hearing him say it hurt like hell.

'I love you, Clara. I have since the day I met you.'

Startled, she looked up, her eyebrows furrowing as she begged a rewind on the previous conversation, her mouth opening to speak then closing again, sure she must somehow have misheard him, or more likely he was about to add a quick postscript: 'As a sister' perhaps or 'as the mother of my child'. But what he said next utterly floored her

'I just can't be second best.'

'You're not,' she croaked, then cleared her throat. 'You never have been.'

'Oh, Clara, you love Kell. Don't try and deny it now. Every time I mentioned his name, tried to find out how you were feeling, you shut me out, Matthew went missing, and who did you turn to? Everywhere I go he seems to be there. Hell, I'm surprised he wasn't the midwife on duty when you delivered.'

A very watery smile wobbled on her lips, but it changed midway and she started to cry.

'When Ross offered me the job I was so happy. I forgot we were supposed to be meeting at the pub and I raced over to the house and there were pictures all over the table, pictures of Kell, and I knew then I couldn't do it, couldn't keep pretending I was good enough, that I was what you wanted.'

'You *are* what I want,' Clara said. 'I couldn't talk about it because I thought I'd scare you off, and as for those pictures... He was getting married, Timothy. I was helping Shelly to put together some photos for Abby, and it didn't hurt a bit, not one single bit. My life was perfect from the day you came to Tennengarrah to the day you left. I love you, Timothy, I always have.'

'So why couldn't you tell me?' Timothy pushed. 'Why couldn't you just say it?'

'Because I didn't want you to feel sorry for me.' Screwing her eyes closed, she pulled her hands from his and covered her eyes, but he pulled them back down, cupping her face and forcing her to look.

'Who hurt you, Clara?' he rasped.

'No one hurt me,' she sobbed. 'Everyone's always been nice, but only because they had to be. I'm sick of being "poor Clara", I'm tired of people asking me for Christmas dinner just because they know I don't have a family, sick of the duty dances because they feel obliged—'

'Clara.' Timothy's voice broke in. 'They aren't doing those things out of a sense of duty. Your parents died fifteen years ago. Hell, where I come from the casseroles and visits end after a couple of weeks, but even allowing for Tennengarrah being a bit more neighbourly, I think fifteen years is pushing things.

'They love you, Clara. Not because of what happened but because of who you are. Good and kind and gentle. For the very same reasons that I love you.

'Love you,' he repeated, just so she could be absolutely sure she wasn't hearing things. 'I don't want to marry you out of duty. Life's too short for that. I want to be with you and only you, and I'm actually starting to believe that you might want to be with me. Can you see that now?'

She couldn't, not yet. He knew that, knew that her pain ran deep, and he held her close as he spoke.

'You didn't just lose your parents when you were fifteen,' he said softly. 'You lost that unconditional love that comes with it. Maybe I don't have the best mum and dad in the world but, as much as I rant and moan, deep down I know that they love me. I knew that when I was sixteen and had the worst acne in the world and no one would even come near me. I knew that when the first of many girls dumped me and even when I'd wasted three years studying for a degree I'll never use, as much as they berated me, they still loved me.

'You never had that, did you?' His eyes were brimming now. 'The confidence that being loved gives you?'

'Everyone was good...' she started, but then she gave in. Cried for all she had lost, all those lonely, lonely nights and the horrible, horrible feeling of never quite fitting in, never being quite good enough.

And he held her, held her and rocked her and loved her until finally, as the shadows on the wall lengthened, the world suddenly didn't seem such a lonely place, his strength, his touch giving her the confidence it took to say the three hardest words of her life.

'I love you.'

'And I love you, too.' Timothy kissed her salty cheeks, kissed her blonde eyelashes and held her tight. 'I got up yesterday and I hated the world without you. Hated the fact I get up now the second the alarm goes off because it's easier than lying in a bed without you, and I knew then that I had to talk to you. That's why I rang, not because you were pregnant—I didn't even know. And not because I felt obliged to, but because I love you and I don't think I can make it without you.' The ringing of the phone made them both jump, scared that somehow, because they hadn't been concentrating for a moment, hadn't been praying hard enough, their little girl might have slipped away.

Timothy got there first, listening intently as Clara hovered anxiously, wringing her hands as he replaced the receiver. 'What did they say? Is she all right?'

'Better than all right.' Timothy smiled. 'Our baby needs a cuddle.'

It was the sweetest moment of them all.

With shaking hands Clara undid her blouse as the nurse gently instructed. 'Your skin's the best blanket of all.'

And suddenly what she had yearned for, ached for was next to her now, the softest skin nuzzling in as the nurse wrapped a bunny rug around them, stepping back slightly as Timothy edged nearer, his camera ready, determined to capture this most precious moment. But in mid-shot he changed his mind and, putting the camera down, came over and held Clara, marvelling in the miracle they had created.

'I'll do the honours.' The nurse smiled, picking up the camera. 'One for the album.'

Clara didn't even look up as the photo was taken, her eyes never leaving her baby.

'Some memento of your holiday, huh?' Clara said softly as Timothy pulled them in closer.

'I wonder if I'll get her through customs.'

And then the joking stopped, the nerves, the shyness disappearing as their eyes locked above their tiny little red-headed babe.

'She needs a name,' Timothy said, his voice thick with emotion. 'We can't let them keep calling her Baby Watts. What was your mother's name?'

'Elizabeth,' Clara whispered. 'But everyone called her Beth.'

'Beth.' Timothy said the name slowly, his face breaking into a smile. 'Beth Morgan—it sounds nice, don't you think?'

Her eyes never left his, confidence, hope, love, tears all shining in her eyes.

'It sounds perfect.'

'She's going to be all right,' Timothy said softly, one large finger stroking the tiny pink cheek. 'More than all right, she's going to be just fine.'

And this time his optimism didn't irritate her, this time his blind faith didn't annoy her.

It was everything she needed.

'We're all going to fine,' he added softly.

EPILOGUE

'YOUR MUM AND DAD would have been so proud of you.'

Bill's voice was gruff as he offered his arm, and Clara leant on it gratefully as he fussed over Beth with all the skill of a new grandfather, his daughter Martha's baby already a playmate for Beth.

'You look wonderful,' Eileen enthused, fiddling with Clara's dress as her heels sank into the dry red earth.

'So do you,' Clara whispered through her chattering teeth.

'At least I've managed to produce a bit of hair for the day.' Eileen grinned, fingering her fine, short hair. 'A bald maid of honour's not the best look.'

'I'm just glad you're here,' Clara said softly, the double meaning not wasted on Eileen as she smiled back fondly. And Eileen truly did look wonderful. Her thin face was filling out now, hope shining in her eyes at the beauty of a future she could glimpse now. They'd decided against a headdress of flowers for Eileen. She truly didn't need them. The wispy locks that framed her smiling face held all the hope of a meadow in springtime.

'Do you want me to take Beth for you?'

Clara shook her head. 'I want to walk up the aisle holding her.'

'They're all ready for you.' Hamo was walking towards her,

unfamiliar in a dark suit, his hair for once neatly cut, the perfect groomsman for Tennengarrah's tiny church.

'Just give me a moment.'

Clara stood for a second gazing at the dusty town she loved, the barn all set up for this magical day, white ribbons adorning it, fairy-lights draped all ready for the biggest party Tennengarrah had ever witnessed. She gazed on the dry, hot land that was her home, knowing deep down that it was time to leave, to follow Timothy's dreams, to help him be all he was going to be.

'We'll be back,' Timothy had promised. 'When I'm a surgeon, we'll come back where we all belong.'

And they did belong, Clara knew that now.

They belonged to the endless red earth, to the family that was Tennengarrah, to the community that had embraced her, not because they'd had to but because they'd wanted to.

Love was never a duty.

But by Timothy's side was where she wanted to be now, where she was needed the most.

Walking towards him, she jumped slightly as the music thundered into life, as the whole of Tennengarrah turned towards her, smiling, taking every step with her as Timothy waited patiently.

Waited and watched as his family walked towards him.

* * * * *

MILLS & BOON

Book Club ♡

Have your favourite series
delivered to your door every month
with a Mills & Boon subscription.

**Use code ROMANCE2021 to
get 50% off the first month of
your chosen subscription PLUS
free delivery.**

Sign up online at
millsandboon.com.au/subscription-2

or call Customer Service on

AUS **1300 659 500** or NZ **0800 265 546**

**No Lock-in
Contracts**

**Free
Postage**

**Exclusive
Offers**

For full terms and conditions go to millsandboon.com.au
Offer expires June 30, 2021

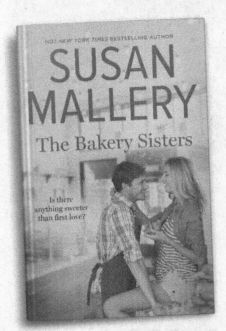
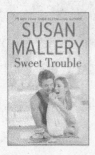